BEYOND
the
STORM

Books by Joseph Pittman

A Christmas Hope

A Christmas Wish

Tilting at Windmills

When the World Was Small

Legend's End

California Scheming: A Todd Gleason Crime Novel

London Frog: A Todd Gleason Crime Novel

The Original Crime, Part One: Remembrance

The Original Crime, Part Two: Retribution

The Original Crime, Part Three: Redemption

BEYOND
the
STORM

JOSEPH PITTMAN

𝓴

Kensington Books
www.kensingtonbooks.com

KENSINGTON BOOKS are published by

Kensington Publishing Corp.
119 West 40th Street
New York, NY 10018

All Kensington titles, imprints, and distributed lines are available at special
quantity discounts for bulk purchases for sales promotion, premiums, fund-
raising, and educational or institutional use.

Special book excerpts or customized printings can also be created to fit spe-
cific needs. For details, write or phone the office of the Kensington Special
Sales Manager: Kensington Publishing Corp., 119 West 40th Street, New
York, NY 10018. Attn. Special Sales Department. Phone: 1-800-221-2647.

Kensington and the K logo Reg. U.S. Pat. & TM Off.

ISBN-13: 978-0-7582-7698-8
ISBN-10: 0-7582-7698-2
First Kensington Trade Paperback Printing: June 2013

eISBN-13: 978-0-7582-7699-5
eISBN-10: 0-7582-7699-0
First Kensington Electronic Edition: June 2013

10 9 8 7 6 5 4 3 2 1

Printed in the United States of America

This one's for . . .
Eduardo Vazquez,
because your smiles
are like sunshine

In our lives there is bound to come some pain,
surely as there are storms and falling rain;
just believe that the one who holds
the storms will bring the sun.

—Anonymous

$\mathcal{P}$ROLOGUE

BEFORE THEN

She awoke early, but even so the dark eyes of fate saw the arrival of dawn first. Today was the day that had possessed her dreams these many months, and so she awakened with a new sense of purpose, despite the damper of heavy clouds hovering in the low-lying sky. The sun would not embrace her today, like a friend gone missing. Still, her newfound energy could not be diffused. From the bed, she unshackled the imaginary restraints she'd felt encumbered by while under the thick covers. Throwing open the window to a burst of fresh sea air, she felt as though her body was able to take to the wind. All in an effort to be with him.

For this eagerly anticipated reunion, she simply could not wait another minute. Even her mother could barely hold her back, knowing her irrepressible, headstrong daughter would be the first to welcome the mariners back home and to the safety of land. So filled with anxiety was she the night before, this spirited young woman appropriately, uniquely, named Venture had given up on her fitful sleep and set out her clothes for the following day. A beautiful dress hung on the back of the door frame; it was her favorite because it was his favorite. In her waking dreams, she imagined the light breeze catching the flowing fabric, unleashing the flowers from the print, rustling against her skin as she ran down the length of the sandy beach in time to meet the ship, the smile lighting his face when he caught sight of her, surrounded by floating petals of red and purple.

The world, though, in its ever-mysterious ways and confounding contrariness, had plans no one could have foreseen, not even our beautiful, driven Venture, a woman whose heart would not be contained by ordinary bounds of flesh and blood. Her soul had wings. Yet something was different today, a feeling in the cool air that permeated through the walls of the clapboard house. The breeze was far fiercer, as, on this dark morning, a storm raged, ripping at anything not tied down to this land, rippling off the silver sheen of the great lake. A storm like this was one thing that would have stopped most people. But not the woman called Venture.

"She was born with unattainable dreams," her mother liked to tell anyone who would listen, "and I don't think she's ever truly woken up from them, not from the very moment we welcomed her into this world and she wailed. It's always felt like she was destined for more than the earth can contain."

The storm today, like Venture, was, indeed, anything but ordinary. Wind howled, nearly bending tree branches midway. Rain lashed the ground, soaking it, swirling around it. Raging water rushed by, gurgling and guzzling all in its path. Later, its deadly swath would tell an angry tale of near-vengeance, of nature's fury unleashed on those unsuspecting of its true power. Even those sensible folks who always thought of themselves prepared for such emergencies were caught unaware, and the devastation they reaped was lived out for years—for some even longer. For a lifetime.

For our Venture and the devoted man she eagerly awaited, they had always envisioned their hopes and their dreams played out differently than others, as though sheer will was enough to achieve life's pinnacle, love. For a time that stretched beyond the limits of what mortals defined the passage of days and months and years, their story would have to wait for one more turn, finally playing out a destiny long thought by others, by them, to be touched by the dust of magic. In truth, all that remained of them was nestled inside a picture frame hung on the wall of the newly rebuilt farmhouse out beyond the coastal village of tiny Danton Hill. As though not only their burned images but their very souls were sealed behind the glass, waiting again for a fierce storm to knock it from its hold, shattering to the floor, releasing them.

How the ensuing tragedy happened would become the stuff of lore, of sadness, the memory left to only one living soul.

How their ending—at least for now—came about, you had to go back to that rain-soaked morning, when not even the blinding wind could hold her feet to the ground.

Venture awakened with what should have been the sun but instead heard the sound of rain beating against her window. For a time, as she placed the delicate material of her beloved dress against her soft skin, the floral print highlighting her auburn locks, nothing could dampen her mood, certainly not some summer storm. Too filled with the future was she, that not even her gut registered the notion that something could possibly go wrong today. A ship on the high seas, really just the Great Lake known as Ontario that loomed above Danton Hill, she never feared for its safety, knowing its crew was the very best the sea had to offer. They could handle anything Mother Nature could dish out, so went her thinking, and as such the only concern that dwelled within her was not being the first to the beach. She had to be the first to catch sight of the giant mast as it crested over the horizon.

Ignoring the pleas of her mother, whom she thought worried enough for the both of them about unnecessary dangers, she took to the nearby beach with the easy grace of the youth. Bare feet padded against grainy sand, her dress whipping in the wind just as she'd envisioned. Rain pelted at her skin, but it was less nature's deterrent than a cold shock of life enlivening her on the in-

side. As she circled around a windblown dune, Venture moved to the edge of the water, where angry waves crashed at her ankles. She screamed out in delight as the seasonably warm loam washed over her, enjoying the fury dancing all around her.

The gray pallor of the sky kept the horizon at bay. Venture gazed out as far as she could, and for thirty minutes, more, she still could not see any sign of the Promenade, *the vessel in which her true love had left aboard nearly nine months ago. No mast emerged through the fog, no billowing sails waved to her in greeting. By now she wasn't alone. Other women—mothers, wives, clapping children—of the village's seafaring heroes had joined her in anticipation of their triumphant return, rich with the spoils of the ocean. The century had turned while these men had been gone, and while industrial revolution was all the rage in the big cities, a quiet place such as Danton Hill still clung to a past that honored the land, the sea, the sky, a connection more in line with written history than unfounded future.*

"Perhaps we have come on the incorrect day, or the weather has kept them anchored offshore somewhere," spoke Anna Revere, a young woman who had once been widowed by the sea and now awaited the return of the new man who had spun her heart into gold. Venture didn't blame Anna for her pessimism, and managed a wan smile as she embraced the stalwart woman. "No, I feel it, deep inside me. The ship may be just beyond our sight now, but it is closer in our heart."

"You love him so," Anna said, more a whisper than words.

Still, Venture heard them and nodded, a smile widening her porcelain features. Then she said, because she could rarely keep silent, "Oh yes, I do, and he adores me so. He'd walk the ends of the earth to find me."

Anna's reply was strange, eerie. "You make it sound like you're going somewhere. You, Venture Mercer, you could never leave behind Danton Hill."

Venture moved forward, oblivious to the words . . . to the idea that swirled around her in the consuming wind. Wandering far down the beach and away from the other women, she never let her gaze stray from the water. She watched as the ripples came in, only to be swept out by the strong tide, following their path until they dissipated beneath the surface.

A speck of light suddenly hit her eyes, causing her heart to skip a beat.

"They're here, out there . . . I see a light. The flickering light he promised."

Indeed, the man she loved had sworn that upon their return he would flash a beam three times toward the land. The first signal was meant to alert them of their imminent landing, the second issued as confirmation that it wasn't a trick of the sun. The third flash was meant only for Venture, a light filled with love. A child-like Venture danced at the edge of the water, waiting for him to fulfill his promise. A flash came, then another flash, finally a third. She knew it was him, that he had come back for her. Indeed, a promise made, a promise kept.

At the far edge of the beach where the residents of Danton Hill stood was a long, rocky pier that stretched deep into the waters, nearly a half mile out. On days when sunshine beamed down and the summer breeze drew numerous beachcombers, the Point, as they referred to it, was a popular meeting place. Today, with the wind as fierce as it was and the water crashing high over the jagged rocks, only the foolish and in love would dare venture out. But, of course, this is where a woman whose dreams often overrode reality was drawn to, and, of course, with a name like Venture it was as though destiny was calling her.

"Venture, dear . . . not today," her mother called out.

"The sea, Venture, it's a cruel lover," spoke Anna, scandalous words at the time but true nonetheless, based on her experience.

Neither woman could stop the headstrong Venture as she lifted the hem of her lovely dress and stepped up on the rocky point. Carefully weaving her way along rocks slippery from the water, damp from the driving rain, Venture made her way along the long, narrow path. Ten feet, then twenty, and before long she imagined she was closer to the ship's bow than she was to the land, like she was offering herself up to either, and whichever first claimed her, won.

Wiping the rain from her eyes, she surged forward, nearly losing her footing on the rocks beneath her. With no rails to steady her purchase, Venture had to rely on her agility, and only at the last second did she manage to right herself. Just then a high wave crashed over her, and she realized—perhaps for the first time—that she had gone out too far. Had she fallen earlier, the wave would have doused her, nearly pulled her to the water.

About to turn back, that's when she caught her first glimpse of the billowing white sails. She would recognize the Promenade's *wooden façade anywhere; she'd watched it sail from her childhood days, when her father would venture yearly to the seas. Across the great lake and up the seaway, finally emerging into the frigid waters of the Atlantic. That's where she got her spirited name, a girl born with her father's sense of wanderlust. And then the man who'd won her heart had also taken to a life at sea, determined to prove his worth and assure doubters that he could forge a good life for them. He would be back for months now, through the cold months, before duty called him back.*

"I knew you'd come back for me," Venture spoke aloud, her words drowned by the wind.

Nature has a way of playing by its own rules, though, and today, as the rain fell and the wind whistled and the mist rumbled over the surface, there would come no exception to this hardened lesson. Crashing waves continued to implode against the rocky pier, which Venture continued to ignore, walking farther out, farther still, until she reached the end of the Point. She waved wildly, her arms outstretched like tree branches as she tried to catch the attention of the seafarers. For the first time, fear came over her, as she suddenly noticed she had run out of space—all that separated her from her man were the foamy whitecaps of the water. Behind her, the shore was gone, lost in the rolling fog. As she turned back, another wave crashed again, loud, angry . . . wanting. It washed completely over Venture, knocking her down. She felt pain as a rock sliced into her side. A second wave followed in close pursuit, pulling at her, like it sought her, and only her. To take her in its embrace. And it did.

Between the wind and the fog, the rain, the fury of all that surrounded them, no one saw what would happen next. Even days later, even after weeks and the years had slipped by, the story of that day would never change. The perilous sea had claimed their precious Venture, as she was never seen again after taking to those treacherous rocks. Her all-consuming love could not have waited a minute longer, to do so would have gone against her own nature. That wasn't who Venture was, and to those who thrived on such stories, such legends of loves found and loves lost, there was no better testament that destiny had a power all its own.

One person who firmly believed in destiny's curse was the soon-to-be brokenhearted man who'd returned home from the sea on board the Promenade, *knowing all along his beautiful Venture, she who would have filled his heart and defined his life, was there waiting for him. They would meet on the beach as prearranged and they would embrace. He would swing her around, and together they would dance to silent music that existed solely between them. But when the ship came ashore and the men disembarked, only this man found his arms empty, and days later too, as he sat by the shore still. He wept at all he'd lost.*

Life sends secret messages, their truths revealed only if your heart understood the coded language. For a man who sailed by the light of the stars, he knew there were mystical forces out there, hidden sometimes by clouds, revealing themselves only when you opened your soul to such notions. That one starry night, three nights since his Venture had left for some other plane, some other place in this world, a piece of her magically found its way to him.

From the water he pulled the billowy object, taking it into his large, calloused hands.

And despite the ache felt deep in his heart, he grinned, because here was proof that she had adored him. The dress that had daz-zled him, one that had initially drawn him to her spirit and en-abled him to see far within her soul, she had indeed worn it on the day he'd come back. Now, even though Venture herself was gone, here was the dress washing ashore, and he knew, instinctively, that they would meet again. This was a clue, a hint from beyond.

He didn't know when or why or how, but in those mystical stars that guided him through life, he knew Venture's spirit would sparkle down on him at the right time. She would return to him, years from now, another time, another century, when she went by an-other name, her soul would still find him and reach out to him. Destiny's secrets, life's reason for taking her from him now, would at last be revealed. The key was in knowing the moment, recog-nizing its importance, and only then would life's eternal promise find them.

"Your Aidan will find you, my dear Venture, no matter where, no matter when," the man said, holding the sea-drenched dress to his face, sensing her presence. He would never show the dress to anyone—his discovery was all he had left and it would remain be-tween the two of them. Upon returning to his home, he went to his thick, oak trunk and unlocked the black padlock with an iron key. He wrapped the sun-warmed material in thick brown paper and sealed it, then placed it inside the trunk. Smiling, a tear slip-ping down his bearded cheek, he closed the lid, knowing one day, perhaps far in the future, that some unsuspecting souls would dis-cover it and unleash its secret power.

For now, at the line in the cool, grainy sand that separated him from her, he had a letter to write. Taking his feathered pen to brown parchment, he began to write what would be the first of many letters.

"My dearest Venture . . ."

PART 1

CHAPTER 1

NOW

Black clouds chased him, threatening him with the promise of its torrential downpour. Sure, he was under protective cover, of sorts, behind the wheel of his rental car, but on this lonely stretch of narrow road, such a fact gave him scarce comfort. Ever since that freak incident on a warm, childhood day, when a dangerous thunderstorm had wreaked havoc on his neighborhood and the high winds had flipped over his swing set and a startling lightning strike had hit a tree, sending it into the house next door to where he lived and claimed the life of his neighbor, wobbly old Mrs. Woodson, he'd hated these sudden summer storms. Now it looked like another storm had come for him after all these years, taunting him, as though it knew his inner fears and was determined to unleash them, much like the rains from its heavy clouds.

His blue eyes hit the digital clock on the dashboard of his white Chevy Malibu: 3:58 in the afternoon. Still another hour or so before he reached his destination, and even still, he'd left little room for delays if he wanted to arrive on time. Pulling to the side of the road to wait out a passing thunderstorm was not on his agenda, nor was the idea of driving through one. Kind of put him between a rock and a hard place.

"Maybe it will blow past," he said to the otherwise empty car.

A booming crack of thunder let him know his wish was just that. As life experiences had taught him, those dreamed-upon thoughts tended not to come true all that often. Still, at least the rain's intensity hadn't begun yet, just a few drops. The road was still dry, and the cruising car sped forward.

What he also noticed on this winding road was that there seemed to be very little in the way of other traffic; he couldn't remember when he'd last seen another car. Such were these old roads up here, they didn't seem to go anywhere until suddenly they did, civilization rearing up over an unexpected twist. His foot pressed on the accelerator and his body felt the Malibu surge as it hugged a long, bending curve. He flicked on his headlights for safety's sake; didn't they say headlights during the day were so other drivers could see you, not to help you see? An accident he'd suffered a few years ago had knocked up his insurance rates and required him to retake a defensive driving course. Some of those lessons remained engrained in his brain.

Age thirty-eight, his dark hair artfully messy, six foot Adam Blackburn had only ever been in that one traffic accident and he'd never received a speeding ticket. Just a simple rear-ending up in Maine one summer vacation with a short-term girlfriend long since gone, both totally his fault. His driving record at least was certainly better than his dating one. Of course, he spent most of his commuting days aboard public transportation, so his ratio of run-ins with law enforcement and actual driving was considerably reduced than those who lived in the suburbs. A city dweller since leaving college, Adam had rented the car for the coming occasion, his reason for being on this seemingly deserted stretch of road stuck in the middle of nowhere. If you're traveling from New York City to a small village in upper Monroe County, situated somewhere between Buffalo and Rochester, at some point you'll have to get a car, and so rather than fly, then drive, he'd opted to splurge on a pricey rental from Manhattan. He'd left the busy city limits this nineteenth day of August around ten o'clock, planning for an eight-hour drive. The event tonight was scheduled to start at eight, which would give him plenty of time to check into his hotel, rest, and maybe have a pre-reunion cocktail before heading over to the school auditorium. That is, if he was able to beat out this looming storm.

Another crack of thunder, preceded by a visible streak of lightning that illuminated the sky as seen through his rearview mirror. The storm was getting closer, no matter the extra burst of speed he gave the car's engine; it was coming for him. Just then the rain began, large droplets hitting his windshield like pale, splattered bugs. He switched on the wipers and opened the vents to allow the blast of air-conditioning to assist in clearing the windows of sudden encroaching condensation. He also paused his iPod, music having kept him company during the long ride. Coldplay's "Clocks" faded, silence grew. Time to concentrate.

More thunder, more lightning.

Adam wiped a cool bead of sweat from his brow. Christ, it was just Mother Nature doing what she did best, so why worry? There was nothing to fear except some lingering memories, fears, from when he was seven years old. But heck, his parents had just trashed the entire swing set during cleanup the next day—and they'd never replaced it. And they'd left him home when they attended the funeral service for Mrs. Woodson. An impressionable boy who liked to hang upside down on the monkey bars and see the world his way tended not to forget such an indelible moment. How often had Mrs. Woodson gazed at him with a dour expression on her face, asking him why he wanted to contort his body like that? Why not, he'd always answered her. Then one day both were gone, the monkey bars and Mrs. Woodson. Always the storm's fault. Yes, Adam Blackburn had an issue with storms. They took things, people.

Glancing into the rearview mirror again, he caught sight of his own expression. He was no longer that young boy, not with his strong jaw, scruffy, darkened cheeks, and thick eyebrows. Yet hidden inside his soft blue eyes were those same inner fears of nature's fury, of the havoc it could create. Taking one last, lingering look at himself, he gauged the growing worry lines on his forehead; was that just a natural furrowing, or had he missed out on the fact he'd aged the last few, troubled months?

The force of the falling rainfall increased, decreasing his visibility. Adam looked out his window to see which direction the storm might be going, hoping it would shift away from him, but then a pair of headlights fast approaching from behind momentarily blinded him. The idiot behind him was not only riding his trunk, but he stupidly had turned his high beams on. Adam instinctively slowed down, an effort that caused the driver behind him to sit on his horn.

"Christ, have you noticed that it's raining?" Adam asked aloud.

Just then the driver behind him gunned his engine, and the speedy red car, a Mustang, pulled out into the lane beside him, the lane that just happened to favor opposing traffic, and there was no broken yellow line. Fear gripping him, Adam took a quick, nervous look ahead, but thankfully there appeared to be no cars coming their way. He watched as the sports car zoomed past him. He wiped at his driver's side window just in time to see the guy flip him the bird.

"I should have flown," Adam said.

Thunder boomed again, producing a near-deafening echo that practically shook the sky's low-hanging ceiling. He imagined himself up in these treacherous, daunting skies, the plane bouncing around as they descended through the clouds, and then changed his mind again about flying. He revised his thoughts once again.

"I should have stayed home."

Staying home, a nice idea. Actually, that had been his initial instinct when the e-mail invitation had popped up in his in-box with the subject line reading: *20th High School Reunion.* He'd barely given that awful time of his life much thought since graduation, and now here it was, somehow, all these years later, with an offer to regroup, reflect, gather to see who had succeeded, who'd gotten fat, who'd remained behind in town, and who had died. Sad, really, to think of his fellow Danton Hill High graduates being defined by the same labels in which they'd entered ninth grade. Did twenty years really represent enough time gone by for all those petty feelings about the teenagers you spent your formative years with to go away? People change, right?

The dual, dueling facts that Adam had enjoyed a modicum of success in life and had decided to attend the reunion kind of answered that one. You always wanted to show off to those who thought you'd never amount to anything.

Nope. Not enough time.

But time was something flexible, bendable. It was why some days seemed to linger longer than others.

He chastised himself, enough with metaphysical things. Forget about tonight and all that it might bring, just for a second. Concentrate on the road.

If memory served him well, there was a turnoff coming up and he didn't want to miss it. Why hadn't he taken the GPS option the rental agent had suggested? Because he was going somewhere he was familiar with, that was why, a place he'd once called home. He imagined he could drive these once-familiar roads in his sleep. This wasn't sleep, this was a thunderstorm.

The blackened sky looked like night's shroud; the heavy clouds seemed to be descending upon him even more, like the sky could no longer support the weight of all that rain. He felt buried inside the car. His visibility grew even more limited. At least there was no sign of that red sports car, one less bad driver to distract him. Adam looked back in the rearview mirror once more, comforted to see he once again had the road to himself. He slowed even more, the mph gauge dropping to forty. He felt the car dip and realized he'd started going downhill. The torrents of rainwater followed after him, chasing him, gurgling beneath his tires. Last thing he wanted to do was hydroplane and slide into the rolling cornfields that ran parallel to the road.

He reduced his speed further. That's when he suddenly saw the yellow sign indicating the turnoff road approaching, just ten feet ahead. Despite his decreased speed, he still hadn't given himself enough time to make the turn without the possibility of careening into a ditch. So he continued on, looking for a place where he could safely turn around. As the road that led toward the village of Danton Hill passed him by, Adam stole a look at the roadside in an effort to remember an identifying marker for when he made his return approach. He didn't want to miss the road to home again.

Lights flashed in his eyes.

Was that lightning again, a streak striking the ground

close to him? No, the glare wasn't followed by any crack of thunder; it wasn't nature's doing. In fact, the harsh light was insistent, not going away. They were coming right at him.

"Get out of my lane, get the fu . . ."

But he was overreacting, wasn't he? The road was simply curving. The other car wasn't in his lane, and he certainly wasn't in its lane. Swallow the paranoia, it was just oncoming traffic, and that was to be expected on a county road that eventually led to a populated town such as Danton Hill. Really, he was going to drown in this anxiety if he didn't compose himself. His nerves were making the situation worse. Just drive, find a place to turn around, and then get back on track . . .

The reunion awaited him.

But the headlights were still coming at him.

He instinctively turned the wheel, his foot applying the brakes. Okay, bad move. That's not what they had taught him in that defensive driving course. The other car swung around, and that's when Adam saw the blinding headlights swing directly into his path. He found himself holding his breath. He had no choice but to brace for impact.

For the entire ride backward in time, toward her childhood stomping grounds of Danton Hill, her mind played with one recurring thought about the reunion: What was she thinking? Hadn't she purposely left this town and this life long ago, vowing never to return to its shores? There were memories here, sure, many of them she would prefer to forget. But there were old friends too, and given all that had happened with her since graduation day, maybe the time had come to look upon her former life with wizened, wisdom-filled eyes. Also, and this was the real truth, there was unfinished business to attend to. Would he be there?

Wait, stop, correct that, she said, the inflection all wrong. Will *He* be there. In her mind she saw that capital *H*, the italics . . . *Him*.

She'd never really forgotten him.

Her heart had; it had felt others, loved others. But not her soul. Souls were mysteries.

Something harkened at her. Brought her back here.

She pushed back her shoulder-length dark hair, opening up her weary, still beautiful face.

Twenty years had somehow slipped by, and that was how long it had been since they'd seen each other . . . well, that wasn't entirely true, there was that one dumb night, an improbable chance encounter eleven or twelve years ago, and . . . well, she put that moment right out of her mind, that entire episode was self-contained, barely worth remembering, but unforgettable nonetheless. Still, it wasn't that she ever expected to get a call or a postcard, an e-mail, a text . . . anything from him. They didn't have that kind of relationship now and they never had. In fact, barring that one crazy week at the end of high school, they barely knew anything about each other, their hopes or their fears or their wishes for the future as much strangers as themselves. No, that wasn't right either, because of course they had talked, that one night, about the future. It's what had bonded them, a burning desire to get out from under the thumb of this town's handprint. Which was why they had gone their separate ways . . . never expecting another thing from the other. They had made no promises. God, I'm a mess, she thought. A walking conundrum.

That would change tonight.

"You hope," she said.

Or did she?

She was alone in the car, and so the running commentary she was having inside her mind really needn't slip out from her mouth, but yet that last comment had. Giving voice to such an inner thought, she had to question just what she really expected from this upcoming reunion. Why was she even going? She'd long ago left behind all her friends, Jana and Tiffany, all of the pointless, useless accolades the school had afforded her—honor society, cheerleader, treasurer of her senior class. Even then, joining those various activities had been laced with subtext, building a résumé of impressive credits that would help her move forward, always forward. She wasn't a "live in the moment" kind of a girl, not then, not now either, and the past . . . well, the past you couldn't change. Even as a kid she had looked to the future: whom she would meet, marry, have children with, what those children would be like. Her career would not define her; she would be well-rounded, ideal. Perfect.

Okay, she allowed herself a bitter laugh.

Perfect.

Vanessa Massey, divorced, childless, at age thirty-eight she was the very definition of a woman whose failed dreams had gotten the better of her. She'd run away from Danton Hill, the pull of wanderlust filling her heart, and she'd never really looked backward. Given all those unforeseen, tricky paths she'd taken in her life, she'd had little choice but to embrace the rare opportunities she'd been given. Not entirely a fair assessment of her person as a whole, but for now it would have to do. For the reunion, she'd have to come up with better answers. Besides, her friends hadn't exactly held back in their belief that *Vanessa* in some other language meant *Dreamer*. The grand adventure always came first, its consequences later. The unlikely idea that she would, twenty years later, return to her old high school and the friends she'd known, well, it was laughable. She did not look back, they always said.

If only they knew. But none of them did. Especially not . . .
Him.

Yet here she was.

She came upon a sign. Danton Hill. Ten miles.

Moving forward now, while somehow moving backward too.

All she'd known, all she'd left behind, was once again so close.

Was the driving rain an omen? There was that day years ago when she knew she would be leaving Danton Hill for a long while, if not for good. Her long-imagined plans for college put off for a season, because she had opted to embark on a journey of soul-searching. Just her, a backpack, a drained bank account, accompanied only by the shell of the woman she'd once been. She'd left for Europe, the whole continent laid out before her, swallowing her into anonymity. And that day she'd left, it had been raining too, as she boarded the airplane in nearby Rochester while clouds rumbled by. Like Danton Hill was unhappy that she was leaving, crying. One of her final thoughts as they lifted off had been about Him. Did she regret not speaking with him one last time? Vanessa Massey had never flown before, and she had to wonder if takeoff was even possible in such weather. Was it safe? She didn't like storms.

Back then she'd arrived without incident at New York's JFK airport, changed to a supersized jet, and taken to the night sky, only to touch down in Paris the next morning, one that came faster in this world than in her old one, her previous life gone but not forgotten amidst the treasures of the great capital, of living a new life amidst antiquities of yesteryear. She'd survived not only that first transatlantic crossing, but subsequent others as well, because here it was twenty years later and Vanessa had touched down once more on U.S. soil. She was back, nearly home, and indeed

seemed changed. Not if the first thought she had upon seeing the reflective green sign for DANTON HILL, 10 MILES,
was about Him. It was almost like destiny had been flying
those planes, bringing her full circle from whence all things
began. She'd left Charles De Gaulle Airport yesterday,
flown back to New York's frantic JFK, and then hopped a
commuter flight to Rochester. Life in reverse, somehow
aging her twenty years.

Vanessa, comfortably ensconced inside her rental car,
made the sharp turn onto Route 14, following the direc-
tions from Google she'd printed out from her computer.
She'd never really driven all that much back in high school,
she always had Danny to ferry her around. She was always
the passenger, the popular cheerleader who waved out the
open window like a politician in training. As soon as she
grew closer to the small village that bordered the windswept
shores of Lake Ontario, familiar images began to find her,
memories falling back into place. She remembered where
she was and how to get there, as though Danny were now
her passenger. She wasn't a fan of riding with ghosts.

"You've come this far."

Switching on the windshield wipers, Vanessa sighed out
of frustration. How many times as a teenager had summer
thunderstorms ruined those languid, humid afternoons
when she and her friends wanted nothing more than to
hang out at the beach checking out hot guys? How many
sultry nights making out with a horny Danny on the boardwalk had been interrupted with a sudden downpour?
Though he needed the soaking before things went too far.
Or when she was alone and walking along the rocky pier
they called the Point, careful of the slippery rocks? That
was life in Danton Hill, a literal wet blanket of a town.

Still, the rain now wasn't really much of a downpour, not
yet, so she could still gaze out her window and catch views

of the passing fields. It must have rained plenty this season, seeing how high the grassy reeds grew right alongside the roads. the countryside carpeted with verdant swaths of golden cornstalks ripe and ready for the picking. She could almost savor the sweetness of the kernels, buttered and salted to perfection. Tastes of childhood awakened her taste buds; picnics by the lake fueled her mind.

As she rounded a particularly winding bend, a car came into sudden view, zooming past her so quickly she only caught a glimpse of it. A red sports car, with an apparent fool behind the wheel. But as she craned her neck in an effort to gauge how fast the guy was going, she saw out of the corner of her eye a big farmhouse on the hill just beyond the cornfields. A bit run-down, her mind imagined what it would look like with a fresh coat of paint, some happy kids running around the front yard, herself situated on the porch, lazily swinging the afternoon away. Funny, in this picture, there was no husband, no man at all . . .

"Oh shit . . ."

Vanessa came out of her fantastical reverie to find her windshield sheeted with rain. The skies had truly opened up at this point, a bad time not to be paying attention to the road. Wiping sudden condensation from her fogging windshield, she righted herself on the road, realizing she was gripping the wheel so fiercely her knuckles had drained of blood to reveal only intense white fingers. Thunder crackled overhead, and a bolt of jagged lightning actually crossed so near her it could have cooked the corn. She jumped, more so in her mind than body, her seat belt holding her firmly in place. She knew this senseless daydreaming had to be set aside, time to concentrate on where the hell she was going.

"You're almost there," she said, nearly saying "home" instead.

Another sharp bend in the road was coming, and Vanessa eased her right foot down on the brake, gently reducing her speed as she maneuvered the car. Tires grooved with the ridges of the road as she smoothly hugged the shoulder. Another boom of thunder sounded above, and she reacted with shock and surprise. She looked up once at the sky, as though trying to ward off the storm, then her eyes focused back on the narrow road. And that was when she saw the other car—coming directly at her.

Turn, turn, turn . . . that was what her mind screamed.

But the car didn't, and neither did hers.

She had control of her vehicle; the opposite seemed true of the other driver.

Vanessa was momentarily blinded by headlights, her mind distracted by the very thought of an accident that seemed helplessly unavoidable.

Another boom. Was that just thunder again, or the awful sound of metal crunching upon metal? Had they already smashed into each other? Why couldn't she tell? She blinked, gazed back out the window, saw the lights again, headlights bearing down on her. But they did not come at her in a fierce rush of confusion and fear, rather with a serene, otherworldly effect, motion slowed for dramatic effect. She felt weirdly disoriented, as though what was happening wasn't really unfolding in her reality. The possibility of a crash had already slipped by, the gods above sparing them.

"Oh, thank—"

She didn't get a chance to finish that last sentence. She thrust her foot down on the brake, and she heard the screech of tires on wet tarmac just before she felt the impact, strong, hard, and violent. She felt a horrible, strangling tightness in her chest as she steeled herself. Then without warning the air bag exploded before her, knocking her back against her seat and headrest. Her hands were flung from their tight control of the wheel as the car spun once, twice, careening off the road, bouncing off the shoulder before plowing straight into the field of corn. It finally came to a stop with the aid of the thick, meaty stalks.

For a moment she sat there, stunned. She couldn't move, trapped as much by the air bag as by the shocking sensations that ripped through her system. And despite the screeching she'd endured moments ago, what now settled inside her car and all around her in the humid air was utter silence. Silence . . . except for the steady drumming of the rain dripping upon the roof.

Vanessa started to move, pushing down at the surprisingly firm material of the air bag. She managed to extricate herself from the bag, and then unclicked her seat belt. She was free of constraints, sort of. Still inside the car, but no longer strapped down. With shaking hands, she depressed the UNLOCK button on the door and heard the doors thankfully disengage. She eased the driver's side open and stepped out onto the squishy ground. Vanessa scanned the area, looking at her car, her location, the direction in which she'd come to a stop, all of it skewed by the steady rain that continued to fall from the sky.

She breathed a sigh of relief. She was fine, uninjured, just rattled.

That was when it occurred to her: What about the other car? The driver, any passengers?

She looked again through the thick curtain of rain, seeing nothing . . . nothing but the cornfield, one that seemed to stretch for endless rows. There was no sign of the car she hit . . . the car that hit her . . . whichever way it happened, there was no sign . . .

"Oh shit," she said.

She finally saw the car, or at least its tires. One of them still spun, as though it had not yet given up on fulfilling its natural existence. It was a wheel, it was round, and thus, it should turn, like life, a steadying force. Located about fifty feet away on the other side of the road, the car had cut a rough, ragged path through the dense, unpicked rows of corn. She didn't even know which direction she faced, which way she'd come from and which way the other car had. All she knew was that the scene before her didn't look right. It was too quiet. Not even thinking, she trudged through the mud, not even looking to see if any other cars were passing, as she made uneasy tracks for the other car.

"Hello . . . anybody, are you okay . . . ?" she called out through the sheeting rain, announcing her presence so as not to further spook the other victim, perhaps more than one. They could still be rattled by the loud crash, especially having tumbled and swerved as they had. She listened carefully for a response. None came.

Suddenly Vanessa stopped short at the fearful sight of the smashed wreckage before her. The car was turned on its side, passenger side facing down. A bloodied, masculine hand was dangling out the driver's side window, a man's watch evident on its wrist. The other thing she could tell, even from this distance? That hand wasn't moving. She wondered who this man was, what he'd been doing out on this rain-soaked road, and whether he was alive. Where had he come from, and what forces had brought him crashing, literally, into her world?

CHAPTER 2

THEN

He showed up for lunch just after one o'clock looking like a successful bum. Dark scruff coated his cheeks and a pair of designer sunglasses hid his eyes. Worn jeans with a rip at the knees that may or may not have been done deliberately hung off his trim waist, and a wrinkled button-down shirt that seemed to have broken up, or at least had a bad argument, with its iron flapped open over a V-neck T-shirt. Despite his stylized look of the downtrodden, he arrived at the tavern wearing a big shit-eating grin as he plunked down beside his friend Patch.

"Adam, you look like shit."

"No, I don't, and you know it."

"What would the boys on the thirtieth floor say?"

"They'd probably be jealous that I'm not wearing a tie and want the life I have."

"Yeah, until payday comes. Then they'd miss out on fattening their wallets."

Adam shrugged. "You make do. In this economy, you have to."

Patch, in his pin-striped suit and blue rep tie pinching his thickening neck, signaled to the hovering, blond waitress.

"Can I get a refill on my drink, and oh, can you find my real friend? I don't know who this slacker is."

"I'll have a Foster's. Pint," Adam told the waitress.

"Foster's?" Patch asked. "What happened to Johnny Black?"

"Beer is cheaper. And Foster's is Australian for beer, mate."

"Too much time on your hands, what are you doing, staring at the television all day?"

"Did you realize *General Hospital* has been on the air for, like, fifty years? That guy who plays Luke . . . what's his name . . ."

"I'm sure I have no idea what you're talking about."

"Well, whatever. He's aged, but man, that's what I call job security."

Patch Grimes, intrepid trader at the investment firm of Koch, Franklin, and Cohn, which had employed him steadily for over a decade, was Adam's best friend and former co-worker and only watched sports whenever the job afforded him a break. He still had his job; Adam didn't. Patch greedily knocked back the rest of his vodka martini, chewed an olive with the contempt of a snooty banker, and eagerly awaited his refill. It was, after all, lunchtime, and while for some people the day of the double martini lunch had gone the way of bonuses and expense accounts, Patch liked to think of himself as a student of the old school. He wore fancy suits and blue shirts with white collars and cuff links, even on casual Fridays.

Adam's sleeves were rolled up to his elbows. Every day was Friday for him, or better yet—Saturday. His mode of dress was certainly more suited to the low-rent surroundings of the Blue Room bar found at Second Avenue and Sixtieth Street, not far from where Adam lived and about half an island away from the prying eyes of Wall Street.

"So," Adam said, after the beer had been placed before him and he'd taken the first sip of the day. "You called this meeting, Chairman. What's up?"

Patch slid an e-mail he'd printed out from work. Adam noticed that his name appeared in bold near the subject line, causing his blue-flecked eyes to gaze up with surprise. Patch raised an eyebrow with more than a hint of mischief. "Interested?"

"What's this?" Adam asked.

"Did you forget how to read?"

"Patch, I'm not working . . . which means I don't want to work at anything."

"Fine, I'll translate business speak for you. Geez, it's been what, six months . . ."

"Eight months, three weeks, two days, a few minutes. Oh, and one more beer. Not that I'm counting anything, days or drinks," Adam said, taking a big, satisfying, post-noontime gulp of his cold brew. He signaled over to the waitress for another; by the time she arrived with it he'd be ready. "Look, Patch, if the subject of that e-mail is what I think it is, you can forget it. I'm not going back to work, certainly not now. I'm enjoying myself way too much. I kind of forgot who Adam Blackburn was, and it's taken me this long to really get a feel for how to do nothing."

"Regis is in the morning, Oprah is in the afternoon, a six-pack for lunch?"

"Cynic. Besides, both of them left their shows and are trying something else."

"How do you know all this?"

"Gotta do something while you drink those beers."

"Seriously, who are you? Now, just read the damn e-mail." He pushed the piece of paper back at Adam, who this time had no choice but to accept. Raising his fresh glass in salute, ⠂

his eyes wandered over the e-mail exchange between Patch and a guy named Topher Anderson.

"Topher? Seriously?"

"He and I go back to prep school."

"Of course you do, with names like yours."

"Adam?"

"Yeah, man?"

"Just keep reading."

He gave in and began to absorb its contents. From the business speak on obvious display in this message, Patch was pounding the pavement pretty hard, but not at all for himself. After the financial meltdown at the investment firm that insiders called KFC, Patch was one of the few execs who had done amazingly well. Promotion to senior vice president, corner office, two assistants and a secretary, the freedom to come and go and enjoy two-martini lunches, there was little reason for him to seek other employment. Only one thing he hadn't been able to do at the firm was save Adam's neck and butt, trying but unable to convince the partners to offer him a position on Patch's team. At KFC, the only thing fried was Adam's career.

"So this guy, uh, Topher, he wants to meet with me? Why, is he trying to commit career suicide—or worse?"

"What happened wasn't your fault."

"Tell that to KFC. Whatever. Moving on."

"Hey, Adam, everyone knows it's a tough world out there. All of our reputations took a big hit after the scandal. People still hate banks, bankers, the lot of us. What they don't dislike, though, is money, and we've got it. Look, the industry is trying to bounce back, and it needs smart people who always put company before the individual."

"That's my reputation? God, now I want to commit suicide. Ugh."

"Adam, that's not a very good interview word."

"Which, *suicide?* Or *ugh?*"

"You're in a mood."

Adam raised his glass, drank. "Good thing I'm not on a job interview," he said.

He saw Patch's expression falter before he could cover it with his martini glass. Was that an effort to hide what he was thinking, or was he just needing the sharp hit of booze?

"Uh, Patch, what the hell's going on?"

"Not that I was looking, but I've received an offer, a good one . . . no, wait, make that a fucking fabulous one from Topher's investment firm. Offices around the world, London, Paris, Hong Kong, hell, Sydney—all the Foster's you want. Topher says I can write my own ticket—which includes handpicking my staff. You're my number-one man."

"No, I'm not."

"Adam, high six figures, bonuses, hot chicks at the bars . . ."

"Been there, done them."

"You're going to turn down the job?"

"I don't know anything about it, and truth of the matter is, I really don't want to. The corporate life left me behind, and I'm happy to keep it that way. So you can tell, uh, this Topher buddy thanks but no thanks."

"You got some grand moneymaking scheme I don't know about? You win the lottery last night?"

"It's not about money right now. I saved, I'm fine. I'll sell the weekend house."

"Are you crazy?"

Adam shook his head, his eyes growing distant in the dim lighting of the bar. "Patch, have you ever wanted to just live the quiet life in some stupid little town that time forgot, maybe in a farmhouse somewhere?" He took a healthy swig of his beer while pouring over the menu.

"Now I know you're crazy. Drunk, too."

"Nope, I'm just me."

"Me. That's so existential."

"There are other planes than just the one we live on."

"Oh yeah, corporate jets too."

"You're not listening to me. I said no. It doesn't feel . . . right."

"Okay, now you're scaring me. Tell me more, Guru Blackburn."

Scuffling to dig something out of his jeans pocket, Adam eventually pulled out a piece of paper, unfolding it, smoothing it down. An e-mail of his own, his own surprise to spring on his friend. It was his turn to slide the paper forward. With a scowl on his face but not another word, Patch scooped it up and began to peruse the words, Adam watching as his friend's face grew wide with absolute horror. He thought he detected a new facial tic, a twitch of his eyelid. Finally Patch looked up, and despite his rule about two martinis and no more, he waved his hand high, ordered a third, and didn't say a word until it arrived and he'd taken a sip. Adam suspected his friend wouldn't mind being that olive right now, wanting to dunk himself inside the high-stemmed glass and drown himself.

"Where the hell is Danton Hill, anyway?"

"Upstate somewhere."

"Like Westchester?"

"No, Patch, really upstate. Lake Ontario."

"That's Canada."

"Sort of. Look, Patch, I don't know why I'm intrigued, but I am, and so I'm going."

"To your twentieth high school reunion? Upstate New York . . . in August?"

"Hey, not my decision, that's when the class decided to hold it. We were even polled on our class Web site for the best available month, and August received the most votes. June had too many graduations, July too many vacations. September . . . everyone busy getting on with their lives." Adam paused, shrugged. "So, August. I'm going. Back home."

"You can't go home again, isn't that what they always say?"

"Why not?"

"That's not an answer. Unless you're five years old."

Adam, about to open his mouth, hesitated, wondering how much of his motive he should reveal to his cynical friend. And then he thought, what the hell, Patch already thought he'd gone bonkers, why not carry it through? So he explained about his home of Danton Hill, the tiny lakeshore town he'd grown up in, and how he hadn't back in years. His family no longer lived there, his parents having moved down to Clearwater right after he'd graduated from high school. "But isn't there always this desire to go back home, see whether it's the town that's changed or simply your perspective on the world? In Danton Park, just before you hit the beach, there's this grassy hill that rises above the town, and there's a story that long ago it was used as a lookout point. Like a hundred years ago, when the original Danton family lived there. Seems one of its sons left for some adventure, or trip, or futile war, whatever, and he never returned. It still didn't stop his mother from journeying daily to the hill to keep watch until he came back. There are all sorts of stories from years ago. Danton Hill was a seafaring place, they lost several people to the elements. Speaking of . . ."

Patch interrupted him. "Gee, Adam, that's real touching about those soggy old tales, you thinking of jumping into the lake and creating your own legend? Or are you just content to play the prodigal son? Is that wistful mother still waiting on the shores of the great lake?"

"Patch, where's your romantic side?"

"I banged Susie Cooper last night, does that count?"

Adam shook his head sadly. "I said romance, not sex."

"Are you kidding with me with this? Oh wait, let me guess . . ."

Adam blushed, unable to hide it. "Well, yes, there was this girl . . ."

"Ah, geez, isn't there always," Patch said. "Adam, do you really want to show up at your high school reunion a current and future failure, looking like a reject from *The Bachelorette*? No rose for you. That's surely the way to impress your old high school sweetheart."

"Oh, the woman in question wasn't my girlfriend," he said, a bit wistful, that faraway look once again glossing over his eyes. "I just did her a favor one night, she did me one, too, and . . . well, the way it ended is not the way our story should have ended. There's unfinished business between us."

"Twenty years, you still think you can bag her? She's probably forgotten all about you. And if she has any sense—unlike you—she'll have the smarts to stay far away from Loser Hill. Something you would be considering too, had you not already lost your mind. Come on, Adam, forgot this nonsense, come work for me. Get back in the game."

Drinking the last of his second pint, Adam Blackburn said, "No offense, but I think I'd rather be dead than go back and work in that snake pit we call Wall Street."

"Bullshit. You just want to get laid, and you think this girl you non-dated in high school will punch your ticket."

"She's not like your Susie date. Look, I don't even know if she's attending the reunion," he said. "Really, Patch, it's not about her. Not her specifically. At least . . . I don't think so."

"So sure of yourself, huh?" he said sarcastically. "Want to explain that one better?"

He leaned forward, the empty glass caught between his two hands. "Did you ever get the feeling you'd met someone before?"

"Plenty of times, the next morning. We'd sober up and realize we'd met before, screwed each other on other occasions."

"Nice story, one for the grandkids no doubt," Adam said. "No, I'm serious, what I mean is . . . this girl, she reminded me of someone, even though I don't know who . . . or even why. Okay, Christ, even to myself I'm starting to sound crazy. Look, I've just got to go back to Danton Hill and see what happened to her. I've got to quiet this itch I feel."

"I know all about those kinds of itches, think I'll give Susie a call when we're done, see what she's up to. With three martinis in me, I think I'm not going back to the office, if you know what I mean," he said with a leering smirk. Adam said nothing, just stared at him. "Fine, this chick who time forgot, does she have a name?"

"Vanessa."

"Oh, sexy," Patch said, gulping down the rest of his martini.

"Patch?"

"Yeah?"

"I think you're drunk."

"Better that than sober and returning to work . . . or worse, back home to Loser Hill. Man, Adam, what the hell are you thinking—and besides, you look like hell. You want to impress a lady, get an iron, work a razor over that scruff . . . then buy a clue. You can't nail the hot chick from high school looking like something the cat dragged in."

"Well, girl, look what the cat dragged in."

"Sorry I'm late, luv. The tube was late in coming, the platform was packed, and I nearly gave up and walked the bridge from Waterloo," the newly arrived woman said, barely pecking her friend's one cheek, then the other.

"Excuse me, you who works for the wife of an ambassador, you took the . . . tube?"

"Face it, it's the fastest way around Central London, not to mention the cheapest . . . though that second one, not by much. Transit fees in this city are getting way out of hand. Reva, you know that better than anyone. How many times have we been stuck in traffic inside a taxi and you've muttered, 'Damn if we shouldn't have taken the bloody tube.' And now you're giving me a hard time about having done just that? So I wouldn't be late in meeting you?"

"Fine, whatever, ride among the huddled masses and wind up smelling like them. I hope you didn't catch any germs or infections," she said, fluffing her curly blond hair in an apparent gesture of ridding herself of any diseases Vanessa might have passed along to her with her air kisses. "Oh, and what's with sending me that text message to meet you here, and with such utter urgency? The Phoenix Club, honey? They stopped stopping people long ago, they'll let anyone in now as long as you're not already drunk." She paused. "They prefer you to get drunk on their booze."

"Reva, you're such a snob."

"Four-letter word, hon, we all use them."

"God, I need a drink."

Located on Charing Cross Road just a block up from the Leister Square tube station, the exclusive underground club was just a short flight of steps down from the theater whose name it shared, playing to a world of actors, performers, and artists, not your usual raucous public house crowd found in nearby Piccadilly Circus. Reva and Vanessa ordered their wines, a pale pinot grigio for Vanessa, a blood-red cabernet for Reva, then settled at a round, back table away from a bunch of squealing girls who looked like they'd just finished up their first day in publishing. "God, were we ever that young?"

"Reva, are you admitting to your age?"

"I don't age," she said, taking a healthy drink, "and neither do you. This keeps us young. Now, what's up, chicky? Tell me you're still flying to Amsterdam with me this weekend. Aren't Mrs. Slave Driver and her ambassador husband off somewhere glam and she's given you the weekend off, right? Wait, don't say a word, I've always been able to read your expressions and today's is not making me very happy. No, not happy at all." That last phrase seemed punctuated by periods after each successive word. "God, I think I'd rather be stuck on the tube with a smelly brute than hear you say you're not coming."

"Take your pick, Tottenham Court or Piccadilly?"

"God."

"You say that too much."

"Christ."

"Reva, I'm going to miss you."

"Color me intrigued. Spill, chicky. What's his name, and on the hotness scale of one to ten, what's his number?"

"You don't miss anything, do you? And no, it's not about a guy . . . not really. Okay, so, I got this e-mail recently and I just ignored it. Or at least, I tried to. But lately, the past week or so, I've been thinking about it. I didn't share it with you because I didn't want to give you a daily opportunity to talk me out of it. And besides, I wasn't even sure I was going to attend until, well, just the other day I talked myself into it. In the end . . . well, here, read for yourself. I'm going to the loo."

Vanessa Massey really didn't have to pee, she just wanted a moment's peace to herself while her friend realized the horror about to rain down on her life. Damn, but she would kill for a cigarette right now, and she was tempted to borrow one from those giggly girls too. There was something about being back in London that made her vices go into overload. Crave all the bad things in life, booze and butts and men's butts. Like rereading a book that had the dirty parts earmarked. For now, she'd have to settle for one out of those three vices, returning with fresh drinks after her stop to freshen herself up.

Without a word, Reva accepted the new drink in the spirit it was given: as a bribe.

"I know what you're going to say."

"Oh honey, you thought when I read this I'd go crackers on you, try and talk you out of going? You've been running from this place since you hopped that flight out of the States twenty years ago and came to Paris. Who knows, maybe going back is the right thing—finally get you to let go of your past and move on with your life. It's all connected, you realize, every decision you make, even if you won't admit it, has to do with your past. Oh wait, what do you call them . . . oh yes, your issues. Coming to Europe, that lingering dalliance with Dominick . . . the baby . . . your whole life, chicky. Vanessa Massey, go back home if you feel you need to. But this time, make sure you free yourself of that tether so when you come back to reliable ol' Reva, that's the end of it. There's still too much fun in the sun to be had. Even in rainy London."

Vanessa, pushing back her dark locks to reveal her catlike green eyes, tossed her friend a curious look. "Rev, we're on a fast, downward slide toward forty. Is that what you want, to go from aging party girl to predatory cougar? And to keep taking me along on the hunt?"

"God, cougar. Such a vulgar term, so American."

"Rev, we're both American."

A look of absolute horror crossed her friend's made-up, ruddy-cheeked face. She quickly gazed about the crowd to ensure no one had overheard such an offensive comment. They'd be tossed out of the Phoenix Club on their ears for sure, this time unable to rise from the ashes.

"When do you leave?"

"This coming Thursday."

"So, it's back to Danton Hill, huh?"

"Yeah."

"You think he'll be there?"

Vanessa visibly blanched. She recovered, though, because she needed to, realizing if she was going to bravely go back she had to work on that poker face of hers. No way could she wear her heart on her sleeve, not here, and definitely not later. "Maybe, probably, I guess so."

"Gee, so definitive."

"Okay, call it a hunch."

"You're using up an awful lot of frequent flier miles on a mere hunch, dear? God, don't you remember, you didn't even like him . . . he was just a stand-in at the last minute, and from what I remember from your stories, he was rather . . . ordinary. What kind word did you use to describe him, 'cute' . . . ? Like a puppy?"

"He was cute, in a little brother sort of way," Vanessa said. "But that was twenty years ago. He's grown-up and he's more than cute. You remember?"

"Sort of," she said, taking a drink from her wine, her red lipstick sticking to the rim of the glass. "Too many of these, I suppose. Then and now. But dear, he may have grown up but is he mature? Why should he be when you're not?"

"Reva, you're such a bitch," Vanessa Massey said, again pushing her hair away from her face, as though with such an action she had stopped hiding behind it. She was ready to show her confidence to the world, or at least to the corner of the world known as Danton Hill. "Now give me a damn cigarette. One last indulgence before I return to the land of the perms and sweatshirts worn off the shoulder. And may God have mercy on my soul."

"You're going home. So clearly he doesn't."

"Who?"

"God," Reva said.

"You say that too much."

Reva laughed, the deep sound flavored with a lifetime of smoking and perhaps a tinge of regret. "So, you're going back to find out if the boy you didn't like was actually The One? And then what? You two go off into the sunset together? Chicky, I'm going to miss you so much."

"Reva, I'll be back."

"With him in tow? Like in a movie, the music swelling as the credits roll?"

"It's Danton Hill," Vanessa said wearily. "The only thing that will be swelling will be the sewers. It rains more there than it does here."

"Hmm, let's hope your taste in men is better than your taste in destinations."

CHAPTER 3

NOW

He was still alive, or at least he thought he was. He couldn't exactly say he was familiar with what death felt like, having been alive all these thirty-eight years. Still, evidence suggested he'd survived the initial crash and impact: His eyes were blinking, and even though maybe he could feel the gooey wetness of blood, he couldn't pinpoint from where on his body it flowed. His current position of being trapped upside down in the car wasn't really ideal for a thorough examination. All he knew right this second was how numb his body felt and that the driver's side window had smashed, turning the once-solid glass into jagged slices, some still imbedded in the frame, other shards dangerously close to him. Rain continued to pour through the opening. He could feel neither the heat of any injuries nor the cool rainwater. As for what he could see, not too much. The world was askew, making it appear as though through the cracked windshield the towering corn was growing sideways, its husks like tentacles reaching out to him.

"Great, I'm stuck in a cornfield, probably going to die here among the stalks."

For a fleeting moment he felt a bit like the wily, supposedly brainless Scarecrow in *The Wizard of Oz*. Adam too had no clue in which direction to travel or even look, and his arms were just as twisted in confusion. But he had the brains to figure his way out of his predicament surely, rattled as they were from the accident.

Adam shook his head, trying to reduce the fuzzy haze behind his eyes. He blinked again, felt better as raindrops helped wash out any soot or specks of glass that might have slipped underneath his eyelids after the car had turned over. Darkness lessened and the overcast world came back into view, giving him a chance to review what had happened.

Another car coming at him, while his went seemingly out of control . . . skating on a sheet of water. Impact, collision, swerving, turning, twisting, finally resting. That was a lot of violent action in a short amount of time. Still, despite the fact his car had actually flipped over—how many times he wasn't sure—the seat belt and air bag had held him locked in position. He couldn't imagine where and how he might have landed had he not been wearing the seat belt; might have been tossed into the cornfields and had all his stuffing knocked out of him. Second best decision he'd made when getting the rental, putting safety ahead of comfort. First thing had been agreeing to the insurance. He had a feeling the car was totaled.

So then why wasn't he?

Adam shifted in his seat, wincing at the pain he felt on his side. The seat belt strap had ripped through his shirt, left him with a nasty burn. He could feel the edges of the rough cloth digging into his skin when he moved. Maybe that's where he was bleeding from, just a slight scratch or two. Just then his eyes blurred again from more intrusive raindrops. He wiped them away, noticing one of the droplets came away as a red smear on his fingertip. He dabbed at his forehead, felt more thick wetness.

"Great, a head injury," he said, touching it again. Still bleeding.

There wasn't much he could do about the wound right now, first he had to free himself before he could attend to any cuts and bruises. But was that really the smartest thing to do, trying to free himself from the confines of the twisted car? What if he had damaged his spine or had a concussion? Any sudden movement could worsen his potential injuries, leave him paralyzed or with lingering headaches.

"Geez, Blackburn, you sound ridiculous. You're fine. Get out of the damned car before the damn thing blows."

He supposed his rental car exploding into a huge orange fireball was a more realistic piece of paranoia than a spinal injury, a leak in the gas tank catching a stray spark. Or worse, lightning striking the stationary car and frying him to a crisp. Closed casket for him. Deep-fried corn on the cob for the guests. He laughed despite his situation, gallows humor indeed.

Adam looked up through the window. Jagged pieces of glass still clung to its edges. He didn't relish risking further injury by exiting through the window, even supposing his body could slip through the tight space. Instead, he reached up and tried the handle, hoping the door hadn't suffered too much damage when the car overturned. He pushed at it with strong, determined hands and a staining face streaked with rivulets of blood. Nothing, no give.

"Crap," he said.

He'd have to wait for someone to rescue him.

He wiped away the blood again, smeared it on his jeans.

That's when it occurred to him to wonder about what had happened to the other car. Was the driver okay? He'd caught a faint glimpse of a woman behind the wheel of the car, but no passenger. Though he supposed there could have been a child, a kid in a car seat in the back, someone you wouldn't see sitting beneath the dashboard. A mix of fear and worry for the other car punched his gut. He had to get out and assess the damage, call for help . . . where the hell was his cell phone? Not in his pocket and not clasped to his leather belt, because he was driving and the law said only hands-free devices were allowed. So where was it? In his weekend bag, in the backseat? No, he remembered taking it out at the last Thruway rest stop, placing it on the front passenger seat. Great, with the car rolling and rolling in the mud and field, that cell phone could be anywhere. And he wasn't exactly expecting anyone to call, so he wouldn't hear it ring even had a friend decided to find out what was up. Patch had wished him well, call me when you're back. Otherwise, radio silence. And for what's up, Me, he answered. Upside down.

No, he had only one choice. Get the hell out of the car.

Adam struggled against the fleshy material of the air bag, his hands finding the release of the seat belt buckle. He felt the pressure against his chest ease, a certain amount of flexibility returning to his body. Wiggling his way upward, he again winced from the pain in his side. Still, pushing through the searing pain, he managed to get a better grip on the door. A rush of adrenaline coursing through his veins, Adam pushed, pushed harder, grunted for extra effort like a tennis player returning an angry serve, and finally he felt the first give of the door. A scrunch of metal sounded against the quiet backdrop.

"Come on, come on, move, dammit . . . why won't you let me out?" he yelled, his voice echoing out beyond the confines of the car, the sound caught by wind.

Apparently the wind knew how to answer.

"Hello?" he heard.

Adam stopped pushing, going silent again. Had he heard something? Someone? Did he just answer himself back, or was there actually someone outside his car? Was it the driver of the other car? Perhaps another car whose driver witnessed the accident? Or maybe a paramedic, already come to his rescue? How long had he been out, unconscious from the car flipping over? He didn't recall losing consciousness; hadn't only a minute or so passed since the car had come to a crunchy rest within the stalks? With one hand still pushing against the door, he stole a look at his watch hand. Just what time was it? He wasn't going to get an answer because the face of his expensive, prized Rolex was cracked, the time stopped on 4:08 in the afternoon. Shit, as far as Adam's world was concerned, time had come to a standstill.

Or maybe it hadn't. There came that voice again.

"Is anybody in there, can you answer me?"

Okay, Adam heard that clear enough, a woman's voice calling through the storm, and it was near. Perhaps she was just outside the car, attempting to gain access to the upturned vehicle. Figuring out how to assist the person trapped inside.

"Yeah, hello, I'm in here, kind of trapped," he called out. "Alone . . . it's just me. I need help with the door . . ."

"Roger that," replied the woman. "I'm coming. Are you hurt?"

Again, the question begged at him. Was he? Aside from the burning sensation on his side, the bleeding, dribbling cut on his forehead, he appeared none the worse for wear. No back pain, no broken limbs. "I guess I'm okay. I think. Some blood and aches . . . just help me get out of this damn car . . ."

"I'm here," he heard next, realizing the voice was so clear, cutting through the rain and the clouds and the muck and the twisted metal of his Malibu. How close was his savior, her voice golden like sunshine, or so he imagined. Adam looked up and blinked away raindrops and there she was, a wet, muddied, but striking vision looming out of the shadows, looking down at him through the broken driver's side window. All that was missing was a halo of sunshine, but of course on a day like this, such heavenly apparitions weren't in the cards.

"Hi," he said.

"Hi," she said back.

Adam watched as a strange look gathered on the woman's face. His mind searched for the right word to describe just what she might be processing, and in the end his own scrambled brain settled on the word *incredulous*. The way she looked at him. It was like she knew him. But how was that possible . . . no one in Danton Hill was even expecting him, he'd even replied "maybe" to the reunion e-mail. Commitment with an out clause.

"Adam?"

"Excuse me?"

"You're Adam Blackburn."

This was the second time he heard his name spoken aloud, and it was not said in the form of a question. She stated it as fact.

How unreal was this, his savior knowing him? En route to his twentieth high school reunion in a town he'd barely called home for all these years, and now, just miles from his destination his rescuer not only knew him and somehow recognized him, but seemed to carry a look of disbelief about the strange coincidence herself. Which meant, deep down inside him, in a place he seldom allowed himself to venture, he knew exactly who this was.

"Oh my God," he breathed, the air escaping his lungs perhaps from injury, perhaps from the onset of shock. Or perhaps this lovely creature that was staring down at him with wide, green eyes had simply taken his breath away, just like it happened on the soundstages in the Hollywood dream factory. This wasn't the movies, though, there was no director to call cut, this was real life and despite how much it hurt, he could do only one thing: laugh. He felt a burning in his chest hurt, then coughed up rainwater. Still, he continued to laugh anyway, and when his body ceased its convulsions, Adam smiled slyly up at the woman he'd come all this way to see.

"So, some reunion, huh, Vanessa?"

"You could say that again," Vanessa Massey replied, staring down at the man she'd come to see, ignoring the rain that washed down around her.

"I would, but I think it would hurt more," he said, a coughing fit erupting the moment his laughter had subsided.

"Ooh, that doesn't sound good. Come on, let's get you out of there."

"Gee, you think?"

"I don't remember sarcasm being part of your repertoire."

"You didn't know me that well."

Vanessa decided a response to such a pointed remark would be counterproductive to their current situation. She knew it was important to get Adam free from the wrecked car. Still, this moment in time gave her pause. She marveled at life, at its unlikely twists and its devilish turns, not unlike the winding road she had just traveled. It was one filled with unexpected encounters. Of zooming sports cars, towering stalks of corn, that lone farmhouse up on a hill, and a fleeting memory of a man who had inadvertently changed the direction of her life all in one night. Those were the flickering images her mind had seen, and as it turned out they were as real as the accident. Because what were the odds that both of them had decided to return for the reunion, heading for Danton Hill at the very same time, crashing their cars into each other?

An explosive reunion indeed, more than she could have envisioned.

"Hey, Vanessa, a little help?"

"Oh right, sorry."

Caught daydreaming again, allowing her mind to wander down paths long covered by the hazy overgrowth of many yesterdays. Adam needed her assistance. Wiping rain away from her face, Vanessa reasserted her hold on the vehicle, her feet planted on the overturned tires, hoping to gain traction. She instructed Adam to try and push the door again; meanwhile she grabbed at the outside handle, and together they worked the door open, the sharp cry of metal screeching as the hinges separated from damaged locks drowning out all noises. Finally, the driver's door thrust wide open, nearly causing Vanessa to lose her fragile footing and fall six feet into a muddy puddle. Not that she didn't already look her worst after the accident and the drenching she'd received from the incessant rain, but hey, you meet up with a guy from high school you'd once danced with at the prom while colored lights circled around you and suddenly you're America's Top Klutz, two left feet. She somehow managed to hold on and found herself suddenly presented with his hand, strong yet craving a true connection. What would this first touch be like? Would it send electric tingles through her body, or would she feel . . . nothing?

"Uh, Vanessa, can you focus please?"

"Right, sorry, where's my head?"

As their hands clasped, she found Adam looking straight into her green eyes. He paused, seemingly to take a moment to search for the appropriate words in this situation. "Vanessa, are sure you're okay? I mean, is it safe to assume you were driving the other car?" When she didn't respond, he knew it to be true. "Anything hurt, any bruises? Another one traveling with you?"

"Thanks, no, I'm fine, surprisingly okay. And I'm alone," she said, "and just a bit shaken by the impact. Good thing for seat belts and air bags. The cornfields broke my fall. Now, come on, let's get us both off this car."

He emerged onto the top of the car with an assist from Vanessa, and there the two of them stood, seemingly on top of the world, or at the very least towering over the fully grown cornstalks. Beyond them in the near distance, the waves of the lake crashed against the shore, churning from the passing storm and eating away at the banks. For them, though, looking down at the ground, they realized the best way down, really their only option, was to jump. Vanessa insisted on going first, since they couldn't be sure how well his legs would hold up. So, as she leaped into the air and splashed down into a thickening puddle, muddy water further ruining her clothing, she positioned herself best to catch him. Well, not catch him completely, just kind of help to break his fall. It was obvious he wasn't the puny little kid from school anymore.

"Here goes nothing," he said, taking a leap into the air.

"Adam . . . no! Wait, I'm not ready . . ." Vanessa exclaimed, still trying to secure her footing. The mud sloshed around her ankle, causing her to slide. He was going to land right on top of her, and his weight would . . .

A second later Adam landed awkwardly in her arms, twisting his ankle and crying out in pain. Vanessa had trouble holding on to him, and with the slippery ground there was going to be only one result. They were going down. And they did, in a big wet splash. Mud swirled around them, instantly coating them in a brown mush. Neither one of them spoke a word as they just absorbed the impact of the ground, the slushy feeling of the mud, wetness and cold enveloping them. God, they must look a frightful sight. Vanessa had envisioned various ways she'd meet up with Adam this weekend, and this certainly wouldn't have made the Top Ten list. Not even the top hundred, if she wanted to be honest.

Being honest, now there was a scary notion, even while in his strong arms. Her encounter with Adam had come far sooner than she'd expected, and without warning. Like this was no accident, the fates having their brand of fun instead. As she and her high school prom date sat in the mud twenty years after the event, each staring at the other, she found that words would not come. Wiping brown muck away from her face, she supposed it was a good thing she couldn't talk. She might actually end up literally eating her muddied words.

"So, fancy meeting you here," Adam said, finally breaking the silence.

"Yeah, funny, huh?"

"You sure you're okay?" he asked.

"A filthy mess. But yeah, I think so."

He nodded.

She stared at him.

Awkward silence fell between them. Vanessa looked away out of nervousness, and then stole a glance back. His eyes hadn't moved from their position, a hint of blue against a gray sky.

"What?" she asked.

He shrugged. "I don't know, I mean . . . you look great."

Vanessa laughed aloud. "Oh yes, covered in mud, looking like a drowned rat. Brown is so my color. Just how I want to appear at my high school reunion."

"Yes, well, you're not alone there."

"True, you're kind of disgusting too. But hey, at least . . . you know, we're alive."

Adam was getting ready to respond when the sky spoke for him. Thunder rumbled again, fierce and loud, dark clouds settling directly over them as a new band of the relentless storm sought them out. Lightning struck again, streaking the low-hanging sky with angry flashes of blazing yellow. They both stared upward.

"Think help is on the way?"

Vanessa looked around at their mangled cars. In the encroaching darkness they were not easy to make out, and soon the stalks would claim them for the long night. Other than that, there was no sign of other people, no passing traffic, no sirens blaring in the near distance.

"Doesn't look like it. You wanna call nine-one-one?"

"I'm not sure where my cell phone went," he said. "Got thrown when the car overturned. Yours?"

She shook her head. "Not working. The plastic shell shattered in the crash."

"Convenient," he said, sarcastically. "Seems as though we're in quite the pickle, and with no one around to help us, looks like we're gonna have to figure something out alone, uh, together," he said. "Got any brilliant thoughts? Any idea what people did before we became slaves to our cell phones? We should probably seek some shelter. I'd say your car or mine, but we know that mine is rather uninhabitable at the moment."

"Come on, let's see what we can salvage from mine."

Somehow she managed to get up from the slippery puddle, then helped Adam to his feet. He hobbled along beside her, wincing still from the pain of his freshly injured ankle. She hoped he hadn't broken it during his landing, she wasn't sure she could carry him, much less balance his weight against her body. The insistent rain continued to fall on them, and the threatening dual presence of lightning and thunder continued; this was the most persistent summer thunderstorm she could remember. Shouldn't it have passed by now?

The two of them made their way across the road to Vanessa's car, inconveniently parked in the cornfield. Mud swirled around the tires; it was clear the car was going nowhere without the assistance of a tow truck. And she rather doubted one would magically appear, not when they'd seen no sign of an ambulance or police or any kind of Good Samaritan. For the moment, the world was theirs, the two of them doing battle against the elements.

"I suppose we could wait out the storm in my car," she said, "making more of a mess of it than I've already accomplished."

"Not much choice. We need shelter."

"But we also need to get out of these clothes . . ."

Adam grinned. "Why, Vanessa Massey . . ."

She blanched. She couldn't help it. No reminders, not this early.

"Sorry," he said. "That was inappropriate."

An attempt at a brush-off laugh, Vanessa said, "Get your mind out of the—"

"Mud?"

They shared a genuine laugh, awkwardness fading between them for the first time. It felt good, like a breath of fresh air.

Still, Vanessa suddenly looked away, embarrassed by the heated, sexual connotation of not only what she'd said but also Adam's quick reaction to it. Were her cheeks reddening? Could he feel a change in the air, in her? God she hated her lack of a poker face. Reva was always calling attention to it on those occasions when they gambled, either in the casinos of Europe or in the love department. She felt like Adam could read her mind right now, and that was not a good thing. Not now. Perhaps not ever.

"Really, I'm sorry, I didn't mean . . . it's just . . . I didn't mean to offend you."

"It's okay, Adam. You just caught me by surprise. I mean, given our past . . ."

"Vanessa, forget I said anything," he said, making an attempt to touch her shoulder but pulling back at the last moment. The sweet gesture was intended to comfort her, and Vanessa decided to make nothing more of it than that. Adam didn't give her the chance anyway. He was ready to spring into action, his ankle notwithstanding. "Come on, let's focus on here and now, getting us out of this storm and into some dry clothes. I could go back and get my suitcase . . ."

"Wait a minute," she said. "The farmhouse!"

"Okay, you got me there. What farmhouse?"

"About half a mile back, I noticed an old farmhouse situated up on the hill. A big house with a porch, a swing, expansive lawn. We can make it there, I'm sure, and ask the people who live there for help. Surely they have a phone. Not like it's the eighteenth century. What do you say, your ankle up for a quick hike?"

Thunder rumbled once more.

Adam looked up; rain washed over his muddy, bloodied face, leaving streaks.

"I hate thunderstorms."

"Storms always did me in too," Vanessa said.

"Every summer in Danton Hill," he said.

"Almost like every day during a Danton Hill summer."

Their shared memories had already begun.

"One storm ruined my swing set. I was five."

"You've changed."

"God, I hope so."

"That farmhouse, it had a porch swing, I saw it, moving in the breeze."

"Lead on," he said. He smiled and she attempted one back.

The two of them started forward down the stretch of

road, sticking to the shoulder for safety's sake but looking for any sign of a passing car. They walked side by side, not touching, not even attempting one . . . at least, not until she slipped on a rock and nearly fell in the ditch beside the road. Adam went to grab her. As their hands touched, she felt the spark between them give deeper heat to the humid night. She looked into his face and realized she was not in the company of the innocent young boy from her high school days but a handsome, strong man who produced within her something that had gone untouched for years. Almost a re-awakening of something hidden deep inside her. Like she wasn't even the woman she'd known these thirty-eight years. She felt a fleeting rush of emotion that had once ex-isted between them flare up inside her, making a sudden re-turn, and with such a sensation racking her body, she figured such heat could dry their clothes and possibly melt her heart too.

Don't get ahead of yourself.

He doesn't know everything. She wondered if he knew any-thing, about them.

They forged on, together.

Shelter awaited them just around the bend in the road. So too did the unforeseen.

But hadn't she lived with a notion of uncertainty for twenty years?

CHAPTER 4

NOW

The farmhouse, with its wraparound porch and Old World–style cupola jutting up from its angled roof, turned out to be nearly a mile from the crash site. By the time Adam and Vanessa had made their way to the protective covering of its gabled porch, few words existed to describe just how soaked to the skin they were. Their clothing resembling mere tatters of cloth now, soggy, muddy, and wearable never again. For Adam, he was never more grateful to see shelter, something he'd never even given any consideration. He'd always had a roof over his head. He kept an apartment in a high-rise steel building in Manhattan, and currently still owned a summer home in the rolling mountains of the Catskills. Life had been kind to him and he'd tucked away a good amount of money, which had allowed him to take full advantage of every chance afforded him. The idea of being caught without a place to stay or to keep him protected, without any way of communicating with the outside world, seemed positively barbaric. Add to this his balky ankle and Adam Blackburn suddenly found himself being thankful for the little things in life.

"Here we are, at last," he said, dropping to the porch steps from exhaustion. "Thank God we made it. I wasn't sure how much longer my ankle could hold out."

"I was beginning to think I might have to carry you on my back," Vanessa said, suppressing a rare smile. Not that they'd had much reason for them given their situation. "Rest your weary self, I'll knock and see if anyone's home. Though from the looks of the uncut lawn and the empty driveway, I'm not sure anyone has called this place home for a while."

"Gee, great. What more could go wrong?"

Adam gazed around. No cars in the driveway, the grass overgrown, the slats of the porch in desperate need of a fresh coat of paint. The porch swing was the only evidence that someone called this place home, its gentle rocking in the wind a tease of life recently lived. Vanessa was right, they may have just stumbled upon a place that could offer covering but little else in the way of amenities. No clothes, no food or beverages . . . that probably meant no working phone or electricity. Like the fates of fortune continued to fail them. Still, it felt good to not have the incessant rain pelting down on them like a continuous form of Chinese water torture.

As Vanessa made her way to the front entrance, Adam untied his shoe and freed his foot. Rubbing his ankle, he noticed just how swollen it was. He moved it around a bit, grimaced again from the shooting pain. It wasn't broken, that was his sense, otherwise how could he have made it this far? He'd only had to lean on Vanessa a short while until he'd felt he could put his weight on it again. He wondered: How was it that during their thirty-minute walk through the storm en route to this deserted farmhouse they hadn't come upon another living soul, not a single car or a wayward individual out for a walk during nature's wrath? Not even a barking dog. The world, as far as they were concerned, had gone quiet.

"Hello, anyone home? Hello?" Vanessa said, rapping her knuckles on the screen door.

From his position on the porch, Adam watched Vanessa knock again, this time opening the weathered screen door and hitting the thick front door harder, all while peering through the glass. She knocked again, calling out once more. What came back in response to her gestures and words were hollow sounds, an echo of her own self that rang inside the old home. If someone was home, they were deaf, a deep sleeper, or dead.

"Nothing," she said, turning back to Adam. "Got any ideas?"

He shrugged. "Try the doorknob. Maybe it's unlocked."

She tried it. The knob did not turn.

"Got any other ideas?"

"Break the glass, then turn the knob from the inside."

"Adam, I'm not breaking and entering into someone's home."

"Hey, Vanessa, we're not exactly criminals here."

"Still, I can't do it."

Adam groaned as he stood up, hopping over to the front door while hoping to avoid getting a splinter in his exposed bare foot. He knocked loudly with his fist, calling out, "Hello, we need some help here, anybody home?" Waiting two beats and getting no response, he shrugged once in Vanessa's direction, and seeing the anticipation cross her face, he used his elbow to crash through the square window. The glass shattered easily and fell to the floor in dangerous shards, unlike the window of his wrecked car. Adam stepped away from a nasty slice that nearly impaled his foot. Then he reached in, careful to avoid the lingering glass, turned the dead bolt, and then pushed open the door. It swung wide with a slight creak of age or neglect, letting a musty smell drift outward, as though the air inside had been trapped and desperate to be freed, now taking to the wind with a exhale of relief.

Adam and Vanessa gave each other one last look before stepping inside the musty home.

"Hello?" Vanessa called out.

"I think we've pretty well established that no one's home," he said. "Come on, I don't know about you but I could use a shower. Wash this mud off me."

"Let's see about finding a working phone first," she said, moving farther into the house. "The sooner we find help, the faster we're back on the road. There is our reunion to attend. Isn't that why we're here?"

"The reunion—I think it's already begun," Adam remarked.

Her eyes shot him a nervous look, fingers absently tugging at her damp, limp hair, before gazing back inside the house.

Adam closed the door behind him, not bothering to turn the lock. Why bother? What were the odds someone else would stumble upon the house? As he followed behind Vanessa, he noted that the living room to the left of them was still furnished, albeit covered in clinging white sheets. Like only ghosts wafted about, living here beneath a coating of dust. They made their way toward the rear of the house, coming upon a sizable kitchen, obviously the heart of the home where family played, worked, talked, ate. Adam could almost envision the occupants, a kindly older couple making large, old-fashioned meals for their visiting children, grandchildren, distant relatives. He could see the woman of the house standing over a large pot, boiling the fresh corn she picked just that morning from the side of the road. Adam's stomach grumbled loudly in the quiet of the room. He wouldn't mind an ear of sweet, buttery corn right about now. Heck, he'd even eat the stalks.

But what most interested him right now was what he found on a wall separating the kitchen from the pantry. An old rotary phone, complete with the twisting black coil that connected receiver to base, was mounted on the wall near the stove. Like something reaching out from the set of Mayberry. Where was Aunt Bee along with some fresh-baked cookies? Vanessa reacted first, picked up the hard receiver and putting it to her ear. Even had her expression not faltered, Adam could have guessed the phone wouldn't work. Because in the silence of this house, even a dial tone would have been deafening.

"I think that phone only calls the nineteen-fifties."

She frowned wanly.

"Well, so much for that brilliant idea," she said, leaving the receiver to twist in the air. The way it swung off its cord, Adam was reminded of the weaving porch swing and how it had given off false hope of life. This house seemed to embody the idea of souls having left the building, like they'd just missed whoever called this place home. The images in his mind were not unlike those depicted in movies about a full-fledged Armageddon, leaving the world empty. A hollowness pervaded the room. But nothing destructive had happened in the world, only a fierce summer storm had swept by, wreaking its vengeance on a small part of it, catching Adam and Vanessa in its wake.

"So, got any fresh ideas?" Vanessa asked.

"I'd like to go back to my original one of a shower. Might help clear my mind."

"Fine, you get cleaned up first, I'll see about some food. Got any favorites?"

Adam smiled. "Spam and baked beans, at the rate we're going."

"Go shower, see about that cut on your side. Your shirt is sticking to it."

Adam had nearly forgotten about the streaks of blood on his side from where the seat belt had shredded both shirt and skin. The cotton material was probably caked into his skin, peeling it away would not be the prettiest of things. Hopefully the shower had hot water and could help melt away the pain.

He started off, but quickly turned around. "Hey, Vanessa?"

"Yeah?"

"This is kinda weird, isn't it?"

"You could say that."

"I did."

She laughed at him, the sound filling the cozy room. "Thanks, Adam. After the stress of the accident, I think I needed that kind of release."

"I think we both did. We need to laugh. The other option is . . ."

Vanessa quieted him by placing a finger to his lip, the physical act so quick but intimate. Adam nearly kissed her finger in return, but something held him back. "Go. I have a strange sense we're not going anywhere for a while, so there's plenty of time for talk . . . you know, later. Guess we're going to have our own reunion." She paused, and again her eyes glazed over with a faraway look. Then what came out next was but a whisper of emotion. "A private reunion, and one a long time coming."

"Our cars crashing like that, you think something else is at work here?"

"Like what?"

"Fate? Destiny? If you believe in such things," he asked, his words like a question.

"Do you?"

A strange, uncertain look crossed over Adam's face, his eyes darting around the spacious kitchen and homely feel of yesteryear. A chill hit him, despite the humidity floating through the house. "I feel like I've been here before."

"Well, we did grow up in Danton Hill."

"No, no, I mean this house."

She shook her head. "I don't think so, at least, nothing strikes me as familiar. You?"

Adam continued to look around at the old-fashioned country kitchen. What stared back should have been home-spun, old-fashioned warmth. Instead, that chilling sensation remained, digging deeper into him. He shivered. "I guess not."

"You want to know what I think?" Vanessa asked. "You banged your head good and it's making you think weird thoughts."

He wanted to be convinced. The uncertainty, though, was beginning to settle in.

"Still, it's like something brought us here."

She pushed him away. "Stop spooking me. Go, get cleaned up."

As Vanessa began to pour over the kitchen supplies to see about getting some food into their systems, Adam made his exit. He hobbled back down the hallway and, with a strong grip on the railing, began to make his way up the long wooden flight of stairs near the entrance hall. With sweat now mixing with the mud and blood, he at last came to the landing on the second floor, sensing that shower spray just down the hall. Opening door after door, passing bedrooms and, thankfully, a stocked linen closet. He grabbed a couple of clean towels, and then continued to the next door, where he at last found the bathroom. There was both a separate shower stall and a large, claw-foot tub, and while the idea of luxuriating in a bath was appealing, what he needed right now was the pelting spray of the shower to wash away all the mud and muck. As he adjusted the nozzles, he thought of the irony of going from outside rain to shower, how one had sullied him, the other would cleanse him like a baptism. Adam then began to remove his clothes, stopping short at the shirt, which still stuck to him. He left it on and stepped into the shower.

"Ohhhh," he said as the spray of heat hit his body. "Thank You, Lord, the boiler works."

He let the steam swirl around him until the stall was fogged up, and then he doused his body with hot water, stinging his side. He peeled the shirt off, grimacing from the pain. But at least he was free of it and he tossed it over the side. Time to clean up, dress his wound. He must have remained within the confines of the shower for a good twenty minutes, watching as the water turned to brown, only to return to a more favorable pink coloring as his body was rinsed clean. With the help of a stray bar of soap he found in a drawer, he washed his bloody side and for a second the water turned red; he'd reopened the wound. The sting from the soap made him cry out, but he was grateful to feel anything after the numbness his body had felt when he'd been trapped inside the upturned car. Setting about cleansing himself one more time, he made certain he wiped all the caked mud out of every nook and crevice. At last he turned off the shower nozzle, wishing he could have remained for hours. But who knew how long the hot water would last, and he didn't want to deprive Vanessa of the same bliss he'd just experienced.

Adam stepped out of the shower and grabbed the towel, wrapping the thick terry cloth around his waist. Leaning into the mirror, his fingers probed his hairline where he'd just noticed a small cut intersected with his forehead. Blood had dried here too, and the gash remained opened. He peered in even closer and detected a miniscule piece of glass inside the cut that the water hadn't washed out.

So that's where the blood had come from that had leaked down his cheek.

"Oh, nice," he said, wondering just what he should do about it. The wound didn't hurt, but he was afraid if he jostled the shard of glass he might start to bleed again, or even worsen the injury. "Leave it alone for now," was what he said to his reflection.

The wound on his left side was far more in need of immediate attention. Looking down, he could see the red welt he'd received from the seat belt when it pulled at him when the car had overturned. Small droplets of blood still seeped from the streaks on his side. Guess the shower wasn't going to be the easy fix he'd hoped for. Grabbing for a washcloth from the side basin, he dipped it into hot water, then gently pressed it against his skin. Immediate pain shot through his body and he pulled the cloth away.

"Shit," he yelled.

Just then he heard a knock at the bathroom door. "Adam, you okay? I heard that . . ."

"Yeah, I'm fine. Just, I'm going to need some bandages . . ."

"Well, you're in luck," she said.

The door opened and in walked Vanessa, a package of white gauze in her hands. "I had a feeling you might need some aid . . . oh, sorry, I didn't realize . . . I'll come back . . ."

Adam, still only wrapped in his towel, turned to her and smiled.

"Vanessa, hey, it's okay, come in. After what we've just been through today, I don't think we need to stand on ceremony.

Besides, you can play Florence Nightingale and help wrap the gauze around me. Did you find any tape with it?"

Vanessa stood there, indecision taking charge of her brain. She'd just casually walked in on a semi-naked man and her instinct now was to back away. Yet her feet remained frozen on the slat between the hallway and the bathroom. She felt stupid for just barging in, and now she was embarrassed by her inability to just suck it up and help him. But here was the man she'd hoped to see at the reunion, Adam Blackburn, clad only in a towel. And he looked good in it . . . *stop it*, she said, *he needs your help*. Of course, Vanessa had seen him in far less clothing than what he was wearing now, but that was a different time, that was the past, a lifetime ago. He'd been practically a kid then, her too. But now, this feral attraction caught her by surprise. Was this something she'd had in mind when she decided to attend the reunion? Had she been hoping for a repeat encounter of their intimacy? Or was it just a natural response of seeing a man without clothes on? It had nothing to do with him.

Him.

She realized she had to do something, say something, because at the moment it appeared that all she was doing was staring, gawking. He looked good. Despite the grin he'd added to his wardrobe.

"I . . . Adam, aside from the bandages, I was really coming to tell you that I found some food that we can actually eat, and surprise, surprise—how about a bottle of wine? Haven't found the corkscrew yet, but maybe I'll look again. Yes, that's what I'll do, I could use a drink right about now." She paused, took a step back, then took one step forward toward him. She placed the gauze on the edge of the sink, stole a look at an obviously bemused Adam, and then made a bid for a hasty retreat. She closed the bathroom door with a bit too much force.

As she walked away, she could hear a chuckle coming from inside the bathroom.

"Jerk," she muttered.

Still, on her way back down the long staircase, clutching the wooden rail in an effort to steady her nerves, the picture of Adam in that blue towel kept popping into her brain. A reunion, a car accident, no phones, just her and him and alone in an abandoned farmhouse, and now she'd mentioned a bottle of wine. Now to top it all off she'd just seen him nearly naked and all she could think of was: *Give me some of that.* He'd looked sexy, for sure—sexier than she could have imagined. He'd aged well. Her pal Reva would have told her to make a play for that trim, athletic body, with well-defined muscles on his arms and a shock of dark chest hair to run her fingers through. Adam Blackburn had grown up a lot, both physically and emotionally, since high school. He'd been almost still a boy back then, and now . . .

She almost missed that last step.

"Focus, girl. That's not what this weekend is about," she said.

But wasn't it? What was her purpose in traveling all these miles—across an ocean for goodness' sake—for the reunion? To see her old high school gang of Jana and Tiffany and Davey and Rich? She was in touch with them already, she spoke with the girls regularly and e-mailed with the guys, and so getting together with friends you still knew could hardly be considered motivation for going to your twentieth high school reunion. No, she'd thought about it in the car, and she was thinking it again now. She'd come purposely to see Adam, but she'd wanted to see him not so she could experience some kind of sexual reawakening. No, she'd come to settle the past with him, to talk, and he was clearly unsuspecting that there was anything to discuss. Her motives were hidden. His intentions looked quite apparent given that supercilious grin he'd adopted when she'd backed out of the bathroom. Though why he would suspect they had unfinished business, she didn't know. She was the one with the secrets. Adam Blackburn knew nothing of what had happened to her.

"The wine, must open the wine."

As she returned to the spacious kitchen, she looked at the plates of food she had prepared. Tomato soup, simmering on the stove, a tin of Vienna sausages that opened with the ease of a pull-top lid, and that bottle of red wine, standing like a sentry on the middle of the counter. With renewed vigor, she hunted again for the corkscrew; there had to be one, why else buy wine if you didn't . . . maybe it had been a gift, maybe the wine was years old and had turned to vinegar. God, chicky, she hoped not, and then let out a laugh, realizing she sounded like her friend Reva. What would she think of this situation? Enjoy the wine, she'd say, and see where things go from there. Which, of course, was why Vanessa was jumpy, she knew herself. The soothing velvety feel of the wine would go a long way toward settling her nerves.

Rummaging around in one drawer, then a second, she found every possible utensil and kitchen aid possible—vegetable peeler, cheese grater, chip clip, everything except the damn corkscrew. She slammed the drawer shut, the lack of a bottle opener manifesting itself into frustration over this crazy, unlikely scenario. This was not the kind of high school reunion she had imagined when she'd answered yes to that e-mail. She was playing house with the one man she should not be doing it with.

"Good afternoon, darling, what have you cooked up for us?"

The sound of Adam's voice coming up from behind startled her, and she nearly jumped out of her skin. "Adam, don't scare me like that . . ."

"Who else did you think was coming? Did we invite the neighbors?" he said.

"Gee, you're funny."

"It's obvious we're alone, so I think we can relax. We're fine, and given the storm is still raging outside, I'd say it's going to be that way awhile. What they call an all-day soaker. Seems to me this old house is someone's second residence and that at the present moment, well, they're probably at their primary. Surely they can't be summering in Florida in August, only to return and spend the winter in Upstate New York. What kind of masochists would they have to be to endure something like that?"

Vanessa realized he was right, they should just relax and enjoy whatever was going to happen. When the world gave you a time-out, take it, enjoy the decompression. She turned to him, laughing at the unexpected sight before her. Adam was standing before her dressed in checkered pants and a striped shirt—looking very much mismatched and ridiculous. Like a Scotsman had thrown up on him. "You planning on going golfing?"

"Yes, I know how silly I look," he said, giving himself the once-over, "but the people who live here, whoever they are, have strange tastes."

"Tell me about it. They have wine, but no corkscrew."

"Is that what's got you so flustered? Here, let me see about it. Wine would be great right about now."

"I told you, I looked . . . twice."

"Vanessa, so far this afternoon we've had to think on our feet, use our ingenuity. Climbing out of an overturned car, walking a mile in the rain—with a bum ankle and against the wind. Seems like we have to step up our game again and think creatively," he said, approaching the counter. He grabbed hold of the bottle, began to undo the red foil at the neck of the bottle. It easily came off, but then there was that seemingly impenetrable cork. "Got a knife?"

"*That* I found in my search," she said, and handed Adam a sharp steak knife.

So he began to dig at the cork, taking pieces of it out in annoying little nubs. But after a couple of minutes, he'd managed to cut through about half of the cork. That's when he placed the knife in the center of the bottle and instead of digging more at the cork, he pushed it down. Gently, easily, so as to not splash any of the precious liquid. The contents might have to go a long way, like the old Bible story of the loaves and fishes. Finally, the cork began to give. Vanessa watched as the remaining piece slid down inside the neck of the bottle until it broke free and settled inside the wider part, plunking into the wine. A few drops splashed out of the top, running down the front of the bottle, staining the label. Adam wiped at one of the drops, looked at it on his fingertip. It was like blood.

"Want the first taste?" he said, holding his finger out in front of her.

Vanessa took a step back, frowned at him. "Just taste it."

He did so, eagerly. His finger in his mouth, he gave her a wide smile of delight. "Yum, fruity. Not bad at all. But I suspect a bottle of vinegar would have done about now. So, shall I pour you a glass?"

"Actually, as tempting as that wine is right now—and trust me, I appreciate your efforts in getting that pesky cork out—what's more appealing is how refreshed you look. Makes me think maybe a shower is a good idea, get all this mud off me." She patted his arm. "So, why don't you finish heating up the soup, it's nearly done anyway, and then you can set the table. Excuse me."

As Vanessa started to slip by him, she felt his hand reach out for her. She stopped, looked at his fingers wrapped around her wrist, not hurting her, but strong enough where she could feel his pulse, he hers. That's when she gazed up at him and their eyes connected. A deep, penetrable look spoke volumes in the silence.

"Everything's going to be just fine, okay? We'll get out of this," Adam said, his voice soothing, the blue glow in his eyes offering comfort. "We're safe, we're uninjured for the most part. Someone will come to our rescue eventually. We didn't come this far only to fail."

"Speak for yourself," she said, her voice laced with an unexpected edge.

And then without an explanation for her cryptic comment, she walked with determination out of the kitchen and wound her way upstairs, no doubt leaving behind a suddenly confused Adam. She'd done that before, run from his kindness and into a self-imposed darkness. Twenty years ago it had been, the night of the senior ball.

How had that even come about, the two of them attending as unlikely dates?

It was like Adam had questioned tonight, were there fates out there controlling our lives? Was yesteryear one of those moments when the world had been working its magic, pushing them together even then? Had they failed to understand the true implications then? Were they just not ready?

Images flooded back to her as she recalled in bright detail the series of circumstances that had led them to dance that slow dance, all while the rest of the class looked on in surprise. It had been Adam Blackburn's one crowning achievement, socially speaking, in high school, and she was certain he recalled the moment fondly, perhaps proudly. Well, thought Vanessa Massey, her eyes darkening as she closed the bathroom door, shutting him out, shutting everything out, the world today and the past that never left her, she doubted he knew everything, and if he did, his life might just shift off its axis.

Rendering him never the same again.

Something else they would have in common.

CHAPTER 5

THEN

He'd already said no.

"Come on, you've got to ask her."

"You need to ask her."

"Trust me, dude, you definitely want to ask her." That last comment was snaked with a knowing wink that only a high school boy on hormones could command.

"You're such a perv."

Finally, a comment not being sent Adam's way, albeit temporarily. They all turned back to him after the slight distraction.

"Really, Adam, she'll say yes. I just know she will."

This last request, it was the only demand peppered with a degree of earnestness. He felt his resolve begin to weaken, despite having told them all no, no, a thousand times no, shaking his head and wishing them gone. They had ganged up on him about ten minutes ago outside his locker, and he was tired of their pleading. What they were asking made no sense. What did they really want with him?

"Why me? It's last minute. It's too late."

The kid who'd called him a dude, he fielded that one. "What you mean to ask is, it's last minute, why *not* you?"

Adam's face reddened. "Meaning, I'm free. No plans."

"Well, yeah, meaning . . . okay, fine, yeah, like, you don't have a date."

"And do you know why?"

"Yeah, 'cause you're a dweeb."

Someone smacked an arm. Adam wished they'd all just smack each other and leave him out of it.

"No, because I'm choosing not to go," Adam said with more defiance than he expected. "I wasn't planning to go—ever."

"Times change. Tenses change—you are going."

Peer pressure can come in many dangerous forms, especially when you're a teenager and your natural insecurities are ripe for easy manipulation. You give in, too quickly, because you want to belong to those who decide what's cool, who's cool—and who's not. You don't want to be the sorry victim of any behind-your-back snickering. For Adam Blackburn, smart kid and graduating senior who still bore the youthful appearance of some unsuspecting freshmen, it had been a long four years since he'd felt part of a gang of friends who didn't judge you based on clothes, pimples, or the kind of car your parents drove. Not that he was fooling himself into any form of social acceptance now; the four people surrounding him were only looking to help their friend. They didn't care for him.

Jana Stevenson, Rich Monk, Davey Sisto, and Tiffany Jones were four of the coolest kids in this year's graduating class. They ruled the busy hallways, the grounds, and the playing fields, while handing out instant approval—or disapproval—to anyone who dared attempting to enter their exclusive world without permission. On a sunny Tuesday afternoon in June, just after the final afternoon bell had rung, they had all practically pushed the unsuspecting Adam up against his locker, tossing their verbal volleys like a sadistic sergeant dealing with a vulnerable new recruit.

"I don't know, I mean, sure I know her a little bit . . . who doesn't, and yeah, we've been in each other's classes since first grade," Adam said, nervously, "but we haven't exactly been friends since then—she's barely said one word to me since we entered these hallowed halls of Danton Hill High."

"You know why? Because you say stupid shit like 'haloed halls.' Geez, Adam, you want her to say yes, don't talk like that, okay?" said Davey, the same guy who moments ago had called him dude. Davey Sisto was already six feet tall and wore a patchy blond beard on his cheeks. He was their leader, their idea man, an artful genius at getting the most out of doing the least amount of work. Adam was surprised to find that this guy even knew his name. Perhaps he'd been coached.

There'd been a time in his life when Adam Blackburn wondered where, if any place, he'd ever fit in. Time was he'd enjoyed the daily ritual of school, back in middle school when he'd been semi-popular and had an easy smile that seemed to draw people to him. Such were the simple years of tween-dom. The sliding social scale had all began to change, however, the moment he hit high school, when hormones and other uncontrollable matters in the universe took over and turned good kids mean, best friends into distant acquaintances, boys to men and girls to women. From ninth grade onward, Adam wondered why the world's axis had shifted, why the familiar had seemingly left him behind. At five feet seven and still apple-cheeked and innocent, it appeared that not even his hormones had befriended him.

And now, one week before graduation, three days before their crowning moment, the big year-end prom, he was being mercilessly dragged inside the lair of Danton High's self-appointed "inner circle." Why, he couldn't say.

"Why me?" he asked again, curious.

"Do you have a date from the prom?"

"I told you, I'm not even going. Why would I ask some-one if I'm not going?"

"But why aren't you?" asked Jana, touching his shoulder. "I mean, really, Adam, who doesn't go to their prom? Every-one and their brother is going."

"Some girls are even bringing their brothers."

"Yeah, the fugly ones," Davey said.

Someone slapped his arm again.

"Look, I'm just not interested. Why would I want to be one of those wallflowers that everyone makes fun of? I could just see it now, I'd never live that one down, probably twenty years from now at some dumb reunion everyone will be like, 'Hey, it's the dude who stood in the corner all prom.' Assuming I'd actually show my face to any such reunion."

"But, Adam, you'll get to go to both of them, the senior prom and the reunion and you'll be remembered as the guy who had Vanessa Massey as his date—and who knows, maybe she'll still be with you for the reunion, right?" stated Jana Stevenson, head cheerleader, debate captain, and one of Vanessa's closest friends.

"Yeah, you know, if you play your cards right," said Davey, who sounded like he wanted to get in Vanessa's pants more so than Adam.

Warning bells began to clang inside Adam's jumbled mind. Putting aside the juvenile innuendos that hung in the air, he concentrated instead on what Jana had said. He would be remembered, and not for four lousy years of higher education but for one night when he was given the privilege of escorting one of the prettiest, most popular girls in school to the prom. Now, if that tease wasn't the ul-timate in teenage manipulation, expertly handled by calcu-lating friends rallying around someone they loved, then nothing was. Trouble was, Adam wasn't the someone they loved, Vanessa was. He was a mere pawn in what he assumed was a bigger game.

"Just ask her. She'll say yes."

"You're sure?" Adam asked, still wary but beginning to come around to their side.

That's when Tiffany moved front and center, her feathery blond hair nearly touching his innocent face as she placed manicured hands on Adam's shoulders. "Look, our Nessa got handed a bad deal, you know—hell, the whole school knows—that Danny Stoker dumped her last week, told her he'd wasted his whole high school life on her and what an f-ing waste it had been. I mean, could you be a bigger jerk?"

"Yeah, he can," Jana said, "because he's taking that skank Lucy Walker to the prom."

"Look like Danny Boy wanted to make sure he gets laid that night," Davey stated.

"Honestly, Davey, is your mind ever out of the gutter?"

"Screw you," he said.

"As if," Jana replied.

"Nice to have you in the gutter with me."

"Ugh."

"So, Adam, sweetie, what do you say?" asked Tiffany, ignoring her friends' pointless banter, and concentrating instead on Adam.

He didn't provide them with an answer. He had enough of being emotionally jostled by this gang. He turned, pulled a couple books out of his locker, tossed them in his knapsack; he had some homework and major studying to do for finals. He closed his locker, turned the dial on the lock, and started off down the hall. Ironically, a banner was hanging nearby announcing the time, place, and theme of the big event, the Senior Ball. Adam thought the sign was poking fun at him, just like his so-called new friends. As he turned a corner, none of those four conspirators chased after him; nor did the sign. But one of them spoke before he was out of earshot.

"She's waiting out on the hill by the water tower," Tiffany said. "Just go over there, ask her, and I promise she'll say yes."

Adam looked back, but said nothing. What more was there to say?

Will you go to the prom with me? A simple enough phrase, for sure, but fraught with the drama that came with high school.

Somehow he didn't see those words coming out of his mouth.

Vanessa Massey hated him, so much so she could spit. If she saw him, maybe even spit on him. In fact, as she sat on the grassy hill up near the water tower where she'd spent so many of her perfect high school days, she angrily yanked a dandelion from the ground and contemplated its fragile state. She plucked the delicate petals, saying, "I hate him, I hate him more. I hate him, I hate him more." When she'd totally decimated the flower and the loose petals caught the wind and fluttered away, she realized she felt no better despite the fact that last petal had fallen victim to one last "I hate him more." Only in her depressed state of mind could she consider that result to be the best thing that had happened to her all day.

She thought about the prom, looming just days away. Her mind filled with pictures of the dress she'd already bought for the big event. Her mother had helped her shop for it, a flowing gown of violet, flower prints dotting the fabric; it would go perfectly with her dark coloring, her tanned skin and silky raven locks. She knew she would be among the most beautiful girls at the dance—and that's what she was aiming for. Not pretty, pretty these days was considered nothing but a backhanded compliment. Like you were still a mere child, carrying a few extra pounds of baby fat while all of the other girls had transformed into glamorous women. Beauty was her aim, especially now, given the fact that Danny had dumped her—dumped her!—just a week before the prom, and all because . . . well, of course it had to do with doing the deed. Didn't it always boil down to sex when it came to boys?

She remembered the conversation between them word for word, and she was certain she always would, even long down the road when she'd gotten married to a decent guy who didn't want sex, he wanted to make love, and they would have kids, she would experience the joys of married life and motherhood, probably even after the great beyond claimed her, Danny's words would haunt her. She would re-member the humiliating moment in school when her boy-friend broke up with her, in the middle of study hall, a week before the prom because she wouldn't "put out." So typical. Like a John Hughes movie with a bad soundtrack.

"Vanessa, come on, honey, you know you want it," he'd whispered that fateful night.

Oh, by the way, he always called it "it." Never sex, cer-tainly not making love. That last one was too advanced a concept for such an inept jerk like Danny Stoker. He'd said that small, but significant word last Friday night, down in his parents' finished basement, Nirvana playing in the back-ground, his fingers playing explorer with her body. Not the most romantic music in the world, hardly effective for such a sloppy seduction. But of course saying, "You know you want it," certainly didn't qualify as seduction, not in Va-nessa's book. It sounded like a rehearsed line. Like he'd been standing before the mirror, swiping on deodorant and splashing cheap cologne on a hairless chest while checking out his expression as he spoke the words. Exuding confidence that such a line would work.

"Danny, we've talked about this. You know I'm not ready."

"I know you've said that . . . a lot, and I've been more than . . . you know, really patient and understanding. But come on, babe, prom is next week, graduation's a week later, and then two weeks after that I'll be eighteen. I'm not turning eighteen still a virgin."

See, that was part of the problem. It was all about Danny, his needs, his wants. To him it sounded like whomever the woman he was with didn't matter, just so long as he broke through that adolescent rite of passage to officially "become a man." How many times had he said that laughable phrase? Too many. Like he'd know what being a man was all about.

So that night, the scene played out like so many other nights had, yet with one vast difference. After a satisfying make-out session—that she didn't mind, he was good at that, and some exploratory touching—all aboveboard and above the waist, that's when Danny had gone in for the big kill. Pressing her hand to his . . . down there. And she had reacted fast, pushing him away to where he nearly fell back over the sofa. That's when he delivered his ultimatum.

"You're such a tease. Okay, so here's the deal, Vanessa," Danny had begun, "I've put up with your spoiled brat routine all throughout high school, and now when I need you most—look, you're not there for me. I can't believe I've wasted all this time with you, all these Friday nights when my parents were out at their bowling league. So, this is what's going to happen—we're going to have it, and by that I mean right now, or you can just leave and we can go our own ways. It's your call. I'm done waiting. Either we move on together, or I move on without you."

Vanessa, fighting back sudden tears, got up from the sofa

and stared down at Danny, the boy who had made her swoon her freshman year, the one who had been at her side all four years, and now . . . now, it had come down to this. His handsome face, with its strong, angular jawline and chiseled cheeks, he'd been about the most striking kid in their class, male or female. As the years had passed his good looks had only increased, and problem was, he knew it. Now he just looked ugly to her.

Now, four days after they'd broken up, she still hadn't the heart to tell her parents about their breakup. But everyone at school knew, that was for sure. Watching a smirking Danny walk down the hall with Lucy Walker on his arm, she wasn't even subtle the way she kissed his neck while staring daggers at Vanessa. *Bitch, she can have him. Probably already has done "it" with him.* That was why today found Vanessa sitting far from the school, immersed in her old self-wallowing. She watched as the kids got on the school buses or into their cars, speeding off like freed inmates for home. While she was still in solitary confinement.

Wait, correct that. Someone was heading her way.

"Oh shit," she said aloud.

Gawky Adam Blackburn, hiking up his jeans like he'd left his belt at home.

That's when she realized, with dread, the horror of her current situation. She was sitting here because Jana and Tiffany had told her to go here, get away from prying eyes and just leave everything to them. They would make it right. Vanessa had insisted this morning that she wasn't going to the prom, no way would she put up with that kind of humiliation. Nor was she going to college as expected. Her entire life's course had been altered; she'd taken a detour. "I think I'll just run away to Europe and see the world, forget all about Danton Hill High and . . . boys. Find the real Vanessa Massey that lives inside me."

"You do that later, Nessa," Jana had said, "right now, you need to plan for the prom. It's our last big day together."

"I thought graduation was."

"That part's for the parents. Prom is for us."

So, this was their brilliant idea for her to get back at Danny? Sending the clumsy kid with the pimples who'd sat in her homeroom all those years? The kid who was chosen last in gym class? The kid who was always assigned a lab partner because no one trusted his nervous hands with a beaker and chemicals. He was just too quiet, too introspective for her. She liked a guy with personality. She liked to laugh. Don't get her wrong, she knew Adam was sweet and kind, but he still looked like a kid, Doogie Howser, Graduate; she doubted a razor had even met his face yet. He probably still wore clothes his mother laid out for him. Still, considering the prom was just a few days from now, the beggar in her couldn't exactly become a chooser; most everyone had hooked up. *Please tell me it's a mistake, that's he's just headed through the fields on his way somewhere other than at her side.*

Nope, wrong. He came straight for her.

"Hi, uh, hey, Vanessa."

"Hi, Adam."

"So, I guess you know why I'm here . . ."

Oh my God, was he really just going to lurch right in and ask her to the prom without any kind of . . . well, Danny would call it foreplay. Adam stood there as awkward as always, his hands in his pants pockets and his knapsack threatening to topple him. He was fidgeting too, and for a second she felt bad for him. Like he'd been sent to the lion's den where the lion was hungry, and angry. She pictured, briefly, Adam's head atop a dandelion.

"No, I don't, Adam. I couldn't possibly know."

Why was she being a bitch? Where had that come from?

"Oh, really, sorry, it's because Jana and Tiffany—Rich,

and that jerk Davey Sisto—they came by my locker and told me that . . ." Just then he closed his mouth. Vanessa saw him burn red beneath the collar of his shirt. He started to back away from her, wiping sweaty hands against his jeans. "Oh, I see, I get it now, this is just a setup—but not the good kind. Get me to humiliate myself, but you never intended to go through with it. Here, I thought you were different from the others . . . well, never mind . . . Vanessa," he said, spitting out her name the way she wanted to do with Danny. Adam made a sudden retreat, starting down the hill, but then suddenly he stopped and turned back toward Vanessa. What he said struck right where Vanessa hurt the most.

"What Danny did to you, and in front of your friends, that was pretty rotten. You deserve better," he said. "You always have."

His words surprised her and she felt a sudden emptiness, like she didn't know who she was. Words failed her as she watched Adam set off, shuffling like a defeated man who'd seen his team lose to a walk-off homer. Vanessa felt a lump in her throat and was reminded of how crushed her feelings were the other night sitting on Danny's couch. When Danny had tossed her aside without any regard to their past, or their history. So she was stuck, instead, in the moment, as unsure of anything as she could remember. Her legs reacted before her mind, as Vanessa got up from the ground. She went running after Adam, calling his name.

She caught up with him in the long shadow of the water tower, the glare of the sun gone, the two of them temporarily lost to the rest of the world. The only heightened sense she felt was her sense of smell; she suddenly took in the brine of the lake, its crashing waves wafting over the wind. She thought of summer, of fun-filled days at the beach, Danny at her side . . .

This situation was crazy, how had her life gone from

everything to nothing so quickly? How was it she and Adam Blackburn had been thrust together by circumstances orchestrated by others? She struggled to find the right words, any words, to soothe his hurt feelings. Why was she suddenly so concerned about him when it was she who had been dumped? Still, she felt a pang of sadness envelop her, knowing she would be more miserable staying home and trying to explain to her mother why Danny was dating Lucy Walker. Better company than loneliness, right? Oh hell, might as well just give in, blurt it out. Like her legs earlier, her mouth acted before her brain. That's when she spoke a simple phrase.

"I'd be happy to go to the prom with you."

Adam, facing her with wounded eyes, swallowed hard, blanching at the abrupt nature of her acceptance. "But . . . but I didn't even get a chance to ask you."

"Well, then I guess I'm asking you, what do you think about that? Adam Blackburn—will you go the Danton Hill High School Senior Ball with me?"

He smiled an unexpected wide grin. "Maybe the prom's theme has something to it after all. It's called the 'Forever Yours' Ball."

"Kid," Vanessa said, her use of the word ironic, not meant to be an insult, "that kind of sappy sentiment doesn't exist in real life. I outta know. So let's forget any sort of talk of destiny or forever or any kind of foolishness like that, okay? Friends, you and me, at least for one night. Oh, and so you know, I'm wearing a gown and heels, so I'm going to be taller than you."

"Everyone is taller than me."

She scrunched her nose at him. "That's a curious thing to say."

"Why? It's true, has been all my life," he said, "and besides, it's a case of perfect symmetry. All through school I've looked up to you, while you've done nothing but look down at me. Sounds like we're a perfect match."

"That's not fair . . ."

"It's okay, Vanessa, I know it's just high school. There are always cooler kids than even you, less popular kids than me. I don't hold it against you, it's just the way things are."

She smiled at him. "Why didn't I notice you freshman year?"

"Maybe you couldn't see me."

She laughed, perhaps the first honest laugh she'd had all during this miserable week. It felt good, better than good.

And then the two new friends linked arms as they walked back toward the school and the waiting yellow buses to take them back to their respective homes. They shared a conspiratorial smirk, followed by a laugh of solidarity. Despite the differences between them that went beyond issues of height, they knew all would be fine for just one night. They were just two people lucky enough to find friendship on the dance floor, and then there would be nothing more beyond that night. Their lives would never again intersect, nor would they need to. Forever yours only held true for a few hours. Forever never lasted for as long as people thought it should.

CHAPTER 6

NOW

Despite the mid-August humidity, a noticeable chill pervaded the creaky steps and peeling walls of the house, accompanied by a certain dampness perhaps created by the rain and intensified by cracks in the walls of the old farmhouse. As Vanessa showered, Adam set about finding kindling that would help him get a fire started in the brick-fronted fireplace located in the living room. First he checked to make sure the vent was open; last thing he wanted to do was fill the house with smoke, forcing them back out into the nasty outdoors. In a side cabinet he located a bundle of dried logs and discarded newspapers. They were dated from the previous year, most from the daily *Rochester Democrat and Chronicle*. Whoever lived here, certain clues suggested they were planning on coming back at some point. Maybe they were off visiting relatives today and were planning to arrive home later this night, or perhaps tomorrow. But then why would they have covered the furniture with white sheets? No, they'd been gone longer, but could return at any moment, right? Would he and Vanessa still be trapped together, and if so, wouldn't that be a hell of a surprise to come back to?

Back in the kitchen, he found a box of stick matches. He returned to the fireplace, where he'd built the wood and kindling into a pyre lacking only flame. That all changed with the strike of a match and the fiery crinkle of newspaper. Orange flame flared up and sweet, cedar-smelling smoke began to drift its way through the old house. Adam immediately felt a heated change of temperature in the room. How about that, he got the fire going on the first attempt, not bad for a city slicker such as himself. Now, one last touch remained and all would be perfect for when Vanessa came back down the stairs. He wanted to set up the food and drink, a makeshift picnic set before a roaring fire. Damn, but if not for the accident and the small piece of glass embedded in his head wound and the gimpy ankle and the sliced skin on his side, this scene could be interpreted as a premeditated seduction. Except for the fact that he wasn't as clever as all that, nor would he have endured such excruciating pain, not voluntarily, in order to secure the romantic setting. It was just happenstance.

A few minutes later, steaming bowls of tomato soup were positioned on place mats before the crackling fire. The wine followed, with two jelly glasses having to suffice for fancy, stemless stemware. The folks who lived here didn't appear to have any crystal. Lastly, he brought the tinned sausages over, spread out on a plate with crackers that were probably stale. Only one way to find out and frankly, he could wait.

So the scene was set. All that was missing was Vanessa.

Standing at the base of the stairs, he called up to her.

"Be right down," she said from one of the rooms upstairs. Her voice carried on the wind.

It took another five more minutes before she reappeared, but from Adam's point of view the wait sure was worth it. Refreshed, showered, pampered even, Vanessa's raven hair was thick and fluffy again, just like he remembered, and she was dressed in a pair of loose-fitting jeans and a blue dress shirt she'd left untucked.

"I didn't like anything the lady of the house had to offer," she said with a throaty laugh, explaining her wardrobe choice. "All frumpy stuff, pale colors. So I went with the lazy guy look."

"No, frumpy definitely would not suit you, and you're the prettiest guy here," he stated, embarrassed to have spoken such a corny line. She waved it off and accepted his proffered hand. She came off the last step and followed him toward the living room. "If you'll follow me, miss, our three-course reunion dinner awaits us."

"Three course?"

"Well, that's what we paid for. I checked off the chicken plate, that's always a safe dish at reunions and conventions, right? You probably ordered the salmon and rice, and yes . . . no doubt the fresh corn, and the chocolate dessert. Sorry, but this feast of ours will have to do. You did all the hard work anyway, cooking with such limitations. But I added the crowning touch."

That's when Vanessa saw the fire blazing, and she sighed with pleasure while cozying up to its inviting warmth. "Can I be honest with you, Adam? I was hoping you'd think to light a fire. I mean, I know this is August and we're in Danton Hill—or as close as we're going to get to our old town tonight—but I just can't seem to shake this chill I've felt all afternoon. Not even the shower was able to remove it entirely. So . . . thank you. I like the heat."

He let that last comment slip by. "No need to thank me. It's to our mutual survival; least I can do is contribute to the cause. Grrr. Man make fire, woman cook," he said, testing out his best caveman voice.

She laughed. Guess it was pretty good.

"So, how about that long-awaited glass of wine? I waited for you."

"From caveman to prince," she said.

"Evolution is a wonderful thing," he said. "Like us, to not-quite-friends to pretty-awful-dance-partners to . . . now."

"Adam?"

"Uh-oh. What'd I say?"

"No, that's not it, you're fine. Just . . . no strolls down memory lane, please. At least, not yet," she said, pointing to the wine. "Just pour."

He did as she commanded, handing over one of the round jelly glasses to Vanessa before pouring some wine for himself. Raising their glasses to the air, they paused, wondering just what they were drinking to. Neither said a word for a moment, letting the silence fill the room and shorten the distance between them. Suddenly too much time had elapsed and they still hadn't toasted and they hadn't taken a sip either. That's when Adam cleared his throat and said simply, "Let's toast to tomorrow."

"Tomorrow? That's a strange thing to toast to, Adam Blackburn, considering you and I only have the past in common. What do you think tomorrow is going to bring?"

"People, life, civilization? Who knows what else," he said with an aimless, uncertain shrug. "That's why I think it's the perfect toast. Look at us, we already know what happened yesterday, and we already know what happened today, at least the today that has already happened. Seems like forever since I left home, driving for hours to get . . . here. But I have a feeling that for the next few hours it's just you and me and nothing but you and me. Well, and the fire and the wine are nice contributors. Tomorrow, the dawn will rise and the sun will shine and wash away the storm clouds. We'll be able to see more clearly where next life takes us."

"Wow, that's quite a toast," Vanessa said. "Have you secretly taken poetry lessons?"

"Ha, a financial genius like me. I'd never hear the end of it."

"Oh right, you're in finance," she said.

"Was."

"Was?"

"Long story."

"I guess we have time."

"Hey, Vanessa?"

"Yes, Adam?"

"You still haven't clinked my glass." His glass hung in the air, waiting expectantly.

"Oh. Right. Well, then, to . . . tomorrow."

"Tomorrow."

And finally the rim of her glass reached out, touching against his, where a gentle clink echoed in the cloistered room. They drank, each of them keeping their eyes on the other, waiting to see if the wine was good, bad, or worse, spoiled. Adam's mouth puckered, but Vanessa handled her first taste like a poker player. Setting down their glasses at the same moment, Adam pointed to the blanket and invited her to sit down and be comfortable. For support, he'd placed some throw pillows he'd found underneath the sheet that covered the sofa.

"You've thought of everything," she said, settling down.

"Just enough to stay warm and dry," he offered.

"You're not good with compliments, are you?"

His brow furrowed. "What do you mean?"

"I just gave you a compliment, thanking you for thinking of everything. You sheepishly looked down, embarrassed. All you needed to say was thank you."

"Oh, right. Uh, thank you."

"Five words, Adam."

"Excuse me?"

"It took you five words to say the simplest two."

"Should I move to the sofa? You going to psycho-analyze me?"

"It was just an observation. I didn't mean to touch a nerve."

Adam waved it off, as though it didn't matter. "How's the wine?"

"It's as good as you are about changing the subject."

"Ouch. That bad?"

"Relax, Adam, I'm not here to interrogate you," she said. "Trust me, the last thing I want is for you to turn the tables on me. 'Cause that ain't happening."

"Ain't? Mrs. Miller wouldn't be very happy to hear you mangle the English language."

"Thank God we're not in third grade anymore," Vanessa said.

"School, what a weird concept. Because it's the accepted thing to do, parents send their kids off to perfect strangers for the day, trusting them to educate them."

Vanessa nodded. "Less responsibility for them, which in my house was a perfect recipe for success. Independence was practically the first word I learned."

"It's amazing to think it's been twenty years since we graduated from Danton Hill High. I don't feel like that much time has passed, do you?"

"Time is both a stranger and a friend. I still feel like a teenager some days . . . well, not feel, but probably I act like one. Like, oh my God, you know?"

He laughed at her valley-speak. "That was never you back then."

"No. Some of my friends were, but I knew they sounded like idiots."

"I think we were all idiots in some way . . . back then."

"Things change," she said.

"People change."

"You certainly have," Vanessa said with surprising conviction.

"How do you mean?"

"Do you remember a short, skinny kid with an occasional pimple who wore clothes that had gone out of style three years long before he wore them, who always had a book in his hand and his head buried in it? Do you remember an awkward boy in gym class who didn't have the muscle strength to properly dismount off the uneven bars?"

Adam turned red at that forgotten memory. "Well, come on, they were uneven . . ."

Vanessa just laughed at him.

"So, okay, yeah, I grew up. God, I hope I did. Guess I was one of those late bloomers in life, not filling out until I went to college, but of course that doesn't help when you're sixteen and gangly," he said. "Once I went away to college, or maybe it was getting away from Danton Hill, it was like my hormones finally caught up to me. I'll never forget orientation at college, they handed us guys a box of toiletries we would need. Razors, shaving cream; I barely needed such items. My roommate already had a thick beard; I swear whenever we hung out it was like I was his younger brother tailing after him, some kid desperate for acceptance. But the world eventually balanced out. Like you said, I grew up." Adam paused, shaking his head at the images flashing in his mind, the boy from high school and the man-boy from college. He'd been dumb then, innocent and naïve. "Tucker, that was my roommate, I'll never forget that first night when the RA was giving us a speech, all about safety on campus and safe sex and all that stuff. Tony was the RA's name, total Long Island Italian who thought he was God's gift to women, and I can still see him pulling out a condom package and saying, 'You wanna play, make sure you don't pay.' And then Tucker speaks up and says, 'Hey, what if that thing won't fit?' And you know what Tony did? He unwrapped the condom and rolled it over his forearm, all the way up to his elbow. Man, you should have seen Tucker wilt back into the shadows."

Adam was laughing, taking a drink of his wine, almost like he was back in college again reliving the experience. The bendable laws of time, suddenly transporting him back to halcyon days. He realized, though, he was the only one grinning. Vanessa had set her glass down and was staring with glazed eyes into the fire, lost in her own private thoughts. He could barely read the expression on her face; she was impenetrable.

"Hey, Vanessa, did I say something wrong?"

"Oh, oh no. Adam, I'm sorry. It's just . . . will you excuse me?"

As she rose from the blanket, she tripped over the uneaten bowl of soup, didn't even notice that it spilled onto Adam's checkered pant leg. She ran from the room and hastily made her way toward the front door, throwing it open with fierce determination. A strong gust of wind howled through the house, as though it had come to claim them. He watched as she struggled to draw deep breaths into her lungs. Running to her side, he placed his hands upon her shoulders, but she wrenched free and stormed out onto the porch.

He didn't know what to do. Should he follow her?

Adam decided best to give her a moment alone. Which was a good thing, it gave him a chance to review what they'd been talking about and what might have possibly set her off.

But he came up empty, just dumb, nonsense talk about high school and college. He went back to the fire, shaking his head with confusion. Taking a sip of wine, he stared at the room, at the white sheets that covered the furniture, wondering about the folks who lived here and of the ghosts that floated in the halls and the rooms and in the nooks and crannies of the old walls. These were the ghosts that caught memories, only to remind you of them when you least expected. Who lived here, what was the story behind this house and its original owner? Who had built it, and what had his life been like? Adam felt that same chill Vanessa had spoken about earlier, like he'd just walked over someone's grave.

As he waited for Vanessa to return, he had to wonder about the fickle hand of fate. It was clear to him that he and Vanessa were supposed to meet over that accident, that they were supposed to have found this house. Their story remained unfinished, but for a second Adam had to wonder, when had it begun? This reunion within a reunion, something had made it happen. What came after that, he couldn't begin to suppose.

"What's going on?" he asked the room.

The ghosts, this time, they said nothing, as though holding back. That sound he heard was still the wind, whipping through the open door. The fire flickered and the last thing he wanted was for the flames to disappear with an exhausted poof. They needed all the heat they could muster, to battle the cold and the ghosts and the memories, and perhaps to embrace some secrets the netherworld didn't know.

He had to wonder, were there secrets that Vanessa knew?

Was that what had spooked her?

The truth of the matter was this: Adam might have thought he was simply rambling about some musty college memory, but in reality he'd hit way too close to home for

Vanessa's comfort. She didn't want to talk about it; God, she didn't even want to think about . . . it. But how to explain her abrupt departure from what had been such a lovely moment, a crackling fire and warming wine and the food she hadn't even touched? Could she explain herself without delving into things she didn't want to? She was hoping the fresh air would help clear her mind.

The rain had finally stopped, the storm quieted. Gray clouds still hovered and as a result she couldn't guess at the time of day—end, beginning of night, or just a moment in time lost to the silent revolutions of the clock. A cool, hair-ruffling breeze rushed by her, taking her back to those early summer nights in Danton Hill when she had never felt more alive. Located on the shores of Lake Ontario, the chilled winds that swept down from Canada were as much a part of her life growing up as were school, friends, hanging out. It was the backdrop to her seemingly perfect life. She'd left them all behind right after high school, but here they were again, her friends only miles away, and the scent and the smell of sea and sand sweeping over her, awakening memories long dormant.

They were inevitable, weren't they? Those memories. Sepia-colored truths.

But facing these buried memories, weren't they her sole reason for coming home? Wasn't that what she'd confessed to Reva? That no matter how far she had run, across countries and continents, Danton Hill still held her captive, keeping her soul tied to its shores while the rest of her thrived in worlds she could only have imagined as a child. She'd told herself too, on the long plane ride and even on the drive that had led to the accident, the truth was back home and so was she. Now she was in the company of an unsuspecting man who had no clue how much he'd impacted her life. The man who sat inside, no doubt perplexed over her actions.

There was another truth here, one she freely admitted to. That grown man inside named Adam Blackburn, so gentle with her today, so caring, that was really all she knew about him. His name and how he'd treated her today. Not about his life, his loves, not his hopes and dreams and desires, the things he'd lost, the things never achieved. Was he as much a victim of Danton Hill, or had he been able to let go and be happy? Was this her chance to find out? Would it even matter, change how she felt?

Finally rising from the porch, Vanessa strolled out into the driveway, under the protection of a leafy oak tree that trapped her in its shadows. The occasional leftover raindrop fell, dripping down the nape of her neck. She welcomed the cool, tingling sensation; it felt different from the consuming chill inside her bones. The raindrops made her feel alive. When she turned back to the house, she noticed a yellow light had been switched on, beaming down from the porch ceiling, a piece of the sun amidst a world of gray. Adam was rocking quietly on the swing, patient, understanding. When had he gone there? She hadn't heard a sound, and only now could she hear the squeaking of the chains of the swing.

"Hi," he said.

His voice was soft, lacking intimidation. That was a nice approach, taking away any hint of confrontation.

"Hi, yourself," she tried, not sure how steady her voice was.

"Was it something I said?"

"Yeah, sort of."

"Want to talk about it?"

"Not really." She paused. "Not yet."

"You keep saying that. Not yet. Is there a better time than now?"

"A better time is never."

"Okay, at least you're not being enigmatic."

She suppressed a grin. "I don't mean to freak out on you. Adam, you know what?"

"Won't know till you tell me, I believe is the phrase."

"Despite our . . . past, what happened that night between you and me . . . we really don't know much about one another, do we? Seems that life throws us together for a limited amount of time, short bursts of experiences that we can either take advantage of . . . or deny the signals and move on, forget. And then life takes us away again. And the things we've done . . . shared . . ."

"Weren't exactly our shiniest moments."

"Right."

"Yeah, right," he said. "So, you want to get to know me, is that what you're saying?"

"Is that a line?"

"No," he said, stifling a grin. "But this is: your swing or mine?"

"Didn't you use that with our cars?"

"I did. Men are like that, we use the same tired lines until they work."

"How's that working out for you?"

He grinned. "There's only one swing. Why don't we call it ours?"

"Smooth, Mr. Blackburn, very smooth," she said. "Can we consider it neutral ground?"

"This whole house is neutral. Doesn't it feel that way?"

She gazed back at the farmhouse, with its wraparound porch and swing, the picture like something conjured from Rockwell. Comfort and familiarity issued forth, at least it appeared that way for Adam. For her, she felt the chill again.

"I'm not so sure about that. You seem to be adapting to our situation better than me . . . you opened the wine and you started the fire. All I did was run. But right now, I think I prefer the swing. I prefer to remain outdoors."

He waved her back up the porch, and she found her feet moving without thought, almost as though he was guiding her, pulling her toward him with the surging power of suggestion. She effortlessly glided up the steps and sat down beside him on the wooden slats of the swing. No cushions. He'd brought the wine, and his inviting smile, for comfort.

"Smart man," she said, happily taking back the glass she'd left inside.

"So, where do we start?"

"With yesterday."

"Literally?" he asked.

"Yesterday, your current life," Vanessa said, thinking yesterday couldn't be so bad. A day consumed, like hers, with anticipation for the reunion. It was easier this way. Rather than harken back to the prom and all that happened that night, she thought going backward in time would ease them into old worlds. "So, we'll start with what you've been doing since we last saw each other . . . oh, how long ago was that, anyway?"

"Eleven years," he said.

"You remember that quickly?"

"I didn't. But I've had time today during the long drive to reminisce about a few things," he said. "Plus, it's one of the reasons I didn't return for our tenth class reunion. What happened, neither one of us would have been ready to face the other. I suppose I felt not enough time had gone by. How was it, by the way?"

Vanessa nearly spit out her wine. "Excuse me?"

"Uh, Nessa, the reunion, I mean. Numero Ten."

For a moment she was taken aback by hearing him speak

such an unfamiliar name, one she hadn't heard in two decades. "Wow, you called me Nessa. No one calls me that anymore."

"More of the reinvention?"

She thrust her glass outward seeking a refill.

"We'll have to pace ourselves," he said.

"Just pour."

"As long as you do the same."

She retorted quickly. "I thought this was your turn to talk."

He nodded as he refilled her glass, then his. The bottle was down halfway. Silently they drank. Vanessa, though, could not help but look at Adam's face as he drank. There was a tender grace to his actions, a gentleman's sip where he appeared to savor the taste, and not just swig it down like a beer or a shot like some eager frat boy. Different from the last time they met, those eleven years ago. That night had been crazy, ridiculous; it was a miracle she even remembered it considering all she'd consumed. Now time had progressed, and so too had they, from innocent teenagers at the dance to drunken twentysomethings during a chance meeting to . . . what, well-heeled, behaving adults? That wasn't exactly how she felt. She felt adrift, like she was floating in a sea that had claimed her as its own to the point where she wasn't even sure who she was anymore. Which was a good thing, she surmised, knowing that Adam was going to tell his tale. The night wasn't dark enough yet for her story; she wasn't ready.

Just then she saw Adam's face leaning close, so much so she could smell his manly scent, a musky breath. She froze, unsure what to do. Was he really going to try what she thought?

Just then she felt his lips touch hers.

Yup, he was.

Her body stiffened and her eyes closed, but surprisingly neither happened with her lips. She responded to the sweetness of his gesture, wondering what had sparked such a move on his part, acceptance on hers. She felt dreams open up before her, laced with colorful sparks.

His lips lingered; they must have sensed a hint of approval.

At last she pulled away, and of course she had to be the one to initiate the separation. His face remained inches from hers. She could smell the wine on his breath, taste the velvet bouquet on her own tongue, but other senses grew heightened, drawing her to him. A gentle sweetness hovered between them, as though ropey vines, entwining them in their ripening, fruitful embrace, connected them.

"You okay?" he asked.

"Uh, yeah."

"Should I apologize?"

"Uh, no."

"You got anything else to say other than 'uh'?"

"Uh . . ."

He kissed her again, quickly and more deeply, with more passion. The tentativeness of that earlier kiss was gone, replaced by confidence, or perhaps a sense of the inevitable unleashing before them, like a storm's deluge. As he drew her closer to him, his hands caressed her face, her hair. As their lips parted, foreheads rested together. She could hear his breath, words forming out of whispers, his words a sotto symphony.

"You are so sweet, Vanessa, and so beautiful, so much more so because someone greater than us put us here in this situation, throwing us together in this crazy moment. It's like this meeting was something dreamed up by the stars, something meant to be, something years in the making. It's something to be appreciated, treasured."

"Adam . . ."

"I know, I know, this is lunacy. Like we're teenagers, making out like it's our first time."

"No, that's not what I mean," she said, pulling back, gazing about with wonder written across her open features. "This moment, it feels more like we've been married for decades, you and I, and for us to be on this swing on the porch of this farmhouse, there is no more natural feeling in the universe."

"So, what do we do about it?"

She stared deep into his eyes. "Like we've done before, maybe we need to listen to the sky and allow the fates to tell us what to do. You and me, we're not so good at those decisions. Let the demands of our reunion dictate what comes next."

He took her in his arms again, and this time he didn't kiss her.

He held her, making her feel as safe as she'd felt since the storm had hit.

Since their cars had slammed into each other, jarring them out of the world they knew and into one filled with all the wonder and uncertainty and hesitant first steps, like a first dance at a prom called Forever Yours.

Forever might have just finally arrived, leading two people beyond their tenuous bond.

CHAPTER 7

NOW

The lights remained off as the early night fell like a curtain being drawn, closing them off even further from the darkened world outside. The fireplace crackled with a flickering glow cast upon empty, faceless walls. Yet despite the ever-present shadows they knew swarmed around them, in this moment and on this lone plane there existed only two people in the world, and they came together, standing, staring, wondering, waiting for whatever next step they took. The heat of the moment on the swing had deepened to something far more meaningful, and it was as though by recognizing such a connection existed, both of them had retreated, nervousness and tentativeness overriding building passion.

From the moment he'd taken hold of her cool hand, lifting her from the swing and inviting her to join him back inside, his heart had been beating, his veins pulsing beneath heated skin. He'd been with women, and he'd even been under the mistaken impression that he'd loved some of those women, but also there had been this eagerness, this carnality that accompanied his journeys to bedrooms he'd known, those that were strange to him. Now, though, he felt a shift deep inside his soul, a feeling inside him long gone untapped. What was soon to pass between them, he knew there was magic dust swirling behind it, and he wasn't one to question the driving passions of the body, not now, perhaps not ever. Sometimes the world handed you a gift and you had to be open to receiving it. Vanessa was his gift.

He cupped her face in his hands, her silky skin soft upon his touch. Gently caressing her tear-reddened cheeks, a wide, knowing smile crossed his face, offering up anticipation, appreciation. The smile spread, from his lips to hers, and what she returned to him beamed in the closing twilight. As he leaned down, his lips touched, pressed against her cool forehead; they continued down, kissing her dancing eyelids, the tip of her nose. Brushing her lips with a hint of what was to come, she reacted as though tickled.

"Adam . . ."

"Sshh, not now. No more words. Say it with a kiss."

She did, eagerly bringing her own soft lips up to meet his. Their mouths opened wide, tongues played, toyed; again the ripeness of the velvety wine wafted up, infusing their embrace, intoxicating them. They kissed more. Adam had known no such combination of tenderness and heat before. Not even when he made such declarations to others, he knew how false those words were, spoken in the moment, meant to intensify the exchange. This time it was different; he and Vanessa were truly connected. His body was alive with a wanting desire. He pressed against her body, letting her know just how she made him feel.

She broke the kiss and looked up at him, her green eyes leading them down to the blanket he'd set for their earlier picnic, soup bowls pushed away, the space cleared for them and them alone. As her head rested against the pillow, Adam lay beside her, his fingers tracing a line first on her upper lip, her lower lip, and then lower still, against her chin and down her elegant neck. He felt her shiver from his touch.

As they kissed again, Adam's fingers toyed with the buttons of the blue dress shirt she'd discovered in the closet upstairs. There was nothing sexier than a woman in a man's shirt. And he told her so, his whispering lips so close she reacted with an arch of her body to the stubble on his cheek. Buttons slipped through holes, and Adam drew back both flaps of the shirt, revealing Vanessa's slim frame, her supple breasts. She wore no bra. She breathed deeply as he hesitantly touched the crook of her neck with his fingers.

"You okay?" he asked.

"Perfect."

"Nervous."

"No."

"You?"

"Incredibly."

"Okay, good. Me too."

He shifted his body over hers, his lips again finding her neck. She arched her back as she again felt his unshaven face, scruffy and rough. He heard her react, heard her groan with desire. Felt her fingers clutch at him through his shirt, digging into the muscles of his back. Kissing her with a new, enveloping passion, he tasted salt and sweet on her neck, in the deep crevice between her round breasts. As his tongue encircled her jutting, enticing nipples, one, the other, he again tasted heat, an electric sizzle they had spontaneously ignited between them. As he took her left nipple in his mouth, his fingers gently rubbed and toyed with the other.

"Adam, oh, oh," she whispered, "the way you touch me . . ."

He could feel her hands caressing his back, foraging upward and running them through his hair. Her words, her touch, both and so much more fed his growing energy. He rose up on his knees, his body straddling her sides. They grinned at each other, but neither said anything and such nothing spoke volumes. They wanted more, they wanted each other.

Vanessa reached up, grabbing at the buttons of his shirt. She started from the bottom and Adam started from the top and at last they met in the middle, and together, fingers entwined, undid the final button, peeling it off his shoulders, and letting the shirt fall against the floor. She drew her fingers across his chest, ruffling the dark hair that covered it, following an equally dark trail down his flat belly until it teasingly disappeared beneath the waistline. Turning him on his back, Vanessa took control, kissing his neck and his ears. Adam felt warm sensations take command of his system, sending rippling messages to his synapses. My God, she knew just how to touch him, just where to stroke him. Her mouth found his nipples. She slid her hand over his chest, grazing her fingers through the thick mat of hair.

"So sexy, so surprising," she said as she pulled away.

He reached for her, kissing her again as their bodies switched positions. Blue eyes met green, they connected again, and both knew what was still to come as an impactful decision loomed before them. Were they really going to give in to their passion? Was this the smartest thing for them to be doing right now? But what was to stop them? Why should they? Not one soul had come to their rescue and no one was going to be coming for them, not for the remainder of tonight. So should they limit themselves to talk long into the night, deny the deep connection they were experiencing now? No, this moment in time was theirs, not like when they were foolish teenagers, not like that awful night in New York eleven years ago, the two of them exerting power over the other. No, this was here, now, and it was urgency taking hold of them. An undeniable attraction had been unleashed, one either to be doused by the storm or quenched by the fire. The difference today was how they felt. Knowing . . . believing this was meant to be. Time finally catching up to them.

Adam snuggled in beside her, his body tight against hers. He kissed her earlobe, tasted it.

"Are you sure?"

"More than ever. You?"

"Yes, me too."

"I can tell," she said, trying to suppress a laugh but failing.

Just then Vanessa popped up from the blanket. A sly grin crossed her face, an appealing look that drew Adam to her every action. She slid the loose-fitting jeans down her legs, kicked them to the sofa. Adam just stared, at her alluring smile and the curves of her body, the way the former seemed to enhance the latter. Whatever had possessed her to run out into the storm a short while ago, she'd either released it or buried it, but no matter, her mood had deepened. The playful girl transformed into a wanting tigress. And as if to prove that there was no going back, she slid off the last of her clothing, the pale, delicate panties, revealing her most sacred self.

He gulped, stared. Reached out.

"Well?" she asked.

"Well?" she repeated.

Adam's body appeared locked, his mouth open but his words hidden inside. Vanessa was thankful to be given a moment to truly consider what they were doing. Was this what she had envisioned when she'd accepted the invitation to attend the reunion? Point-blank, had she come all this way expecting to have sex with Adam Blackburn? Was it really that simple? Had she not grown up at all after twenty years? And just where was that romp supposed to take place, certainly not in the coach's office of the school's gymnasium, so maybe on the grassy hill by the water tower where once upon a time they'd agreed to attend the dance together? In a hotel room, with her secretly passing him the key card to her room during one of the evening's boring toasts? Each scenario was ridiculous, tinged with the impossible. She knew she wouldn't have had the guts to go through with any of it, not there. Because she promised herself this time when she saw him, it wasn't going to be about sex. It was going to be about telling the truth.

Which, she reminded herself, she still hadn't done.

Not even close.

But there was no going back now. She'd revealed her complete self to Adam. She gazed at his handsome face and strong jaw. She loved how strangely secure the touch of his chest hair made her feel, like she could roll herself up within him, feel his warmth. She stole a glance at the obvious rise in his pants, which, moments from now, she knew would no longer be held captive inside. Again, she liked what she saw. There was a long night ahead of them, and she doubted sleep held much interest for either of them. Sex, sex, sex, that was fine, and when they had exhausted themselves, talk, talk, talk they would, long into the night and into the waking hours of the dawn. That was when all would be revealed. So she promised herself. The physical would come now, emotions later. Yes, she would give herself now, indulging her body's physical needs, but later, she would go someplace even deeper. Vanessa Massey would attempt to give him her heart by revealing her secrets. Revealing her betrayals.

For now, she just wanted to feel alive.

"Take me, Adam," she said.

He held her, kissed her fiercely. His tongue felt like fire suddenly, dipped in the embers that crackled near them. She gripped him, her fingers digging into the nape of his neck. Her legs she curled around his waist. With her whole body she pressed tight against him. Adam pulled away, reaching for the button of his pants. He ripped it open, slid the zipper down, and tossed the pants aside, the shorts quickly following. Lying down on the blanket, fully revealed, his erection pressed hard against her.

"Do we need . . . ?" he started to ask.

"No."

"Why?"

"I don't know . . . I mean, I do . . . we don't . . . trust me . . ."

An actual tear slid from her eye, and Adam bent down, absorbed it with his kiss.

"It's okay . . ." he said.

She nodded, stared deep into the windows of his eyes, and saw only comfort. And that's when she opened herself up. She could feel the urgency inside now, her desire for him, his for her. Heat giving way to desperation, desperation to desire. True moments like this, they were few and far between in the messed-up life of Vanessa Massey, that much she knew and she remembered a series of incidents with bright clarity, as though a catalog of wrong choices and bad men were flipping wildly through her mind. Those images, rather than kill the moment, only made her want this one even more, because it was with Adam, with a nice man, a sweet man, a sexy one, and a giving one, and a . . .

"Ooohh," she said, thoughts gone, the past released to now and only now.

She felt all of him, sliding inside and filling her, resting inside her to allow her body the chance to adapt to this new-found presence. She squeezed her eyes shut, waiting a fast beat of her heart while taking a breath, exhaling sharply. As she opened her eyes, she saw his beautiful ocean of irises seeking hers, peering in, at the soul she seldom let out.

The connection held, their eyes locked, he pushed more, going further. He slid back, slid in, slid back, again, more still. She was so ready, so moist, she welcomed him and she urged him to not slip out, to not deny her the passion. He kissed her, surprising her with the touch of his lips. She had known men at this point who knew what they wanted and tended to remain focused on their own pleasure. Adam, though, let her know this was more than physical release, this was unrelenting truth. An ache inside her, inside him, that had been waiting . . . for how long? Again, the kiss of the ocean wafted around her, enveloping her, a sensation unlike any she'd ever felt. Adam kissed her once more like a wave washing over her, and then he thrust, he pushed, more, each time with building energy and passion. Each eager motion built upon the last, and before long he was panting, hard, fast, an engine's fuel powering him. Vanessa took each thrust easily, with a wanton desire matched only by his thrill-ing, unleashed actions. Words were spoken to the quiet walls, emotions revealed, energy was expounded by grunts and groans, the bodies nearly shaking the long-set founda-tion of the old farmhouse, chasing away those lingering shadows.

She was lost in the moment; nothing else mattered. Not yesterday, not tomorrow, not the regrets that lived within her. She barely knew where she was or who she was, she just gave in to the swarming passion stinging at her body. Tiny, rolling orgasms pinged through her as Adam kept pumping, thrusting. Kept loving her, kept looking at her. She urged him more, her fingers grabbing at his back, nipples rubbed red by the springy mat of his chest hair hovering just over. Another wave of blistering heat swallowed her, and she arched her back in anticipation. She knew this one was bigger, better, an explosion that threatened to send her to the other side of the world. She urged him, faster, deeper, hungrier . . .

Adam drew breath, filling his lungs for the final push. And he did, again thrusting deep inside her. She screamed again, her mouth biting into his shoulder, her nails scraping his back. She could hold back no further, no longer, and suddenly the room was filled with her voice, her inner self revealed and exposed, left open for the world to hear and to know and to wonder why such color is so often drenched in black and white. Her tightly controlled self, she left it behind, perhaps as far behind as her home in Europe or inside the wrecked car sinking into the wet cornfields, or maybe some other place to be found in some faraway land she didn't even know existed. She unleashed the power and just let it drift away on the electric currents of the wind.

She felt Adam grow thicker inside her. She knew he was climaxing soon, she could read it in his eyes and feel it in his breath, taste it on her tongue. And then in an amazing rush that had him crying out with that otherworldly combination of pain and shock and surprise and heat, he released himself. He thrust, more, more, and she urged him on, tightening her legs against his backside, not letting him slip out, not just yet.

At last his body came to rest atop her, his breathing labored. Her chest heaved against his. Sweat dripped from her brow, off her chest, pooling between her breasts. Adam lifted his body, his body slick with sweat, chest hair matted. With her tongue she teased his nipple.

"Oh my God, enough, enough, let me catch my breath . . ." he said, rolling off her and landing with a satisfying thud against the blanket.

And Vanessa, seeing his reaction, did something she hadn't done in quite some time. She giggled, like an impish school-girl who just spotted from afar the cutest boy in the class and he'd caught her secretly gazing in his direction. Well, she wasn't going to look away, not this time, she wouldn't let this newly invigorated woman who felt more alive now than she had just an hour ago, a day ago, for some time, taste fear. This was about opening up, body, perhaps more. She felt like water had washed over her, threatening to take her in its wake. She had fought back, though. She had re-claimed herself, and by doing so, reclaimed him.

"Uh, okay, wow," Adam finally said after minutes of si-lence.

"You could say that again," she said, sidling up beside him, resting her chin on his chest.

"Actually, I couldn't," he said, still catching his breath.

She laughed while playfully hitting his arm.

"So, Adam Blackburn, is that how you show all the girls a good time?"

"You know, usually it's the moment. This time it's the woman."

"Sweet."

"Honest," he said.

"Ooh, I like that. Brave man."

"What? For being honest? What do you call what we did?"

"You mean the sex?"

"It was more than sex, Vanessa, and you know it."

Her eyes softened, and she kissed his shoulder. "Yeah, I know it."

Neither spoke a word for quite a while, even while it appeared time didn't move. They just enjoyed the crackle of the fire, the silence of the house. Not even the steady breeze outside was making shutters creak or curtains flap. She realized Adam was right, sometimes it was the moment that took the ordinary and made it extraordinary, and now, this time and this moment, when all the world existed beyond them, leaving them alone, she knew they had redefined their lives, the ones they had shared, the ones they had lived apart.

Suddenly she bounded up from the floor, looking all around her.

"What'd you lose?"

"Not my virginity, that's for sure," she said, offering him a quick, surprising laugh and hoping he would follow suit. Quick check of him showed that he was grinning and not making her feel like an idiot for such a dumb thing to say. That was a good sign, they understood each other, their quirks and fallows. "Have you seen the wine bottle? Don't tell me we finished it."

"It's on the porch, with our glasses. Fear not, there's still half a bottle."

"Perfect," Vanessa said, "I'll be right back. And then I want to hear all about her."

"Excuse me?"

"Adam Blackburn, don't think you've landed yourself in the arms of a foolish woman. A giving man like you, you can't have lived without at least having fallen in love once. I'd like to hear about her. How you met, what was good, and why you're no longer together."

"Now? You want to hear about her now?"

"See, I was right."

"Vanessa, after what we just experienced, you want to hear about another woman?"

She kissed him once, then said, "With what we did, and with such intensity behind our actions, I would hardly think there could remain any secrets between us. Certainly not a little old story about finding the wrong woman."

Rising up, resting on his elbows and forearms, Adam said, "Fine, have it your way. But definitely fetch the wine, because I'll need some reinforcement if I'm going to tell you my sad woes. Oh, and when I'm done, it's your turn."

Vanessa's back was turned to him at this point as she, gathering up a sheet from an old recliner and wrapping it around her naked self, headed toward the porch, and that was a good thing. Her confidence suddenly wavered, and she felt a bit of wind dip out of her sail. But as nervous as she suddenly was over that prospect, she knew one thing: Adam was right. Hearing his story would be easier—mostly because it didn't involve her in the least. He'd gone on without her. As for her own story, now that was really quite the opposite. What happened to her had everything to do with Adam.

She thought they might need a case of wine to get through that one.

Still, she pulled herself together by setting aside her problems. She wanted to know more about the life Adam Blackburn had lived, and when she returned from the porch with the wine and those silly jelly glasses and an eager expression on her face, she said, "I'm not going to interrupt. Like you said, my turn will come later. For now, Blackburn, you have the floor . . ."

"Yes, with you all covered up," he said.

Vanessa instinctively tightened her hold on the sheet, all while Adam remained naked.

Exposed.

He didn't see her eyes darken, her pupils hiding as the

light from the fire died down. Adam laughed nervously as he made his way to the fireplace, tossing on another log, lighting another match.

"It always starts with a spark, doesn't it," he said. "Her name was . . ."

CHAPTER 8

THEN

". . . Sarah Jane Stockdale. Blond, tan, athletic, the apple of her father's discerning eye, a woman who struggled to please everyone around her, all while failing at her own hopes. But that's what you get when you lived in such a world. Sarah Jane was the youngest daughter of the lead golfing partner of one of my firm's senior management staff. Had all those connections, all those high-powered labels, he was envied by many to his face and disliked by most behind his back. It all comes down to money, and lots of it. In a world where everything was for sale, I suddenly found myself being put up as the latest commodity. I was dragged in, hardly kicking and screaming, but before it was all over and done with, my name had been dragged through the mud as well. The kind that stains. The kind you can't easily shower off."

From the moment he first heard her name, Adam knew he would hate her. Okay, not her personally, he had nothing against the woman; heck, he didn't even know anything about her and had to assume she was well-mannered and well-bred, the scion of a family who actually knew what that word meant. The exclusive, pampered world she belonged to was quite another matter. Probably had a cousin named

Buffy or Muffy, Adam surmised over drinks one night with his friend Patch, who offered up "poor you" remarks as he poured down tequila shots. No doubt the Stockdales summered in the Hamptons and wintered in St. Moritz and groaned about not being at either during the spring and fall. Bracing from the lime and the salt, Adam asked Patch, "When did the seasons become verbs?"

"These are people who have no trouble buying vowels," Patch said. That had been the night before the up and coming in the firm Adam Blackburn was scheduled—yes, scheduled!—to meet the aforementioned, and apparently available, Sarah Jane Stockdale. "They can do what they want. Good luck."

The circumstances surrounding the meeting between born-on-the-wrong-side-of-the-tracks Adam Blackburn and blue-blood, DAR Sarah Jane Stockdale was to be handled in the form of a corporate outing, assuring both parties that nothing untoward could possibly happen. The lofty investment firm of Koch, Franklin, and Cohn was sponsoring a fund-raiser in support of cancer research, and all partners and junior level people were expected to attend. What nobody knew, certainly not Adam, was that the entire afternoon's soirée was a mere front—its sole purpose was to find college-grad Sarah Jane a husband. Wait, correct that, a suitable husband. If they happened to raise money and awareness for cancer in the meantime, all the more power to them, not to mention clocking a tax write-off doubling as a debutante ball. Now, here's the other thing Adam didn't know: He wasn't the only potential suitor being carted out before the prize steed. Of course, that wasn't how it was presented to him the day before the cruise.

Five o'clock on a warm, humid summer Friday, in the high floors of the lower Manhattan offices of the so-nicknamed KFC, Adam was tidying up some details on a few last-minute transactions his clients had begged for before the long holiday weekend, and he couldn't think straight. Numbers were a jumbled mess on his computer screen. He was looking forward to a weekend away from the rat race, from the idiots he worked for, and from the whole financial circuitry that consumed most of his waking hours. Of course, knowing his escape was imminent meant his bosses would suddenly conjure other plans for him, and true to their nature, a knock came at his door, and before waiting for a response . . . a welcome, his door opened. In walked one of the senior partners, Carpenter Franklin, his bald, shiny head adorned with beads of sweat on a high brow. His cheeks were flush. These high-level guys who made it this far up in the firm's hierarchy, they all had names that sounded like presidents and bodies one stress test away from a heart attack.

"Burnie, cancel your plans this weekend, you're busy."

"Uh, sir, you're right. I am busy."

"And now, Burnie, you're going to be even busier."

This Burnie thing, it was annoying as much as it was unavoidable. His immediate boss had this habit of calling everyone by their last name, but with Adam he'd decided that Blackburn possessed too many syllables. So it was shortened to Burnie, despite the fact it took just as long to say that as did to say Blackburn. Half the company thought his real name was Bernie.

"Let me guess, sir. Black tie."

"Wrongo, Burnie, break out the prep-school wear," he said.

"I didn't attend prep school, sir."

"Ohh, keep that detail to yourself. It won't win you any friends."

"I've done fine so far."

"So far being the key phrase."

Franklin also still sounded like a frat boy, even though

he'd been bald longer than Adam had been alive. "Regardless of your background, this is a cruise. Daytime. Adapt."

"Ah, time to drag out the J.Crew uniform. I'll have to go
shopping."

"Tomorrow. Two o'clock. Don't bring the sarcasm."

"What's the occasion?"

Carpenter Franklin grinned, like he'd scored a big wind-
fall. "Your future."

Adam's future was not to be found on any New York Wa-
terways ferry to New Jersey—hardly. This was a private lux-
ury yacht afforded only by the disgustingly wealthy, set to
hove off from the piers on the West Side for a daylong cruise
around Manhattan Island. As Adam boarded the gangplank
the next day and hoping not to befall a fate with these moneyed pirates—boat shoes on his feet, navy blue sweater
wrapped jauntily around his Oxford-cloth white shirt, khaki
pants perfectly ironed—he knew he was a far cry from the
paddleboats of Lake Ontario. Danton Hill really was but a
distant memory, and as he meandered around the upper
deck with a glass of champagne, the whole world turned
shiny, like new money gleaned through his sunglasses. Still,
he could not have asked for a better setting to put his best
(boat) shoe forward. Growing up in a coastal village, Adam
was acquainted well enough with the water, its swells and
smells, the rocking motion created by waves both natural
and human. He was equally adept on large watercraft as he
was in a canoe. From childhood, boating had been something he was at ease with, and so feeling the gentle motion
of the yacht on this day was equal to a calming breeze off
the lake.

Looking around, Adam watched as dozens of well-
turned-out people mingled, most of them coming from an
older, preserved generation—the partners, their tanned wives,
mothers, aunts, possibly a few younger mistresses tossed in

to make it interesting. He'd hate to see this yacht crash against the pier, the folks here would stain the Hudson a royal azure, what with all this blue blood coursing onboard.

"Ah, Blackburn, very good."

In short order of being found by the senior partner, Carpenter Franklin, Adam was whisked away while simultaneously being handed a fresh glass of pricey champagne. It was cold and it woke him up, the bubbles reminding him this day was not without some purpose. He was escorted to a lower deck and a private stateroom, figuring he was about to find out. He was told to stand before another tastefully decorated man who wore an ascot. Adam grabbed the sleeves of his sweater, made sure it was secure on his shoulders. There were also three other men, all approximately Adam's age. He recognized one of them from his own firm; he was tall and tanned and his blond hair was perfectly coiffed, so much so the windy seas would not be much of a challenge to it. Who the other two "chosen" gentlemen gathered were, Adam hadn't a clue. His guess, they were rising stars at other, competing firms. He felt he was on a high-priced version of *The Dating Game.*

"Gentlemen," the ascot-turned man said, not bothering to introduce himself. He had an air about him that assumed everyone knew who he was. "Thank you for being here on this fine Memorial Day weekend. I realize the timing of this matter came as rather short notice and the method quite unorthodox, but I believe that if you strike when the iron is hot, you can avoid any unnecessary wrinkles. My lovely daughter Sarah Jane, a breath of fresh air on any ocean, is home from the Continent for two weeks, and it is my duty that she be properly entertained during her stay. She is, of course, onboard today, and each of you will be afforded a chance at getting acquainted with her. Keeping things in nautical terms, my Sarah Jane is precious cargo, and she is to be handled . . . accordingly. Thank you."

With that, Whoever He Was left the stateroom.

"Should we have saluted?" Adam asked.

Only Carpenter Franklin, who had remained behind in the shadows, frowned. The other three men didn't move a muscle and Adam had to wonder if they'd already suffered from too many Botox injections. At this point, they all appeared like they wouldn't want to be caught dead with Adam; the smart-mouth with the bad attitude was always trouble. Without a word, they just cleared out of the room. Apparently the pistol had gone off, the gates opened, and the race was on for the fastest thoroughbred to put his best hoof forward in search of the winner's circle. Adam was the last to leave the stateroom, but not before he drank down his champagne in one gulp. He left the glass on the table, and also left behind a head-shaking Carpenter Franklin. Perhaps his boss was questioning having chosen Adam for this highly sensitive project.

But enough with the first race. He'd lost that one.

He knew he would soon be trotted out to meet the lovely Sarah Jane Stockdale.

She wore a vibrant hue of blue that day, which, when backed up against the sunlit sky, made her blend beautifully into the background, challenging nature's beauty. The whole picture complemented her honey-blond hair and her apple-cheeked goodness. She was prim and she was proper and she also knew her father was watching her every move, from the upturn of her lips when she laughed to her hand reaching out to touch someone's sleeve. Her grandmother too was ever-present, one of those miserly old broads who could make God count his blessings. Sarah Jane laughed when required, shunned a second cocktail, pretended to be cold, only to be embraced by the sweater off the shoulders of the men fortunate to be chosen to dwell in her company. But when it was Adam's turn, and really what other term was there, he put on his best upper-crust attitude and acted properly by extending a hand, being polite and charming but not overly forward. He offered her champagne, and her reply took him by surprise.

"You too? Oh, I expected different. God, I'd kill for a scotch."

Adam paused, momentarily distracted by her forthright, as well as her unexpected nature. As he leaned against the deck's rail, ironically staring at the very building in Lower Manhattan in which he worked, the one that provided him his livelihood, his decent bank account, his freedom, then considered his answer very carefully. "No hard stuff, not here. On our first date? I'll take you to a place where you can drink whatever you want and swear like a sailor."

"Oh, goody," she said, clapping her hands. "I knew I was going to like you the best, Adam. You don't seem as . . . prepared as the others. But you'll have to wait, I still have to suffer through one more horrid introduction, but trust me—it won't take long," she said, rolling her eyes enough to make one seasick. She pointed to the boat's stern. "Do you see that blond helmet he calls hair? It doesn't move, I don't even think a shower dampens it. And his name is Skipper. I think his parents hated him when he was conceived. Or each other."

Ouch. She didn't take any prisoners, this surprising Sarah Jane Stockdale. Still, Adam put on his best smile because, in truth, who knew what she'd said about him to one of the other money models. Probably some comment about a fish out of water. Adam would happily jump back in, swim his way back to the shores of reality. But no, he told Sarah Jane,

"I'll be waiting right here." Then he paused, for dramatic, and effective, effect. "Sarah."

He didn't add the "Jane." On purpose.

She smiled widely over that. Not a social gaffe, turns out, but a turn-on.

So, not only did Sarah Jane Stockdale, heir to some kind of bean fortune, get to drink as much scotch on her first date with Adam Blackburn at a bar in Hell's Kitchen, blocks from the piers where they had met, she got to swear up a storm and make a fifty-ish man who'd been in his share of bar fights blush, and in the process she relaxed and let down her hair and much later, she even took off her clothes and got fucked all night by the renegade trader whom her parents and grandmother would have passed over without a shed of doubt, one she'd deliberately chosen for the same such reason. Her word, calling him a renegade, all while asking him to take her back to his place.

"This I could get used to," she said as she lay in a sweaty mess amidst tangled sheets.

Adam stared at the ceiling, wondering just what the hell he'd gotten himself into.

And then, at her urging, he'd gotten himself back into her.

All while thinking, how about that, Adam Blackburn, once a refugee from remote Danton Hill, now a sexual toy for one of New York's society girls. She confessed that he wasn't the first man she'd been with, it wasn't her first time, and Adam confessed that he could tell. Nor would it be her last encounter with Adam, whom, in the afterglow, she admitted, her father had referred to as the "long shot."

"Gee, thanks," he'd said. "That bodes well for our future."

"Pay no attention to my family. They don't make my decisions."

"Didn't seem that way on the yacht."

"Daddy is a pushover," she said. "Adam Blackburn, you rock my world."

"So you're choosing me over Daddy?"

She kissed him, stroked him.

"Who says I have to choose?" she said with easy petulance. "Now, just make me forget where I came from. Nothing proper."

Adam threw himself into her demands.

A sensational whirlwind romance ensued that became small pieces of gossip in the *New York Post*, and in the corridors of KFC's Manhattan offices. Privileged Sarah Jane Stockdale and an unknown trader named Adam Blackburn, who got ink and photos because he was handsome, especially beside the blond and beautiful heiress, they were never without plans after work, on the weekends. Dinner parties at her demanding grandmother's penthouse on Sutton Place, stuffy weekends of tennis at the sprawling estate in Greenwich, Connecticut, each visit accompanied by an interrogation by her family, always politely disguised as curious, enlivening conversation. *Where do you see yourself in five years? Where will you summer? How many children do you see yourself stuffing inside an SUV?* Like there were choices listed on the million-dollar menu, one from column A, one from column B. Frankly, Adam always felt tempted to answer that he saw himself with the American average of two-point-five children, but of course rich people didn't like handicaps. So Adam said the right things, he was courteous and attentive and even played against—and lost to, graciously and willingly—Grandmother in a few gin-soaked rounds of gin rummy. At tennis, with his weak backhand

and failure to follow through on his swing, he let his prospective father-in-law triumph handily on the family's clay courts, as the man ended each match with a slap of Adam's shoulder and saying, "Next time, maybe I'll let you win."

But of course he didn't, he couldn't, or he wouldn't allow himself.

Just like Grandmother.

The Stockdales were only happy when they won.

As a result of his newfound association with the privileged, competitive Stockdale family, Adam Blackburn's own stock began to skyrocket, both in society and in financial circles. Not only did he and Sarah Jane get invited to the swankiest, most exclusive parties in town and out in the country during the season, new clients at KFC who considered "wealthy" an understatement started consulting with Adam on what to buy, what to sell, who to crush in the ever-demanding arena of stocks, investments, portfolios. To these movers and shakers, the stock market was their personal game of Monopoly, and like when he played with the Stockdales, he knew to let them win. They'd better win. They all wanted Adam to purchase them Boardwalk.

Of course, as it would turn out, they would barely escape with Baltic Avenue.

And Adam Blackburn, sucked into this world and unable to extricate himself when things began to swirl downward, well, to keep the famed Monopoly game metaphor going, he nearly needed that "Get Out of Jail Free" card.

CHAPTER 9

NOW

The word *jail* loomed between them, especially considering the prison they found themselves in today, albeit one filled with temptations of the vine and of the flesh. Adam had rarely spoken of the incident, surprising himself that he had just dropped such a bomb on an unsuspecting Vanessa, given the look of surprise evident on her open face. The flames of the fire flickered, casting shadows on the walls, and on her face too. Like she didn't want to know the truth, the shadows delving deeper into his story. But he knew he had to continue, he wanted to share with her.

"It's okay, ask away. I know you want to."

She hesitated before saying, "What does that mean, jail? What did you do?"

"Oh, there were never any official charges filed, nothing ever turned serious. Just a lot of threats and supposition and suspicion. And, well, a couple of depositions. It could have been worse for me, and it was worse for others."

Lying beside him, her fingers had been dancing lazily in the tufts on his chest as he'd told his tale of the proper young woman with the edgy personality and of their grand romance, feeling almost a part of the heat he and Sarah Jane

had experienced, pulling away only when he'd spoken about
legal trouble. She couldn't help her reaction, she'd lived her
whole life reacting with natural instinct. She recognized that
Adam picked up on the change in her mood, the loss of her
silky touch. Building a wall, and he recognized the materials
required.

"Still, to even sniff prison . . . Adam?"

"You're wondering whether I really went to jail?"

Wondering why I'm such an idiot around you, was more in
line with her thinking. "No, no, it's just . . . well, the end of
your story took me by surprise. Here, I thought you were
telling me a tale of a doomed love affair, and instead . . ."

"It was real life."

She understood that comment. "Were you detained by
police, arrested? Lawyers?"

"Like I said, depositions. But, Vanessa, I'm not a crook."

"Adam . . . I didn't mean to imply . . ."

"Never mind, I did just kind of drop that bomb," he said.
"There I was, telling you about Sarah Jane Stockdale and
our whirlwind courtship and how she liked to knock back
scotch when not in her family's presence, and next thing I
know I'm mentioning being carted off to jail. Just one night,
but it was enough to make me realize my life had spiraled
out of control, and it all came about once I met the Stockdales. Keep in mind, the transition from almost-fiancé to
jailbird wasn't quite as abrupt as I make it sound. Sarah Jane
and I did have some good times. But when you're involved
with someone like her, you're involved with her family, and
with her family comes a bigger association: money."

"So what happened?"

"Easy. The stock market crashed, big-time, and bankers
became Public Enemy Number One. The recession hit, and
the greed-mongers on Wall Street nearly threw the country
into a second Great Depression. Jobs were slashed, unem-

ployment skyrocketed, and investment firms and banks were suddenly seen as the devil. Once upon a time I could mention that I made my living as a stockbroker and it was my ticket to anywhere cool in the city. Clubs, bars, parties, I had money and cachet and life was damn good—no, better, it was great. I was having a blast and could afford most anything I wanted. You read any cautionary tale, though, you know the hero is going down at some point. He needs to learn his lesson until he can appreciate where he came from." He paused. "Where I came from. Danton Hill."

Vanessa nodded. She understood.

"I'm glad to know you think of yourself as the hero."

"Yes, ever the hero, dashingly naïve to the end. Like a sailor coming home from the sea, a bit damaged but still himself for having conquered the world, his fears. Home to the lady he loved."

Vanessa's eyes blinked, once, twice. "Why would you say that?"

"Say what?"

"The sailor . . ."

"We're here in Danton Hill, the lake is just miles away. When you think hero, you think something swashbuckling. One who triumphs over evil, or maybe just over nature? Like we did, today, battling the storm. That accident, it could have killed us. We never would have had this . . ."

"Our private reunion."

"It's going well."

She deflected his comment, brought the conversation back to his tale.

"Is that what happened to you? You beat evil at its own game?"

"Actually, I sort of quit playing. Maybe I'm not such a hero. Maybe I should avoid the swirling seas and stick to safety of the land, stick to my own cautionary tale." Adam

spread his hands before him. "So, anyway, you asked about
the big love of my life. That's the story."

She nodded, drank down some wine. "I don't know what
to say."

"Sometimes, I don't either," he said. His fingers sought
out hers, entwined around them, tying them together.
Alone in this farmhouse, nothing to occupy their time but
sharing their lives, talking about missed opportunities, regrets, wishes, Vanessa suddenly felt awful for having doubted
him moments ago. For having pulled back. He'd been nothing but gentle with her: the fireplace, the wine, the lovemaking. Their impromptu reunion had been special, far
more than she could have anticipated when she'd decided to
return home to Danton Hill. She hadn't given tomorrow a
single thought. That was how much she wanted today to
last. A sudden emptiness found its way to the pit of her stomach, and that's when Vanessa realized that tomorrow was a
strange, uncertain concept, a word without definition,
twisting in the storm-ravaged wind. Lost in this singular
world of theirs, no sense of time passing, barely a sound emanating from outside the farmhouse, a wave of claustropho-
bia threatened to sweep over her. Her body wavered, her
head felt dizzy. She pulled the blanket tighter around her.

"Hey, you feeling okay?"

"I feel . . . odd. Cold, but not really. Sort of disconnected
to myself."

"You barely ate. Why don't I reheat the soup . . ."

"Adam, it's fine, I'll be fine."

"Maybe I should go down to the road, try to flag someone down. We could be deluding ourselves here, lost in our
own cocoon, that we're both fine after the accident," he
said. "Maybe what you're feeling is some post-accident symp-
toms . . . a concussion, shock?"

Adam uncrossed his legs, pushing himself up from the floor.

Vanessa reached out and grabbed his arm. "No, no, Adam, there's no need. Really, I'm fine. It'll pass. I think I was just feeling . . . I don't know, maybe sad? Melancholy? For you, for how things worked out with Sarah . . . Sarah Jane. Gee, I don't even know how to refer to her after hearing your story."

Adam laughed. "Join the club. Sarah was always an enigma, stuck between what she wanted and what was expected of her. Two identities."

"So, you believe she was the one, huh?"

"I don't know, guess not. She was more like the half."

"Like one of your imaginary children?"

"No, no . . . but hey, that shows you were listening. No, with Sarah, it's funny, when it was just the two of us and she could be just Sarah . . . wow, she was everything I thought I ever wanted. A partner, an equal, proper when needed, aggressive when unleashed; we supported each other emotionally and could always depend upon the other to be there when we needed a pick-me-up. But then we'd be around her family and . . ."

"She became Sarah Jane."

"Big-time."

"So, which one do you really think she was?"

"Ultimately?"

"Honestly, Adam. Your gut."

Without hesitation, he said, "She was a Stockdale, through and through. If she had to do it alone—and by alone I mean live financially independent, it's not as if she couldn't survive, she simply wouldn't want to. She'd never get so far as to make that choice of defying the wishes of Daddy Stockdale . . . of her family. Sarah Jane Stockdale had blood as blue as her grandmother's. She just liked to occasionally feel scotch run through those same veins."

"The rebellious girl who would eventually settle down and do as was expected."

"Bingo."

"Using you. Poor Adam."

"Oh, don't feel too sorry for me," he said. "Perhaps a part of me knew the relationship was doomed even as it was getting started. I doubt her family would have granted me full membership into her world—their world. Guess I was on a guest pass that summer. When Sarah and I finally realized we wouldn't work long-term, we parted. Our breakup wasn't about love or lust or betrayal, it was just we'd been left no other choice. Once everything went down at KFC, I would have been lucky to date the cleaning lady."

"So what really happened?"

"Not here."

"Huh?"

"Come with me," he said, extending his hand.

"Where? Adam, I'm not even properly dressed . . ."

"I'm not dressed at all."

Still, Adam tossed her the now-wrinkled blue dress shirt, and she quickly buttoned it over her otherwise naked self. He donned the goofy checkered pants. Half-dressed but respectable. Before whisking her away from the comforting fire, he took her into his arms and held her, kissing the top of her head. She sighed while feeling the heat emanating off his body, burying her face in the comfort of his chest. They could have remained there, but when a blast of wind rocked the house they parted and gazed at each other. Wordlessly, he led her out of the living room and up the stairs of the old farmhouse, one creaky step at a time. She attempted to ask where they were going, but he put a finger to his lips, then asked her to trust him.

"Your questions are just delaying our adventure."

"Adventure? What kind of adventure could be waiting for us inside this house?"

"Don't you like surprises?"

Her eyes darkened, just slightly. "Not always, no."

"I heard a story once," he announced. "Now I'm wondering how much of it is true."

"A story about what?"

"Destiny."

"Oh, great, that again."

"You're such a cynic."

"And you're not?"

He grinned as he looked upward. "Perhaps not. Perhaps in the long run I'm a lost soul, still seeking out the great romance of my life."

"And you think it's up these stairs?"

As he took her hand in his, he said, "I think anything is possible between two people."

"Now I think you're the one suffering from some post-accident concussion," she said. "Adam, where are you taking me?"

"Vanessa, venture with me, upstairs."

"That's a strange choice of words," she said.

"What, what did I say? Come with me, right?"

"Never mind," she said. "Lead on. Let's get this over with."

"Aren't you having fun yet?"

On the second floor of the house, Adam led them down the back hallway, where a small doorway revealed itself. He tested the knob, found it opened easily. Before them was a winding staircase, cobwebs caught in their cast-iron curls. The lightbulb didn't work, so Adam guided Vanessa up and around the curve of the stairs, climbing high, higher. At last they emerged inside the farmhouse's dusty, but surprisingly spacious cupola. It was bare of furniture except for a large wooden trunk with iron fixtures tucked into a dark corner. Moonlit rays streaked through the dirtied windows. The storm seemed to have cleared some, but still they needed a moment for their eyes to adjust to the darkness.

"Adam, this is beautiful . . . like a hidden fort."

"The perfect escape," he said.

"Haven't we already done that?"

He smiled, holding her tight from behind, his strong arms encircling her body. With a swift, easy motion he brushed back her silky hair, kissed her neck. "It's strange how being here makes me feel. I was trying to remember when last I felt this content, you know . . . my mind, my body, at peace. Strangely, I think it was the last night I spent with Sarah Jane. A warm summer night had fallen upon us after a storm had swept by, not unlike the one today. I was out in the Hamptons, at the Stockdales' summer place, and Sarah Jane had just told me that, and I quote, 'It's just not going to work out between us,' which was doublespeak for 'You're not good enough for me, for my family, anymore.' Her parents, namely her father, had decided that his precious Sarah Jane needed someone who understood the value of money—who was part of their world. Which meant someone who already had money, and lots of it. It was just too much hard work to integrate me into society."

"That's ridiculous . . ."

"Truthfully, it was liberating."

"Still, after what you'd shared. How you helped her escape that perfect little existence."

"Vanessa, in their world they believed they were perfectly justified. I'd just been fired from KFC, and no other investment firm in the city would hire me. I was branded an outcast even in my own world."

"Adam, can you tell me why?"

"I need to. For nearly nine months I've buried everything, pretending to enjoy my life but still stinging over life's betrayal. But here, in this cupola with only you and the cracks in the walls to hear me, I think I can speak of what happened." He paused, clearing his throat. "Okay, so here's how things played out. As I said earlier, I was working under the guidance of one of the partners, Carpenter Franklin. He was one of those moneyed executives who found himself, after KFC nearly went bankrupt, under investigation by the SEC for fraud, embezzlement, mishandling of corporate funds, whatever else they could think of. He denied all the charges, but the evidence was overwhelming. He was guilty as sin and the company had already decided he'd become their sacrificial lamb. Ultimately . . . well, perhaps it was true, or perhaps he simply didn't want to deal with the publicity . . . we'll never know."

"Why not?"

"Carpenter Franklin jumped out his office window at work."

"My God . . ."

"We worked on the thirtieth floor."

Vanessa's hand flew to her open mouth, her mind doing its best to shut out the image. "Adam, why are you telling me this—here, and why now?"

"Carpenter Franklin was a jerk, a toy for the industry and the firm, a yes-man who would do whatever it took to get the job done. As a result, he rode my ass daily, urged me to make more money—his attempt at setting me up with Sarah Jane was just his way of insinuating himself into Stockdale cash. I joked once about that phrase being engraved onto his headstone—MORE MONEY, ALWAYS MORE. And you know how he responded? 'Good way to go.' The man, faults aside, he loved who he was. And so, coming up here to the highest point in the house, I guess I wanted to look at the sky, but also be able to look down at the ground too . . . and ponder what Carpenter must have been thinking seconds before he ended his life." Adam paused, his expression tinged with regret. When he resumed, his voice was quieter. "Yeah, in business he was a total suck-up, but he wasn't a bad guy when you shared a few good scotches with him outside the office. He just got caught up in the world as much as I did, probably more. He was a good fifteen years older than me, so for him, KFC—the stocks, investments, money— represented the sum of his entire life, one that offered no escape other than the one he chose for himself. I'd been granted clemency, both from the senior partners at KFC and from the Stockdale family. From the SEC too, thank God. But I was still one of Franklin's men. Taint by association. So I was out. I was finished."

Words seemed inadequate right now. Vanessa just allowed him to hold her; she snuggled tighter against his body. Like their bodies were conjoined, connected.

"The week after I'd been fired was when, out at the Hamptons, Sarah Jane handed me my other walking papers. She said I could come back to bed for one last night. Like I should be grateful that I got another roll on the golden mattress. I didn't go back to her room, I didn't even pack my bag. I just set out on foot and left the Hamptons that night, waited at the train station for the first morning train back to the city. I promised myself I would never look back and I didn't. Sarah Jane got married three months ago to the son of a British lord, if you can believe it. The wealthy Stockdale family needed to find some new old money for their baby girl."

"And you, Adam? What have you been doing since then?"

"Nothing."

"You're not working?"

"Not since my last day at KFC."

"But that's been nearly a year . . ."

"Yeah, how great is that? It's been good for me, mostly. The time off has given me a chance to find out who I really am—or maybe I'm just rediscovering myself. Who I might have been, who I'd like to be again. To see what else awaits me in this world."

"You talk like you've got other lives to live."

"Or that I've already lived some."

"Really? You believe in stuff like that?"

He shrugged. "Sometimes I wonder . . . don't you ever feel that sense of déjà vu?"

"Yes. But that doesn't mean it's because I existed in a previous life."

"But what if it did? Vanessa, what if you and I knew each other before?"

"We did. We were both stupid teenagers."

"No, I mean, before that . . . before we were born," he said, turning to face her. "What if the prom all those years ago was our chance to remember a different time, and we failed to recognize the signs? What if the universe is now giving us another shot?"

"A high school reunion? Is that our 'shot'?"

Adam let out a snort of disapproval over her cynicism. "Maybe it is—or maybe, I don't know, just maybe, the accident, our finding this farmhouse, maybe this is our moment? We needed to grow up first, experience the world before we could find what was in front of our faces years ago. We were too young, too naïve, back then. It's funny, but when the invitation to attend the reunion popped into my in-box, I nearly deleted it. I mean, I'm jobless, unemployable in my chosen field, and the woman of my supposed dreams dumped me because ultimately I wasn't good enough for her fancy family. Gee, that's the perfect scenario to chat up people at your high school reunion. A real proud moment. Living up to the promise I had way back then."

"You sell yourself too short."

"Again, just like high school."

"Adam, is everything a joke?"

"About then. Yeah, mostly."

"So why did you decide to return? This other-life thing?"

"Not really, no, it's something fun to speculate about, when you're alone, or with someone you trust . . . someone you can admit crazy things to . . . but in the end, no, I'm me. Adam Blackburn, a product of Danton Hill High. Can't change that, that's not only the past, it's truth," he said, a nervous laugh accompanying his denial. His eyes had adjusted to the darkness inside the old cupola, and Adam found himself moving around the small space. He wandered over to the wooden trunk, sitting down upon its lid. He heard a sharp creak, but it was just the wood settling, adjusting to his weight. "Who knows? Maybe I need to take a step back in order to take that next step forward in my life," he said. "Being humbled is a great place to start. And who better to leave you humbled than the people who did that to you on a daily basis years ago?"

"So you're willingly taking a step back into the past to find out what you should be when you grow up?"

"Something like that."

"At thirty-eight?"

He shrugged. "It's never too late to grow up, isn't that what those self-help gurus say? It's never too late to become the person you always envisioned you would be, just follow their easy ten-step program," he said. "But it's also never too late to remain young. The beauty of life is you don't really have to decide between young and old, you just have to live." He pounded on the wooden trunk, a hollow sound echoing from within. "You can't keep yourself locked up. Sure, you can pack the bad stuff away and think it's gone. But it's not really, it's always waiting to be unlocked."

"So why not do that?"

"Do what?"

"Unlock it?"

"What are you talking about?"

"The trunk you're sitting on. You keep speaking in maybes, so let's play your game even further."

"I'm not following you."

"You keep speaking about fate, destiny . . . stuff like that. Let's indulge ourselves, Adam, play out your fanciful scenario of you and me in another time, another place. Say that you and I were meant to be, even before the prom came calling. Now other forces have pushed us together again, first by having our cars collide and then in finding this house. Like invisible hands have been guiding us, pushing us toward each other. Well, perhaps the universe further directed us upstairs to this cupola, and the reason why is because we're supposed to find this old trunk. We're supposed to see what's inside. Aren't you the least bit curious? If the owners are gone, why leave the trunk behind? Come on, let's open it, and see what's inside."

"Sounds like we could be unleashing Pandora."

"Now who's the cynic? *Maybe* it's just the opposite," she said. "Not everything in life has to turn out badly. Not that I have much experience in that, but hey, all those storm clouds outside, perhaps one of them has a silver lining?" She paused, watched as the sky above them darkened, the light fading from inside the cupola, barely leaving them with their shadows. She shivered once, wrapped her arms around herself. "Look, Adam, the two of us are here—alone—and the world seems to have halted on its axis. Or at least, that's the way it feels. Let's go with your gut instinct and find out what all this means." She paused, and her eyes connected with his in a way she'd never before felt with another soul. Like their eyes truly were windows to the outside, and they'd just opened them to something new, something amazing. Adam still hadn't spoken a word, and so Vanessa said with more drama to her voice than she intended, "Go ahead. Open the trunk."

There was no lock on the front of the trunk, making its contents available to anyone who dared to open it. So Adam bent down on one knee and unlatched the metal clasps. They were rusty, the hinges squeaking from rusted neglect. But finally they popped open and the trunk lid jumped up a few inches, like a spring uncoiled. Outside the cupola's windows came a streak of lightning, thunder rumbling across the sky seconds later. Was the storm on its way back, coming for them? Both Adam and Vanessa looked upward, suddenly wary.

"Coincidence?" he asked.

"I think the universe is telling us something."

"Yeah, but was that encouragement—or a warning?"

In a move of solidarity, Vanessa sat beside Adam, and again they looked at each other, as though confirming their next step. Words went unspoken but somehow they were still in sync, communicating, urging the other to take that next step. They did so, together. Four hands lifted the lid of the wooden trunk, again a creaking sound swallowing up the room. Darkness gave way to light as the contents of the trunk were exposed. Vanessa took a deep breath and then spoke.

"Look at these," she said pausing, her fingers gliding over the bundles before them, "letters, stack of letters. There must be hundreds of them, sealed in envelopes and wrapped in red ribbons. Look, they all have dates on them. Someone was a very busy writer."

Adam lifted one bundle to further examine the letters.

"That's curious, they've never been opened. They've never even been mailed."

Vanessa pointed to what was written on the envelope. "Adam—look?"

It was a name, written in a handsome script. Still, the name was unmistakable.

"*Venture,*" he said, his voice almost reverent.

"How strange . . . what kind of name is that, and why does it sound . . ." Vanessa began to ask, her whispered voice trailing off as soon as they passed her lips. She felt cold rip through her body. After hearing the name grace Adam's lips, she felt as though her feet had lifted off the ground, her body floating high into the air. Into the rumbling clouds. She felt disoriented, and reached out to steady herself. Then . . .

That's when the world went black and she fainted.

*I*NTERLUDE

B̶EFORE T̶HEN

He knew he had to write to her one last time. A final letter, but hardly a final good-bye. Knowing time was of the essence, the old man set about his weekly ritual.

Appropriately enough the cool rain was falling hard from the dark sky, the wind tilting its droplets sideways. The kids on the far side of the street would think him crazy going out in such weather, but traditions were called such for a reason, and he was not the kind of man to be deterred by the whims of Mother Nature. Especially not at this last stage of his life, when every day, nearly every hour, seemed precious and fleeting and special all at the same time. First thing he did was seek out his yellow rain slicker and hat in the front closet, thinking with a smirk how the protective gear transformed him from hobbling old man to a fair imitation of that guy from the seafood commercial. Trust him, trust yourself. He even had the thick white whiskers to go along with the classic image. The only difference being that this man was not fiction, he who ascribed to his daily ambitions with earnest zeal. He was a sailor who had lived his life upon the churning seas or somewhere near where the water could offer him comfort. Always . . . the water was there. Like it called to him, a gurgling whisper.

But that had been a long time ago.
Almost another life.
Almost.

His name was Aidan Barton, and for forty years of hard, honest living, the expansive Great Lakes and the roiling oceans had been not just his mistress, but his temptress and the only love to which he could cling, and only then was its hold tenuous at best, slipping through his fingers with the crush of a wave. She was untamed, much like the spirit of the woman he'd once anticipated sharing a life with. Alas, life had seen fit to explore other plans, seek out other paths, other ideas, and so the man named Aidan went about his days and his nights alone, at least when it came to the piercing matters of the heart. That was the thing about a life at sea, you had to have patience on your side as much as luck; no one could rush anything and achieve success. Patience taught his lonely soul that he would one day see his beloved Venture again, on a day when the world gifted them the chance to become entwined as it always should have been. Now, at seventy-four, retired nearly fifteen years from all he'd known, he had retreated to the big farmhouse on the hill, where the breeze off the lake kept him in good spirits, allowing him the chance to relive both those charmed moments he'd been afforded, the tragic ones too.

He'd created his own moments too, upon setting up home in this rambling old house.

The letters. Always the letters were there to keep his mind occupied.

Today, this late Friday afternoon in late August, while the sky darkened with the onset of the summer storm, Aidan knew he had to endure the travails of this journey. Would it be his last? Only time and God knew and neither was giving up answers, but he was practical that the day was soon upon him. He mustered up enough strength to walk across the wooden floor, turn the knob of the front door. Once outside on the porch, he saw the rambling old truck turn into the driveway. His ride, perfectly timed.

"Good evening, Mr. Barton."

Aidan smiled. Mr. Barton, indeed. As much as he insisted that she call him by his first name, she absolutely refused. Her mama had raised her to respect her elders, and she held dear to such traditions, just as much as her charge did. As a man steeped in tradition, Aidan Barton had no choice but to appreciate her dedication. Her name was Myra Ravens, she was a local girl. Raised in Danton Hill, one who never felt the gravitational pull of the outside world, content to finish her studies here, learn her craft, devote herself to helping others. She was a nurse's aide, she had been coming by to see "Mr. Barton" for well over a year now, and the two had grown close. Aidan might be in his seventies and Myra only in her late twenties, but they had forged a bond that traversed decades nonetheless. It was six months before she was privy, though, to his one secret, the letter writing.

That's when she started showing up during her off time, to assist him.

She knew how important his errand was, and she was determined to never miss one.

Tonight was one such errand, perhaps his last, if you were to believe his crazy talk.

"Stop that nonsense," was how Myra responded to such an idea.

Now, Myra Ravens, pretty but not beautiful, with thin blond hair that never stayed over her ears, emerged from the dry safety of her truck and bounded toward the steps of the porch. Aidan was already attempting the first step down, his aged hand clutching the rail as firmly as he could.

"Nasty night for going out, Mr. Barton."

"I've seen worse," he assured her.

There was truth to his words. Summer storms here in the lake-soaked land of Danton Hill were infamous, especially in the oppressive late days of August. Aidan had lived through his fair share of those. So that's why he took her comment with a grain of salt, and she just accepted things as they were. She knew the importance of this brief trip.

She helped him down the remainder of the stairs, neither of them bothered by the falling rain, and finally she got him settled into the passenger side of the cab. The step up was the hard part, but Aidan, with a steely, deep breath, was able to manage the feat. Determination had that effect on him. Myra joined him on the driver's side, turning up the blower to fight off the condensation building across the windshield. Then she looked at him.

"How are you feeling?"

"Chatter only delays our mission. Let's just go, my dear," he said with a gentle nod, and then he paused and she looked at him because both of them knew some worldly piece of wisdom was forming on his tight lips. "The clock runs on its own time, and we are merely slaves to its endless revolutions. Time doesn't end, only those who lived by it." Myra smiled sideways at him while Aidan stared forward, and then they were off, wipers battling the rain so they didn't have to.

The treacherous drive along winding, country roads to the shores of Lake Ontario took fifteen minutes. Danton Hill's lakeside, once wild and free, had now been claimed by the State Park Service of New York, and as such you had to pay to get in. "Even for a quick ten-minute visit?" Myra, rolling her eyes, had asked the first time she'd taken Aidan here, but he'd merely waved away her concerns and handed the woman working the booth the seven-dollar admission fee. Today was no exception, and Myra, still with that roll of her eyes, quickly passed the money along before resuming her drive into the deeper regions of the park.

Few cars were parked in the lot; the rain had been long predicted today and served to keep away most summer revelers. Once they parked, Myra helped Aidan out of the truck. He took in a deep breath, allowing the brine of the sea to infiltrate his insides, fill his lungs with the familiar scent of his life. Then he started forward across the wet, green lawn, determination again written across his handsome, weathered face. Myra followed close behind, bypassing abandoned picnic tables and damp grills, the beach their obvious destination.

Aidan made his way across the sand, his eyes focused on the line of the horizon way out in the distance. The gray sky above limited just how far you could see, but his mind had plenty of images from over the years, taken both from this beach and beyond, out on the calm waters. To his left was the rock-lined jetty used today by fisherman and young children wishing to brave the slippery stones in search of a day's catch. Aidan had no business there, even if his footing was secure. It was that rocky pier that had led to his Venture being taken by the sea, which in turn had led him to these weekly visits, as forced upon him as the grief he'd felt upon his return all those years ago. Encroaching upon the water's edge, Aidan withdrew from his pocket a small glass vial and unscrewed the black top. He bent down, knees aching, and placed the object in the lake. Water gurgled in quickly, and just like that it, the vial was full, his mission completed.

He turned back to Myra, who was waiting just a few feet away.

"You loved her that much," she said.

A twinkle sparkled from his eye, the only light in an otherwise gray day.

"And now, my dear Myra, I have many thoughts to jot down, a very pressing letter." He held up the vial of lake water, a broad smile crossing his face. Yet again he'd captured a part of Venture's spirit, a necessary thing to have at his side as he sat down to his old desk.

The water connected him to her, it was where she'd gone to rest.

Except he didn't believe she had ever found peace.

Venture, even in the afterlife, surely lived up to her name.

My dearest Venture:

The clock ticks toward midnight. It is
August 18th and the languid days of summer
are in full swing. I write this letter to you—a
final one, my love—in the comforting glow of
candlelight, which flickers against the walls.
Shadows act as my companions, as they always
have since you left me, bouncing off the walls
like young children in need of discipline.
These shadows, though, they are silent and
allow me my meditations, my mind's musings
before I set words to paper.

You are in my thoughts, of course. You
always are, but today is different. For so many
years we have been separated, and I feel the
time is fast approaching upon our reunion.
That is my hope. That is the faith I keep
clenched inside my heart. Life is a mystery, for
certain, and death is perhaps its ultimate
secret. What will I know once I pass? What
will the universe reveal to me? Only time will
tell, goes the old expression. The clock's bell
will toll for me.

I think back to that day I returned from my
journey upon the sea, waiting to sweep your
lithe self into my arms. Instead it was the great
waters of the lake that swept you away, taking
you from me. Those days after when I sought
solace at the edge of the lake, when I felt I had
lost everything, I wasn't sure how I could go
on. How cruel could my lifeblood be, taking
from me all I worked for? What would I do?
You, of course, know all this, I've detailed it
over the years in my letters. The anniversary

of the day you were taken from me, on your birthday, the day on which we met, they all served as constant reminders of all I had lost.

But know this, my Venture, it was that day on the beach when hope defined itself. I knew you'd sent me a message. You weren't fully gone from this world, and you were waiting for me to join you. When your lovely dress came ashore, the one you were wearing when first we met, practically wrapping its entrails around my legs, your presence was felt. The dress remains with me, stored inside this old trunk along with the letters I wrote to you over these many years. If the universe allows it, we will one day return to the farmhouse I built for us, and together discover the precious contents of this trunk.

We may not recognize our meeting immediately, for how could we? I will not be Aidan, you will not be Venture. We will, of course, be other people in another time, but our souls will remain ours, buried inside until such is the time for our reawakening, our destined reunion. For now, I just await that time. The clock ticks again, midnight has come and gone and a new day has arrived. Darkness still swirls, the sun hours from rising. Time is short. Our time is coming.

Good night, my sweet, dearest Venture. Know that you share my whole heart and possess my soul, now and always, in the light of day and under the cover of darkness, in the calm of a moonlit sky or in the throes of the deepest, darkest storm. Forces of nature are unstoppable, and I knew from the moment I

met you that we were one. Venture, you were
a true force of nature the world could not
contain. Your soul may have left us that day,
but your spirit remained. I feel it now at my
side.
    You blessed my life. Bless me once again,
Venture, in my looming death.

I remain, forever yours,

Aidan

*He set down the quill pen, knowing he would never again dip
its black tip into the inkwell. What followed was as much a part of
his tradition as anything: the sealing of the envelope, its intent
clear, and his motions symbolic. First, with difficulty because of his
aged fingers, he folded the sheets of parchment into thirds, paying
particular attention to the sharp creases. Once they were smoothed
to his satisfaction, he gently slipped the letter inside the thick,
ivory-colored envelope. Laying the envelope down flat on his desk,
its back flap sticking up, Aidan reached over with shaking arms
and took hold of the small bottle of water. Sprinkling a bit of the
lake's tears onto the strip of adhesive, the old man with the heavy
heart then folded the flap down, pressing it tight against the envelope. There he sealed his words from the world, allowing them to
be discovered only by its intended. It was as though with this action, her spirit locked his heart inside.*
    One final touch awaited him.
    *Turning the envelope over, he took hold one last time of the
quill pen, for certain this time. And with his hand unsteady, he
still somehow managed a perfect scripted word:* Venture. *He underlined the name with a flourish, and then, staring at it, feeling
tears well up in his eyes, he bent down and pressed his lips to it,
letting them linger. The ritual over, he placed the letter atop a*

small bundle of other envelopes. He'd written one letter each week since Venture had left him, all of them gathered here inside this trunk. And beneath them, a small package wrapped in protective plastic contained a dress that had not been worn since that fateful day just after the turn of the last century. More than fifty years had passed, the world had moved on, except for one man and his memories of a love that had defied time.

The man named Aidan Barton rose from his rickety chair, taking hold of the candlestick as he did so. His movements were slower now than they had been over the years, this was natural, all of time was an unstoppable, forceful progression. Using one hand to assist him with the handrail, he made his way down the crooked steps from the cupola and into his bedroom. He set the candlestick on his nightstand and blew the flame until all that remained were smoky entrails. With only fresh moonlight guiding him, Aidan shucked his bathrobe and got into bed. Once under the covers, his head comfortably resting against the pillows, he let out a heavy sigh. Today had been a busy day, the preparations he had taken care of all day, the trip up to the lake, the strained writing of Venture's letter. They were the hardest part, translating thoughts into words. Sleep would come quickly tonight, and he felt in his tired bones that eternal sleep was not far behind him. His breathing had grown shallow, his heart no longer strong. He'd shunned doctors lately, knowing that what he needed could only be called nature's cure, one prescribed by the universe and not by some educated professional.

He was still smiling when he drifted off.

If he awoke tomorrow, fine, such was the way of the world. If not, he was content with the life he had lived, the dedication in which he had served his fellow man, and the one woman whose spirit filled his soul. For now, though, he'd ensured his future way beyond this concept called death.

Because he'd left one secret behind, still to be discovered.

PART 2

CHAPTER 10

NOW

Vanessa Massey's eyes flickered open, hesitantly at first, then open wide and filled with questions. About her location and about what had happened, neither of which she gave voice to, bothered by the persistent chill that had seeped into her bones and still held tight to her body. A cool wetness was draped against her forehead, a single drop sliding into her eye, like shedding a tear in reverse. As it hit her eyelid, she blinked and then she stirred, fully came to, and then, at last, she spoke.

"What happened . . . where am I?" She paused, light finding her, as though she had realized her situation. "Adam . . . are you here?"

A soothing voice settled over her.

"Yeah, I'm right by your side, Vanessa. I only left you for a brief moment to run down and get a cold washcloth from the bathroom." He'd placed the cool, damp cloth on her feverish forehead, and now it peeled off and dropped to the wood floor of the cupola as she sat up. He paused, staring at her, watching as the light of life came back into her eyes, those green irises widening as he came into focus. Her wandering gaze indicated she was unsure where she was.

"Still at the farmhouse, it's only been a few minutes since you went blank on me."

"I passed out?"

"Fainted dead away," he said. "But I think you're going to be fine. I don't think you'll have any lingering damage, your head barely hit the floor. I caught you just in time."

"Just the idea of that sounds like it could have hurt. How long was I out?"

"Like I said, just a few minutes."

"A few?"

"Maybe five. Really, that's all."

"I don't understand what happened. Why would I faint? I'm not a fainter by nature, nor am I some retiring type from the Victorian era. I've always been strong."

"Yes, you can handle anything."

He had no idea. She knew he soon would.

"So why this time?"

"Something took you by surprise. I saw your eyes roll up inside your head just before you went for a header."

"Pretty picture. But really . . . something? Thanks, Adam. That's very specific."

He let out a short bark of a laugh that echoed down the open stairs. "At least you haven't lost your biting sense of humor," he said. "We went upstairs to the cupola, I wanted to show you the stars. Do you remember discovering the letters inside the trunk, the name written on them?"

She nodded. "Venture."

"I said her name, and next thing you know . . . you were lights-out."

"I don't understand."

"Probably coincidence, that's all, you were already a bit light-headed. Your fainting spell had more to do with the heat up here in the cupola. Windows closed, no fresh air.

What I think you most need is some food . . . nourishment. Who knows when last you ate, you've been flying for a day, then you barely ate anything earlier. Not that I blame you, the soup and sausages were hardly appetizing. Let's get you downstairs, maybe open the front door and get some breeze circulating in this house. Between the accident, the humidity outside, and the mustiness of this old cupola, the lack of solid food, maybe the effects of the wine too, and the, uh, energy we expended, it all created a perfect storm and out you went."

"Don't say storm," she said.

He nodded, agreeing with her there. "Sorry, poor choice of word on my part. Come on, let's see if we can get you back on your feet."

Her knees a bit wobbly, she happily accepted help from the stalwart, steadying force that Adam represented. He took hold of her arms and practically lifted her up. Holding on to him with one arm, her other grabbing at the railing, she eased down the first step, then a second. Immediately she felt a rush of cool air swirling up the staircase that helped clear the cobwebs from her mind. Still, before leaving the cupola she stole a look back at the old trunk, still open, the stack of envelopes piled about. He'd jokingly spoken of having a connection between them, and then they had gone and opened the trunk and discovered all those unread letters. Was there a link? How did it all connect, and why should it? She guessed that neither of them had any answers.

"Once we get you settled, I'll reheat what's left of the soup and this time you'll eat it," Adam said as they made their way to the hallway on the second floor.

Vanessa shuddered at the memory of the makeshift meal she'd prepared. "Condensed soup made without milk? I think I deliberately knocked it over."

"The sausages?"

She looked suddenly green. "Even as I opened the tin I knew I wouldn't eat one. Am I too grown-up to say *ick?*"

"Just don't faint on me again."

Still, Adam had to agree with her about their meal, cold soup and greasy sausages were not exactly a gourmet's delight. The kitchen cabinets, though, had been as bare as the rest of the house, offering few options. He thought about the reunion surely taking place now, mere miles from them in the auditorium of Danton Hill High. Drinks were being served along with hugs between people who hadn't seen each other in five, ten, perhaps twenty years, hungry former classmates chatting jovially as they piled their plates high with meats and salads, fresh local corn. Sounded nice; stomachs grumbled. His mouth watered over rich, fragrant, but imaginary smells. Vanessa's voice broke him from his brief reverie.

"What are you thinking about?"

"Honestly? The reunion."

"There was salmon on the menu," Vanessa said.

"Salmon . . . from Danton Hill? That famous Great Lakes Salmon?"

"Okay, I doubt the fish is the freshest . . . still, I'm so hungry I could eat anything . . . except soup and sausages. What else was in the cupboards, I can't remember."

"Not much."

Just then, inspiration struck Adam, the proverbial lightbulb going off over his head.

"Corn."

"Corn, in the cupboards? I repeated: ick. I hate canned vegetables. Adam, my stomach is growling, my mind is numb, and my body is feeling that deep-in-the-bone chill again."

"No, that's not what I mean. Think about it, Vanessa,

there's fresh food right under our noses, literally—directly outside, in the fields that surround the farmhouse. How come we didn't think of it before? We were only trapped in the midst of all those stalks this afternoon."

"The cornfields, Adam! My gosh, right from the stalk . . . fresh and sweet and juicy . . . my mouth is already watering at the very thought . . . and the corn is at its peak in August. It will be perfect." She brightened, color returning to her cheeks. "I think I'm coming to."

"You do look a little better, the outside air might be just what you need," Adam said.

"Or a little exercise," she replied.

"Huh?"

Vanessa picked up their pace as she neared the bottom steps, and suddenly she was off, racing through the house, not unlike before they had made love, when something had spooked her and she'd run from the house. This time her mood was bright, her energy pulsing.

"Hey, wait . . . take it easy . . ."

So much for the fainting spell.

An impromptu race was on, the two of them charging through the kitchen and out the back door, nearly leaping onto rain-soaked ground and splashing their way through grassy pools far from the house and the road. Vanessa leading the charge, they journeyed into the towering, silk-topped stalks that grew from the edge of the yard. As the cooling night air prickled at their skin, they waded their way into two parallel rows of stalks, each of them picking out several ears still encased in their thick husks. Peeling away the soft silk and rough-hewn stalk, the exposed kernels were a mix of yellow and white. Vanessa dug a fingernail into the sweet meat, producing a bubble of juice. She brought it to her lips and closed her eyes as sweetness enveloped her.

As they sought out the perfect ears, they paid little attention to the fact that their legs were once again splattered with mud.

Like pirates on the high seas finding a long-sought treasure, they laughed and shouted out in surprise. Gathering husks of corn into their arms, Adam at one point leaned through the stalks and planted an appealingly sloppy kiss on Vanessa's lips. She giggled like a young girl before running through the tall rows. He chased after her, dropping ears with each unsteady step. At last he caught up to her, tossing the freshly picked ears into the air to free his hands for a near tackle, grabbing her as she threatened to lose her footing. After her fainting spell, he didn't need to risk injury to her. Still laughing, she greedily accepted his kisses, his touch, as if this intimate exchange was the very nourishment her body had been craving. For a second it felt like the rain had returned, only to realize they were being showered by droplets that clung still to the giant stalks, released to the air by their happy tussle.

"I think our isolation is turning us crazy," she said.

Smiling at her, he said, "Let's keep it that way."

"What, isolated or crazy?"

"I don't know about you, but I like not feeling like part of the world. Solitude for two."

She paused, gazing into his eyes. They held the moment.

Finally they returned to the here and now, noticing the ears of corn they picked were now lying muddied on the ground and in need of a good wash. They laughed at the sight of not just the corn but of their happy selves, never imagining that their return to the Danton Hill area would have brought about such surprises. That the simple task of picking corn would turn the heat up between them, sweeping away the cool air with a pleasant warm front and plenty of sweat-inducing humidity. Neither paid the world around them any attention, they just kissed and touched and touched again and kissed, right there in the middle of the cornfield, with no care other than the hunger they needed to feed.

A distant, howling sound caught their attention, forcing them to break their embrace. A dog or a wolf, whatever creature lived out there, was angry at having its home disturbed. It was the first sign of life they'd encountered since the accident.

"Uh-oh," he said, pulling away, looking deep into the cornstalks.

"Uh, yeah, well said."

"Shall we take this back inside?"

"The corn, yes."

"Not just that . . ." Adam said, then the second those words had escaped his lips he knew he'd spoken the wrong thing. Even the wolf-like thing howled again, like it knew the mistake he'd made. Don't push things, all that had happened so far had grown organically. What they had reacted to was a spontaneous burst of passion, with neither of them giving thought beyond what each was feeling. Speaking words, and as such giving credence and voice to the passion exploding between them, only served to put an end to their emotions. Like raindrops drowning their sizzle.

"Okay, I know, sorry to push you . . ."

She put a lone finger to his lips. "No, you have nothing to be sorry about. Look, Adam, I can't tell you what an amazing time I'm having, with you . . . us, here at some lone house that no one seems to live in, but that still has managed to clothe us and comfort us and . . . well, nearly feed us. This is a far better reunion than I could have possibly imagined, not when I got the invitation, not on the plane when the pilot suddenly announced we'd begun our descent into the New York area. I hadn't been back to the States for some years, and the apprehension I felt nearly paralyzed my heart. But the truth of the matter is, and I don't think you'll deny it, something odd is going on here—something bigger than both of us. It's almost like we're both supposed to be here, just the two of us. It's like the play . . ."

"*No Exit.*"

"Sartre, right, all that existentialism. We're trapped, with no chance of escape. I mean, look at what happened to us in the cupola, what we discovered."

"You think those letters are a clue?"

"I . . . I don't know. I'm curious to know all about those letters, but right now something bigger demands our attention." She hesitated, searching for additional words, hoping they would help explain her feelings. "Before we look at those letters, though, we have unfinished business between us, and if I'm ever to give myself to you again—honestly and truthfully and with no barrier built up between us—then I need to tell you my tale. Like you told yours, I think it's my turn. Will you allow me that chance? Will you listen?"

"That's all I've been waiting for," he said, "but I wasn't going to push it. Look, Vanessa, I know something happened to you, either when you first left Danton Hill after high school or once you arrived in Europe, and whether it was good or bad is not important. I can tell that it changed your life forever, like today . . . is changing us. What happened altered your perspective, perhaps even your soul. It took from you, from your family and friends, that popular girl from high school who gave no thought to climbing to the top of the cheerleader pyramid. Like climbing atop the world, you feared nothing. Suddenly you became someone who questions all she does and beats herself up afterward for not being stronger. Am I close?"

"I believe it's called a sea change," she said.

"The sea. Water, again. We're close."

She could smell the brine of the lake wafting through the air. Almost like the house was built upon this hill for just such a reason, to feel the daily currents of water-soaked wind. "Way too close."

"Come on, let's get back to the house and get ourselves cleaned up, and then we'll cook up some of this corn. I doubt there's butter in the fridge, but if not, there's got to be salt. Put some flavor on our tongues, get some substance in our bellies. And then, my dear Vanessa, the floor is yours. Just as you gave me space to tell my story, I won't talk, I won't react. I'll just listen. And I certainly won't judge. Sound like a deal?"

She hesitated a moment, staring down at the ears of corn at their feet.

"What, is something else the matter?"

"Adam, I have a confession to make."

"Okay . . ." he said, hesitantly.

"I'm a terrible cook."

Having feared the worst, Adam felt relief wash over him as he let out a laugh that rivaled the wail of whatever creature had howled them back into reality. He assured her he would boil the corn and maybe find something more in the kitchen to satisfy their cravings. If she really didn't know her way around the kitchen, perhaps she'd missed some tasty morsel earlier. Maybe even another bottle of wine was hidden in a bottom cabinet just waiting to be uncorked. Like the past, it would provide a velvety comfort. She admitted that the latter would be a great find.

"I'm on the case."

As they headed through the soaked yard back toward the rear porch, Adam's foot tripped on an upturned root. He fell to the ground, crying out with sudden pain.

"Is it your ankle?"

"No, no . . . I bumped my head against something. Something hard."

Vanessa reached down to help him up. As he righted himself on the ground, he touched the wound on his forehead he'd incurred during the accident. He still felt the sharp piece of glass imbedded beneath the open skin beneath his hairline. He hadn't reopened the wound, thankfully, as no fresh blood dripped. Just a sharp pain had wafted through his system, no doubt from the impact of his head hitting hard against the stone.

"You okay?"

"Yeah, I'll be fine. Just, what was that I hit?"

He looked, and Vanessa looked, and what they saw was unmistakable.

"Oh my God," he said.

What revealed itself to them in the glow of the moonlight and in the high grass was a lone grave marker. Jutting out of the ground was a thick granite stone, a simple inscription chiseled onto its hard façade. With the aid of the freshly emerging silver moon's glow, they were able to make out the letters. Each of them read the epitaph silently, their minds giving quiet reverence to their discovery. What they saw was this:

AIDAN BARTON
Death is just the beginning.
August 19th

Finally, the wind quieted down and the silence was all the more apparent.

Vanessa was the first to speak. "Adam, look at the date . . . it's today."

"More than fifty years ago . . . but you're right, August nineteenth. That's kind of creepy. And an odd coincidence." Adam paused. "If you believe in such things."

"I think you do," Vanessa answered. "All your talk of fate, and it lands us here."

"The fact of the grave's existence still doesn't answer who lives here now. Aidan Barton died long ago, the house could have changed hands countless times."

"And yet his grave remains."

"What a curious epitaph—'death is just the beginning'?" Adam said, his mind turning over meanings for such an enigmatic phrase, like it was offering up hope of tomorrow. "He must have loved this house or Danton Hill itself to have asked to be buried here. Do you think he's the guy who wrote all those letters? That woman . . . whom he called Venture, she must have been the love of his life, but I don't see a grave for her. He lies here, alone."

"What I think is I want to go inside now," Vanessa said, again wrapping her arms around her for needed warmth. Or perhaps, she thought, for protection. Adam watched as she stared down at the stone, wiping a single tear from her mud-stained cheek. "To think he's all alone here, how sad. I'm glad that on the anniversary of his death someone is here to remember him. Thank you, Mr. Barton," she said, "for giving us shelter. We'll take good care of your home."

Adam smiled at her, reaching out to clasp his hand in hers. "Come on, let's get you some food. I think you'll feel better after we eat. You shower again, I'll cook. And then maybe we'll go see what our Aidan Barton wrote about in all those letters."

"Aidan Barton, how strange," Vanessa said, testing the name out on her tongue, feeling a sense of the familiar.

"Adam Blackburn. Do you realize the two of you share the same initials?"

Vanessa returned to the kitchen after having taken her second shower of the night, looking younger, red-cheeked, and fresh as a daisy. Her dark hair was still wet and clinging tight to her head, and a rare, genuine smile gracing her face let Adam know all his efforts had been worth it. She had also found a blue terry-cloth robe in a back closet, so she was warm and toasty and said she almost felt like she'd warmed up, that she felt all cozy.

"Perhaps this robe gave some lady friend of Mr. Barton's some comfort," she said.

"Kind of ratty, then, if it's that old. But the sight of you wrapped inside the robe makes you look like you live here. The mistress of the house."

"Home. Not a concept I'm completely familiar with at the moment," she remarked.

Adam allowed the cryptic comment to slide by. She was full of these curious phrases that dropped into the ether without explanation, making him all the more curious about the life she had led, the secrets she kept. She obviously had issues to deal with, and with his patience they were getting there. "You hungry?"

"Duh. Starving."

He smiled at her. "Good, we're ready."

That's when she saw that the wooden kitchen table, which seated eight people easily, had been turned into an intimate setting for two, with place mats and linen napkins that he'd found in the side cabinet, and two thin, scented candles that flickered and burned, their smell wafting through the dimly lit room. Silverware, plates, utensils, all had been set out, each one kitty-corner to the other. No opposite ends of the table here, this was a dinner served up close and personal. Adam escorted her to her seat, pulling out the chair so she could slide in with ease. He got her settled, and then took the vacant seat.

"What have you done?"

"Well, for starters . . . under this towel is a basket full of banana bread. There was a mix in the cupboard, and thankfully some cooking oil and some butter in the fridge—I checked the date, it was fine. Alas, no milk or eggs, but I think it'll taste just fine enough. And under this one, the corn we picked, freshly shucked and steamed perfectly. And last but not least . . . it's not a red, but a white wine will have to do."

Vanessa looked at him with bemused wonder. "What is this, the story of the loaves and fishes? I think perhaps, Adam Blackburn, you have the ability to walk on water."

"If that were the case, neither of us would be here now," he said, thinking back to his car and how it had hydroplaned on the highway just moments before the crash. The rainwater had not been his friend then, so why should some preternatural power possibly possess him now? He pushed the images aside and concentrated instead on the meal, the wine, and most especially, the company.

"So," he said, "let's dig in and get some food in our systems, and when you're ready you can tell me your story. Let me guess where it begins. How about the day after the prom, as you were getting ready to leave for Europe? You were so excited that night, your first trip out of Danton Hill. I'm anxious to know what happened next."

Vanessa was buttering her bread, when all of a sudden she dropped the knife to the plate. She gazed back at him, the light in her eyes doused. "Why there, why start there?"

"I don't know, it's just what came to mind. It's where we

ended, the prom, even though we'd barely started. Not that
I was expecting us to, it was just one night. But this is your
life. I want to hear all about it, so feel free to begin wherever."

She nodded her head, resumed spreading butter on the
piece of bread while stealing glances at him. "Thank you,
Adam, and I'm sorry to . . . jump all over you. This isn't
easy for me. And no, my story does not start after the prom.
This one is different. You told me about Sarah Jane, so I
want to tell you about the man who shook my world . . . are
you ready for this one? His name was Dominick di Paolo
Alighetti."

"That's quite a mouthful."

"He was quite a man."

"Was?"

"Oh no, it's nothing that tragic. He's alive, that's for certain."

"Ah. So your use of past tense . . . describes his personality."

"Something like that."

"Did he hurt you?"

She paused to take a sip of the wine, never letting her
eyes leave the inside of the glass. Like answers floated inside
among the fermentation, confused by the intoxicating
aroma. Adam felt his heart constrict with sorrow as he
waited for her inevitable, unfortunate answer.

"Yes, Dominick did hurt me, he hurt me very much,"
Vanessa said, and in a surprisingly tender voice that belied
her earlier words, continued with the dual personality rela-
tionships can possess. "But before he did that, first he daz-
zled me and then he loved me and invited me to be the
center of his life, to be his everything. But I'm getting way
ahead of myself, though. Before you can understand Do-

minick, you have to understand Vanessa. To know where I was coming from. What I'd been doing all those years.

"And what I'd been searching for."

Vanessa began, her own mind drifting back, finally, to yesteryear.

CHAPTER 11

THEN

Hopeless romantics will tell you that there's no greater notion than love at first sight, when that instant and unsuspecting attraction immediately sinks deep into your pores and into your heart and down deep into your soul, shifting your perspective on the world, on yourself. For too many years, an adult, wounded, vulnerable, and uncertain, Vanessa Massey had resisted what others believed. The fantasy that, when it came to love and sex and men, was just that, something born of the fantastical. She hadn't exactly been living a sheltered life during her transformative years in Europe, but as she worked, partied, lived—her free-spirited twenties somehow slipping into her early, sobering thirties—she refused to settle down with anyone, much less settle for anything but the very best that life had to offer. She had left Danton Hill on her own terms, determined to see herself grow beyond those imaginary but ever-present walls of small-town life.

She recalled her last night there.

"I can't believe you're leaving. When will you be back?" asked her friend Tiffany.

Vanessa assured her that she would be back, soon, "because my parents expect me to go to college eventually, and I guess I have to honor their request, and besides, we promised years ago that we would attend school together."

Even to herself, she sounded thoroughly unconvincing. A broken promise, and not the first she would fulfill.

When her other best friend, Jana, showed up, she produced from her overnight bag a bottle of wine and a fifth of cheap vodka to celebrate the "gang's" final night together. In Vanessa's basement, they talked for hours. They drank, Jana and Tiffany, but not Vanessa. She wanted to remain fresh for her long day of flying, she explained. She wanted to keep her wits about her and experience the thrill of lift-off. The friends hugged, and a pang of regret hit Vanessa as she felt her friends' warmth. Because she knew she'd been lying to them all night.

And then came that next day, just three weeks removed from the prom and high school graduation and all the juvenile insanity that came with being an entitled senior: being dumped by the cutest boy in school whom she imagined was the boy of her supposed dreams, going to the prom with a near-stranger and enduring the embarrassment of that night, being handed a diploma that felt as light as it did hollow. It was under such cover of darkness and remorse that Vanessa Massey said good-bye to Danton Hill.

Vanessa had gone on to live in the great capitals of Europe—London, Paris, Brussels—for the better part of a year and was glad she had done it. Wanderlust was a feeling never satisfied. Back home, no one had understood her desire to seek out a life without borders, and after a few months the wordy letters to her friends had become postcards, and then they had ceased. She moved around too much for any letters to find her in return. Taking a year off before college had been a great way for her to taste what was possible, to know what she really wanted and discover who she was, where she was going. An exotic sojourn in life, the result meant recharged batteries and a zest and zoom to life that she hadn't previously thought existed. Frankly, living on the crowded streets of Europe where anonymity ruled had given her a chance to get away from all she'd known in Danton Hill and become not a merely more mature version of herself but a different one altogether, her eyes widened by experience found beyond the shores of Lake Ontario. Now, having lived near the banks of the Thames and the romantic Seine, and in the bohemian neighborhood of Saint-Gilles in Brussels, drinking, smoking . . . living, amidst students and revolutionaries who spoke languages that spanned the globe, she realized there was so much more to the world than Friday fish fries and bingo tournaments in the church basement on Saturday nights with your mother and grandmother looking to see if they had five in a row. There was excitement here, bright lights and strange languages and strong drinks and aromatic cigarettes. What there wasn't, she knew, was love, and certainly not at first sight.

On a dark night while sitting outside the Parvis de Saint-Gilles metro station was where Vanessa would look back no further. Only tomorrow mattered, and it came in the guise of a woman who became her best-ever friend on the planet, the unconquerable, unpredictable Reva Jenkins. Two years older than Vanessa, adventurous to a fault and filled with knowledge that belied her years. Reva had done the same thing upon leaving school that Vanessa had done, and by happenstance had landed in the unheralded city of Brussels, living with a wild-haired, bearded guy who liked to smoke pot and speak out about the corrupt government and imperialistic king, but in the end just didn't have the fortitude or guts to attract any kind of following. They parted ways, he gone to the fragrant freedoms of Amsterdam, with Reva staying behind, often hanging out at the cafés where she would meet men, women, whatever she was in the mood for. Attraction was found not in the sexes, but in the people. So on that fateful night in September, as the sun went down and the night air chilled the great European capital, Vanessa and Reva found themselves sitting next to each other as their mutual friend Elio celebrated his birthday. It was a Sunday night, and few of the outside tables in the square were occupied. Just a few random folks lost in their own passions, a writer busy with his pen and notepad who sipped at a beer and jotted furiously; a local, gray-haired man who puffed too hard on his cigarette, like it was his last one; a couple once in love but now disconnected, lost in their own thoughts. The group Vanessa was with kept expanding as new people arrived and additional chairs were brought over, drinks were replenished and Jupiler beers were downed, a cloud of smoke gathered above them. Finally the curly-headed blond girl named Reva looked at Vanessa, she in the midst of a coughing fit, and said, in English, "You don't smoke?"

"No."

"I sense an American accent."

"So do I."

"Don't ever say that again."

Vanessa was intimidated. This Reva was a force, one who was thrusting a hand-rolled cigarette her way.

"Consider yourself a smoker now. This is Europe. Get used to it. Everyone does it."

Vanessa had experienced her own small-world version of peer pressure back at Danton High, usually resisting. This was different. You couldn't say no.

Vanessa accepted, she tried, she puffed, coughed, coughed more, then settled down as she realized no one at any of the crowded tables was judging her. That's what she liked most about these Europeans, they were so consumed with having a good time they couldn't be bothered with other folk who weren't. From that night on, as midnight came and the drinks continued, she and Reva became inseparable, so much so they eventually shared a tiny apartment around the corner on the narrow Rue de Rome. They told each other everything about themselves, leaving nothing out, not with such freedom of speech afforded them, and for the first time Vanessa felt like a terrible weight had been lifted from her hunched shoulders. She found herself standing proud. Never again would she have to shy away from certain topics, and never again would she have to go through anything alone. Reva was there, Reva was always there.

It was another fateful night about six months after they had met and named themselves best friends for life that had the two ladies gambling the night away, or as Reva liked to refer to it, "earning next month's rent." When the idea of venturing to a casino had first presented itself, Vanessa's base instinct was to say no, thinking of her parents and bingo nights, then thinking of her dwindling bank account. "I don't have the money or the clothes for Monte Carlo, much less the cost of the flight." Wasn't that where anyone who was anyone went?

"To hell with Monte," Reva responded with her usual sobering disdain. "Where we are going is much closer and much more exclusive. We're going to Luxembourg City. Just wait, it's perfect."

Whether that three-hour train ride to the Grand Duchy was a good idea or not, it certainly ended up changing Vanessa Massey's life for forever. As the two women crossed over the expansive Pont Adolphe, Reva, laughing, smoking, dared her friend to look down deep at the lush, verdant park set deep in the gorge beneath the bridge. As Vanessa clung to the railing and felt a hit of vertigo possess her, Reva suddenly embraced her friend and said, "Whatever happens tonight, say you won't ever leave me."

"You're crazy. What could possibly happen?"

"You could be swept off your feet."

"I get swept off my feet, all I'm doing is falling into that ravine."

"Forget the gorge. The men here, they are all gorgeous."

"Awful, Rev."

"Like I said, promise you won't ever leave me." Her voice was tinged with sorrow.

Those were prophetic words, and words Vanessa would have trouble living up to.

Inside the bright and busy Casino Luxembourg on the Rue du Notre Dame, just blocks from the train station, Vanessa was attempting a simple game of blackjack when she realized her gin and tonic had gone dry, ice melting. Needing something to occupy her nervous hands during the tense standoff with the dealer, she reached for a cigarette, only to notice her lighter had gone missing. She heard a soft voice whispering in her ear, and she had to admit that she liked the accompanying accent, his statement inflected with the hint of a question.

"Allow me."

Shit, Reva had been right. Vanessa turned to gaze upward into the dark eyes of perhaps the most gorgeous man she'd ever set her eyes upon, his handsome, appealing face thick with a week's growth of dark beard and brown eyes that looked like Belgian chocolate. She nodded at him after catching her breath, approving his want to light her cigarette. After all, he was the one who had hijacked her lighter, and now he held it before her in his large hand, tempting her with the promise of desired heat. What he did instead surprised her and annoyed her and ultimately delighted her.

He cavalierly slipped the lighter into his pocket and then plucked the dangling cigarette from her pursed lips, crushing it underneath what turned out to be a pair of very expensive Italian leather boots.

"You may thank me now."

"Why would I want to do that?"

"I just added five years to your life."

"Why would I want five more years of life? So I can just gamble my savings away?"

"So you have more time to spend with me." He said it like he meant it.

Intrigue punched her in the gut, and so, having been forewarned by Reva, Vanessa decided to play along with this hunk, wasn't that what happened in such exclusive places as this? You indulged whoever caught your eye, you played your cards, and you gambled on a whim and hoped you came up a winner. She swirled around in her seat, ignoring the dealer even when he asked if she wanted another card. "Spend time with you? And why would I want to do a ridiculous thing like that?"

"Because, as they say, life is a gamble, and sometimes you take that other card," he said, an aimless finger stroking his stubbled chin. "But sometimes, you stay, confident in your hand."

"Oh, and what are you recommending I do?"

"I'm a very safe bet."

"And who, may I ask, are you?"

"Dominick di Paolo Arghetti. Can you say that three times fast?"

Her heart skipped a beat, maybe twice. "I'm not sure I can say it once," she said. "Can I just call you Dom?"

"My mother calls me Dominick."

"Then Dom it is, most definitely," she said, flashing a

playful smile that seemed to further intrigue the sexy stranger standing before her.

And sexy he was. Half-Italian, half-Portuguese as it turned out, which would account for his smooth, near mocha-like skin. His dark, expressive eyes hidden beneath thick brows gave him an appearance of having to look up, even when his six-two frame stared down at her. He invited her then for a drink, and just before she accepted she turned around and asked the patient dealer for that next card, just to close out her hand. She'd been holding firm at a measly sixteen, but now she took that gamble. Queen. Dealer wins.

"Guess you're buying," Vanessa informed him with a batting of her eyelashes.

Problem was, Vanessa hadn't taken the hint Dom, or life had given her. She'd lost her bet, could she afford to play this next hand? Even as he held his out to assist her down from the gaming table.

They flirted the rest of the night, with "Oh My God" expressions being mouthed all night from Reva, who was hovering nearby with newly made friends, whether at the bar or at the craps table. She tried eavesdropping as best she could on their hushed, intimate conversation and grew frustrated when Dom would lean in and practically whisper into Vanessa's ear. When later that night Vanessa showed up, alone, at her and Reva's meager hotel room, the question asked was, "Why are you here, and why is he not?"

"A girl's gotta play it the way she sees it."

"Chicky, I saw that man and I saw the way you looked at him. Everyone did. He's not interested in playing games, despite the fact he was in a casino," she said. "Not the way he was into you. He's talking real life, big dreams. Even though you just met, I could see it in his eyes. He sees you in his future for better, for worse, for richer."

"What happened to poorer?"

"Don't think a man with four names knows the word."

"This is ridiculous," Vanessa said, even though she was still a bit tipsy from the champagne they had consumed and feeling like a girl at the prom with the right guy. "I'm not the type to fall for that overly romantic crap and killer accent and I'm surprised to find that you think I would—or that you're smitten for this guy for me. I mean, who but you taught me the joys of cynicism? Reva, honey, everyone promises they'll be there in good times and bad, but truthfully no one really wants to deal with worse. That's why divorce was invented."

"Tell me you got something more out of tonight other than that. That on the night you met Prince Hunky you're not already thinking divorce."

"Oh, don't get me wrong, Rev. My boy, Dom, he's one hell of a kisser. A girl could get used to that."

"You bitch!"

"Yeah," Vanessa said, giggling, plopping down on the bed. "I know."

Vanessa Massey decided to play her cards close to the vest when it came to this burgeoning relationship, being ever-so-coy about her interest. Or at least, she would try her best to resist Dom's natural charms for as long as she could hold out. He arrived in the lobby of their hotel for breakfast the next day, then whisked her for a drive in his Maserati deep into the hills of the tiny country for a day of joyriding and getting to know each other. The next night, a romantic dinner for two occurred, made even more so by the fact he'd bought out every table and had closed the restaurant. In a matter of two quick weeks, they were inseparable, causing great consternation between the two friends.

Reva had grown accustomed to having her wing girl at her side at all times, and now that just wasn't the case. A whirlwind weekend on the lush Amalfi Coast, shows in London's bustling West End, strolls down the wide, café-laden sidewalks of the Champs-Elysees, Vanessa's life went from pedestrian to princess, and she was going to enjoy herself for as long as she could. As she told Reva on a rare night back in Brussels while Dom dealt with some family business, she asked to "let me have fun with my charming Italian stallion. I'm sure he'll tire of me eventually, especially since I haven't put out yet." That truth slipped out after five weeks of dating.

"I couldn't resist that," Reva confessed.

Five weeks and one day later, Vanessa finally agreed with her friend.

His touch upon her naked skin was remarkable, soft and gentle, sending thrills curling up her spine. Sexy and giving, understanding a woman's body with remarkable ability, he was the ideal lover. Patient when she needed it, full of stamina when she cried for it, and after that first night barely another escaped when they weren't indulging each other's unquenchable passions. Vanessa Massey, late of Danton Hill, New York, United States of America, had ceased to exist, and in her place was this newly crowned sophisticate of the continent, adorned in the finest threads from pricey designers that Dominick could afford, which was considerable.

It was on a Thursday night four months after their initial meeting, inside her and Reva's apartment while her friend sat at the nearby bar in which they had met, smoking, drinking, and feeling jealousy consume her, that Vanessa announced she had news. They were scheduled to fly to Milan the next day and then drive up to the family villa on the upper shores of Lake Como, an eager Dom ready to introduce her. What she had to say was that she was two months' pregnant. Trepidation accompanied her telling him, like butterflies on crack, fearing the worst response possible. His reaction was anything but bad, as he took her into his strong, hairy arms. He hugged her, kissed her belly, explaining how pleased his mother would be.

"But won't she be . . . disapproving? She's so . . . staunch in her beliefs."

"My mother knows all, and so she knows certain things before you. She knows you are to be my wife."

Wife, the four-letter word reverberated in her mind. But it also left an empty pang in her stomach. She should be overjoyed, but the baby growing inside her kept her steeped in reality. Dominick was, of course, oblivious to her feelings, the uncertainty that had kept her awake the week she had found out, because he had all that he wanted. In seven months' time Dominick would have even more, a child . . . an heir. Perhaps she should have seen this as a sign, possession winning out over passion. Maybe she even did. Maybe she just chose to believe in the fairy tale, for once believing in happy endings.

"We must travel to Como and tell them at once."

"Wait . . . Dominick, there's something I have to tell you . . . really, we should wait before we make any kind of announcement . . ."

Dominick downplayed her concerns while Vanessa's head spun from the sudden change of direction in her life. She could hardly believe the little towheaded girl in the pigtails had run away from home and forged a life in Europe, met what was essentially an Italian count, and was now going to be married to him and live forever in the glamorous capitals and cities of the world. Just three years removed from high school, dreams she hadn't even envisioned were coming true. When at last she did meet the stern-faced Mama di Arghetti, as well as Dom's distant father and sisters and cousins and aunts and uncles, she'd been assured all would be well, they would have the most perfect life, he and she and their soon-to-be-born child. Vanessa still worried about his mother's reaction to the news of her pregnancy—they were Catholic and she and Dom were kind of putting the cart before the horse here. Same held true for the Arghettis, but she was here, this was real. Danton Hill ceased to exist. The first thing that happened, upon hearing the news, was Mama Arghetti touching her distended belly.

"Sí, Dominick. Sí."

That, in Mama Arghetti's world, meant approval.

A few weeks later on a night back in Brussels, when Dominick was away on business and Vanessa had a rare moment free in which to spend time with the only friend who had stood by her through thick and thin, through the skinny jeans phase to the newly purchased maternity clothes, Reva sat her down in their old flat and proceeded to warn her of the perils of success. Of money. "The problem with having big dreams is, they can come true."

"What is that supposed to mean?"

Reva took a drag on her filthy cigarette, blowing the puff of toxic smoke away from her expectant friend. She refilled her glass of flat champagne, poured more Perrier for Vanessa. "You arrived in Europe three years ago with the hope of finding yourself. What I have to ask you may not want to hear, or answer. Have you done that, Vanessa? Do you know who you are, and what you want? Or have you just become what Dominick wants? Or worse, what Mama Arghetti wants."

The wedding occurred on the shores of Lake Como, and practically every person in town was invited for the daylong feast. Dominick led the celebration with glasses of chilled Prosecco and his mother followed suit with plate after plate of pastas and cheeses and meats. They settled in the Trastevere neighborhood of Rome, where Dominick went back to work for the family's company. They grew and sold olives and sunflowers and their oily by-products, and apparently prospered quite well thanks to their international appeal and reputation for fresh products. For Vanessa, she felt a bit like a modern-day Rapunzel, relegated to the quiet of the urban apartment, watching from the window as the crowded trams passed by, the noisy bleat of horns they made as pedestrians crossed in front of them. Still, it was life outside her window, leaving her trapped. She was still only five months' pregnant; the wedding having been rushed for appearances' sake, they didn't want her showing too much in front of the nosy villagers. Nor did they want to wait months and have the wailing sounds of a baby overtake those of the priest at the ceremony.

One night, with Dominick still out, Vanessa spied the first bit of spotting.

She knew immediately what was happening.

She called Reva first.

She told her to call Dominick.

She did, reluctance filling her newly empty soul.

While she waited for Dom to come rescue her from her tower, she admitted to Reva that she was afraid, deeply and deathly. "You were right, Rev, you told me to be careful of those dreams coming true. I've been living in a bubble, a very rich and fancy one. But there's no different, rich or poor, sometimes bubbles pop and pierce your heart and you wake up and what's left is an awful bloody mess of a life," she said, staring down at the bed in which she lay, the bed she shared with the man who'd created those dreams. Who, with love and with tenderness and an urgent desire pulsing through him, had created the child within her.

Dominick arrived home an hour later, sweaty, concerned, then rushed her himself to the hospital by motorcar. But by then it was too late.

Way too late.

CHAPTER 12

NOW

"My God, he didn't . . ."

"What? Divorce me because I miscarried his first child and heir? Come on, Adam, what kind of fool would I be not to recognize a man of such bad character?"

He heard the words, but there was a biting, cutting commentary behind them. Like there was more to her story.

"Of course Dominick saw me through the difficulty of that night and beyond. He helped me recover both physically and emotionally from the trauma, and trust me, that's what it was. I was a devastated wreck. I even got a month's holiday at the villa up Lake Como, with his mother doting on me every single second, almost cloyingly. She wouldn't leave me until I ate, then sat by me while I slept the days away. Even Reva came and stayed for a week, Dom financing her trip. He understood and he cared."

"Okay, so what happened? How'd it end?"

"Simple. I never got pregnant again," she said with the barest hint of emotion, as though distancing herself from the words even as she spoke them. "Oh, the doctors, all kinds of Italian and Swiss specialists, they ran a battery of tests that made me feel simultaneously like a guinea pig and a baby-making machine, given no other purpose on this earth than to bear Dominick's prized Junior. Reva was of course right, in the midst of the whirlwind romance, I hadn't found my true self at all, and in the process of marrying Dominick and becoming Mrs. di Arghetti I'd lost all sight of the reasons why I'd escaped to Europe. If I wanted to just play housewife and pump out babies, I could have easily done that in Danton Hill . . ." She suddenly stopped talking, her mouth closing like a steel trap.

Adam sat there in the hard-backed chair in the kitchen, one leg curled underneath him, the other jutting upward; his arms crossed over his chest. As though he was trying to hide from the truth being revealed, while seeking heat and comfort, fighting off a noticeable chill that had pervaded the room all during Vanessa's story. The highs of their courtship, the lows of her not finding herself, they had left him drained. His emotions remained on the edge because he didn't know how . . . or why the story ended. He wanted to embrace her, but somehow he couldn't move. The timing was all off, anyway, her confession only half complete and hanging between them like something unattainable, something untouchable. To reach for her now would be to smother her against the words that still floated in the fragrant scent of the candle. He recalled her word for Mama Arghetti: cloying. Now he decided to give her air.

"Dominick was as patient as he could be, even while he was determined to get me pregnant again. He would come to my bed . . . often, like we were something out of a Victorian novel, existing separately, until the night bore down on us. That's when he would knock, enter, and . . . enter. But the routine wore thin as the months, then years progressed, and finally after six years of marriage . . . well, there was no baby, no heir for him to hold up to his expectant family." She laughed. "Sorry, poor choice of word."

"So he stopped coming to your room?"

"No, he continued our lovemaking, believing he had more power over nature than I did and could magically convince my body to produce . . . to reproduce," she said. "But guess what? No baby . . . there would be no Vanessa either."

"He divorced you because you hadn't been able to have a child?"

She nodded, wiping away a stray tear. She appeared annoyed that she'd shed yet another tear for her failure. "And never would. The doctors all confirmed that it was unlikely I would carry a baby to term."

"My God . . . Vanessa, I don't know what to say."

"That's okay, Dominick spared me no words—in both English and Italian. He claimed I deceived him, that I must have known that I couldn't have had children. He said I knew how important children were to him and his family and still I married him. How important they were to his mother— his precious Mama Arghetti. She had plenty of words for me too, but she barely knew any English so I escaped her wrath by the sake of never having learned Italian. Still, her tone barely needed translation. It was clear mother and son were in agreement about what to do with me." She paused, suppressing a misguided laugh. "I'm not sure how to say it in Italian, but annulment was the term they bandied about."

"After six . . . seven years of marriage? You can't annul . . ."

"The Arghettis' money could, and it did. Marriage wiped off the books, and so Dominick Paolo di Arghetti was free to marry again for the first time, while I was quickly, quietly shipped back to Brussels and Reva's tiny apartment and the stale smell of cigarette smoke. In all that time, while my fairy tale was exploding, Reva was a steadying force. Her cigarettes saw me through some dark nights." Vanessa coughed, as though those hazy, smoke-filled memories swirled around her right now. "It's funny, Adam, you and me."

"How's that?"

"You and Sarah Jane, me and Dom. We both ended up with people who wanted only what they wanted, or had been told by their parents what was expected of them. Their own lives were defined, in order, by money and identity and perception, by family, and ultimately, by self-love. No room there for anyone else, certainly not an outsider who couldn't provide them with a future. If Dominick had told me right off the bat that all he wanted was someone to sire him the next great Arghetti son . . . I don't even know how I would have responded to him. Probably I would have held at that blackjack table. Maybe I might have had the satisfaction of beating the dealer."

"Where is Dom now, do you know? It has been ten years."

"Oh, he's married now to a nice Italian woman, slightly plump with hips ideal for childbearing. Three kids and counting, including two boys. You can't compete with that, no way, no how. Not that he ever told me about his new family, but in Europe, in the bars and cafés, even the casinos . . . you just hear things. Look, I'm sure Dominick is a good, doting father, and maybe he's even a decent, giving husband. But the rumors of him getting action on the side have increased since the arrival of the kids. So, who knows? All I learned was that he's a lousy human being." She paused, drank a healthy gulp of the white wine, which fortunately came from California, and then said, "There's more, though."

Adam shook his head emphatically, essentially shutting down this tortured, sad trip down memory lane. "Not now, there isn't. Vanessa, you should give yourself a break. We can resume your tale later. Right now you've put yourself through too much already today, both physically and emotionally. Give your body and your heart and your soul a well-deserved break. Give them a chance to heal."

"Hasn't happened yet. I don't see that happening in just these few hours."

"Don't be surprised," he said, offering up his best smile. "This night has already seen magical things happen. I doubt we've seen the last of them."

"Fine, Adam, play the romantic, but me . . . I could use a cigarette."

"Now you're joking," he said.

"Yes, I'm joking. Sort of. Maybe. Probably I'm just channeling Reva, suddenly envious of the life she still lives. Not a care in the world, no responsibility, no headaches. Or heartaches. See, Adam, I haven't lost everything, my sense of humor is as intact as my cynicism," she said. Then she rose from the table, surveying the dirtied dishes before them. "So, while we wait to see what other rabbits you'll pull out of this farmhouse's hat, why don't I clean up this mess."

"I think those can wait till morning. New light, clean house . . . fresh start."

"Smooth line. You should have been in advertising, Adam, not finance. Look, doing the dishes is busywork and right now that's just what I need, something mindless. Didn't you ever learn that cleaning is considered a form of therapy? There were days my mother practically slept with the vacuum she was so stressed. I guess I inherited that from her."

He did as requested, stating he would see about the fire, maybe it needed another log. He paused, got no response from her as she made her way to the sink; he wasn't even sure Vanessa heard him. He walked out of the kitchen, but not before stealing a look back at her. She was busy at the sink, not a whistle to be heard while she worked. Though her back was to him, he could tell from the slump of her shoulders and the listless way her arms went about cleaning that her smile had dissipated. For a moment he considered the impact this strange day had had on her, whether she had suffered some internal injury from the accident that hadn't yet revealed itself. About to return to the living room, he paused once more. What he thought about were the letters upstairs in the cupola and the gravestone outside, and the loneliness that permeated the walls of this house. Were they contributing to it, or helping to fill the house with fresh sounds of life?

Back in the living room, Adam gazed around at the white ghosts of the furniture. The fire had indeed diminished to mere remnants, now only a hint of the enervating heat that once was—not unlike the two of them, he noted. But for the first time since arriving at the farmhouse, he really took in his surroundings, trying for a glimpse into the lives of the people who called this place home. No photos of the Barton family adorned the mantle, nor did any paintings or other accoutrements decorate the walls. The covered furniture again left him unsettled; this was very much a home in transition, not unlike his and Vanessa's lives. Perhaps the Barton children had only done so much with closing up the house after their father had died. Turn off the phone, he guessed that made sense. Keep the heat and electricity turned on for convenience's sake. Piece together all of this evidence and an answer to the mystery inside this house still failed to reveal itself.

Sparking the sizzling embers with the metal poker, waiting for the new log to catch on fire, Adam found his mind drifting. Thinking again about Vanessa and all the heartache she'd been through. As difficult as the breakup with the Stockdale family had been—and that's what it was, a separation from each generation, not just from Sarah Jane—nothing compared with losing the child you were expecting, your husband, and the life you had forged together. He'd never committed to Sarah Jane, not even gotten close to proposing to her, but Vanessa, she had believed the fairy tale and jumped into the prince's arms without blinders. And fallen hard off the lily pad. Her marriage had ended, by his count, eleven years ago, right about the time he'd joined KFC. What he most took from that time in his life was . . .

"New York," he said aloud, as though the mere mention of the city he called home summoned up images of a chance encounter, a mistake. With one half of Vanessa's story told to him, he had been granted a greater insight into what that night eleven years ago had been about. When he and Vanessa had met again under circumstances that could only be called coincidental. Or maybe not? For some reason, Vanessa Massey kept sneaking into his life, making an impact when only a dent was called for. First the prom, then the night in Manhattan, finally the car accident that had landed them here. Did there really exist a deeper connection between them? Was there something to this notion of having known her before . . . ?

Was that what had kept him, all these years, from locking down his desires?

Still, Vanessa had seen far worse. He might have missed out on dreams, even let them elude him voluntarily, but she had both achieved and then lost hers.

Adam liked to joke about having the proverbial two-point-five kids, but that didn't mean he never envisioned himself as a father. And not that his chances were over, he could still meet a woman and fall in love, and she could . . . he stepped dead in his tracks as the most tortured image rushed into his mind like a dam unleashed. A woman, any woman, just as long as she bore him a child . . . he shuddered, realizing how that made him sound, made worse by the fact that in his mind he immediately pictured Vanessa as that woman. Was that what today's twist of fate was all about, finding a tomorrow, possibly one with her? While the world spun outside, what exactly was happening inside

the confining walls of this farmhouse? Was it a passing reunion, one more fling between two people who found momentary attraction, or was there more to her and him and
the future and yesterday and too many unasked or unanswered questions?

Could what they started today be just that, a start?

Or was today like before, another random exchange of
heat and anger? Meant to bury their pain as much as their
previous encounters had? Lonely souls, broken people, the
world was full of them, all them looking to prove something
to themselves and to others. I matter, I'm important, I feel
better now, I feel wanted. Was that all? An affirmation of
self, fulfilled with the aid of the first available body? Was
that how he would be able to justify the intimacy they'd
shared today?

Adam felt conflicted. The fireplace taken care of, with
fresh, warm crackling filling the house, he found himself
standing in the hallway somewhere between the living room
and the kitchen, caught between the past and present, and
he couldn't decide which way to venture. That word stirred
him, awoke something in him. *Venture.* That was the
strange name written on the letters. Mr. Barton had written
them, but why? Who was Venture, and what did he have to
say to her in all those letters? Had he loved her? Had he lost
her?

Adam found himself with a decision to make. Should he
be like Aidan Barton and keep his feelings sealed in an envelope? Should he just sit and wait for Vanessa to return to his
side, let her finish the story of her life, or should he throw
caution to the wind, rush upstairs, and tear open the letters,
return to the kitchen and sweep her off her feet and an-
nounce he was never letting her go? The other option, of
course, was to open wide the front door and never look back,
never to be heard from again, not in the lake-scented land

of Danton Hill or the life of alluring, beautiful, broken Vanessa Massey. For some reason, the day's puzzling vents had made him question the big picture, the important questions. Life-changing questions. Maybe smashing his car into an accordion and sticking his forehead with a piece of glass like he was a pincushion had made him wake up and smell the acrid cornfields. His car was totaled, not unlike his career and maybe his life, and the only thing left was what he'd come back to Danton Hill to find. So he remained just where he was, still caught between then and now.

That's when he heard the explosive sound of shattering glass and a shriek that broke the silent night.

"Vanessa?"

His thoughts suddenly dissipated into the ether, he ran into the kitchen just in time to see the back door clacking once, twice, a lazy third time before finally resting against its frame. A broken jelly glass lay in sharp, dangerous pieces on the floor. Alongside a smear of blood, that trailed down the door.

Adam ran out into the night.

Impulse driving him, possessed with determination and the power to make everything right, for once, he screamed into the wind, "Venture!" and then felt a strange, unnamed emotion wash over him. The name swirled in the air around him, like it was a boomerang, launched, only to return to him an echo. She had to have heard it.

Still, the response he got was the voice of the mute.

She'd run out on him, yet again.

Damn if she didn't have a penchant for disappearing.

Like she acted first, thought later.

"Vanessa?" he called out once more.

Neither woman was responding to him.

*   *   *

One minute the jelly glass was secure in her hands, bubbles washing off its surface with the force of the water from the faucet. The next thing she knew, the glass had slipped from her hands, hit the counter, and then smashed on the hardwood floor. A wayward shard of glass imbedded itself in her bare foot, blood bubbling out of the cut immediately. It wasn't pain or embarrassment that made her run, but rather, an overwhelming, newly unleashed frustration that had been building inside her since her fainting spell took hold of her. What had that been about? Had it really been the heat, the lack of food, or had something . . . spooked her? What was it about the name Venture that so chilled her, startled her? And then to revisit her life with Dominick, sharing it with, of all people . . . Adam. It had been necessary, part of her plan . . . still, having gone there was different from thinking of going there. All she knew now was that she had run, again, out into the wet, dark night, her breath becoming labored the harder she pushed herself. At last her feet came to a sudden stop, her lungs seemingly ready to burst from lack of oxygen. She had to admit, looking around at the enveloping darkness, she had no idea where she was.

Clouds had moved in again, making the moonlight slip away from view. She had to hope a trace of light would return soon and act as her guide. All around her blackness continued to move in on her, so much so that she blinked and then blinked and still she was lost. Her breathing became labored, like she was having an anxiety attack. Suddenly shapes and forms emerged, her night vision kicking in and offering up the comfort of the familiar. Cornstalks loomed before her. She was lost among the endless rows of cornstalks, and worst of all, with her beating heart and fear of something she didn't understand, she couldn't help but think about that Stephen King story they'd made too many sequels of, most of which she and Danny had watched at the Danton Hill Quad. She needed his hand now, his comforting touch, to see her through the flickering glow of this new form of evil.

Danny wasn't there for her. Neither, at the moment, was Adam.

Adam.

What the hell was she going to do about Adam?

She knew what she needed to do, and that's probably why she had run. She'd already confessed to him her marriage to Dominick and the disaster born from that—or not born, for that matter, she thought with a taste of gallows humor on her tongue. There was so much more to her story gone unrevealed. She had tried to tell him, before he shut her down with a request to eat, get some strength and nourishment into her system, and he'd been right. Her current frame of mind was still too fragile to tell the rest of the story. She was a jumble of emotions, ricocheting between past and present and some other plane she couldn't quite put her finger on. She had planned on telling him, on revealing all, that was the point of this entire stupid journey home. As though her body had left Danton Hill, but her spirit had remained locked here, the past unsettled. The reunion. Ha, what a foolish venture. But she had hoped to tell him the whole truth after a night when the entire class had laughed and reminisced, grown sad over those they had lost and looked to tomorrow for hope and the promise that they would reunite again five years down the road. Vanessa had even contemplated taking Adam back to the lake and to Danton's Hill, the scene of the alleged . . . incident. To Mercer Pier.

But she knew the farmhouse was located nowhere near the Hill. Even though she'd run off into the night, her instincts said she hadn't traveled that far, perhaps only in circles. She was still near Route 20, within shouting distance of the old farmhouse, her body as turned around in these damn cornstalks as her mind was. One looked just like the other, each of them bending in the currents of the wind. Which was the only sound she could hear, that cool, rustling wind and nothing more—no howling wolves or dogs or whatever nocturnal creature had pierced the night. And, surprisingly, no Adam. Not that she wanted him to come to her rescue, she just sort of expected it. What she knew about him from high school and that unfortunate encounter in New York, and then now, today, when he was tender and loving and gentle and amazingly in tune with her needs . . . she knew Adam Blackburn was honorable to a fault. As though no matter what mistakes she made, he was always lurking in the shadows of her life. She didn't expect him to land right before her dressed like Superman, but at this moment with her arms wrapped around her body to fend off the chill and the loose, muddy dirt staining her cut foot and bare legs, well, it would be nice to feel his strong arms envelop her.

This was stupid. Why did she keep running away from him? Why couldn't she face the choices she had made in her life? She was as much responsible for her actions as he was.

And why was she in the middle of Nowhere, New York, home in the distance but yet unreachable, dressed only in a ratty old bathrobe? What made her keep running?

Her foot absently kicked at a loose rock in the field. Bending down to massage her hurt toe, she made contact with the offending stone and grabbed it, hurling it through the air with a fierce and loud grunt, her anger and frustration finally unleashed.

"Dammit, why is this happening?"

Her voice echoed, followed by a thunk and the tinkle of breaking glass. Her ears perked up as her eyes sought the direction from which the sound had come. Focusing, locking on to the scent of smoke wafting up from the farmhouse's chimney, she suddenly knew where she was. She started off through the cornstalks, her bare feet oblivious to the pain of rocks and dirt and fallen stalks the sun had burned stale. Running again, laughing uncontrollably, she finally let go of the tight control she'd clung to all day, and damn if it didn't feel good, liberating, like she was Alice and she had found the hole that would relieve her of the craziness that was Wonderland and return her to the normal, natural world.

At last she broke through the clearing and very nearly tripped when her feet hit cement.

She'd found it, the highway.

Her car. It was nearby, wasn't it?

Maybe she'd been wrong, maybe her phone did work. Maybe right now Jana and Tiffany were calling, leaving their ninety-ninth message of the night, asking where she was and what she was doing, and why wasn't she trying to force down the overcooked salmon like the rest of their classmates. Oh, how she wanted to hear those messages, her friends' voices that seemed so unchanged after twenty years, or better yet answer those questions directly, eat the inedible fish. She wanted to be at the reunion. She wanted to dance and feel like a kid again, to be that happy girl she hadn't been since that damn prom had reared its haunting promise. "Forever Yours"—that had been the ridiculous, time-defying theme—and to Vanessa it was more than just another banner from high school she'd helped decorate with glitter and bunting; it was a lifelong taunt.

The road was dark and the moon hadn't yet reemerged from the fast-moving clouds; the shoulders devoid of street lamps on these quiet, rural roads. At the moment no bright shadows emerged, no encroaching headlights caught her in their glow. The night still belonged to her, she was alone with no stars and no moon and no future. Just herself, wandering unseen, as though she'd been doing it for years . . . for forever. Forever yours . . . more like forever mine. She sought out objects other than tarmac and field greens and at last she scoped out a rectangular shape in the near distance. Edging forward, bravery winning out over foolishness, she was careful of each step, knowing that if she were to stumble upon the scene of the accident there was bound to be broken glass and random pieces of metal that could inflict far worse damage than a thin shard from a jelly glass she had used to drink wine.

At last she came to the field where her car had gone off the road. She saw no skid marks and quite frankly couldn't remember ever hitting the brakes. Though she must have, there was no way even those hearty stalks were strong enough to stop a car hurtling out of control. As she approached the darkened car, her heart began to beat fast again. Whether anxious memories of the crash or tasting hope at the idea of ending this strange, lingering night, she didn't know. Still, she forged ahead, newly unafraid of what she might find. Telling herself that anything was possible when you swallowed your fears.

Luckily her car hadn't flipped over like Adam's. She was able to try her hand at the driver's side door. It opened easily, but of course it did, she hadn't experienced a problem getting out after the crash. The air bag lay deflated, like a sad Big Top left by a decamped circus. She began to forage around the interior, a raccoon digging through a Dumpster. She found gum wrappers and a half-empty bottle of Diet Coke. What she didn't find was her cell phone. Her fingers searched beneath seats, cushions . . . finally she felt something small and plastic, under the mud flap. She ripped it up to unveil the wayward phone. There was no glow from the screen, no blinking light announcing a message. The phone was dead. Still, she fingered the red button and waited for the sound and the light associated with the phone powering up. Nothing happened. The sheer plastic window was cracked, the inside wet and muddied. As she had known but somehow had hoped differently, the thing was useless.

"Dammit, dammit," she said, throwing the phone into the air and listening as it shattered into pieces, microchips reduced to granules of sand. Dust to dust, a lifeline reduced to silence. She sobbed as she stared at the broken pieces. Her hair fell over her face, covering it, hiding her. She wanted to be swallowed up alive, right now. *Just end this night or let me go.* The smell of the lake wafted over the flatland, and for a second she imagined the cold water washing over, claiming her. Yes, please . . . no more of this middle ground, this land without answers.

"Is that what you did with the glass?"

She spun around at the sound of a voice sneaking up from behind her, shoulders raised, defenses up. She very nearly screamed out, but her rational self seemed to return as she recognized the only person who could possibly have made such a comment. Who else knew about the broken glass? Adam, who had come to her aid.

"How did you find me?"

"I followed your laughter. You sounded like a mental patient who'd just been released."

"You know me so well."

He attempted a smile that the darkness claimed. "You okay?"

"Beats me."

"Let's start with physically."

"I'm fine. I think running around in the mud has been good for my cut foot."

"We should get you back to the house. Get it cleaned up just in case."

"I don't know where it is."

"I do."

"Of course you do. My hero, home from the sea."

"Why did you say that?"

"I don't know . . . I just thought it . . . no, not even. I felt it wash over me. Before you arrived, all I could smell was the lake. Like it was calling to me. And then there you were."

"Is that what you want? To venture up to the lake?"

"Don't say . . ."

"What . . . venture?"

"Adam . . ."

"Sorry. I don't mean to tease you. Do you want to stay here?"

Vanessa looked around at the dark sky and the dismantled car whose tires had sunk into the mud, and the shattered cell phone and the lack of any signs of life on the open road. All that existed was them, this time, and somewhere in the distance, the crashing waves of the lake. She let out a small giggle born of nervousness, tiredness. "Kind of foolish to remain here."

"Come on, let's go back home," Adam said.

"Home?"

"For lack of a better word."

"Fine." She paused, thinking. "If we go back there, we're going back for a reason."

"And what's the reason?"

"The truth. The past. Us. What happened. Things you know, things you don't," she said, not meaning to be enigmatic. He deserved better. She paused. "Things neither of us know, but maybe . . . maybe, deep down, we do."

"Sounds like a long night," he said. "Where do we start?"

She didn't even hesitate. "With New York."

"New York."

"Eleven years ago."

"Oh," he remarked. "That. Okay. Let's go. Let's get that memory out of the way."

He was right, this one they had to face, sooner rather than later, before other secrets could reveal themselves on this endless night. So she allowed his strong, secure arms to encircle her, lead her down the darkened road and back toward the farmhouse. She steeled herself for the journey, each step bringing them closer to what some people called the past. What she might call a mistake. Of course none of it would have occurred had not Adam been there to begin with.

Destiny teasing them again.

CHAPTER 13

THEN

The meeting place was sophisticated, super trendy, and so not like any place he'd envisioned an older-generation Wall Street executive to choose for a meeting. That's why a skeptical Adam Blackburn wondered if he'd been told the right place. Plus, it was a Saturday, early evening, just near seven, the oddest time for a job interview he'd ever heard of, but then again, in the cutthroat world of investment banking, secrets had a way of getting out to the wrong people. Every precaution was taken in keeping the gossip to a minimum.

The meatpacking district of Manhattan was just awakening for the coming night. It was that nebulous time of day when the regular city folk secured tables at fashionable restaurants for "early seating," just after the hour when visiting Euro trash had finished shopping in nearby SoHo and the chic, stylish set hadn't yet ventured outside for their nocturnal pursuits. The sun was drifting down from the sky, an orange orb in the west that preceded nightfall. In his fashionable dark suit by Hugo Boss and wearing a brand-new gold striped tie he'd purchased only today from Brooks Brothers, Adam entered Le Bain, one of several places to imbibe inside the exclusive Standard Hotel, High Line, and informed the hostess at the bar whom he was meeting.

"You are the first to arrive, sir, follow me."

Adam did so, liking how promptly he was taken care of. Service that money bought. As he settled into a back booth far away from the growing, glowering crowd at the bar, he surveyed his surroundings and decided there was much to this lifestyle he could get used to. Outside the window he saw panoramic views of Manhattan, folks below walking amidst the lush greenery of the High Line park. He imagined his new office would have similar, stunning views. Assuming, of course, he scored the job, but the fact he'd secured an interview not only with Koch, Franklin, and Cohn but with the middle partner of the three was considered a major coup. Having been at his most recent job nearly four years, it was time for a change, time to take that big leap into the big-time. So he'd brushed up his résumé, sent it to a headhunter, and a few weeks later here he was, ordering top-shelf scotch in anticipation of a meeting between two good old boys.

A harried Carpenter Franklin arrived the moment Adam's drink did, and lo and behold, there were two glasses positioned on the tray. Adam said nothing but he had the sense this scene was orchestrated, prearranged—no small talk to endure while waiting on that first drink. Franklin was probably fifty, balding, florid-faced and paunchy from either too much red meat or too much stress. Didn't bode well for a future at KFC. No chickens need apply.

"At last, the famed Adam Blackburn," Carpenter Franklin said as he sat down.

"Sir? Famed?"

"You think I haven't had my research done on you, kid?" Kid. Not a good start, but probably meant to intimidate. So

Adam waited, and he listened. "We could have just gone the regular interview route, had you meet with those clueless imbeciles in HR and you would have waited what, three, four weeks for an answer, and it would have been thanks but no thanks, no openings, you're not right for the job, too green, not sharp enough, etc. Every once in a while I look through the résumés we've received, and when I see something—or rather, someone—who stands out, I pull it, find out about the individual, then pretend I had nothing to do with setting up the interview. Standard Hotel, nice, isn't it? People can see you peeing from the High Line."

"Yes sir. So I've read."

"You like the good life?"

"I don't fancy living in a cardboard box."

"There is a happy medium."

"Medium, yes, happy I'm not so certain about."

Carpenter Franklin raised his glass of scotch, the two ice cubes tinkling against the crystal glass, and the two men cheered. After he drank, he said, "Adam Blackburn, you need to come work for me."

"I'm grateful to hear that, but aren't I supposed to be selling you?"

"Kid, if I hadn't already been sold on your coming to work with me, we wouldn't be here. Isn't that the secret to a successful investment? Scouting it out before jumping in with blinders on? What do they tell those pain-in-the-ass pissant lawyers when they enter a courtroom? Never ask a question you don't already know the answer to. Well, I'm going to ask one anyway, and I don't want to hear you hesitate. I'm not a fan of those who hesitate."

"I'm listening."

"Adam Blackburn, when can you start?"

"Sir, I don't even know what the job entails."

"It's what you already do, but on a higher level and answering to me when it all goes ka-flooey." He drank a healthy gulp of scotch, closed his eyes to savor its smoky flavor. "Oh, and by the way, business should never go all ka-flooey, because chances are I'll already know about the fuckup a week before your dumb brain has discovered it, and your ass will have been kicked to the curb long before your head stops spinning."

"Wow, sir, that's a lot of body parts," Adam said.

The man guffawed loud enough to catch the attention of other drinkers, then drank down the remainder of his scotch. "Retain your sense of humor and you'll do well. Welcome aboard, Blackburn."

"Call me Adam."

"Ha ha, not anymore, Burnie," the man said, rising from the table with surprising alacrity. "Enjoy yourself tonight for as long as you want, the bill has been taken care of by KFC—oh, and if you ever use those initials in such a way, I'll have you banned from all company picnics. I always bring fried chicken, just a little private joke between partners. Ha ha!" He slid a thick manila envelope Adam's way. "These papers include the terms of employment, including what I'm sure you'll agree is generous compensation. Read them over, don't question because I already know your present salary, just sign and fax to me by tomorrow morning. I'll see you two weeks from this Monday, my office, seven A.M. Sharp. And by sharp I mean six fifty-five. A real pleasure, Blackburn, I'm sure I'll make a lot of money."

"Don't you mean we'll make a lot of money?"

"Oh Burnie. You've got so much to learn."

The portly but nimble Carpenter Franklin laughed again, shaking his head as he left the bar, the lobby, the hotel, leaving Adam Blackburn, apparently now christened

"Burnie," all alone with a half-finished drink and his head seemingly swirling like a weather vane during a storm. Had this interview really only lasted seven minutes and forty-two seconds? Adam had timed it. Had he really secured himself a major new job with major new money and major benefits? Adam had done his research. He knew this guy Patch Grimes who already worked there and the car he drove and the high-rise apartment he lived in and the hot women he slept with, all top of the line. Adam Blackburn had been in New York City for five years at this point, and at last he felt like he'd hit the big-time. Time now to celebrate.

"Another scotch," Adam said, but before the waiter scurried away, he asked just what brand he was drinking.

"Some fancy label," the waitress said. "It's like . . . I don't know, a hundred years old. Certainly older than the guy you were seated with."

As Adam savored the perfect smooth flavor of the scotch, he noticed the bar had begun to fill up. Beautiful people in stylish clothing hugged the shimmering glass bar, whispering into the ears of friends and grinning and pointing and then laughing, as though this was sport to them, picking out the losers who didn't belong. Maybe when he'd walked in, but not now. He belonged. Adam wondered about himself and whether he was already emitting that glow of money, the looks from the barflies tinged with envy, as he sat in an exclusive booth, drinking the most expensive thing on the beverage menu . . . but doing it all by himself. So okay, that last part wasn't so cool.

Turned out, life had additional plans for him, and it revealed its hand not long after. Two young, sleek-looking women hovering near the bar, holding thin-stemmed martini glasses in delicate grips, had taken notice of him. They waved, he nodded, and that was the signal for them to make their way over to his spacious booth. In addition to designer labels adoring their slim frames, they wore a predatory look on their faces that stated they were in search of "fresh meat," and wasn't this the part of town to find it? Dressed to the nines in silky material that clung to their bodies like a second layer of skin, they approached with the confident appearance of ladies not accustomed to paying for their own drinks.

"Hi," said the curly blonde. "I'm Reva."

"Hi back, Reva. I'm Adam," a smiling, appreciative Adam replied, the taste of newfound assurance on his lips, transferring its addictive feel as he kissed the hand that had been extended his way. He turned to the other woman and said, "And how about you . . ."

Words failed him and he was glad not to have been holding his glass, otherwise he'd have been sporting a fancy suit that smelled of fancy scotch and sparkled with thin shards of fancy crystal. He closed his brown eyes and then they reopened, rebooted, but the image was still the same. A woman his own age with long dark hair curving against her heart-shaped face, pretty in a petulant way that looked all too familiar, even years later. He had a feeling when she smiled, the whole effect would transform her look. He should know, he'd seen it before.

"Vanessa Massey," he said.

"Excuse me?"

The woman named Reva turned to her friend, tossing her a curious look. "You know this guy, chicky?"

"Uh, no . . . I don't think so," the woman said, her voice not as certain as her words.

That's when Adam stood from the booth, buttoning the jacket of his suit, and with the same gentlemanly wave of his hand that he'd used to entice the ladies over, he invited them to join him. His mind was spinning and his eyes remained focused on Vanessa, who still failed to recognize him. "I beg to differ, but please, have a seat and we can restart our Forever Yours reunion. I mean, it's the least I can do for the girl who let me take her to the senior prom . . ."

Vanessa's eyes widened, but she said nothing, sliding into the booth with a nervous push back of her hair.

"You're shitting me, you're that Adam Blackburn? God, I am so taking a front-row seat for this one," Reva said, quickly settling her sexy self in the comfy booth while Adam remained standing, waiting for Vanessa to acknowledge him. An already tipsy Reva insisted he sit in between them, so quickly she got up and practically pushed him down, his body nearly scraping against the exposed skin of Vanessa's arm. Still no comment, all she did was stare at him, which kind of pleased Adam because she seemed to be searching for the little schoolboy she knew and not the grown man before her. He'd been what they called a late bloomer, and little trace of the once-upon-a-Danton-Hill meek Adam Blackburn remained inside his sturdy six-foot frame. When at last all three were cozily settled and fresh drinks had been ordered—Grey Goose martinis for the ladies, he sticking with the KFC-bought scotch—Vanessa spoke her first words.

"Holy shit."

Reva nudged her. "Took you that long to come up with that?"

Reva went ignored, by both of them.

"Small word," Adam said, "for such a big city."

"Smaller than Danton Hill," Vanessa managed.

What followed for the next two hours were conversation, drinks, flirting on the part of Reva, and a whole lot of pouting on the part of a still-shocked Vanessa Massey. Sure, she managed to get some words in, oftentimes trying to steal the spotlight by highlighting one of her achievements in high school, experiences only she remembered, and as such leaving both Reva and Adam left out. Like she was experiencing her own reunion, sometimes her eyes wandering into some far-off place where neither could reach her. Adam was forced to explain to Reva that the two of them hadn't exactly traveled in the same social circles back at Danton High. He admitted to not being a cool kid, not quite a geek.

"Just one of those students, assigned to anonymity by others."

"You know, Adam, from where I'm sitting, you look more than a bit yummy," Reva said, touching his arm, and not for the first time, "and yummy happens to be one of my specialties. But poor you, you've been sitting here in between us this entire time and still you look positively and dreadfully dressed for that interview. Let's get that jacket off you, and while we're at it, that awful corporate tie as well. It's Saturday. Aren't you suffocating? God, ties bore me, they look like they'll strangle you. And I would hate to see that happen to you, to see life hold you back. Though I have to say, ties and suits like yours, mean big bucks in the corporate scheme. I'll forgive it, for the salaries—those I adore! Adam, wherever did you get that stuffy tie anyway, Brooks Brothers?"

When Adam admitted that he had purchased it just that day, Reva squealed with delight at her knowledge and immediately began to unknot the silky cloth. Adam initially protested a bit, but then with the scotch swirling in his mind and the fact that his new company was footing the bill tonight and two attractive women were nearly fighting over him, one with subtlety, the other with animal-like aggression, he resigned himself to going with the flow. With her tongue stuck between pursed lips, Reva grabbed the undone tie and pulled it out from under his collar, wrapping it around her neck instead like a scarf, a lascivious look plastered upon her made-up face. She leaned over, her lips close to his, as she undid the top button of his shirt, then a second.

"Ooh, what kind of luscious surprise do we have here," Reva said, sliding her hand through the newly exposed triangle of dark chest hair. "You see this, Vanessa? I don't remember you telling me about this part of Adam, or for that matter . . . this part." He turned to her with utter shock on his face, because she'd just grabbed at his crotch. "Oh, don't worry, Adam, my girl Vanessa here told me lots of other things about you, about what a sweet date you were that prom night, and how you helped her show up that idiot Danny Stoker . . . owww. Ow, ow, ow, chicky."

She'd been kicked under the table, and none too lightly by Vanessa.

Excising her hand from inside his shirt, Adam awkwardly tried to slip out of the booth, Reva finally letting him, said he had to see a man about a horse.

"I bet you do," Reva said.

"Ladies, order whatever you want, our tab is taken care of by your most-hated corporate sector," he said. "Oh, and Reva, I'll need that tie back later, it's my good-luck charm now."

"You bet it is."

An alcohol-buzzed Adam bid a hasty retreat from the bar, found his way to the men's lounge, where he passed up the series of urinals for an available stall. He needed to think, to catch his breath. He sat and thought about the crazy night unfolding before his very eyes. The job interview itself made for a good story, but combined with the oversexed antics of Laverne and Shirley out there, well, he'd have a good tale for his buddy Patch's ears. That's when it occurred to him, he should call Patch to maybe help get Vanessa out of his hair. Reva was the wild one, and tonight that's what he was feeling, what he craved. She fit the occasion for a wild roll in the hay, not like Vanessa, the safe choice, someone with whom he shared a checkered history. God, was he even contemplating sex with either of them? *God, I'm starting to talk like Reva.*

Just then he heard the wrong tenor of voice inside the men's private den, one so soft and seductive he felt his body begin to react. "Adam Blackburn, where did you go?"

Could that really be the impulsive Reva entering the men's room, come to claim him here? There was an edge of danger to that one, and with too much scotch in his brain, he was excited at such a prospect. Time to go about his business. "Uh, usually I pee in the urinal," he said. "Regardless, it's still an ongoing process."

"Hurry. I can't wait."

"Gee, that's a comfort to my bladder."

She must have followed his voice to the last stall, because all at once she was knocking on the door. "Quick, let me in. There's a guy at the urinal giving me a strange look."

Let her in? What the hell? He looked around the intimate stall, feeling stupid even as he did so. Obviously there was only one way in or out of the stall. He didn't want them getting thrown out, so he unlatched the door and grabbed her hand to pull her inside before they were discovered, knowing he looked ridiculous with his pants still down around his legs. Turned out that was the least of his concerns, because the woman in the stall with him was not the sexy Reva. It was the safe Vanessa Massey.

"Vanessa?" he said, rising from his seat.

"Just shut up, Adam," she said, grabbing at the open folds of his shirt. She kissed him without warning, hot lips on his, her teeth nibbling, pulling, gnawing on his lower lip. He knew he should push her away, but he was slightly drunk and she was more than slightly hot and very aggressive, and besides they did have a history and why else do people study history but because it's a way to remember. He grabbed at her hair, running his hands through it, and he felt her breasts, which easily popped out of the dress she was barely wearing. Licking exposed, ripe nipples, he tried to be quiet but it didn't matter, Vanessa was making noises enough for the both of them to be discovered. He tried to quiet her with kisses, but she pulled back. She unbuttoned his shirt hastily, digging her nails into his hard pecs.

She leaned in, whispered into his ear. "Take me, Adam, take me here and now."

"Uh . . ." he stammered.

He realized she had produced a small square package in her hand and he also knew what it was and thought about how well prepared she was, like she had planned to get laid and who the chosen one was didn't much matter. With one quick motion she brought the packet up to her lips and tore it with her gleaming teeth. Not even looking where she was going, like she had a map to the treasure memorized, she grabbed hold of him and slid the condom down the length of his growing shaft.

"I said, take me, Adam. Now."

He stopped for a moment, his eyes locked on hers. She looked familiar, that's for sure, but there was also something different, something . . . primal here. Something beyond the two of them. A new era was dawning between them, not the past and not tomorrow, one that existed in this frozen moment of time. It was almost like he was a different person and so too was she, both of them victims of some crazy possession that had taken them from Danton Hill and from New York, and into an existence where only they breathed. He detected hollowness behind her eyes and an empty soul living inside her body, almost like death had settled inside her.

Don't do it, don't do it . . . he told himself.

He felt her lips upon his chest. His body surged with heat . . .

. . . and then he plunged inside her.

A hungover Vanessa awoke that next morning and hadn't a clue about a lot of things. Where she had slept was chief among them, followed by what time it was, what city she was in, and just how many vodka martinis she drank last night. Her last question was really more a realization, because in the deepest and most fuzzy regions of her brain, she knew she'd had sex and for the life of her she couldn't remember a single detail about the guy she'd done it with. She called out to Reva, who was always there but who wasn't there, and that's when Vanessa popped up from the bed, saw the garbage can beside it, and nearly retched into it based on the sheer convenience of it. Nothing happened, just dry heaves, and she lay back down, hoping that today could suddenly become tomorrow and she'd be that much further removed from a night to remember that no doubt she wouldn't. Reva would have fun reminding her, though.

She stole a look at the clock, the numbers blurry. Her eyes blinked, focused. 10:37.

Not bad, she could go back to sleep and . . .

She bolted out of bed.

"Shit," she said. "Shit, shit, shit."

Tossing back the covers, she rushed into the bathroom and looked at the mess that stared back at her from the mirror. She repeated her earlier curse words, tossing in a few harsher ones. She was very nearly late for the real reason she'd come to New York. Twenty minutes until her appointment, that much she remembered. Trouble was, it was uptown and she was downtown (wasn't she?) and more than miles separated the two destinations, especially if she were to make herself presentable. She had a choice, be late and look great or be on time and look like shit.

"Shit, shit . . . shit."

She tossed on whatever clothes she saw lying around, grabbed her purse, and was down in the lobby of the SoHo Grand Hotel moments later. Outside she hailed a cab and told the driver there was a big tip in it for him if he got her to Sixty-Fifth and Fifth in ten minutes. Fortunately it was Sunday morning and traffic wasn't as bad as it could have been during a weekday and Vanessa reached her destination with two minutes to spare. She tipped the cabbie five bucks.

The pre-war building was one of those fancy addresses along the exclusive avenue that lined the eastern edge of Central Park. Somewhere inside the massive stone building was the very forbidding Eleanor Stillwell-Abramson, wife of the ambassador to some country Vanessa could not recall at the moment; she was lucky she came up with the wife's name. As she entered the building, the doorman inquired whom she was seeing. She could already feel contempt burning from his eyes; she wondered what Mrs. Stillwell-Abramson would think of her appearance if she was getting the stink eye from the doorman. *Great, I look like a party girl who can't control herself and who stays out till late and doesn't take anything in life seriously, so why should I even be considered for a position as this privileged woman's personal assistant?* She could just hear that upper-crusty Fifth Avenue voice and see the pince-nez with her beady eyes wide inside them casting judgment down upon Vanessa. She should just turn around now.

Except she couldn't do that to Reva; her friend had pulled a major favor from a friend of a friend of a friend to secure this interview for Vanessa.

She passed muster and found herself shooting up to the twenty-fifth floor.

"Ms. Massey, please come in," a waiting Eleanor Stillwell-Abramson said as the express elevator opened up directly onto the penthouse-level apartment. The regal-looking woman with perfectly coiffed white hair standing before her was sixty-ish, smartly dressed in a blue tailored suit with a set of pearls wrapped around an aging neck. Her lips were held tight, her makeup nearly undetectable.

"Thank you, Mrs. Stillwell-Abramson, very kind of you." Vanessa attempted to get the words out, her tongue's clarity trapped somewhere after the hyphen.

"Dear, it's okay. I know it's quite a mouthful. Why not call me Eleanor."

"Thank you."

"Some tea, coffee, water . . . uh, aspirin?"

There was no hint of sarcasm, just kindness.

"Oh, three of those four would be wonderful," she said, an attempt at humor.

"I assume that last choice is between tea and coffee . . . hmm, let me presume that if you're interviewing for this job you probably have a thing for London and its penchant for afternoon tea, and if that's the case you'll be drinking and serving a fair amount of Earl Grey to thirsty highbrows . . . how am I doing so far?"

"You're reading me very well," Vanessa said. "I apologize . . ."

"Dear, please have a seat. I'll get the aspirin."

Vanessa did as instructed, especially since the tender but firm voice reminded her of a school's headmistress. She returned a moment later and the two women settled down to talk as tea was served, as were those promised aspirin. Mrs. Stillwell-Abramson outlined the details of the job: the lucky candidate would live with her and her husband in their stylishly appointed flat in Mayfair, overlooking London's expansive Green Park. She would arrange Eleanor's schedule, get her to her appointments on time, help when it came to shopping, clothes, travel arrangements, etc. Sundays would be her one day off, otherwise, she would be on call 24-7, but she'd be handsomely compensated for her potential lack of sleep. The woman, eyes steely and serious, asked if Vanessa understood and she said yes, shook her head, and said how much she would enjoy the job.

"You're American."

"Yes, ma'am."

"Please, call me Eleanor," the woman said, then added, "Americans have no taste."

"Indeed, ma'am."

"Are you agreeing with me?"

"Yes?"

"Then why would I possibly hire you for a delicate job that requires not just taste but manners?" Her tone had turned chilly, like a wind suddenly sweeping down from the north, off the lake, a feeling Vanessa knew quite well and had experienced recently. "If you're American and Americans have no taste and you are in agreement with me, then it very much implies that you, dear, sweet and pretty and as unkempt as you are even for this interview, have no taste."

"I had taste enough to answer your ad and to ask Reva Jenkins to get me the interview," she said, "and quite frankly, I still have the guts to be sitting here in this pretentious apartment on Fifth Avenue, answering ridiculous questions that really have no merit when it comes to the job qualifications. And can I say, you should really be living in Notting Hill, not Mayfair, it's much trendier, way less . . . stuffy."

"Are you calling me stuffy?"

"You are planning to reside in Mayfair, aren't you?" Vanessa asked, a broad, confident smile widening her curious face.

Mrs. Stillwell-Abramson pursed her lips in a way that made them hard to read. "You're hired."

"I am?"

"Dear . . . I appreciate good conversation, and even more so I appreciate someone who will challenge me. All the other girls I've met with, they were all raised properly by their parents or their nannies or their Upper East Side schools, so they want to say the right thing, dress the right way. I could do with a breath of fresh air . . . a dose of reality. Not quite a tornado, mind you . . . But, Vanessa dear, keep this in mind. The partying lifestyle you indulge in goes by the wayside. Time to clean up your act. You're how old?"

"Twenty-eight."

"Time to grow up."

"Yes, Eleanor."

"You're married?"

"Divorced. Not a good breakup. He was Italian. I was independent."

"Say no more."

"I wasn't planning to."

Eleanor simply nodded.

"So you've been living in London?"

"Yes. But Brussels before that. And Rome and the Lake District when married."

"A jet-setter."

"Hardly. Just trying to find where I fit in."

"A rebel then." Before giving Vanessa a chance to reply, she asked, "What brought you back to the States?"

"I had some personal matters to attend back home. Up-state."

"Westchester?"

"No, real Upstate. Lake Ontario, a small town, forget-table."

"From your expression, what brought you back was nothing to your liking."

"A funeral."

Again, Eleanor Stillwell-Abramson simply nodded. "I'm sorry."

"I'm not."

The woman waited for more, but Vanessa was done with that line of questioning. She'd offer up no further details.

"In that case, we leave for London next week. My husband is already there, working."

"I'll be ready tonight," Vanessa said, and for the first time she smiled since waking up in that disheveled hotel bed with no memory of the night before. She recalled her visit back home and all the awfulness that trip had brought, and then she saw images from last night start to creep back into her memory. Reva, the Standard, running into Adam Blackburn and thinking the sexy man in front of her couldn't possibly be the same boy who had taken her to the prom. Endless drinks, endless innuendo from Reva, and then seiz-ing her moment, begging Adam for sex and feeling him in-side her, knowing at once it was the same Adam. All of them had been stupid mistakes that only managed to bring her even further back home, inextricably linking her to Danton Hill for forever despite her continual running away. Then she said, setting down the cup of tea and wishing for two more aspirin, "I can't get out of this city—this country—soon enough."

Eleanor paused, as though waiting for what more was to come.

Vanessa Massey said, "I'm ready to be someone else."

Chapter 14

Now

"What time is it?"

Adam, pupils darkened by night and by forgotten memories, was unaware not only of the time but that Vanessa had ceased talking before posing her question. Unknowingly, they had allowed silence to hover between them without thought toward filling it. They had each told their respective stories of lost love while sitting out on the front porch of the farmhouse, avoiding the romantic pull of the swing and the sexual entanglement it had earlier led them to. This late hour felt like a moment for revelations and truths, not explosive passion that served only to delay such truths. Sitting opposite each other, leaning against the sturdy wooden posts, they had talked and they had listened, and then it was as though their words had dried up with the rain, secrets held over them by thickening clouds. As though the space separating them now represented eleven years passing of when they hadn't seen, talked, thought much, or heard about the other.

Almost like that night in New York had never happened.

"I'm sorry, what did you ask?" Adam asked.

"The time."

He checked his wrist instinctively, but he wore no watch. It didn't work anyway, broken in the car accident. "I don't know. Eight o'clock? Midnight? Does it matter?"

"I was just wondering what was happening at the reunion."

"Probably it's just getting started . . . or it's over."

"Adam, time doesn't mean much right now, does it?"

"Guess not."

"Still . . ." she said, her voice drifting off.

Adam filled the void building between them. "Lark Henry is probably giving a speech, just like she always used to when she was voted class president; two years running, if I remember. Standing up in front of the gang, maybe hint of gray in her hair, saying how great it is to see everyone and thanks for the great turnout . . . you know, the same words she spoke twenty-plus years ago when she was first elected."

"What does she do for a living anyway?" Vanessa asked.

"School principal. At Danton Hill High."

"Scary. But perfect."

"Leader that she is, she's probably gathered everyone together for a moment of silence in remembrance of our classmates who have died," Adam said. "She's a good soul."

Vanessa nodded, withdrawn for a moment, lost in thought, before her eyes lightened up with a sudden roll of her eyes. "Jana and Tiffany are probably thinking of adding me to that list. Because my no-show just means they'll kill me," she said. Then quickly added, "What about you, Adam, were you close with anyone in particular in high school? Anyone you still keep in touch with or were anxious to see at the reunion?"

Adam shook his head. "Not that I've kept in touch with. When I went away to college, everything changed for me. Like I woke up from some awful dream and for the first time I saw the sun shining. I acquired some much-needed confidence about myself—who I was and what I wanted from life. No longer was I content being that sniveling, weak boy looking for acceptance from anyone who would look toward him. Danton Hill kind of suffocated me. Leaving allowed me to breathe. What about you, what do you remember most about Danton Hill?"

"The town itself? So much, the football field and sneaking out during lunch period to eat our sandwiches on the bleachers, the fact that we had to travel like twenty miles to get to a mall, that playground . . . up on Danton's Hill. Running with friends along rocky Mercer Pier inside Danton State Park. I remember all those times. But God, I suppose the place I remember best is that stupid, old-fashioned soda shop. The Sno-Cone . . . the woman who ran the place was so old we called her . . ."

"Sno-Crone, I remember."

A bit of reminiscent laughter escaped their mouths. "We used to hang out there all the time, when school let out or after football games on autumn Friday nights. We'd get one of those old-fashioned egg creams or a sundae or sometimes just a soda and fries. I mean, there are other memories too. Not all fun and games. Like my demanding parents and the house we lived in on Sanders Street, the dog we had when I was younger, whom I named Yellow because he was. My room with those horrible posters of movies and bands that everyone liked so I liked, even though I really didn't. My grandmother's death and how quiet the house was after that. No one talked about death, they just . . . accepted it as they did a summer storm. Just one day she was gone and I didn't understand and my questions went unanswered. I was so naïve back then, so innocent . . . not like when I got to high school. When I hit the ninth grade, like you said about college, everything started to change."

"You changed."

Vanessa tossed him a strange look. "In a good or bad way?"

"Neither. You were you, or at least trying the newer version on for size."

"I wasn't very nice to you."

"Vanessa, even when we were in third grade and I believed you still had cooties, we were never friends."

"Sorry," she said.

"No, no, that's okay," he said. "You know, not everyone can be part of someone's circle, sometimes those circles close for no reason other than you didn't like the color pants I wore that day. It made no sense, but that was school. Fitting in socially was harder than homework."

"My parents preached independence, but not in any proactive way. I was just an excuse for them to ignore me. As I hit my teen years, I could come and go pretty much as I pleased, and trust me, I did. I started dating Danny Stoker the very first day of high school. He asked me out right there at what became our regular booth at Sno-Cone. We were sitting with friends and someone, I think it was Davey, said high school was all about social status, not grades, and so you better choose your gang wisely or you're in for a miserable four years."

"I think I chose unwisely," Adam said.

"Adam, you want to know the awful truth? You don't choose, none of us did, even the so-called popular kids. You get chosen, mostly based on looks and appearance and where you live and how much money your parents make." She paused to look up at the sky, searching for the twinkle of stars that should be transporting them back to those days, maybe another time of their choosing. All that hung over them were clouds, the moonlight forgotten, just as they appeared to be. "Eighth grade, we were all still finding our way, naïvely playing and plotting without understanding its repercussions. We all knew that after summer passed, the crazy jockeying for popularity would begin again, and this time on a tougher, much bigger playground. Fortunately, my body filled out that summer. So that first morning at my locker when I heard my name and it was Danny and he said, 'Whoa, where'd those knockers come from?' I knew I'd be fine. Crude and shallow, but you take my point. Danny was the best-looking guy in school and he'd chosen me. Well, initially he had chosen my boobs. For the first few months we dated I don't think he knew the color of my eyes."

"Green, with tiny specks," Adam said, staring at her. "Like unearthed emeralds."

Vanessa deflected the obvious compliment, again pushing her hair away from her face like she had that night at the hotel lounge in Manhattan. "When Danny realized he actually liked me for me, he used to joke that he was getting three for the price of me. Direct quote."

"Idiot."

"Yup."

"So why did you continue to go out with him?"

"Are you really asking that question?"

Adam acknowledged the stupidity of asking. "Right, got it. Good-looking, great hair, quarterback of the football team . . . am I missing something?"

"Really good kisser," she added, and then looked like she regretted saying that.

"Vanessa, you don't have to worry about offending me. You're allowed to remember the good times you and Danny shared together. It's not the past if you deny something ever existed. Everything happened, experiences don't just disappear because you don't want to remember them."

"I'm not denying it . . . him, it's just . . . here now, with you, I just don't want Danny Stoker intruding on this . . . uh, unexpected night of ours. It's like the prom we really never had—or were promised. No guarantees, huh? Guess

I've learned that. But still, Adam, the prom should have been a time when you could dance at will, laugh like you hadn't a care in the world. When the night ended it's like you'd endured a rite of passage. You got through graduation . . . anything was possible."

"I still think anything is possible."

"Even without a job, or prospects for a future?"

"Hey, I'm only thirty-eight. I've still got time to figure it out."

"Adam, you're just being flippant."

"Lighten the mood," he said. "Not everything we talk about tonight has to be soaked with meaning. Sometimes you just have to make a joke at your own expense."

"You want to know something?"

"Sure, let me hear it."

"I don't have a job either."

"But . . . Mrs. Stillwell-Abramson . . . who will dress her and keep her schedule . . . and . . ."

"Her husband is no longer ambassador. New president, new appointments. They moved back to that stuffy Fifth Avenue apartment six months ago."

"And you?"

"I moved back in with Reva, but this time in a crappy but cool flat in Putney—not quite Central London but good enough." She laughed. "Like I'm regressing. Maybe that's why I decided to come back for the reunion. Maybe I couldn't believe twenty years had somehow passed and I was still living with a roommate, drinking, smoking again, wasting away the days because I still didn't know what I wanted to be when I grew up."

"So, we're kind of in the same boat."

"And sinking fast," she said, looking away as she said the words, wishing she could take them back. Why was the sea . . .

or the lake or ocean or whatever body of water was nearby, why did it keep washing into her thoughts, tangling them with its discarded entrails? She'd never quite taken to the water, and she hated to swim. Were these allusions mere illusions? Turning back to him, she said, "Tomorrow may be coming, but that doesn't mean we know what comes next. Heck, don't know what I'm doing a minute from now, much less tomorrow or six months or a decade from now."

"Then let's take the night a minute at a time. No sense rushing time when it doesn't seem to be moving anyway."

"Doesn't stop me from worrying about tomorrow when it happens," she said. "You want to know something, Adam? What this night means? Why we're telling these stories? Because I don't think we're ever truly done with the past. It shapes us, perhaps defines us, and right now it's consuming us. So let's embrace it the way it wants. Come on, I've spilled my guts enough. For now. I think it's your turn again."

Adam steeled himself, wondering just where this was leading.

"What do you want to know?" he asked.

"Anything," she said. "Surprise me."

"You want me to open up my letters and share with you what I wrote?"

His words chilled her, this feeling almost like a sharp stab at her abdomen. Was it cold from the night air, or fear at what lay beyond these borders? And if fear, of what? Of the unknown? Why had he used such a metaphor, when earlier the idea of the letters had brought about her fainting spell? But as she studied his expression, there didn't seem to be any hidden meaning behind his bemused look. So Vanessa wrapped her arms around herself, forged ahead, and did as he asked. She delved into his past, his psyche.

"Tell me about your high school."

They, of course, had gone to the same one. Yet she could tell he knew exactly what she meant. "Why go there?"

"Adam?"

"Yes, Vanessa."

"Spill."

"Remind me again why we're doing this?"

"Because we've talked about everything else—life and love, sex and babies, spouses and lovers, things we've lost or things we've never had. Things that might have been, or might have happened in some other time. So here's where we are, the only logical place for us to return to—high school, the prom. This is supposed to be a high school reunion, Adam, right? And we were both planning to attend it and I think we were each looking for the other. Instead the fates, as you believe, have thrown us together for our very own reunion. I shared my story, tell me yours."

"High school sucked." He paused. "End of story."

"I'd like to hear what happened during your pause. Your eyes . . . they darkened."

"Do you know what it meant to get that job at KFC, to land clients who trusted you, who had faith in you and unflagging confidence that you'd make them rich? Absolutely fucking great. I had left all of my old life behind, and I found a place where I fit in."

"You fit in before . . . just, you know, in your world. With your own friends, pursuing your own interests. You just weren't comfortable in your own skin yet, it wasn't like you wanted to be someone else. Don't you get it? That's the lesson, Adam, that envying other people's lives just makes you miserable. So don't think that nobody cared . . . that you didn't matter. Thinking that you don't fit in anywhere, that's an awful outlook on life."

"It was an even worse way to live. Vanessa . . . can we not do this?"

She crossed over from her side of the porch, sat beside him, her hand caressing his arm. The cool night allowed the temperature to flare up. "Tell me."

"You sure know how to get a guy's attention, then—and now," he said. "Okay, well, for starters I hung out with the math geeks. We played stupid games. Get this: One kid would toss out random numbers and the others had to add, subtract, multiply, divide, at will, and if you got it wrong everyone forced you to recite the Pythagorean theorem. For fun. Sounds cool, just like a date at Sno-Cone, huh? I didn't even like math, I sucked at algebra. But there I was. You were out socializing with Danny, drinking your malteds and probably sneaking booze under the bleachers while he was trying to unbutton your blouse, and I was drinking flat grape soda at Hank Goldman's house. No wonder we were nicknamed the Zit Club."

Vanessa let out a laugh, then quickly apologized. "Sorry, I forgot about that."

"Where's the wine?"

"Now you sound like me."

"That's why we get along," he said. "I think it's still in the kitchen, I'll be right back."

Adam left her to her own thoughts. In the craziness of the day, all the events that had occurred between the two of them—first thrust together by the chance accident and then by some untenable passion—she hadn't actually thought about the true nature of their relationship. Where had it even begun? On the grassy hill beside the school's water tower when he asked her to the prom . . . or, more accurately, where she asked him? Or even before that, when neither of them knew who they were or what the universe held for them? They did have a surprising amount in common, including that overwhelming desire to get out from under where you grew up, redefine yourself as you saw fit. No one to judge you, your decisions. Not once today had they lost patience with each other, lost their temper. Well, more so Vanessa than Adam, but never at the other's expense. But there was more than that pulling her toward him. No doubt she found him attractive, that wasn't up for debate. She wondered what would come with tomorrow, under the new light of a fresh morning.

Answers to such questions would have to wait, the night still held more secrets.

Clearly those secrets were close to revealing themselves.

Adam returned with the wine, two new glasses.

"Don't break this one, we're out of jelly glasses."

"At least the glass was empty when I dropped it."

"The rare occasion when the glass being empty was a positive," he said, raising his glass with yet another toast.

"Now what?"

"We would have had to endure even more toasts at the reunion. So just run with it."

"Okay, toastmaster. Toast away."

He thought before speaking. "Actually, let's cheer to us."

"Us?"

"Yes. For what we've been through, and what we've become."

"Stronger?"

"Wiser."

"Drunker," she said, and laughed with the sound of someone grown suddenly content. In this life, this crazy world, you took what you got, you made memories out of moments, and you locked them in your mind so no one could steal them from you. She sipped, looked up at Adam to guess what he was thinking and found him staring out into the blackness. What hung back out of their reach was sealed up and unforeseen, like those letters upstairs, but that didn't mean it failed to exist. Memories she chose not to remember, they had a way of sneaking out.

"So . . . math club?"

"It wasn't an official club . . ." He stopped, smiled at how ridiculous he sounded, trying to defend a decision he'd made more than twenty years ago. "Look, let's not dwell on Danton Hill High. Those kids were my friends when I needed them, and then I moved on because I couldn't see myself drinking grape soda the rest of my school days. So I drifted away, but not anywhere where I found solid land. Just islands, many of them my own. I wasn't athletic, my singing was bad enough for the shower to turn off automatically, and I didn't smoke or do drugs, so . . . you know, no hanging out behind the school with those kids."

"Sounds lonely."

"I survived."

A comfortable silence enveloped them even as the cool air swirled around them. Vanessa sensed there was something more he wanted to say, he was just taking his time getting there. Rather than rush the moment, she would offer him the same consideration he had shown her, so she could wait till the right time. So she remained sitting, drinking, waiting, thinking.

He spoke at last. "Sophomore year, I still looked like I could pass for a sixth grader. You know, get in for less at the movies? Which everyone thought was a cool thing—well, the math guys, anyway. They would calculate how much money I'd saved with such a scam. But that's not the story . . . it's . . . yeah, sophomore year . . . I was so naïve, dumb even."

He took another sip, checked out the bottle's contents. Enough for one last round.

"It was February," he said. "Actually, the fourteenth."

"Valentine's Day," Vanessa said, realizing just where this stroll down memory lane was taking them. Because in a flash she remembered that day too, the square red envelope, the red and white card littered with golden sparkles that fell all over her dress when she opened it. She knew before she read the cramped signature line that the card had been from Adam; the way he'd looked at her queerly all day long, as though waiting for a chance to talk to her when friends didn't surround her, classmates . . . Danny, he'd been waiting to give her this.

And lost his courage.

"Do you know that I gave you a Valentine's card?"

"Actually, you didn't give it to me. You *left* it for me, sliding it right through the upper slots of my school locker. I found it after football practice—I always stayed after school to watch Danny. He said he tossed better when I was cheering him on."

"I put it there at the end of the day. I almost didn't."

"I'm glad you did."

"You are?"

"Remember in grade school every Valentine's Day our teachers would have us cut and paste cards? Glue everywhere and inevitably one of the kids would cut himself with those cheap scissors and go bleeding his way down to the school nurse, but in the end we all got those little makeshift cards made and passed them around to classmates and family and even some teachers. It was a pretty corny tradition. But still, as forced upon us as they were, there was inherent sweetness to getting loads of valentines." She paused, pouring a bit more wine into her glass. "That sophomore year, the only Valentine's Day card I received was the one from you."

"But Danny . . ."

She waved off his comment before he could say anything

more. "But Danny nothing. I remember that night clearly because he went out with his buddies. Someone had a fake ID and so they drank a case of cheap beer and probably puked their guts out later. Not that they didn't deserve it. Happy Valentine's Day, Vanessa!"

"What did you do?"

"I sat at home and ate a pint of rocky road and held your card."

"It was corny."

"Yup. It was sweet too. I remember what you wrote inside it."

"You couldn't possibly . . . ?"

"You start, I'll finish."

"'From the land to the sea . . .'" Adam began.

"'You are all I see,'" Vanessa completed. "I knew it was from you."

"How could you know? How did I sign it?"

"You signed it . . ." She paused. She sought an answer in her emerging memories. Could she picture the card, the awkward, juvenile lettering? A surprised expression crossed her face and she looked up. "There was no name, no signature. Just . . ."

"Just what?"

"Initials."

Adam nodded. "What initials?"

"A.B."

"See, could have been anybody."

She tossed him a look of genial annoyance. "Not likely. I knew then, and I know now, it was the initials of one Adam Blackburn."

He went along with the idea, for now. "Okay, fine. So I was hiding behind an alias. You figured it out. A.B. was Adam Blackburn. Guilty as charged. I was a dork."

"Yes, you were," she said.

"Gee, thanks."

"Danny saw it."

"What?"

She'd gone there, might as well continue. "The Valentine's card. He came over to my house a couple days later and your card was still on my dresser, right beside my earring tree and jewelry box."

"What did he do?"

"Oh, he tore it to shreds, tossed it into the air like it was confetti."

"I'm sorry."

She looked away, almost shamed. "You can't go back. You can't change who you were. Not you, not me, definitely not Danny."

"He was, is, and probably always will be a jerk."

Setting her glass down, Vanessa stood up, her feet taking her a distance from Adam, her arms encircling the columns of the porch for support, for something to lean on. She, like Adam before her, stared out in the darkness, and even though her eyes couldn't be certain what she had found beyond those blackened borders, she knew what images her mind saw. She saw Danton Hill, eleven years ago, the last time she'd ever set foot on its soil. The week before her interview with Mrs. Stillwell-Abramson, just a few days before she would coincidentally run into Adam at the Standard and screw him in the men's room because she just wanted to forget. She had returned home that time—thankfully with Reva at her side—for a funeral.

"Adam," Vanessa said, "Danny Stoker's dead."

"Oh, uh, wow. I'm sorry. I didn't know."

"That's why I came back to the States, that time when we met up in New York."

"You'd gone home?"

"All the way to Danton Hill."

"So, a little part of you, maybe you still loved Danny? Loved the memories of your fun times in high school, not how it ended or what happened after that . . ."

"No," she said, shaking her head. Pain stabbed at her heart. "I didn't love Danny Stoker, and I doubt I ever did. You know why I went back?"

Adam was still seated on the porch. She could feel his eyes bearing down on her, but she couldn't look back at him, she couldn't reveal the awful emotions boiling inside her heart. "No. But I think you want to tell me."

"I just wanted to see it for myself. I wanted to see him lying in that casket."

Her focus was elsewhere, so the sudden warmth of his arms surprised her. She welcomed his touch, invited him closer. He held her, and she held him, and she allowed a tear to fall from her eyes and slide down unchecked upon her cheek. She did nothing to wipe it away, it would have meant breaking free from his embrace and that was the last thing she wanted. Right now, this time and this moment, amidst clouds and blackness, equal parts mystery and darkness, she needed to feel something other than pain.

Just then Adam broke the embrace, but still never let go of her hand.

"Vanessa Massey," he said, taking a step back. "May I have this dance?"

"Excuse me?"

"I want to dance with you."

"Adam, there's no music."

"Hey, our cars got to dance, the music of crashing metal."

"That's not even funny."

"So stop questioning reality, it's not real, not now," he said. "Only the two of us exist in this moment, and we can make any noise we want and no one will hear us. Music surrounds us if we want it, it's in our hearts and our minds. We can feel the beat between our hearts, the heat between our bodies, the rhythm of our emotions whenever we want. Feel it now, Vanessa, feel the music with me."

She thought he was crazy but maybe crazy was good, maybe right now crazy was perfect. She accepted his lead, taking hold of his strong hand. He led her around the width of the porch, one step, then two, then three and then four in classic ballroom fashion, and she was the lucky girl in the swirling gown and he was the handsome boy who smelled of fresh cedar, and with the waltz playing somewhere way back in their past but somehow seeping through an encroaching glint of moonlit darkness and into this dreamy moment, she suddenly laughed and shouted and waited with giddy anticipation before he twirled her around, not once and not twice but a third time, until she dizzyingly collapsed into his arms.

"Oh Adam, I wish somehow this night could last forever."

Sealing her wish with a kiss upon her lips, he finally broke and said, "Forever yours."

CHAPTER 15

THEN

It was the day before Danton Hill High School's "Forever Yours" senior prom, and a nervous, sweaty Adam Blackburn knew the approaching night would end in unmitigated disaster, just one more lousy high school memory that he would hopefully banish from his mind once he skipped town for college and the fortunes that awaited him beyond these borders. If that was the case, why then was he actually going through with this foolish venture? What possible reason existed for him to be escorting the beautiful, alluring, but ultimately infuriating Vanessa Massey?

Good question, one he'd silently been asking himself countless times since the afternoon he and Vanessa had agreed to attend the dance together, like a deal made with the devil. No one in school was supposed to know about the unlikely coupling of Adam Blackburn and Vanessa Massey, save for her insider gang who had pressured Adam initially to come forth with the invite. Sure, they all knew, but they had also been sworn to secrecy on threat of being disowned by their cool friends. Adam had just a few true friends himself, and he hadn't spoken a word to them. He had made a promise to Vanessa that he wouldn't talk about their non-date, and she promised too, they had even shaken hands over it, their first touch of intimacy of any nature.

So then it was a total and not too pleasant surprise that Adam found himself cornered in the empty corridor outside the lunchroom by four guys led by a pissed-off Danny Stoker on that Thursday afternoon before the fateful dance. He was positioned ironically beneath one of the prom banners that hung throughout the school when they approached him. Danny took the lead, of course; as the captain and quarterback of the Danton Hill Great Lakers football team there was an automatic deference to his leadership—what he said went, and who he picked on . . . well, his gang was right there beside him.

Toby, Kyle, Frank . . . and Danny, lead singer and backup, ready to doo-wop on Adam.

Danny, all six-two of him, strong, agile, with thick dark hair and more than a hint of razor scruff on his nearly eighteen-year-old face, leaned in close, intimidation on the menu; Adam could smell the cigarette smoke on his breath. The threat, and what else could it be—certainly not a friendly exchange between pals, not with this body language, not with their respective status in school—was simple, intimidating, and straight to the point. "Cancel your plans Friday night, you ain't going anywhere near the gym."

Adam never felt smaller than in this guy's presence, like the sun had been blocked and he was living in its shadow. An image flashed in his mind, of him and Vanessa dancing across that gymnasium floor and how ridiculous it would look when the picture everyone had expected to see was one of Danny and Vanessa, the ideal high school couple enjoying their final moment of glory. King and queen, ready to be crowned, suddenly upset by a stunning coup.

Or in Danny's language, an interception.

"I don't know what you're talking about," Adam found himself saying.

Danny Stoker looked surprised; no one ever questioned him.

"Punk, what did you just say?"

"What makes you think I'm going to that stupid dance?"

"You think I'm dumb?" he asked.

Adam couldn't help himself, he gave the smart-mouth response. "Changing topics?"

Danny Stoker's face scrunched up, confused and annoyed, probably because the latter informed the former. He raised his large hand, usually perfect for throwing the ideal spiral with the football, and thrust it under Adam's tight throat. He pushed upward. Adam felt his feet rise slightly off the ground.

"Listen to me good, punk. This conversation is over. You've been told what you have to do."

"You mean, what I don't have to do," Adam said, wondering where this shot of bravery was coming from.

That same angry scowl came across his new enemy's face, now red from embarrassment. "Show up here tomorrow night and you'll live to regret it."

"What if I do show up, and what if I'm not alone?"

"Oh, then you'll have no more regrets. Because you'll be dead."

Released from his hold, shoved against a line of thin metal lockers, Adam's feet gave out and he slid to the floor in pain he tried not to show. The four guys headed off down the hall, laughing and high-fiving, walking tall like the king and princes of school that they were. Jerks.

Cut to the next night, and Adam was alone in his bedroom, staring at the taunting tuxedo that hung from that little hook on the back of his door. He was scheduled to pick up Vanessa in twenty minutes, and she lived fifteen minutes away on the other side of town. Which any math geek could tell meant he had just five minutes to don the tux, and that included tying the bow tie, no clip-on here. Of course he'd been standing, pondering, debating for the past half hour, still unconvinced he was actually going through with the "date." Danny Stoker's threatening words reverberated in his ears. But could he really end his high school days on such a low note of cowardice, of leaving the pretty girl who had invited him, even if it had been last minute and really didn't mean anything outside of her revenge on the boy who'd broken her heart? Could he go out a loser and let her go out shamed? These were big issues for someone of his tender age, and he had no one to discuss them with. No friend who would understand, neither of his parents suspected anything was wrong. He knew what he had to do: face the music, whether Danny's or the orchestra's. It was fight or dance, but no matter what happened, in the end he couldn't leave Vanessa in her dress, standing on the porch waiting in vain for Mr. Temporary Charming.

"So, it's been a good run . . . some people think death is the better alternative," he said to the mirror. The person who stared back swallowed a lump in his throat.

And with such a creed spoken, Adam Blackburn donned his funeral suit.

Four years of being one of the most popular girls in high school, all of her efforts culminated in this one grand moment: the senior prom. So why then did she feel like she was starting fresh, starting over, and her social status had gone from one hundred to zero faster than she'd said no to Danny's insistent advances? She wondered what the big deal was over sleeping with him. Get it over with, she'd have to eventually, so why not with the boy she'd endured the last four years with? Because it just didn't feel right. He was handsome, he was popular, she loved the way his kisses tickled her neck . . . but . . . well, the longer she knew him the more she was convinced what a self-centered jerk he was.

Now, as a result of her actions, her . . . pride, she was attending the "Forever Yours" Senior Prom with sweet, reliable, fresh-faced Adam Blackburn. Except tonight he wasn't exactly living up to that reliable reputation. He was already fifteen minutes late and she was growing antsy. God, what the hell had she been thinking? Did he even know how to drive? Maybe his bicycle had gotten a flat.

A moment later she saw the sweeping glow of headlights appear and heard tires crunch over the driveway gravel.

Vanessa, who had been watching and waiting from her bedroom window, like a prisoner, bolted out of her room, running down the stairs despite her heels and the flowing violet gown that billowed out from under her. She reached the front door seconds before her mother did, opened the front door, and stepped out onto the dimly lit porch.

"Vanessa, dear, isn't Danny coming in for pictures?"

"Oh. Mom . . . uh, no, he had a sports injury the other day, his nose is swollen," she said, conjuring that scene from a corny *Brady Bunch* episode she'd caught on Nick at Nite, turning Marcia's bloated nose to her advantage. "He insisted no formal pictures. We'll take some at the dance, when the lighting isn't so revealing . . ."

"Okay, dear, you know best," her mother said to the fleeing figure.

Such was one advantage of Vanessa's easily won independence.

So that's how Vanessa deflected the question of who was taking her to the senior prom, and good thing Adam was so willing to go along with every covert suggestion she came up with. Don't honk, don't come to the door, wait in the car, drive away quickly. That's what happened when she hopped into the front seat, not even giving him a chance to chivalrously open the door. "Drive," was all she said as acknowledgment to her date, and like he'd done since the moment they agreed to this foolish venture, he did as asked. For the next several minutes, as they drove through the village of Danton Hill, Vanessa fixed her makeup with the aid of the mirror above the passenger seat, and more than once did she stop and look deeper into her red-shaded eyes and wonder why going to this dance even mattered. Wasn't there a big world out there, one that didn't care about the petty concerns of a high school cheerleader who'd lost all reason to wave her pom-poms?

It wasn't until they arrived on the school grounds and he parked that she even looked at Adam, really looked at him. He had opened the door for her this time, his hand outstretched.

"Oh, Adam . . . thank you."

"My mother insisted I act the perfect gentleman."

"You told your mother you were going to the prom?"

"Well, the tux kind of gave me away. And I had to ask my dad for the car, which I never do. They had questions, but don't worry, they don't know I'm with you . . . that you're with me. I told them I didn't have a date, it was just a bunch of friends going . . . is that all right?"

"It's fine . . . and I appreciate your flexibility, Adam." Why was she being so hesitant with him? Why was she so on edge? This was supposed to be fun, one last party with her friends before graduation, before the school sent you out into the world with all those hard-fought lessons, where success and failure were yours depending upon the decisions you made. Grown-up decisions. No more tests, this was real.

That's when she noticed how nice Adam looked, how . . . yes, grown-up. His thick brown hair was slicked back, his cheeks red and freshly shaved, not that he looked like he needed to scrape away the peach fuzz all that often; but still, she appreciated his effort. What she noticed most was the violet-colored bow tie and the red kerchief in the jacket pocket, a perfect match and complement to the colors of her own dress. In her hair she wore a scarlet flower, pinned to the side. With one simple burst of festive color, they looked like they went together, like they had planned this weeks in advance. A perfectly matched pair. But when he presented her with a corsage so bright, so vibrantly purple and alive, right there in the parking lot while others of their classmates headed into the gym, she realized that Adam had put more effort into the night than she had anticipated. As he slid the flower, adorned with a red ribbon, onto her wrist, she felt a passing weakness, like she could faint. She couldn't look into his eyes. She looked anywhere else, at the water tower where they'd agreed to this night, at the football field in the distance where she'd cheered on a dominant Danny and the team, but mostly at the large dome of the looming gym, wondering just what was going to happen inside it.

"Vanessa?"

She didn't even hear her own name, not at first. There might have been an echo and only the reverberation by the wind off the lake brought her back to the moment. She finally let her eyes settle on Adam's earnest face. He looked lost, like he didn't even know how he'd gotten to this point. A wave of remorse swept over her as she realized she was using him to fulfill some dumb girlish fantasy and that he knew it too, and that tonight was as much a memory that would stick with him as it would her. But other matters took precedence. Because no matter whom you went with, not attending the prom represented the ultimate social failure for any high schooler.

"Adam?"

"Yeah?"

"We don't have to go through with this, you know?"

His face remained impassive. He was hard to read. "This is your night. I'm your escort. We do what you want."

Her eyes softened. And her heart melted, just a tiny bit.

"You're so much more a gentleman than . . ."

But he stopped her from saying it, a simple gesture of his finger upon her lips.

"I'm sorry," she said.

"Don't be. It's natural that you think about . . ."

"No names," she said.

"No names," he agreed.

That's when she took hold of his hand, slipped her fingers within his. She ignored the fact that his hand was moist and sweaty. She couldn't blame him his apprehension. Her heart was beating a mile a minute.

"Ready?" she asked.

"Are you?"

She swallowed all those butterflies doing flips in her stomach and thought instead about the day she'd been named head cheerleader. She decided nothing could ruin this night, no one. Confidence swelled inside her. "Adam Blackburn?"

"Yes, Vanessa Massey?"

From somewhere deep inside her, she found strength from a previously untapped source. "May I have this first dance?"

* * *

What Adam had feared most was their entrance into the gymnasium. Would Danny and his gang be waiting right inside those doors, ready to pounce like lions on the hunt? Or would they be lurking in the shadows of bright streamers, allowing the tentative couple to build a false sense of comfort before jumping in and tearing down her dreams and his reputation? There was only one way to find out.

"Ready?" she said.

"Not at all," he said, but he took hold of the door and held it for her, and together Adam Blackburn and Vanessa Massey made their grand entrance. The music swelled and then came to an abrupt stop. Dancers broke their embraces, they applauded politely, and then in an unplanned moment of awkwardness turned to see who the new arrivals were. It was just a small beat, barely a second before the band resumed, but in that moment Adam felt every eye fall on him, a feeling he'd never before experienced in four years of school. For one brief moment, he was the center of attention, and on his arm was a girl so pretty he could hardly believe it. With streamers colored silver and gold floating down from the ceiling, the swirling lights of red and blue and green bouncing off them, the effect was better than any conjured dream. Here was a place of shimmering beauty, the gym transformed from a place of sweaty workouts to a fantasyland of glittering rainbows and endless promise.

As the couples resumed dancing, Adam led Vanessa through the dense crowd, not sure what they should be doing, dancing or getting a glass of punch or perhaps finding some friends in which to lose themselves. They were here, together, but did that mean they were joined at the hip? Just what was expected of him now that they were here? Fortunately, he was spared having to answer that, as Vanessa's friends immediately swirled around them like a protective cocoon, like they'd been coached, the team led by Tiffany and Jana and their respective dates. The girls kissed cheeks and squealed over their dresses, and Adam received a high five from Davey Sisto and a slight head nod from Rich. Adam was grateful for their attention, but that didn't stop him from looking around at his other classmates. Was Danny Stoker even here? Wasn't he supposed to be here with trashy Lucy Walker?

Yup, that's exactly who he was with. Sighting confirmed. Adam could see them amidst the other dancers, though what the two of them were doing could hardly be considered dancing. Their bodies were locked nearly as one, their hips grinding more than swaying. Danny's face was buried in her neck, his face concealed by his mop of unruly hair. Good, keep it that way, don't notice me . . . us.

Just then the song changed to a more up-tempo beat and the gang immediately headed out to the dance floor, Adam and Vanessa caught in their undertow. More group dance than intimate encounter, Adam found himself starting to loosen up, his body gyrating to the music, his eyes alternating between Vanessa, who seemingly had decided to just have fun tonight, her bright smile enough to light the dim room, and sneaky Danny Stoker, whose eyes had just lit up upon discovering the newly minted couple. Adam thought he should look away when his eyes met Danny's but then thought better of it. Don't show intimidation, don't show fear, and don't be the first to break contact. Be strong, be confident . . . you're safe within a group, there are teachers and chaperones around, Danny Stoker would be a fool to try anything here. Still, his threat hung over Adam like a storm cloud readying to release its pent-up rains. The song changed again. The gang stayed out on the dance floor. They were settling in, ready to enjoy the long night. Adam tried to do the same.

Finally, sweat from dancing dotting his brow and trick-
ling down the back of his tuxedo shirt, he whispered into
Vanessa's ear that perhaps they could take a break, grab a
beverage.

"Oh, okay, that would be nice."

He escorted her over to the punch bowl in the corner,
where he poured out two ladles of the fruity drink into red
plastic tumblers. He handed one to Vanessa, hoisted the
other in a toast.

"To the most beautiful girl on the dance floor," he said.

Vanessa's face turned the color of punch, matching the
flower in her hair. "Adam . . . you don't have to say that. I
mean, it's nice and . . . it's just, remember, we're only
friends."

"And friends can't be honest with each other?"

"Thank you. You look very handsome in your tux. Sorry
I didn't say so earlier."

"This old thing?" he said, trying to lighten the mood.

She laughed, her smile helping to evaporate the tension
between them.

"Are you glad you're here?" he asked.

"I think so. It's nice to see how the gym looks—Jana and
I worked on the committee that helped get it set up, but you
never know what it's going to look like until you see it with
those nasty fluorescent lights off and the band playing and
the way the dance balls gleam off the streamers. So, yeah,
I'm glad I'm here. Thank you."

"Everyone is staring at us."

"At me," she said. "Sorry, that sounds so self-centered,
but usually the other kids look at me with envy, but now it's
definitely something else—like I'm part of a freak show."

"Welcome to my life," he said.

"How do you do it . . . being made fun of, people judging
you when they don't know you?"

He shrugged. "I guess you put it out of your mind. You go to your classes, you study, you end up with straight As. And you get a scholarship to an Ivy League school that promises to take you away from all the petty things that high school seems to be about."

"Ivy League?"

"Princeton."

"Wow, I didn't know," she said, sipping her drink. "Congratulations."

"That's how I survived, knowing that once high school was over I could get the heck out of Danton Hill and away from all these people. College opens up a new life, new opportunities to find your real self, free from peer pressure and family expectations. I'll be on my own and that's just how I prefer it. The day after graduation, I'm outta here. I'm going to take a couple summer courses to get acclimated, and then in the fall I go full-time. I can't see myself ever coming back to Danton Hill."

"What about your family?"

"It's just my folks, no siblings, and frankly they can't wait to put the house on the market and move down to Florida. This dance is my swan song to Danton Hill, and frankly I'm honored that I get to leave on such a high note. Being here at the senior prom—being here with you."

"Adam Blackburn, I think you're really special and I'm lucky to have you as my date," Vanessa suddenly said, her hand touching his shoulder as she leaned forward to plant a kiss on his cheek.

He didn't have a chance to react to such an unexpected treat. Someone bumped him from behind and his punch glass went flying into the air, the red-colored beverage nearly threatening to splash against Vanessa's dress. Adam reacted by pushing her out of the way, taking the brunt of the hit. Droplets of punch landed on his tuxedo jacket and shirt, the sugary juice settling in for a permanent stain.

"Oh, gee, did I do that . . . how clumsy of me."

Adam didn't even have to see the face to know the identity of who had slammed him.

"A simple accident, I'm sure," Adam said with more than a hint of sarcasm.

"Danny, get the hell away from us," Vanessa said.

He did nothing of the kind. He just stood there with a disgusting smile on his face, his arm wrapped tight around his date's waist. Lucy Walker's blond hair was teased and curly, her dress low and revealing. Her makeup was overdone, and Adam thought she looked awful, like Danny had found her on some street corner. Comparatively, Vanessa looked the very picture of class, a vision in red and purple. And in the moment, he got it, that Danny Stoker wasn't mad at Adam, or at Vanessa. He was angry with himself for being in this position in the first place; he'd overplayed his hand when Vanessa had rejected his advances. Adam had to believe Danny never envisioned attending this dance with anyone else. He was making trouble to lessen his own pain.

"You look nice, Nessa, really nice," Danny said.

"Hey," Lucy said, smacking him on his arm. "You barely said that to me!"

He ignored his date. "So, Nessa, you wanna dance?" Danny asked.

Adam watched Vanessa carefully, curious to see what she would do. Was this all she desired, to be suddenly respected by the boy she'd swooned over all through high school? He had a feeling deep down that she wanted to accept his invitation and be whisked onto the dance floor, with the crowd applauding the king and queen as crowns were placed ceremoniously upon their heads. He wondered if there was a bucket of pig's blood awaiting him.

"Danny, not if you were the last boy on earth," she said. "Adam, shall we dance?"

She took hold of his freshly sweaty palm. If she noticed, she didn't let it show, and Adam tightened his grip that much more to let her know he was with her, that he appreciated her act of loyalty. But before they could make their way to the dance floor, Adam felt a hard tug on his arm. He turned to find Danny right up in his face.

"Fifteen minutes," he whispered, so only Adam could hear. "The gym office. Prepare to die."

So the two couples had endured their juvenile confrontation, they'd gone to separate corners of the gym, Adam and Vanessa reuniting on the dance floor while Danny and Lucy disappeared into the dense crowd. As they danced, Vanessa tried to get Adam to tell her what Danny had said, but he refused to speak about it, not wanting to spoil any more of their evening. With their friends once again surrounding them, comfort again set in, and the dance continued, even when the band switched tempo and a slow dance began. For a split second, Adam and Vanessa stood without moving, unsure what to do next. But then he took her hand, and he moved her once, twice, a third time around the floor, feeling the music, feeling a rush of emotion accompanying their clumsy elegance. He cautiously avoided eye contact, concentrating instead on the motion and movement of their bodies, letting the language of dance speak the words they were afraid to give voice to. Time meant nothing suddenly, the song seemed both endless and like it had just begun, allowing the two near strangers the chance to connect on a level neither of them expected. Nothing could spoil this unexpected moment.

Except three large boys who walked out onto the dance floor and interrupted their dance. Danny's entourage, football players, linebackers. The same jerks from yesterday.

"Time's up, kid. You had your fun," one of them said.

"Danny's turn," the second offered.

The third kid just sniggered.

Vanessa did her best to intervene, protesting to leave them alone, all while pulling on Adam's arm to keep him from being dragged forward. Her efforts were fruitless, David had nothing on these dumb Goliaths; the weak would not prevail this time. As Adam found himself being led off, Vanessa followed behind, berating them, pleading that they let Adam go, her head swirling, looking for the useless chaperones. The music grew toward a crescendo, drowning out her requests. Danny's friends wouldn't have listened anyway, thugs that they were. Only their leader gave orders.

Adam was thrust inside the small office located at the edge of the gym. Sounds filled the air, grunts, laughter, dirty words whispered only in private. Though the lights were off, his eyes quickly adjusted to the darkness, and he could see two bodies entwined, one of them lying flat on the desk, legs splayed in the air. The other figure hovered above, holding the legs with his hands as he moved, bucked, thrust.

A light from behind suddenly shed illumination on the urgent sexual coupling of Danny Stoker and Lucy Walker, she lost amidst drunken passion, he staring straight ahead at Adam with a wide grin on his face. Adam realized this little show was being put on not just for his benefit, but for Vanessa . . . who stood behind him, her hand covering her mouth in disgust. Danny might be having his way with Lucy at this very second, but the message was more than clear—Danny was screwing with them all, most of all with Vanessa. With the three thugs standing guard on the other side of the door, Adam and Vanessa were trapped, laid witness to what was transpiring, and the only thing they could do was watch, wait, listen.

Adam wrapped Vanessa in his arms, shielding her eyes. She covered her ears, but Adam doubted that would accomplish much, given the vocal performances emanating from the couple on the desk. Finally, the cruel scene came to a finish, with Danny practically tossing Lucy aside as he told her to get cleaned up. "And then get out of here, I don't need you anymore." She retreated out of sight without arguing, like she was accustomed to being discarded.

"You're disgusting, Danny."

"Jealous, Nessa?"

"Don't talk to her, Danny. You got a problem with me, let's settle it. But how you could treat Vanessa this way . . . any girl . . . you're beyond contempt. If you even know what that means. And I realize this little show was for her benefit, not mine. You just used me to hurt her even more."

"Oh, the valiant new boyfriend, standing up for the girl he could never have."

Adam felt a certain power rising within some hidden part of himself. He wanted to rush him, sack the quarterback to the point where he'd never get up and his career would be over, and he'd have to live his life with only this one victory. But it wasn't to be, at least not coming from Adam. He'd hesitated too long.

Vanessa rushed forward unexpectedly, surprising both Adam and Danny. She landed a hard smack to Danny's smirking face, nearly knocking him to the floor. He stumbled back against the chair, and that's when she landed another blow, a fierce kick right to his groin. Danny doubled over in howling pain as this time he did drop. Adam watched as he vomited a spew of red; it was only the punch, laced with vodka. Man, she must have landed quite a blow.

She retreated, her breath coming fast and heavy.

"Vanessa . . ."

But she said nothing to Adam, just ran past him and back out into the dance, the crowd swallowing her up like she'd never existed. Adam realized he was still alone in the office with a doubled-over Danny Stoker, his goons still waiting on the outside. His feet moved forward until he hovered directly over the boy who had threatened his life, told him not to take Vanessa to the dance, who thought he could do anything he wanted. Adam knew this was his moment, control was on his side. Danny looked up at him, and Adam thought he detected fear in his eyes.

"You know, Danny. High school, they call it a microcosm of life. You know what that means? I know, I know, it's a big word but I think you're smart enough to figure it out. So, this little contained world of ours, it throws us all these big issues. Life and death, friendship, love, all played out on a stage where the players are too young and stupid to understand what they are doing. About how their actions affect other people. Some go through these tortured years being told by everyone that they're a loser and will never amount to anything. While others seem to be spun from gold, with the sun shining down on them every day, like they walk on water. They get the girl, they get the adulation. They can do no wrong, kings that they are. But in this moment, at a dance that represents the culmination of our high school lives, the tables have turned. Because I know that my life is just beginning, and the world is filled with possibility. I get to go out on the high note, with the pretty girl on my arm, able to walk with my head held high. For you, it's over. You've peaked. You're nothing but a fucking loser now. A fucking coward who treats women like objects. Look at you, lying on the floor in your own vomit, kicked in the balls by the best thing that ever happened to you. How the mighty have fallen."

"Fuck you," Danny said.

Adam couldn't help it, he laughed. "Clever, to the end."

And then Adam Blackburn walked out, confidently striding past the three thugs who were too busy looking at their fallen leader, still green and sickly, lying on the cold gym floor. The last thing Adam saw before he left the gymnasium, home to the "Forever Yours" Senior Prom, was three linebackers running far away from the brutal sacking. Game over. Season done.

Vanessa Massey, a flood of emotions running through her to the point she couldn't settle on one, felt like she wanted to vomit up that sugary punch also. Instead she ran out of the gym and opted for fresh, lake-scented air, the comforting, briny breeze seemingly helping her recover from the awful scene she'd witnessed inside the coaches' office. The sight of a nearly stripped-down Danny, forced to watch what he was doing with Lucy, to Lucy . . . it just sickened her. It cheapened what sex was supposed to be like between consenting partners, and for the first time since their breakup she was thankful she hadn't given in to his pressures. Was that how he would have treated her? She shuddered now at the thought of his touch . . .

With night encasing her in its warm breath, her senses heightened to the point she could still hear the pulsing music floating out from the prom, she felt a sudden graze of fingers against her shoulder. She nearly jumped out of her skin, turned wildly, her body ready for fight. Like Danny had come seeking revenge. She softened when she saw who stood at her side.

"Adam . . . God, you scared me."

"Sorry. You okay . . . I mean, I don't even know where to begin. Danny . . ."

"Don't say that name. Ever. Again."

"Okay. Whatever you want, you're the boss. This is your night."

"Not yours?"

"I wasn't even going to come."

"I think you're the smart one. Come on, let's just get out of here."

"You don't want to return to the dance?"

She wrapped her arms around herself, shook her head with sudden maturity, like she'd suddenly decided nothing mattered but tomorrow. "I've danced my last tango at Danton. The last four years of my life have been accentuated by everything that happened inside that building just now," she said, with more than a taste of venom spitting forth. "I think I'm finally over high school, classes and proms and lousy ex-boyfriends. Just hand me my diploma and let me get on that plane."

"Plane? Where are you going?"

"Not here," she said. "Drive us somewhere and I'll fill you in. You're not the only one planning to ditch this water-soaked town."

Adam and Vanessa, bonding suddenly over dreams neither of them had spoken of before, before they could ditch the town, ditched the remainder of the "Forever Yours" dance, with Adam aimlessly, silently driving his father's car on the black roads of Danton Hill. Vanessa just stared straight ahead through the darkened windshield, trying to force Danny Stoker from her mind. He kept creeping back in; she could hear him laugh, see his sneer. For a split second she gazed over at Adam, concentrating so hard on the driving he didn't even notice she'd turned her attention to him. He was so sweet and caring, so well meaning and tonight acting the perfect gentleman. An ideal prom date, the boy she'd ignored for forever. She felt a tear seep out; she didn't wipe it away. As her wet eyes settled back on the road, inspiration suddenly hit her.

"Go to Danton's Hill. To the water."

"Now. At this late hour?"

"No one from the school should be there yet, we'll be all alone. The gang was planning to rendezvous there later, you know, after the dance. For the real party."

Adam did as asked, turned off on the next road, doubling back toward the other end of town. They bypassed an old farmhouse, all dark against the moonlit night. At last they made the cutoff road that led toward Lake Ontario and the town's famed landmark. It was really just a grassy hill found at the edge of the Danton State Park, but back years ago the so-named Danton's Hill afforded visitors magnificent views of the lake on clear days, and on moonlit nights like tonight the stars twinkled down like golden confetti. People would wait for the ships to arrive back from their seafaring journeys, the mariners coming home to their families after months adrift. The drive took only a few minutes, and before long Adam had parked and Vanessa was already walking up the hill when he caught up beside her.

"Hey, what's the rush?"

"Sorry, Adam, guess I'm anxious. The more distance we put between that stupid dance and us the better. I'm sorry I dragged you into the mess that my life's become, and I'm sorry that Danny did what he did, and I'm sorry . . ."

"Hey, enough apologizing. Okay? I knew what I was getting myself into . . . well, sort of." He paused before speaking what was going through his brain. "Look, Vanessa, I don't know why things happened like they did—you and

Danny breaking up, your friends thinking I would be the perfect person to escort you to the dance, why you accepted . . . actually, why you ended up asking me when I felt you had rejected my offer. It was just a big mistake from the start, and now we're both paying the price. One more memory to add to our illustrious high school careers—and I'm not sure either of us can claim it as a high point. You especially, since you've had four years of high points. I've had—"

"Adam," she said, putting a finger to his lips. "Don't you ever get tired of putting yourself down?"

"Excuse me?"

"You're a nice guy, you're kinda cute, especially in that tux—it kind of transforms you and makes you look older. For you to take me to the prom like you did shows that you've got guts, character. You followed through on my impulse, which shows you've got integrity. That's a rare characteristic of someone any age, much less a teenager. I've seen the real Adam Blackburn buried beneath that façade of yours, and he's not the insecure, self-deprecating kid you portray him to be. So when are you going to start believing in yourself?"

"As soon as I have that diploma in my hands and Danton Hill is in my rearview mirror."

"Guess what, Adam? It's already in that mirror. The past, even the recent past, is where it belongs. You told me about Princeton, about how your future doesn't include Danton Hill or anyone who lives here. Even your parents are ready to pack it in and say good-bye. So, tonight, take your first step. Right here on Danton's Hill. Come on, take a look out on the water, it's a beautiful, clear night, and who knows how far you can see. I bet your eyes can gaze out beyond the lake, but your mind can reach even further. Your mind always can, because what it sees is limitless. Mine is halfway across the Atlantic already. I'm ready to seek out new ventures to other places—distant places, aren't you?"

Adam took a deep breath, whether to fill his lungs with the refreshing air blowing off the lake or from her words, words that inspired him and challenged him all at the same time. "Wow, no one has ever spoken to me like that before, not my so-called friends and certainly not my parents. I've said it to myself, but only inwardly, I know what I'm capable of. But I've never heard those words said aloud."

"And what does it make you want to do?"

"Recede."

"Why?"

"Because when you put my dreams into words, they somehow lose their power. What I want, is it really something I can hope to achieve? Can I run away from this dumb town and find the man hidden underneath this boyish frame? Am I running to something, or am I running from something? Right now, right here, with you, I just don't know anymore. These last two days, knowing you would be with me for that last rite of passage before graduation, I guess I started to think about what high school might have been if I'd been braver. Did I sell myself short? Do I really lack confidence? Did I let others box me in, only to close the lid myself? Did I willingly accept their labels? How is that strong? How is that knowing who you are?"

A brilliant flash of smile hit Vanessa's face, meant to soothe his doubts. "Adam, I've got one more place we can go to. The gang will be expecting us here, and right now they're the last people I want to see. In fact, other than you, there's not another soul on this planet I'd rather be with." She urged him forward. "Come on . . ."

Adam found himself transfixed by her alluring smile, and he allowed himself to be pulled forward. Down the far end of Danton's Hill they went, running first across the dewy grass to the sticky pink sand of the beach. Vanessa stopped, flipping off her heels, freeing her feet to dig into the cool sand. Adam did the same, leaving behind a trail of shoes and socks. Together the two of them ran far from the dance, far from high school and the memories they had made, intent on new ones that waited beyond the horizon. As they approached the lapping shore of the great lake, Vanessa pushed past a wooden sign situated before the long pier of rocks. MERCER'S POINT, it read, its letters faded, as though it were part of another time and place, a distant piece of some other life.

"Careful, Vanessa, those rocks can be sharp and slippery . . ."

Vanessa didn't seem to care. It was like she was dancing on the rocky pier, tiptoeing her way down its narrow length. Crashing waves washed up against either side, gently cooling the boulders with its foamy spray. Finally, she had edged her way toward the end of the long pier, with nothing between her and the lake and the faraway land on the other side. Vanessa was breathing hard, laughing like she hadn't all week. Releasing her pent-up emotions. Adam stood beside her, drawn to her energy. Like this place, where they were so alone and so together, had infused her spirit.

Then, there, on the very tip of Mercer's Point, nestled beneath the starry night with no one else around them, Vanessa Massey stared deep into Adam Blackburn's eyes, searching for the truth about life. What would she see in his blue eyes? How did he see the world, and would she recognize any of its destinations? Could Adam even reveal his dreams and open up his soul? She felt nervous tingles course throughout her body, a new but somehow comfortable connection between herself and the person before her. She felt overwhelmed, not in control of her actions. A raw power overwhelmed her, some larger force directing them toward each other. That's what she thought, so that's what made her do what she did. And what she did was lean forward to place a sweet kiss on Adam's mouth. An awkward kiss, where her top lip met his lower lip, a slight disconnection, not unlike how this night had come about, forced but in the end acceptable. Her kiss met his again, and this time they got it right, his touch and hers.

In the shadow of the moon, just one hundred yards from where the women of yesteryear once came to seek out the men who had promised to come home but oftentimes did not, Adam and Vanessa gave in to a moment neither could have predicted before this night had begun, but both willingly fed the night's passion. Hidden behind a large cropping of rocks, far from prying eyes, the music of the sea their guide, they kissed and they touched, they caressed and spoke no words because any words might spoil the blossoming moment between them.

At last their lips parted and only their wide eyes met. A fresh longing existed between them, the knowledge that waning childhoods had finally caught up to adulthood, and a decision loomed before them as to which of those entities they embraced. They were locked neither in the past nor the future. This moment was now, and only belonged to them. They touched again, her hand against his cheek, his fingers toying with hers, almost counting them, looking at perfection.

At last, Adam said, "I should probably take you home."

"I don't want to go home. Not now, and probably not ever."

"We both have plans beyond Danton Hill."

"That's why this place is perfect. It's a launching pad to tomorrow."

"Then why are we still thinking about the past, letting

school rule our decisions?" he said. "This is just about getting back at . . ."

"Don't say his name, please," she pleaded, desperation filling her voice. "Only we exist now. It's like time has stopped, like it's only you and me in this world. Mercer's Point and its launching pad to the sea has lifted us, taken us away from all we know, and what happens next only happens now." She paused, a hard lump caught in her throat. "Adam, I don't want to leave for Europe a girl. I want to fly away a woman."

"Vanessa . . ."

"It's one more rite of passage. It's necessary."

"But . . . you wouldn't . . . you know, with . . ."

"Because I knew it was wrong. Because I knew that with him, it wouldn't be special, it would be all about him and his pleasure and I would just . . . I'd barely be a part of it. You, on the other hand, Adam, you understand the universe, how it works, why things happen, why certain connections exist between certain people. That's us. That's us . . . right now. Let's take our last night as kids and grow up together. Adam, right here and now, let's stop questioning everything. I need to feel love, and I know, even in this briefest of moments, you'll indulge me."

"Vanessa, this is crazy . . . just the other day we barely spoke to each other."

"Like I said, the universe had other plans for us," she said. "This place, out on this rocky pier, I would always crawl out here when the rest of my friends were swimming. I never really took to the water—don't get me wrong, I loved its motion, but I also respected its power. So I would come here to the edge of Mercer's Point and watch. But secretly, I'd be wishing to be somewhere else. It's my own private place."

He leaned forward, he kissed her. She kissed him back.

"And now I'm here with you."

"Yes, you are. And it feels right, my sharing it with you."

And then they did as the night dictated, silhouetting their shadows with moonlight that seeped through darkened clouds. They undressed, and they touched, they felt and they explored, and finally, ultimately, she opened herself to him, and he pushed all thoughts from his mind as emotion won the night's battle, their hearts parting ways with the rational. It was wonderful and incredible, even ridiculous as he fished into his wallet for the condom that had dented a ring into the leather from years of carrying it, years of not requiring use.

He gazed at her.

She gazed back, gave a silent nod.

Passion rode the wind that night, gave its cry an echoing finish. When at last they were satiated, a deep realization set in. About what they had done, whom they had done such a thing with. But they only managed to smile at each other, kiss each other. Regrets had no place out here on this rocky shore, those would come later, when neither were a part of the other's life and the implications of their actions grew clearer. For now, they dressed as they realized the dance must have ended and the seniors would soon begin to invade Danton's Hill in droves, ready to continue the party without benefit of teachers and chaperones.

They agreed to stay behind was out of the question. They left Mercer's Point avoiding detection by bypassing the gang, Adam driving her home. In the gravelly driveway where he had picked her up just hours ago, they parted as friends, as onetime lovers who dared never speak of what had transpired between them. They were ready for the future, to move beyond the simple existence of high school life and the world they knew as Danton Hill. By car or by plane, their paths would never again cross. Separate ways they would go, it's how it was meant to be, with neither speaking a word about one day reuniting.

"Good-bye, Vanessa."

"Good-bye, Adam. And good luck. I know you'll be a huge success."

"And you . . . you can be anything you want to be. See the world, find yourself."

The night of the Forever Yours dance ended with the two of them merely smiling at each other, Vanessa beneath the glow of the porch light of her childhood home, Adam leaning against his father's wheels, shaded in the dark. One last connection to the past held them before each sought out their futures, alone. Moments later, he hopped in behind the wheel and the car pulled out of the driveway, its rear taillights disappearing around the bend, car and driver mutually gone from Vanessa's life.

She sat on the steps of the porch, not sure what to think about, who to think about.

That decision was made for her.

Danny Stoker, disheveled, emerged from the darkness, into her light.

"What are you doing here?"

"How was he?"

"Danny, don't be gross. Though I have to admit, it's something you're good at."

He grinned lasciviously, like a man unsatisfied with his earlier encounter. "That's not all I'm good at, not that you'd know. So, what's so special about that loser Adam Blackburn? You give to him what you wouldn't give to me?"

"You were watching us?"

"Gotcha!"

Vanessa stood, attempting to gain access to her house. The door was locked and the keys were inside her closed purse. Not enough time to grab them before Danny was on her, his beer-fueled breath invasive against her skin.

"Don't touch me," she said. "I'll scream. My parents are right upstairs."

"Oh, I'm not going to do anything to you. You proved you didn't want me and that these years meant nothing. If you can live with your decision to go out a loser, so can I. But can you honestly say you're happy? Is this how you want to end it? Us, high school?"

"I don't even know you anymore."

"I doubt you ever did."

"Good-bye, Danny."

"Good-bye to you, bitch."

Vanessa swung at him, her fist connecting with his face. She watched as Danny's head swung upward from the impact, watched as he drunkenly lost his balance. He fell back against the decorative rocks that lined the path to her mother's rose garden. He didn't hit his head, but she heard him cry out with pain. A scrape appeared on his arms, a trace of blood bubbling out of the wound.

"You're nothing but a bastard. Evil, that's what you are. You'll never make anything of yourself, Danny Stoker. The next time I see you, I hope it's at your funeral."

He grinned, showing a line of perfect white teeth, highlighting his dark good looks. He was at the height of his power, still the undisputed king of Danton Hill High School. "Fine by me. That means I can haunt you forever," he said.

That's when he departed, disappearing into the shadows from where he'd emerged. And that's when Vanessa Massey realized she was truly all alone, and not just on her front porch. Her parents might be upstairs, but they wouldn't understand. Her friends were enjoying the after party up on Danton's Hill, at Mercer's Point. And Adam Blackburn and their night together were already starting to fade from her memories. She'd used him for sure, that much she knew, and it left her with an empty hole in her gut. There was not one person she could turn to, no one who understood anything anymore about the girl named Vanessa Massey. The woman, she reminded herself. She was a woman now.

Ten days later, as the plane lifted off the ground, Vanessa breathed a sigh of relief.

She had escaped, with no one privy to the secret she took with her.

Because she wasn't alone on that flight.

CHAPTER 16

NOW

Vanessa's surprising revelation hung between them, seemingly trapped by its own admission.

"What do you mean, you weren't alone? Who went with you?"

She didn't answer, not immediately.

They remained still, sitting across from one another on the porch as another batch of dark clouds rumbled across the sky. The chill in the air had deepened, or perhaps it was the result of the shifting mood, chill gone to frost over her freshly revealed betrayal.

"Vanessa, did you hear me?"

"Yes, Adam, I did," she said, looking away, her face stricken. "I'm sorry, even now this is still so difficult for me to discuss. Aside from Reva, I've never told another soul."

Adam leaned forward, searching her eyes, trying his best to understand her. He pictured the scene after he left her alone in the driveway to be confronted by Danny. She'd rejected him, but at some point must have changed her mind. That important detail she'd left out. So now he was left with the image of her and that jerk together. After what she and

Adam had shared that night, just to toss away their connection with such cavalier disregard. "Why would you do that, put yourself though such an ordeal? I mean . . . after he treated you so horribly, why you would take him with you on your trip? How is that escaping?" At first he couldn't bring himself to say the name, and then finally he did. "Danny Stoker went with you to Europe."

She couldn't help it, she laughed deeply, the sound throaty and guttural in the dark night. Hers was a laugh tinged with both irony and regret and maybe even a bit of revulsion. "No, no, Adam . . . that's not what I said. That night on my porch, after the dance, what I told Danny I meant and I fulfilled it. I never saw him again, not until he was lying inside his open casket, nine years later. There is no way in hell I would have allowed him to travel with me, if he even had the desire to leave. Danny was a Danton Hill boy through and through, so much so I doubt he ever went any further than Rochester."

"So, then I don't get it. Who accompanied you to Europe?"

"Wow, for such a smart guy, you're playing it awfully dumb."

"Vanessa, I think you just need to spell it out for me."

She paused, searching for words that would not doubt pierce, but hurt him the least. If such words even existed. He obviously needed it spelled out, and perhaps she needn't be so coy. She needed to say it aloud too, directly to his face. She reached out, gently taking hold of his strong hands, caressing them, as if seeking safety from the heat they gave off, a contrast to the chill surrounding them. "Adam, here's the truth. When I left Danton Hill, I was pregnant."

"Pregnant." He said the word, heard how foreign it sounded on his tongue and in the air between them.

"Yeah, how about that," she said, letting out a deep breath. "I had company on the flight, but it's not like I had to buy an extra seat."

Realization dawned on him like waves of water, like sheeting rain assaulting his body. It awakened him, doused the fuzziness inside his brain and shook him to his very core. Finally he felt the unsettled chill of the night that had so far evaded him. That cold had previously only seemed to live inside her. He struggled to find the right words and finally said, each word laced with hesitation, "The baby . . . was mine?"

"No one else's."

"Oh, oh . . . wow . . ."

"Yeah, that was kind of my reaction, except back then I was just some dumb high school graduate who was headed to Europe for a year before coming back for college. Let's see, my ex-boyfriend had proved to be a total jerk, and I was pregnant thanks to an impulsive decision and I guess one really old condom. That night on Mercer's Point, we—Adam Blackburn and Vanessa Massey—made a baby, created a life. And I know how shocked you must be right now—Adam, it's okay, whatever you're feeling, I'll understand. If you want to run, like I did, like I always do . . . I've had twenty years to process this fact and you, you're hearing it for the first time all these years later. But whatever you're feeling, please don't hate me, because right now I know I couldn't handle that. Right now I need your understanding and . . ."

"The baby. What happened to . . . ?"

"Her," she said, softness in her voice.

"Her, right. Wow, her . . ." Adam repeated, his voice just as soft and wistful as a summer breeze. "Where is she?"

"Adam," Vanessa said, holding his hands still, squeezing

them as though to make the two of them one, to share together the sad truth of yesteryear. "She didn't live."

He visibly blanched, like his body had suffered a small
stroke. A child had been given to him and just as quickly
had been torn away from his embrace. His mind couldn't
absorb all she had revealed. But he had to know more. He
had to know every damn truth that lay deep inside her.
Every detail. "You miscarried? Like you did later, with Dominick's baby?"

Vanessa, tears forming in the corners of her eyes, shook
her head. "Not that time, no. I carried her to term, went
through childbirth, the whole awful, screaming deal."

"You went through this alone?"

Again, she nodded. This time she wiped away the tears,
wiped away the memory.

"In a hospital in London. To this day, Reva is the only
person I ever told the whole story to. Not Dominick, not
my parents, and not my friends, and certainly I couldn't tell
you . . ."

"Why not?"

"Oh Adam," she said, hands cupping his face, absently
scratching at the dark stubble on his chin. "Let's not do this
right now, these questions and answers. If you really think
about it, you'll know that I couldn't do that to you. You'd already left Danton Hill by the time I found out weeks later,
you'd taken your first step toward your future. You were
summering in Princeton, you'd been given your one chance
to escape the world that was Danton Hill High—how could
I spoil your dream with news that I was having a baby? We
barely knew each other; we certainly didn't love each other.
We were young and stupid and that night I wasn't making
the most informed decisions. We let one night of teenage
drama transform us into the adults we weren't ready to be,

and the result was something . . . someone neither of us was prepared for. There was no magic that night on Mercer's Point, it was just two dumb kids angry at the world. A cruel twist of fate, made even crueler by the fact that she didn't live beyond her birth."

"Can I ask, did you get to hold her?"

"Hold her, yes, I got to hold her, briefly. Feed her, no. She just lay so silent in my arms, an angel in every sense of the word. I touched heaven when I touched her. I never felt closer to another person, and I still never have."

"You named her, of course?"

She nodded, this time with a smile. "Yes. Elizabeth Grace."

Adam could find no more words, ask no more questions. In his mind he pictured a very young, lost, and innocent Vanessa Massey, alone and scared in a foreign country, dealing with the complications of a teenage pregnancy she'd endured by herself. Giving birth, crying out in the hospital room when she began to realize that all was not right with the baby, with the birth. He could picture her holding the still form, envisioning endless tears as she embraced a baby who would never smile, never cry, never find laughter in the simplest of things.

At last, he said, "Elizabeth Grace. That's the most beautiful name ever."

"Adam . . . I'm sorry," she said, still stroking his cheek. She leaned in, and despite the tears that still fell from her eyes, from his, she kissed him gently, tenderly. It was the last thing he wanted, but he knew he couldn't reject her, not during such an intimate exchange. He responded in kind, grateful for the sweet gesture, the offer of comfort. The connection they'd forged earlier still existed between them. What had happened today had served to strengthen a bond that kept them tethered, even if neither had known about why it was happening. Now, with the unexpected news of lovely Elizabeth Grace's existence, they were forever linked. By life and by death, by tragedy, and yes, by grace.

"So, what happens next?" he asked.

"I don't understand, what are you asking?"

"All day, it's been one trip down memory lane after another. We can't keep dwelling on the past . . . eventually tomorrow will come, and with its arrival all of our secrets will be laid bare. Think about it. We've reminisced, we've remembered. We've had our reunion, unlikely as it is, and like all such events, they end with promises made and seldom kept, we just move on. We go back to our own lives and tuck these memories in some place we don't need ready access to. If not for the car accident, our day here, would you have ever told me about the baby? Would we even have had time to talk amidst the swirl of classmates to finally get to know one another? Would we have explored the possibility that our encounters—both at Mercer Point and in New York, that they really did mean something beyond foolish youth or being drunk? Maybe the world was telling us something that neither of us was ready to hear."

"What's this—more of your past-life stuff, Adam? Destiny?"

"No, that's just ridiculous speculation. I can't explain why this is happening."

"I can. It's why I came back. Why I wanted to go to the reunion."

"To tell me all of this?"

She nodded.

"But how could you be assured I'd be there?"

"I couldn't be. I just knew I had to try."

"See, destiny at work again."

"Adam, you've really got to stop with all this crazy talk," she said, looking suddenly to the sky, as if seeking from hidden stars some kind of acknowledgment. Life didn't work the way Adam implied, it held no magic other than the kind you conjured inside yourself. Drive, energy, ambition, power, the world fed off of you, not the other way around. But the sky provided neither agreement nor disagreement, leaving only darkness swirling all around them, cocooned beneath clouds. Like the world had trapped them in this farmhouse, allowing no other soul able to sneak through. It was only the two of them, and at last there lay no further secrets. The past existed where it should, buried inside them.

"Vanessa, do you believe in second chances?"

"Second chances? How about third? Four . . . what does it matter? We make mistakes, we have to move on from them or they'll define us . . . consume us. So, no, I don't believe in second chances. What I know is that I betrayed you—betrayed your faith in me, in myself as well. I'll heal, because I always do. Or at least, that's what I tell myself. What about you? Have I just given, then taken away, something you always wanted?"

She got up from the porch, pacing back and forth, her words more directed at the universe than at Adam. Still, he felt the brunt, he absorbed them as he listened.

"Who knows, maybe my entire life has just been about hiding—hiding from real truths, from fabrication, from what could have been and what might have been. Things happen in life, sometimes awful things, and you just have to move on. When you start to think in absolutes—or worse, in hope—you're set up for nothing but disappointment. I don't get why you're still being so nice to me. I don't deserve it. You should be screaming at me, telling me how much I screwed up your life. That stupid prom, why did people think it was so important? Like your world would crumble if no one asked you and you stayed home. Sometimes disappointment is a good thing, it's the kind of thing that makes you stronger. Adam, I took a part of you away, and worse still—I didn't even give you a choice in the matter. I made up your mind for you . . . about the baby. I set you free when you didn't even know you were trapped. You should hate me, and instead you're . . . what? Reminding me of Valentine's Day cards you left for me? Finding wine bottles that don't exist, only to seduce me beside a roaring fire? Make up your mind—which deity do you want to be? Cupid? Sling your arrow at me and I fall prey to your charms? Or maybe you're Apollo, waiting for the sun to come out so you can take me for a ride on your chariot. Show me the world from Mount Olympus? Myths, that's all they are. I'm mortal, an imperfect being. There's nothing special inside this body, no power to take us beyond today, just one crazy, mixed-up mess. Happy fucking twentieth reunion."

Adam still said nothing. He wasn't convinced she was finished, but the way she had just punched the column of the porch, he gazed upward to make sure the structure wasn't going to collapse on them. Just then Vanessa turned to him, eyeing him with newfound suspicion. She couldn't find another word to say, though. Adam was convinced she'd used them all up.

"You done?" he asked.

"I . . ." she said, seemingly wanting to vent still but realizing the futility of the situation. Was she even angry at him—for being nice, for understanding? Or was she finally just letting it all out, the emotions and the frustrations and the failed dreams, railing at the world for its cruel twists and unfair turns? At last, she let out the deepest breath, and rather than the porch dropping on them, Vanessa did, plopping onto the wood boards with exhaustion.

"Yeah, I'm done."

"Good. Can we focus on what's important now?"

"Which is what?"

"Us. Now. There's nothing we can do about the past, and at the moment we don't seem to be able to do much of anything about the future. All that exists is this moment. So why not try and make the best of it."

"Adam, what are you getting at? Where is this going? What is 'the best'?"

"Everything is out in the open—at least, I think so."

She nodded. "No more secrets."

"Good. So let's just take the rest of this rare time-out and enjoy ourselves. I don't know about you, but I can wait for whatever morning brings. I'll take this night every night. I'll take tonight right now." He paused to stare directly into her emerald eyes; he thought he could see his reflection in her irises. No, more than just his body, he thought he could see the elusive thing called a soul and it was staring back at him, letting him know how right the time was. "Let me take you upstairs. I want to be with you, fully, completely . . . it's time that we . . ."

She put a lone finger to his expressive lips, silencing them. "Time that we made love? That we truly shared ourselves, finally free from the past?"

"You read my mind."

"You opened yourself to me. I get it, Adam. I get you."

"You need to get us."

He took her hand as he rose from his seat on the porch. With one easy motion he brought her close against his body. He felt the heat melt their bodies. He kissed her hard as he embraced her. All around them the night came alive, streaks of moonlight suddenly peeking from behind those persistent storm clouds, the chirping of crickets filling the air with their endless song, the wind answering back with its own swirling effects. They held each other as time stood still. The world was theirs and only theirs.

Adam began to lead her back inside when suddenly her arms enveloped herself.

"What's wrong?"

"I'm cold."

"I'll keep you warm, that's a promise."

"No, no, you don't understand. Adam, this chill, it's been with me all day. Even with the fireplace blazing and the hot shower, the fainting spell I experienced inside the cupola, our dash through the cornfields where I was nearly sweating, all of this warmth and still I haven't shaken the cold I've felt since the accident. Why? What's wrong with me?"

"I'm no doctor, but maybe it's a mild case of shock. Not just from the accident, but from all the secrets you've had bottled up inside you," he said. "You've released them. So now come to bed, let the covers, let me . . . chase the cold night away. Together we'll find warmth before the morning sun provides it."

"You're quite the romantic, Adam Blackburn."

"You're quite the reason to be, Vanessa Massey."

He opened the screen door, escorting her inside. They paused at the base of the stairs, looking upward. Like this was one final climb, one last obstacle.

"I feel weird. It's not our house, not our bedroom."

Adam shook his head. "For tonight, this house is our home. Perhaps it's where we would have lived, you and me and Elizabeth Grace, had life worked out differently. We might have been happy here, instead of spending our entire lives running from truth, seeking out something we never ultimately wanted. And I'm not talking about regrets, because those are for fools. Our lives have happened as they have because that's how it was meant to be. Our friend out there, Mr. Aidan Barton, I think he would approve. He's been very giving so far today, letting us use his house to finally realize the connection that exists between us." He paused, his hand caressing her cheek. "Tonight is meant to be as well. So come upstairs—to our bed, where we'll exist on our own plane and in our own time."

"Adam Blackburn?"

"Uh-oh, I sense hesitancy in your voice."

She nodded. "Right now, as much as I'd follow you to the edge of the earth and probably beyond . . . I think we're forgetting one thing. But you have only yourself to blame, you brought him up and reminded me—about Aidan Barton. Remember when I said that you both shared the same initials? Well, I'm curious about something that until just now had eluded me."

"What's that?"

"The name Venture."

"The name on the letters."

"Venture. Vanessa. Don't you get it? She had the same first initial as me," she said. "So it's got me thinking. What's Venture's last name?"

The crackle of wood from the fire lit orange sparks against the walls, illuminating their faces upon the walls. The illusion was powerful, as though they were no longer two but four, the shadows having moved in to be with the people inside the house.

"The letters," Vanessa said. "We forgot all about the letters."

Adam looked at her and she stared right back.

They were on the same page, and soon would be reading the same pages.

And the race was back on, this time the two of them chasing each other up to the cupola. The shadows followed, curious also to learn the decades-old secrets awaiting to be unsealed.

*   *   *

Feeling already like intruders inside this house, what they were about to do seemed like an even deeper betrayal, a violation of an implied trust. They had eaten the food and drank the wine, they'd showered, worn their clothes. All because it was available to them and fed their needs. But now, just because they had stumbled upon the old trunk filled with unread letters, did that give them permission to open them? The contents of the unread letters were none of their business, so why then was Vanessa sitting on the edge of the top step of the cupola, watching with anticipation as Adam approached the letters with nothing short of determination. He lifted the lid of the old trunk, a discernable squeak filling the space of the small room.

"Ready?" he asked.

"I'm not sure."

He looked at her, a knowing look on his face. He felt it too. The sense that they were overstepping their bounds. But he then looked back at the letters as momentary indecision hung in the thick air. "You give the word and I can seal this old trunk up again, and we can return downstairs and forget we ever found it. We can let Aidan's secrets stay buried for another day, for another person to find them."

That was the practical thing to do. But nothing about this day fit that description. They had gone with a flow as natural as that found on the lake, questioning their predicament but not understanding it. And so it was with the trunk, the letters. They had to go for it, there was no turning back now. "No, I think we're supposed to read them."

Adam nodded. "I agree. Okay, so no more delays."

From inside the trunk he withdrew a bundle of letters and handed them over to Vanessa. They were from the top of the pile, the most recent.

"Go ahead, you first," he said.

Swallowing hard, Vanessa ran a finger across the thick parchment of the envelope before pulling at the red ribbon that held them intact, releasing the letters to the floor in a fanlike display. Spread before her, she noticed they were all of the same quality of stationery, the same word . . . name . . . written across the middle in the same script. *Venture*, they stated, all with an underlined flourish. Vanessa looked up for confirmation from Adam that they were indeed going ahead with this. His eyes said it all, he was eager to know the contents, and she had to imagine that her eyes spoke the same language.

"Here goes," she said.

She took hold of the top letter, turning it over to reveal flaps perfectly sealed. Sliding a nail underneath, she moved slowly across the length of the envelope, not wanting to tear it to shreds. A letter opener would have been easier. But at last the flap lifted, revealing two sheets of paper inside. She unfolded them to reveal the same flowing script that adorned the front of each envelope. Aidan had used some kind of quill pen, the ink jet-black, his handwriting strong and de-termined, yet with the natural flow of a true romantic. She cleared her throat, and began to read.

"My dearest Venture . . ."

The letter took just minutes to read, and as the words fil-tered into the room, filling it, all of nature grew quiet, the reverence clear. Aidan's story to his "dearest" Venture was simple and profound, but his love for her was unmistakable, unmatched. He claimed this was his last letter to her, know-ing the end was near for him. He spoke of the day in which the sea had claimed her, and how he had spent the remain-der of his life devoted to her memory, never once forgetting her. He was confident of being reunited with her, if not today or tomorrow but someday.

"My God, Adam, he was so earnest. So certain."

"That's love. That's faith."

"To think, he spent years—his whole life—writing these letters to her, ending with this one where he believed they were to be reunited in death. How he must have felt, how his emotions must have overtaken him. Look at the date at the top of this final letter, August 18th. Written the day before he died. And the determination behind his words, he knew he was going to die, yet he remained unafraid."

Silence descended upon them as Vanessa thought of what that day must have been like. The old man at his writing desk, his hand wobbly from age but somehow resilient when the time came to jot down his final thoughts to Venture. When she looked up, she noticed that Adam had gotten up from the floor and was now peering out the window. No doubt at Aidan's grave down below.

"Adam, what a privilege this is, finding these letters."

She saw him nod gently toward Aidan's grave. A touch of respect, an acknowledgment that his stories, his dreams . . . they were safe in their hands. "If you don't mind, sir, we'd like to know more about you, and about Venture, and about what you meant to each other."

The wind gave up no hint of objection to his request, and the single bulb illuminating the cupola remained lit. Nature was quiet, power on their side. Vanessa retrieved another letter from the pile, again gently opening its seal. She read silently this time before opening the next, again reading Aidan's expressive words to herself. Adam did not interrupt, waiting patiently for Vanessa. At last, after having read through seven letters, she set them down, a stack of loving remembrances. She gazed up.

"Every letter begins with the same greeting: 'My dearest Venture . . .' But Adam, it's how Aidan signed off, his salutation. It's either a strange coincidence, or it's just . . . I don't know—freaky?"

"We've done freaky today. What's one more instance? What does it say?"

"Forever yours."

Even after a day filled with strange moments and situations neither could explain, this had to be chief among the coincidences. She watched as visible surprise formed on his dry lips. Sitting down beside her, Adam picked up one letter, then another, not because he didn't believe her but because he had to see them for himself. She was right, each letter ended with the phrase "Forever Yours."

"The prom," he said.

"That was our theme. It was called the Forever Yours Senior Ball."

"Well, it's not completely unlikely. It's not exactly an uncommon phrase . . ."

"Adam, you don't get it. The theme—that so-called common phrase? You know who came up with it? It was me. I was on the prom committee, and we all had to submit ideas for the theme. I remember the phrase coming to me in a dream the night after my friends and I spent the day up at the lake. The memory is strong—the water was fierce that day, with strong waves hitting the shore, and it got me thinking. Humans have only a limited time on this earth, but the water . . . the lake, nature, all that surrounds it, it's for forever. If only we could experience such a thing as forever, that's what I thought. Isn't what love is supposed to be, a connection that can't be broken? That's how the theme came about. I proposed it the next day and everyone agreed immediately that it was the ideal sentiment. And now here we are, twenty years later, two people who had no business together attending a prom called Forever Yours, reunited and discovering these letters . . ."

"Meant to be," he said.

"Or maybe your silly theory isn't so silly."

"What? That I'm really the living soul of Aidan Barton? And you're Venture . . ."

"Venture who? We still haven't learned her last name."

"You think her last name begins with an *M?*"

"Don't you?" she asked.

"Yeah, at this point, I can't imagine the alphabet even having twenty-five other letters."

"Speaking of more letters. I'm sure we'll find her name in the letter somewhere. But where do we start? There are hundreds of letters, Adam, he wrote one every week, and he lived for so much longer than Venture."

"Easy solution," he said. "The first one."

The moment became a mad scramble with both Vanessa and Adam making their way back to the truth-baring trunk. Adam held the lid up against the wall while Vanessa systematically removed bundle after bundle, setting them on the floor in neat piles. At last she came to the bottom stack, the envelopes appearing to be surprisingly well preserved. They were nearly one hundred years old, they had to be, and yet they were perfectly kept inside the closed air of the trunk. Only the red ribbon wrapped around the stack had frayed, and it easily fell apart at her touch. She left most of the letters of that first stack in the trunk, only the one on the bottom interested her. Because, of course, it was the very first one Aidan wrote.

"Found it!" she exclaimed.

"I can only imagine what it has to say . . . actually, I can't. Who knows what Aidan was feeling when he first started writing the letters? Was he sad, or angry?"

She thrust the envelope his way. "Only one way to find out—you read it. Adam, if we're supposed to believe this wild story that you are somehow Aidan Barton's soul come back from his resting place, then it's appropriate that you give voice to his words. I'll listen, just as he intended. The letters were meant for me . . . for Venture."

"A little playacting, huh?"

"Or maybe just something we're supposed to do."

"Now who's going overboard with this reincarnation stuff?"

"Adam."

"Yes?"

"Read the letter."

He took her advice, settling onto the floor with the letter in his hand. Vanessa sat against the wall just below the window; she could see a streak of moonlight slip through the window, its beam creating a shadow effect on Adam's face. She thought she could detect fresh lines on his face, the weathered features of a man who lived his life on the rough-hewn sea. Aidan Barton himself had returned to this land, or so she fantasized, and he was at last going to read aloud one of his letters, and its intended was finally sitting beside him, ready, eager, to listen.

"'My dearest Venture,'" Adam said, his voice soft and somber, appropriate to the mood they'd created inside the cupola, perfect for the remembrances that emanated all around them. A setting and scenario just as Aidan might have wished for. These were letters of love, and on their pages were words expressed, sealed so long ago, finally about to be spoken.

And so he began . . .

"I have come home from my nine months' journey to the great seas of this world. It was at times a treacherous journey, laced with danger, crackling with fear. Lake Ontario can be a calm body, but once we entered the St. Lawrence Seaway and ventured onward toward the mighty Atlantic, wild winds and storms were our

near-constant companions. *What kept me going through those rough nights, when it felt almost like the sea would claim our sturdy ship, was the thought of you waiting back in Danton Hill for me. I would think about our secret signal, the third flash of light given upon our return, meant only for you. I knew the day we returned you would see it, you would know that our life together was soon to begin.*

"Life had other plans. Ironically, it wasn't the sea that took me. It took you. And so I am left with a desolate world without you. But forget you I cannot, and will not. In this letter I commit a promise to you that you will remain in my heart, for as long as I live and beyond, till the moment when the universe sees fit to right this wrong and return us to each other.

"There is a secret I must tell you. Days after the sea claimed you, I returned to the shores of the lake, perhaps for the first time afraid of its power. The life of a seaman always comes with risk, and of course you learn quickly to respect the place that provides your livelihood. But never had I dreamed it would betray me in such cruel fashion, taking from me the one person whom I valued far beyond my own life. You, my irrepressible, wild-eyed Venture. You never met a challenge you couldn't handle—until that day. Oh, how your mother railed against the world, against God, when she lost you. She remained that way the rest of her life, despite my efforts in comforting her. 'Elizabeth,' I would tell her, 'we knew our Venture was only truly happy when being defiant, when she followed only her heart and nothing else. She was stubborn, yes, but she was true to herself and to all who had the honor to know her.'

"I will look after your mother, I promise you that. But I will honor your memory also. Though I'm sure you know this somehow, wherever you are, I'll tell you anyway. I came to visit you days after the lake had taken you. On the shore, the lake was calm and the sun was brilliant. The kind of day considered a gift from nature. I crouched at the shore, my feet feeling the cold tendrils of

the water as I thought about you, about us, and all that we missed out on. And then the strangest of things occurred. Several feet out in the water I noticed something floating atop the gentle waves, and I waded out to the point where I could retrieve it. Imagine my surprise when my hands took hold of your dress, the beautiful violet-colored dress with the red flowers, the one you'd worn for the town social and that drew my eye. That was the day I saw you for the first time as a woman, all grown, and I knew then you would be the love of my life.

"You did not come back to me that day on the shore, but in the days afterward, you did. It was a message from beyond, a world I could not understand until I was a part of it. So I vowed that day that I would keep secret the return of your dress. It was meant for me. I have wrapped the dress in protective packaging, and I will keep it with these letters, and one day you will read my words and once again the dress will adorn your lovely, lithe self, and at last my Venture will be returned to me.

"Until then, know that I will not forget you, and neither will your home of Danton Hill. It too lost a true spirit that day, and starting tomorrow you will live forever in the hearts and minds of the villagers. A memorial service will be held for you, and it will take place lakeside. We will speak of your love, your reverence, your love of us, your indomitable spirit. And then we will dedicate the rocky pier that you so loved, and which ultimately claimed you, in your memory. From tomorrow until forever, it will be known as Mercer's Point.

"My dear Venture Mercer. You lived with such energy, with such vitality. But yet also with such gentle, effervescent grace. I will tell you one more secret. Had we been blessed with a child, which was to have been her name. Grace. You would probably object, wanting her to be called Wild or Willful or Fierce, all adjectives that describe you. But a child born of the two of us, she would be unique, nothing short of the very notion of grace.

"Until the next letter, my Venture, I remain . . .
"Forever Yours," Adam concluded.

Neither knew what to say, and perhaps their silence was best. Leaving Aidan's perfect words to linger long within the heat of the cupola was almost ideal, the weight of the humidity the only thing able to hold the power of those words. Vanessa wiped away a tear, and Adam sat in a state of shock. There were far too many coincidences here, far too much that linked Vanessa and Adam with Venture and Aidan, with such eerie notions leaving an ominous feeling hovering between them. Time once again meant nothing, and when finally they spoke they couldn't say how many minutes had passed.

"Mercer," Vanessa said, her voice barely above a whisper. "Her name was Mercer."

"As in Mercer's Point."

"Do you understand what that means, Adam? For us?"

"It's where you took me. Took us—after the prom."

"It's where Elizabeth Grace was conceived."

"Elizabeth. She was Venture's mother."

"Grace would have been the child of Aidan and Venture."

Again, an unsettling silence grew, the implications of such revelations chilling. They had set out to learn Venture's surname and learned it they had, but what came with such knowledge was more than they had bargained for. If the day hadn't already been filled with strange twists, with secrets revealed, Vanessa might be running once again far from the farmhouse, deep into the cornstalks and back into the relative safety of her damaged, rain-soaked car. Was this otherworldly experience really happening, or was it fantasy being fueled by wild imagination? Instead of running, this time Vanessa remained inside the cupola, chilled still while encased in this world of consuming secrets. A participant to a past unleashed.

Just then she seemed to come out of her funk, a further fact washing over her. "Adam, in his letter Aidan mentioned something about a dress—the one that washed ashore. He supposedly left it inside the trunk, but I don't remember anything but letters."

"Well, let's look again, now that we know what to look for."

Back beside the trunk, Adam again lifted the lid and the two of them peered inside. What they saw was what they had seen earlier, bundle after bundle of letters, their accompanying red ribbons like a series of snakes squirming from the exposed light. There was nothing else to be found. The trunk stared back at them, challenging them to learn its final secret.

"The lid! Adam, it kept closing, when probably it should have just sprung open. Maybe there's a hidden panel or . . . I don't know. Just look!"

"Okay, okay . . ." He did as she suggested, lifting the lid even higher above them, letting more light reveal what lay underneath. And there, secured among frayed black straps, was a brown paper sack. "You mean that?"

Vanessa reached in, gently sliding the package from its constraints and into the safety of her arms. The brown paper was faded, the adhesive around its edges long since dried out. It only took a small effort on Vanessa's part for the tape to give way, the paper opening. Silently Vanessa hoped the air wouldn't damage what was inside the long-secure package. She would hate for Venture's prized dress, which had been through so much and had waited so long to see new light, to be destroyed from its exposure to the elements. But, as Vanessa pushed back the brown paper, she held her breath at the lovely sight before her. Yes, the material was old, its edges frayed and delicate. But what held her attention, what caught her breath in her throat and stopped her heart if only for a moment, was perhaps the most surprising moment in a day filled with surprises.

"Adam . . ." she said, unable to come up with any more words.

"I see it. I know."

"It's my dress," she said finally, her fingers touching the soft lace around the edges. "I mean, it's not an exact match, but the pattern . . . the colors. Look at them. Violet, or maybe purple originally. The color has obviously faded from time, but that floral pattern. Red, like the ribbons wrapped around the letters. The flower in my hair."

"The corsage I bought for you."

Vanessa's head turned to him, eyes afire. "My God . . . it's like you knew. Like it was all meant to be. Danny betraying me just days before the prom, my friends urging you to ask me. I didn't want to go with you and I had told myself I would say no to you—to anyone—and perhaps if it had been someone other than you asking I would have said no. Life handed me a curve at the end of high school, and I had to decide if I was going to act like a spoiled girl and not go, or grow up and enjoy one of those rites of passage kids are supposed to go through." She paused, again fingering the soft fabric of the dress. "Venture's spirit has never been quieted. She never got a proper good-bye, and the fact that Aidan held on to her memory his whole life, it's like she was denied eternal rest. Has she been restlessly wandering the shores of Danton Hill all these years, waiting for the right time to come back? Am I she? Or just a vessel? Adam, she and I, we have so much in common . . ."

Adam wrapped his arms around her, nuzzling her neck. "I can't explain any of this. A simple reunion brought us back home, but there was so much unsaid between us, so many secrets to be revealed, so many unfulfilled wishes between us. I think it's pretty clear that we are where we are supposed to be—this farmhouse, discovering all that's been waiting to be found inside. Vanessa, you and I, maybe we weren't star-crossed lovers from the start, maybe we needed to be ourselves for as long as we could, live our lives and make the mistakes we did, and then when the universe saw fit to reunite us, we were given the chance to recognize the signs . . . given a chance to embrace the things we couldn't understand. We were pushed into this situation by forces beyond our control. I know none of this makes sense. So perhaps we should stop asking, stop questioning. Perhaps we should just give in to the moment."

He leaned forward and placed a sweet kiss on her lips. Her kiss back was fast, urgent, the power inside the cupola fueling a sudden, growing passion between them.

"Vanessa, come downstairs with me. No more questions. No past, no future."

"No," she said, touching his face, kissing him again. "I think it's important for the past to be a part of us. Only then will the future reveal itself to us. What tomorrow brings. But you go downstairs first, Adam. I need a minute, just me and these letters. Me, this dress, the memories of Venture and all that she could have had, all that she lost."

"I'll be waiting," Adam said.

"Yes, but for whom?" Vanessa asked, and for this time, for this briefest of moments, for all they had experienced and all that they would experience, Adam was unsure of the answer. Still, he left Vanessa alone, gave her a chance to understand herself. Once he was gone, she took hold of the dress, removing it from the package that had kept it secure all these years.

She draped it against her body.

The fit was nearly perfect.

Vanessa felt that inner chill leave her, genuine warmth spreading through her for the first time today. Because for the first time she believed in the idea of something beyond the practical, she believed that in this world existed the unforeseen, the magical. She released doubt and gave in to desire, her mind swirling with images, of Venture dashing along Mercer's Point, her feet dancing on sharp rocks amidst crashing waves, and of Aidan at his desk, sorrow in his heart as he wrote his impassioned letters to her spirit. That same spirit that was somewhere deep inside her, hidden before, newly revealed. She slipped into the delicate dress and allowed a transformation to occur. Destiny playing out, as only it knew it could. Now, at last, Vanessa was ready to move forward . . . or perhaps, more appropriately, backward.

That was where a woman named Venture lived.

CHAPTER 17

NOW

Normally the picture of calm, the waters of the great Lake Ontario had been churning all day, its quiet sheen stirred thanks to the fierce summer thunderstorm that ripped across normally peaceful lands. Gentle waves that lapped against the sandy shores of Danton Hill now rushed in, crashing loudly to anyone foolish enough to venture toward the roiling lake. The beach was littered with entrails from the sea, cracked pieces of shells that pierced the wet sand, green strands of weed strewn about like the torn remnants of discarded fabric.

The sky was dark, with thick, angry clouds hovering above. Occasional bright flashes of lightning swept across the horizon, deadly streaks striking the ground, blowing tree branches to the ground, highlighting ripples against the surface of the warm water. Whatever picnickers had been here earlier, they had all gone to seek shelter elsewhere, leaving the beach deserted and alone. As hard waves jutted up against the sharp rocks of Mercer's Point, thunder crackled big and loud overhead. Something had stirred Mother Nature; an internal fight between earth and sea had sprung up. It was a perfect storm of time and power; ideal conditions for the return of the sister whom the sea had claimed long ago.

A vision appeared from nowhere, seemingly conjured from wind and white gossamer, her fresh presence still hesitant, ghost-like. Effortlessly gliding over rippling water, she appeared briefly to hover over the slick, sharp stones of the place named in her honor before moving to the safety of the land. Once clear of Mercer's Point, her footprints barely made an impression in the cool sand as she glided with focused determination. She'd heard her name spoken from some deep recess of the world, a place from which she'd waited for the call from destiny. Locked inside her were stories untold, meant to be sealed forever but now opened to reveal their inner truth, their unique embrace.

On her body magically appeared the familiar dress, returned to her as though through the power of forgotten dreams. Its once-vibrant colors of red and violet were long faded, but still she would know its contours anywhere. She remembered the way it draped against her lithe body that morning she'd gone to greet him at the lake's edge. How it had hung from her door frame while she slept, waiting more patiently than she possibly could for morning's arrival. How long ago that had seemed, yet how familiar the image was to her. Her arms outstretched, the fabric flowing in the wild wind, it was almost like the currents took hold of her, lifted her forward, her spectral self-guided toward an unknown destination.

She'd never been there, but suddenly there she was. She was free from the constraints of the sea, her soul returned to seek all it had once desired. She gazed about, her piercing eyes able to see all she chose to. A large house stood before her, darkened against the black backdrop of night. Only a sliver of moon slipped through a cloud, the thin strip of light catching her reflection in a nearby puddle of rainwater. She was real, she could see herself, and it was like she was unchanged after all this time. Her beauty preserved just as much as her spirit remained untamed.

"My Aidan," she said, the sound of her voice hollow, echoing only in her mind.

Still, she had actually spoken the word, and somewhere she knew the word was heard.

Across the expansive lawn she went. Bypassing a swing gently swaying in the breeze, she found herself surrounded by tall stalks of corn. She was in the backyard, at the edge of rows of corn that stretched seemingly for miles. Funny, neither hunger nor thirst demanded themselves of her. Only a deep passion fueled her and pushed her forward. But what did all of this mean, the house and the yard, the porch swing that her mother would have enjoyed? A tear formed at the corner of her eye, the rush of emotions suddenly too much for her.

She fought to return from where she'd come.

This was too hard, she was lost. Control, so much a part of her, was not hers.

The wind struggled with her, and at last she gave in to its whims.

That's when she discovered a fine granite stone set before her.

"Aidan," she said again, and this time it was like she was reading his name.

She was.

For it was his name etched on the stone that she saw. Aidan Barton. August 19th.

The date meant nothing to her, and why should it? For her time was immaterial. All that mattered now was this plot of land, the thick tendrils of grass that sprang from the soggy ground, almost as though somewhere beneath it life fed the good earth. Her earlier tear evaporated, giving way to a heartfelt smile. She reached down to run a hand across the smooth top of the stone, pulling back as she felt a striking heat emanating from its surface. Expecting its touch to be cool, instead the stone was fiery and alive.

"Venture, you've come back . . ."

She turned with surprise, her green eyes expressive in the all-consuming night. Had she heard something, was he somehow calling to her? Or was it a trick of the wind, like her own presence, unreal but real, its sweeping voice howling against tree branches, the rustling sound its own language. Her eyes fell upon the upstairs of the old farmhouse, a light appearing in the attic. She believed it was referred to as a cupola, and inside the square room came a shadow against the window.

"Aidan," she said again. "Have I come back to you? Do you even know it's me?"

She watched the house again. The soft glow of light inside the cupola was doused, with the night once again settling over her. But darkness had a way of heightening the other senses, and so she breathed and tasted the scent of the lake and she listened, deeply, no longer wishing to hear the rushing sounds of the sea, the whispers of the wind. She wanted to hear her name.

"Please, Aidan, answer me. Know that I love you . . ."

There came nothing, and for a moment she felt deflated, as though the next breeze could whisk her away in oblivion.

And then there was this willowy sound, spoken almost like a secret told between souls of those truly meant for each other. Of those who opened their hearts to this elusive notion called destiny.

"My dearest Venture," she heard, a quiet voice from somewhere in the dark of night, "I knew you would return to me. Oh, how I've waited to hear your sweet voice again . . . your laugh that so spun my dreams."

She took another step forward, still floating on air.

She sensed a shadow emerging from the cornstalks.

The transformation was nearly complete.

Deep inside Vanessa's imagination, she could see that Venture Mercer had come back to life, her willowy self miraculously, improbably, floating amidst the cool breeze of night just as moonlight streaked across the violet dress. Vanessa stood before the reflection in the window of the cupola, knowing that what looked back at her was someone beyond herself. Wearing the dress, surrounded by the love letters Aidan had written to Venture still strewn about the floor, Vanessa realized she had unlocked a portion of her trapped soul, knowing at last that she had found what she was looking for . . . whom she was looking for. And he was waiting downstairs for her.

So what was she waiting for?

Looking deep into her reflection, her mind swam with memories. At the corners of her eyes were the lines of a life lived with zeal and with passion, but also tinged by sadness and tragedy. She'd seen it all, she liked to think, and most importantly she'd survived it all. Now, the next stage of her life awaited her in a bedroom that wasn't theirs except for tonight—and for now tonight was all that mattered. Though they had shared their bodies earlier in the day, she was nervous thinking about being with Adam. Because this time they had left all their worries, their secrets, behind them, tucked into a past that finally felt settled. What they had uncovered inside this cupola, amidst all those unread letters, was the notion of faith. You had to take a leap and have faith that life would work out as you wanted. As it was supposed to.

Running fingers through her thick, dark hair, she watched as the locks fell back against the nape of her neck. She imagined his touch, the way his lips had felt on her skin, the tingling sensation that ripped through her body. She wanted nothing more than to feel him again, to touch him and caress him, reach for him and feel the heat of his body against her. So why then was she still upstairs? Was she avoiding him, or herself, or simply what making love would mean to their future?

"Vanessa, you okay up there?" she heard from the base of the stairs.

"Sorry, yeah . . . just, you know . . . girl stuff."

Enough stalling. Enough thinking.

With one last glance at her face in the window, she willed

away her fears and then went to leave. A vision again from outside caught her attention, and her eyes widened, searching for what had attracted her attention. But she saw nothing, just the rustling of trees from the wind. Seemed like the storm was gearing up for another go at them. As she stepped toward the stairs, she doused the candle by which they had read Aidan's letters, and then she spoke a silent thank-you. To Aidan and to Venture, their enduring love a message for all. What she could have with Adam was what they had lost, and she was determined, if nothing else, to honor them.

She emerged downstairs into a glow emanating out of the darkness. She found several other candles lit, the light from their flames flickering against the wall, creating moving shadows of light and dark. Smiling at the lovely setting before her, she padded down the hallway and into the far bedroom, coming to the edge of the bed, where she found Adam already settled, waiting. Leaning against a mass of soft pillows, his bare, muscular body partially covered by sheets, he looked so handsome and sexy, yet boyish at the same time thanks to his grin, caught by candlelight. A mix of that insecure kid she'd known back in high school and the confident man she'd met in New York.

"Wow, the dress," he said, speaking softly. "As though it was made for you."

"It's not . . . weird?"

"It's perfect. Just as Aidan treasured it, so too do I."

He leaned over to take her hands into his. He drew her nearer to him, she climbing onto the bed beside him. His hand reached up, slipping Venture's dress off her shoulders, exposing them bare. She felt a chill rip through her body, then felt a contrasting heat as his hand encircled her breast, one then the other. She arched her neck, felt his fingers dance up her skin, her neck, touching her lips. She took them in her mouth, suckled them, tasting him. He pulled her closer to the point where their lips met; a hot kiss sizzled between them. Her cheeks he cupped with his hands as her own fingers slid up, then down his arms, toying with the hair coating his forearms. The scratch of his beard awakened dizzying sensations beneath her skin.

"Adam, the way you touch me . . ."

He kissed her more intently, and she responded in kind, pressing him down against the softness of the mattress. Her body atop his, she sought out his neck, the lobe of one ear then the other. She could feel him beneath the blanket, and her wandering actions served to feed their passion. Kissing the scruff on his neck, she wandered down further, her tongue tasting the salty sweat that lived within his thicket of chest hair. She encircled his nipples, one with her tongue, another with her finger, squeezing, teasing him. He pulled her even closer, his arms encircling her body to the point where they were indistinguishable. His strong, hairy body sending tingling charges over her soft skin.

"Adam . . . Aidan, take me."

"Vanessa . . . Venture . . . we are together, soon to be embraced as one."

Vanessa slid further down against him, pressing against his hard body. With a free hand she suddenly, quickly guided him inside her, with penetrating tingles rippling through her body. She let out a hearty breath, only to breathe in some needed air as he entered her further. All the time she watched him and he watched her, their expressions locked, serious, intense. At last he filled her, and she began to move, up then down, up then down, while sitting atop him. She gasped aloud as pleasurable sensations danced around inside her. She stroked his chest, teased his nipples. The feel of him inside her was magnificent, hitting all the right sensations within her. Suddenly a small wave of orgasm swarmed through her body. She kept up her motions, giving in to another wave of pleasure, then another, letting them wash over her like the currents of the ocean, gaining strength, impacting against the shore with a resounding crash.

"Adam, Adam . . . don't stop, oh, don't . . ."

She felt him push more, deeper, just as strong hands encircled her breasts. Her eyes closed and she gave herself to the moment, enjoying how and where he touched her, all the while continuing to ride atop him, waiting, wanting . . . desiring his inevitable climax. Her motions increased, she again gasped as he thrust, as he grunted. Theirs was a rhythmic dance that had found its syncopation, and they moved with their own music, just as they had on the porch earlier this night, sounds found only between hearts finding a common beat.

Neither knew how long they lasted, mostly because they had learned time meant nothing, even more so now. Vanessa continued to indulge passion she hadn't felt for too long, and from Adam's energy, his heat, his stamina, she recognized a man with whom she could share her innermost desires, fears. As Venture must have with Aidan, how else could they have forged a bond that defied the boundaries of time? As Adam rolled and thrust, as Vanessa touched and caressed, as they made love in a room lit by candles and moonlight, the past that had threatened to undo them became just that, a past relegated to a place where it could no longer do harm. They knew that even lovers from yesteryear had a future. With his kiss, she felt her old self melt away; with his eager thrusts, she sensed an awakening of a new kind was happening; with each ripple that swept over her body, she longed for one more, another, more and more. She was greedy, and he was giving. She wanted to feel his climax, and he was more than ready.

With his body now atop her, his hips moving with frantic, energetic motion, she dug her nails into his slick back, scratching at his heated skin as she held on, waiting, waiting . . . and then he exploded, his cries shaking the bed, the room, her very soul. Legs wrapped tightly around him, she urged him more, more, asking him to give her every bit of himself. When at last he rolled off her and sought air, Vanessa smiled at him as she rested her head upon his heaving chest, enjoying the rough hair, sweaty but dense like a pillow.

"I think it's good there are no other houses nearby," she said.

"I think you're right," he replied, his words coming between breaths.

Her eyes darted about the room; she noticed the candles had burned down halfway, waxy strips sticking to the sides like frozen tears. For a second she felt at a loss for words, emotions taking hold inside her chest, her lungs. How had things between them progressed so deeply in such a short amount of time? Were the discovered love letters such an aphrodisiac? Her days of one-nighters and foolish behavior were long past her now, she was a grown-up and thus responsible. . . . right? How was it that she lay in bed with Adam Blackburn now, and not for the first time today? Though what had transpired between them this afternoon was a mere footnote compared to the intensity they had brought to their lovemaking just now. Before had been about comfort, about realizing you were alive after the crash of metal, and as such each had brought their own baggage to that earlier passion. Now they had been one; a piece of magic had been conjured at some point this night. Thanks to a tale of lost love, they now were able to open up and experience what they had denied themselves for so long. A simple reunion was all that she had intended, now taken on new depth, new dimensions. As she lay there, safe and secure in his arms, she tried not to wonder what came next, didn't want to ask, hoped her voice would not intrude upon this moment. But she knew it would, and it did.

"Morning's coming," she said.

"Eventually," Adam said, kissing her forehead. "Many hours remain."

"For what?"

"For us, and us alone."

"And Venture. And Aidan."

"Yes. They are here, in our hearts, and maybe our souls."

"You still think it's odd . . . the coincidence of their names, our names. The initials . . ."

"Let's just say if anyone was meant to experience a day like today at Aidan's house, it's us. To discover the old trunk, the letters . . ."

"The dress . . ."

"Yes, the dress. It was us, this was all meant for us."

"It's a beautiful story, and a wonderful lesson they left us. But morning comes, reality sets in. Then what?"

Silence settled between them, as though neither wished to answer the question. Their constant shadows flickered on the walls from the diminishing candles, giving them tenuous life but no voice, as though through their wavering shapes lived an uncertain future. A simple breeze could douse all the light in the room.

At last Adam said, with a kiss to seal his spoken wish, "Can we figure everything out later . . . then? Here, in the golden glow of Aidan and Venture's world, I've found contentment. The real world has no place here."

"Can we beat it?"

"Beat what?'

"The real world . . . your life and mine, we live such opposite ones . . . jobs, friends, cities."

He put a finger to her delicate lips. "Our lives are in

limbo, Vanessa, isn't that why we traveled this far, twenty years into the past and beyond, to rediscover who we are and what's really waiting for us out there? Could we really be the lost souls of Aidan and Venture, finally reuniting? Or are they just a fantasy in which to indulge ourselves? We've already lived separate lives, and now maybe the world is giving us a chance at something new, something together. Is that something you want?"

"Yes," she said, "and yes, I know it sounds crazy to say that, but after what we've been through . . ."

"Words can't explain it," he said. "So let's not look for any."

She snuggled closer to him, kissed his chest. "I don't feel that chill, not now."

He actually let out a little laugh. "How could you? We practically set the bed on fire."

"I like that image, that warmth."

He wrapped his arms around her, pulled her to him, kissed her lips and her neck.

"Again?" she asked.

"You said it . . . morning is coming, and sooner than we would like. I say, let's wake up the sun, show it what heat really feels like."

Vanessa smiled, her emerald eyes finding solace in his earnest face. "I like the way you talk. I like the way you think."

"I like the way you are," he said.

As the candles burned down to stubs and the moon began to descend over the horizon, as the next day threatened to arrive and disrupt what they had staved off so far, Vanessa smiled and she laughed and she opened herself once more, allowing Adam inside her again, inside her heart and deep inside her entire body, journeying to the mysterious place where her once unattainable soul dwelled. Here he was, now, this man who had once changed her life, living inside a portion of her she thought closed off years ago, changing her, opening her, again . . . again, and again.

Perhaps they were themselves. Perhaps the night knew other secrets.

The candles flickered, light suddenly gone to black.

Words reverberated against darkened walls. Shadows returned.

"*Aidan . . .*" came a voice of untold pleasure.

"*Oh, my love, my dearest Venture . . . I knew you would come back to me . . .*"

CHAPTER 18

NOW

Adam Blackburn woke to sheer darkness, as though a blanket covered him, a shroud hampering any available light. Distant sounds caused him to stir, but what those sounds were he could not discern. His eyes sought out anything familiar but came up with nothing. He rubbed at them, hoping to wipe them of lingering sleep. Just how long had he been asleep? Had the night passed and a cloud-covered morning risen? Or was it still the middle of the night, which might explain why he remained encased in this obsidian shield. He reached across the bed, discovered he was alone. Vanessa, who had fallen asleep in his arms, she had left at some point. Why? Had their intense lovemaking tonight . . . last night . . . whatever time it had taken place . . . had it all been too much, had it left her with a hole in her heart? Had they exposed too much to each other? Expected too much after discovering Aidan's secret letters? Had they bought in to fantasy? Was it too soon in their newfound relationship, or perhaps even too late, for them?

Sitting up on his elbows, Adam surveyed the room. That sound came again, like crying. He thought he could detect a whirring coming from the outdoors; it was too far away for him to decipher its source. But at least his eyes were finally adjusting to the darkness; he could see a figure sitting across from him on a wooden chair, a fluffy cushion on its seat. Dressed again in Venture's old, willowy dress, her arms wrapped around legs that rested on the edge of the chair, Vanessa held a faraway look in her eyes.

"You okay?" he asked.

She turned, her gaze falling upon him. He saw her nod, trying for a smile but ending up with a shrug. Indifference or uncertainty on her part, he couldn't be sure. Finally, she said, "Cold, still. Or again."

"Well, you're dressed only in that threadbare dress in an unheated house. How long have you been sitting there?"

"Beats me. I just needed . . . I don't know. To think."

"You could continue your thinking here," he said, smoothing down the ruffled blanket. "Come back beside me, get under the covers, and let me fold you into my arms. I enjoyed that, you know, having you next to me in this bed."

A smile finally graced her otherwise worried face. "Me too."

"But you woke up anyway."

"I don't know how long I slept."

"Time doesn't seem to mean anything right now, does it?"

That she agreed with. "It hasn't all day. Why start now? The sun has yet to come up."

"So I hear," he said.

"You hear the sun?"

"No. It's the rain. I hear the rain."

"Like yesterday," she said.

"Exactly like yesterday," he said.

"Something's weird, Adam. I thought the storm would have swept out by now, that with a new day, I don't know . . . is it too much to ask for some ray of sunshine? I feel like I've been underwater for forever," she said, again curling her bare feet beneath her body, for warmth, for security. "Something's wrong."

Separated not just by the distance in the room but by something indefinable that hung in the air, he knew she was right. "I feel it too."

"Adam, where are we?"

"What do you mean?"

"I've been thinking . . . about the stories we read in those letters, about the onetime owner of this house. About Aidan Barton, whose grave we found in the backyard. He's here, I feel like . . . like he's been watching us. Or better, guiding our actions, wanting us to learn about his undying love for Venture. Venture, I've been thinking about her a lot too . . . I feel bad for her, and for him. For all they were denied. That's why I put the dress back on. In a way, I feel close to her."

"Venture Mercer. Aidan Barton. It's quite a coincidence."

"It's scary, is what it is." She paused, then said, "Plus, everything else that's happened, it's just left my mind swirling, like I'm living inside some cocoon. The accident . . . our finding refuge in this farmhouse, the rain and the fireplace, the fresh corn in the fields and the wine that appears seemingly out of our wishes, no phones and no people, what does all this mean? We've had no communication with the outside world all day or all night. No one, as far as we know, has discovered our cars. It's like we exist on our own plane. Almost like our reunion isn't really ours."

"It's Venture's and Aidan's?"

"Does that make sense?"

"Not a bit."

"But . . ."

"But that doesn't mean I disagree with you. Those silly comments about reincarnation I made, I was just having a bit of fun at our expense and our situation. Now, though . . . it gives one pause. It's like we were supposed to stumble upon that old trunk—waiting for us all these years. And only us." He paused, giving a listen to the rain again. It had grown louder. "I know how weird this has been, but it's definitely morning and I suppose we'll figure out whatever together. You hear that, Vanessa, together. No more running off into the night."

"Into the cornfield," she said, smiling.

"From the porch," he said. "From the fire, from the cupola . . ."

"Why do I always run?"

That he couldn't answer. "What do you want to do now?"

"I wish I knew."

Just then the rainfall picked up. Earlier the pitter-patter sounds were like a cooling shower and now the downpour intensified, beating against the gabled roof, against the windows, threatening to spill over the windowsill and into their world. As he looked out the window, Adam noticed a flash of light outside; he waited, knowing instinctively what it was. Lightning. He was right, because a beat later he heard the deep rumble of thunder, a hearty cough rupturing across the sky. Another summer storm, just as fierce as yesterday's, or maybe, improbably, the same one. For a moment he was transported back to when he was seven when that great storm had knocked over his swing set, destroying it before grabbing hold of poor old Mrs. Woodson and sweeping her down the street to her eventual demise. How appropriate, he thought, for this new morning to start where yesterday had ended, complete with his earliest memory of death. He'd come full circle.

Through the open window came a burst of cool air, causing the curtains to billow inward. Adam saw Vanessa curl up even more in an effort to fight off the chill. Getting up from the bed, he knelt before her, his warm hands rubbing her toes. She smiled down at him, tousled his already messy bed head. It was a sweet gesture between two people who knew actions spoke as loudly as their words, perhaps said even more about the newfound bond between them.

"Is it really possible," he said, "you know . . . us."

"Sshh, Adam, let's not go there. Not now. I mean, I have those same concerns . . . but let's not put those words out there, not yet."

He leaned in, kissed her.

A lashing echo that spread across the morning sky broke their kiss. The same whirring, whirling sound that had stirred Adam from his otherworldly sleep, whatever it was now grew closer. And closer still. He looked up, his ear cocked like a dog hearing something humans couldn't. Even Vanessa heard it now, coming out from her distant funk as she was.

"What is that?" she asked.

It was his turn to shush her. She clammed up, allowing him to listen with more intensity. They were far up on the hill, and the outside sounds were easily deafened by the copse of trees that stood like sentries before the old house. Had they been in the back of the house or living room, they might not have even registered any noise. But on the second floor, inside the front bedroom and with the window open to the world beyond them, sound traveled. It was growing closer, coming from the road.

"It's a siren . . ." he said.

"Our cars," Vanessa said, leaning forward. "They've been found, rescue is just beyond the door. Come on, Adam, let's get back down to the crash site so we can let them know we're okay. They can take us to a hotel and we can shower and eat like . . ."

"Like a normal couple."

Despite the circumstances, she laughed. "Yeah, that I don't think we are."

Quickly he donned a T-shirt and jeans from the floor before racing out of the room in his bare feet. His ankle no longer bothered him. Vanessa too had bare feet, and she was still dressed in the flimsy remnants of the dress. Down the stairs they both went and out the door, beyond the porch and into the cool air. Storm clouds rumbled by, rain pelted at them, but neither acted as a deterrent. There was no telling what time of day it was. No moon and no sun were evident; a gray pall hung over them.

"Vanessa, wait . . ." Adam said, pausing to catch his breath as much to assess the situation. He gave another listen; this time there were multiple sirens, whether ambulance or fire truck or perhaps both, they sounded as though they were nearing the field where they had crashed their cars. The rescue workers wouldn't be going anywhere anytime soon, so what was their rush?

He halted in his tracks, watching again as Vanessa continued toward the crash site. Why wasn't he as anxious as she to be rescued? Because he didn't want their precious time together to end. Could she not wait to be found? Indecision hit him like a brick. A hollow feeling settled inside him as he realized that their night was indeed over, perhaps too all they had shared. They had been living a fantasy inside that farmhouse, and here came reality screaming back into their lives. He turned, looking back at the solemn façade of the farmhouse; how quiet it looked now, unoccupied and alone, almost like the ghost of Aidan Barton was all that remained inside those walls. Against the dark backdrop, it was a mere studio set, ready to be torn down. The movie was over. Or had at least reached its penultimate scene.

That's when Adam regained his traction on the wet,

muddy lawn, and he began to chase after Vanessa, who had already reached the road's shoulder. The grass was slippery against his bare feet, but he knew the paved road would be worse on them. Hell, there was an ambulance on the other end to take care of any cuts or bruises. If bloodied feet was the worst either of them suffered, lucky them.

The hard road had slowed Vanessa down, and so Adam was able to catch up to her. She said nothing, just kept walking with determination, her steps ginger against rough tarmac. With silence walking beside them, they made slow progress along the rain-slickened road. The breeze picked up, nearby cornstalks wavering in the wind. No cars zoomed by. It was still just them alone in the world, at least for now.

As they rounded the sharp bend in the road, the sight they came upon appeared surreal. Swirling red lights illuminated the closed-off road, and three trucks—one fire, two ambulances—were positioned strategically to keep any onlookers, not that there were any on this desolate road, from rubbernecking at the accident scene. The only people who appeared to be present were the rescue workers: several firemen in their protective gear accompanied by a couple of EMTs, all of them scurrying around the crash site like ants under a hot sun. Vanessa tugged on Adam's sleeve, pointing to just beyond the trucks where a lone car had pulled onto the road's rocky shoulder. A middle-aged couple stood beside the car, holding each other with nervous apprehension while they addressed one of the firemen. They were pointing toward a shredded field of corn.

"They must be the people who came upon the accident and called for help," Vanessa said. "Let's go up to them and tell them who we are. That we're okay."

"Wait, Vanessa. Let's just see how this plays out."

"Why? We were the accident victims, we're not going to be in the way."

She started forward, but Adam reached out for her hand in an attempt to keep her back. With one quick motion she wrenched her arm free of him. "Over here," she called out, waving her arms in the air. "We're okay, we're right over here."

No one turned to her. None of those gathered at the accident scene appeared to even hear her. The couple continued to point, and then the fireman nodded before rejoining his team.

Vanessa turned back. "Adam, why didn't they respond?"

"I don't know . . . but like you said earlier, something's definitely weird. Can we do it my way, please, and hang back? See what happens?"

"This makes no sense," she said.

"It hasn't from the start."

She stood beside him, her arms wrapped around her torso, staving off the chill from the rain that continued to fall around them and penetrate their skin. Adam took a step forward, then another. Vanessa asked him what he was doing and he assured her he'd be right back, to just wait there. For once, she didn't run and she didn't argue, she merely stood her ground while Adam inched closer to the accident scene. He could hear the voices of the rescue workers.

"Yeah, chief, the one car is turned on its side," said a burly guy with a thick mustache, a heavy ax over his thick shoulder. "Over there, in that cornfield. Skid marks on the road show the driver tried to apply the brakes at the last minute. Probably what made him turn sideways."

"Let's get the hell over there, see if we can find the driver," said the older chief, nodding, taking command of the situation with authority. He pointed, instructing several of his men to check on Adam's car to see what they could uncover. Adam found himself trailing after them. What he noticed sent an alarming, bone-felt chill throughout his body. Because the fact of the matter was that no one was paying him any attention; his presence had gone undetected. It was like he'd turned invisible, like he wasn't even there. He decided not to attempt to talk to anyone. If they hadn't heard Vanessa and they hadn't seen him, what did it matter?

Instead, he ventured off the road and into the familiar field to get a look at the action. He could see his totaled rental car now, still overturned, the windows shattered, the driver's side positioned against the ground. The same burly firemen he'd seen earlier climbed atop the car, not unlike when Vanessa had yesterday . . . today, whenever that had been. The fireman peered into the passenger window where the glass had shattered.

"Hey, mister, can you hear me? Are you okay, are you conscious?"

Adam blanched, his face going ghost-white. Fear swimming inside him, his head turned to the point of whiplash. Who the hell was the fireman talking to? Adam was right here, he wasn't inside the car. He couldn't be . . .

"I can't be," he said aloud.

Though he was standing a mere two feet from the fire chief, who was speaking into a radio, Adam continued to be ignored.

"Get any response from him, Georgie?"

"Nothing. Guy's out, I see a lot of blood, chief. This doesn't look good."

Adam stood frozen, listening to those words. They reverberated inside him, like a pinball ricocheting off too many targets, his bones and his lungs, his still-beating heart. Firemen and emergency workers suddenly sprang into action, working diligently, quickly, efficiently, but carefully too, at opening the passenger-side door. Crushed glass and squeaking metal drowned out their voices, and when at last the door came free, the lead fireman slipped inside the wrecked car. Time stood still as they all waited for the results of the examination the guy was no doubt performing on the victim. *The victim, who happens to be me, there inside the car but standing here too*, Adam thought crazily. Barely a minute passed before the rescuer reemerged, shaking his head.

"He's gone."

"What do you mean I'm gone?" Adam asked.

"Gone? Who?"

Adam spun around, expecting to see the fire chief but instead who he saw was Vanessa. He felt her soft hand grasp his, damp with sweat and rain. From her expression she knew something had gone terribly, awfully wrong. Neither of them spoke a word and neither asked for an answer to their unheard question. They stood in shocked silence and watched fruitlessly as Adam's crumpled body was pulled out of the car, laid down on a stretcher that had been fetched from one of the waiting ambulances. He looked at himself from this short distance, afraid to go any closer and see the damage up close. What was happening, it was impossible. Wasn't it?

Another emergency worker leaned over his body, again checking for a pulse on the neck, his wrist, searching in vain for any sign of life and coming up empty. The woman looked up, said to those assembled, "Doubt the guy ever had a chance. Look at that gash on his forehead, you can see a piece of glass slicing right into his skull. It's just the beginning of a nasty shard that looks like it went right into his brain. Guy probably died on impact, or shortly thereafter."

"Nooooo!" The deafening voice came from beside him.

Vanessa was screaming as she tried to race forward. Adam grabbed her, fighting against the strength of her adrenaline-fueled body. He held her, pressing his face into her cool neck, whispering that it was okay, it was okay, it

wasn't real, it was a nightmare, they were back at the farmhouse, still asleep, everything was perfect, it was almost
time to wake up and get breakfast before they sought help.
Not this kind of help . . . definitely not, because they were
alive and they were fine and oh God . . . Adam thought, exhaustion giving way to sudden realization. He touched his
forehead, felt the shard of glass still inside him. Why didn't
it hurt? Why didn't it bleed? Because the shocking answer
was before him. The truth. The EMT pulled a white sheet
over Adam's body, covering his entire self, legs, torso, his
blood-streaked face. Like Adam had ceased to exist in this
world . . . their world. It was just like Adam had awakened
this morning, the shroud covering his face.

"Chief . . . over here," said a new voice booming from
beyond the cornfields. "I found the other car. And good
news . . . the vic, she's still alive . . ."

Adam turned to ask Vanessa how that was possible, but
he discovered he was as alone as he'd ever been. How was
that even possible? She'd just been in his arms, crying,
protesting the fact of his death. And now he felt nothing,
not her touch and not her breath on his neck and the comfort she gave him. Not even did he feel the rain that fell
from the sky or the cold wind that ripped through his
clothes and smothered his body. He was dead.

But somehow, and he wasn't sure how he felt about it,
Vanessa was alive.

"Where am I . . . who, who are you . . . ?"

They had already pulled her from the wreckage, easing
her body onto the gurney.

"Sshh, don't talk, miss. Let us examine you. You're going
to be okay, you hear me?"

Vanessa nodded, trying to listen and obey. But she

wanted to talk, and when she wanted something, nothing could stop her. "Cold. I'm cold all over."

"You've been stuck in that car, rain falling on you for over an hour, maybe more. It's not a nice night tonight, the storm's not leaving us anytime soon," said a man with a gentle smile and crinkly eyes. "But we'll get you safely into the ambulance and get you plenty warm, okay? You just hang in there."

She was lying down and staring up at the sky, but she closed her eyes to fend off the rain that continued to dampen her confused state. In her frazzled, rattled mind she tried to process what was happening and what had happened, how long ago . . . but nothing made sense to her. She was tired, for sure, and she was colder than she'd ever before felt in her life. What she wouldn't give for Dominick's lush villa on Lake Como, the blazing heat of the Italian sun bearing down on her tanned skin. But that was when? A lifetime ago, now just a passing memory. She'd been warm other times, she had to have been, sweeter memories . . . she thought then of the Forever Yours Senior Prom, when gawky Adam Blackburn had taken her in his nervous grasp for the first time to swirl her around the dance floor. She'd felt surprising warmth then. The dance, her date, her dress . . . Why was she thinking about those silly memories? Why . . . now, and then it hit her, of course, the reunion. She was headed to the reunion to see her long-lost friends who'd stayed while she'd run. She was going to see Adam, all grown up, and finally tell him everything.

She stopped. She paused. Then she spoke.

"Adam . . ."

"It's okay, miss, please, no more talking. Save your strength."

She didn't understand, but she lay there like a good girl

anyway while they attended to her injuries. A soft blanket covered her body in an attempt to stave off further chills. It didn't help. They poked and they prodded, they applied bandages to her bleeding cuts. Nothing felt right, not her body, certainly not her mind, not anything she had ever previously known. Like she'd become someone other than herself, as though between the time of the accident and being rescued an unforeseen transformation had taken place within her.

She could hear huddled voices murmuring around her, but she couldn't decipher words, like she existed in a vacuum. Opening her green eyes, she saw people standing near her. Two men and a woman wearing official uniforms, firemen and EMTs. They were talking with a couple, both of whom appeared to be maybe fifty years old, not much more; she was dowdy and he was robust, and each of them had the look of people who had lived hard, honest lives. They were explaining how they had come to find the accident.

"Laura's folks . . . the Turners, they lived just beyond the bend in the road up there, big old farmhouse up on the hill. Her father passed away about six months ago and her mother had to be moved to a nursing home. Myra Turner . . . formerly Myra Ravens, she inherited the house from a kindly old gentleman . . . I don't know why I'm telling you all this. The house, we don't know what to do with it. We were coming to close it up for the rest of the season, and we almost didn't come today because of the weather forecast. We knew thunderstorms were in the forecast, but still, Mom needed some of her belongings. As we were coming down the road, we couldn't help but notice the skid marks, they looked so . . . fresh, then we saw a section of the cornfield had been mowed down, and not in a natural-like way. So we stopped and that's when we saw the first car . . . the one where you found the lady. We called you immediately."

"Any idea how long ago the crash happened?"

"Couldn't say. It was five thirty when we came upon the scene."

Vanessa could hear it all, even if it sounded like she was underwater. She could tell them when it happened, the accident had occurred a few minutes after four that afternoon, so based on what they were saying she'd been alone in that car for only an hour and a half, the chill of the rain and the power of the thunder her only company while she waited to be found. But in her mind the timing didn't seem right at all, surely more time had passed. She had the feeling something more had happened.

"Well, thank you for stopping, for caring, Mr. and Mrs. Cross," the chief said, shaking their hands.

"Will they be okay?"

"The man we found in the other car, unfortunately, there was nothing more we could do for him. The pretty lady over there, she's gonna need some attention, so we're gonna take her to Rochester, closest big hospital to handle what must be internal injuries. Can't take a chance with a crash like this. But we're hopeful. Feel free to call the station, ask us for an update. For now, why don't you two get out of the rain and cozy up in that nice farmhouse of yours. I remember your folks, Mrs. Cross, nice folk. Sorry again to hear about your father. Sad day, all around."

"Thank you. They lived full lives when they moved to Danton Hill. They always wanted a house like the one they found. My mother once took care of the old man who built the house, and when he died she inherited it. We never met him, it was before Laura was born. Retirement was good for them. Some nights, they would just sit on the porch swing and watch the world go by."

An image flashed in Vanessa's mind.

Finally, words that meant something filtered deep into her soul.

And then she saw the porch swing.

She saw a couple sitting beside each other.

They were not elderly. They were ageless, spectral . . . but they belonged together.

They were . . .

"Adam," she spoke, her strained voice a whisper, all she could muster. She wanted to scream it aloud, but she didn't have the energy. Did she even need to? Surely they . . . no, not them, him. Surely he could hear her.

"I'm here," she heard inside her mind, like sounds being telegraphed across the wind, and that's when Vanessa opened her eyes again, wide, surprised, the world before her fuzzy. He was leaning over her. "You're going to be fine."

"No, I can't be."

"Of course you are," he said. "Vanessa, I don't know how you can see me. But you can, right? You can see me?"

A smile crossed her face. "Yes, yes, I can."

"Who am I?"

"Aidan . . . no, you're Adam."

He bent down, pressed his lips against hers. "Right."

"What's going on?"

"You can feel my kiss, can't you?"

"Yes. It's like magic, your touch."

He gripped her hand, pressed hard, as though even her weakened pulse could heal him and restore his breath. She recalled the farmhouse, and now she remembered the sirens howling in the morning, how their intrusive sound had made her run from the house. She remembered the blazing fireplace and the sweet creak of the swing, the wine and the fresh burst of corn and the way Adam had touched her . . . she remembered it all, the letters and the story of Aidan and Venture. *Venture*, she thought, and then she gasped with sudden pain. She felt, she remembered it all, the events of the recent past coming back to her like a flood in these cool rains. Cool, she thought . . . cold. Her body shivered.

"It's okay, Vanessa. Just hang on."

"Not without you," she said.

"Don't be silly. You don't even know me. I'm just some kid you went with to a dance."

"No, that's not true," she insisted. "You waited for me, somehow, all these years. I didn't know, I didn't believe. Inside, you knew . . . how did you know? Adam, you and I, we danced, yes, back then, but we also danced yesterday or today or whenever this now is. We danced on the porch, and there was no music except between us, and you kissed me and you held me and you made love to me, and we talked, and you learned about what I had done, what I denied you. What the world denied me. You convinced me that I was more than just me, that my heart was yours and my soul was Venture's. Adam, how is any of this possible?"

"I don't know, I can't explain anything. Perhaps when tragedy strikes it allows life the time to clear your mind before you pass . . . before you're ready for whatever waits on the other side. Maybe it gives you a chance to reconnect with who you once were before you become the who you'll forever be. We're free now, I know what happened and I have no regrets. Nor should you, because it's time for you to put your demons to rest and finally be free of them. Live your life, Vanessa Massey."

"Not without you. Not after what we shared."

"No."

"I can't. We just found each other. After all these years."

"It wasn't real," he said.

"But it was, I felt it. You did too."

She heard him laugh. "But I'm dead. I can't feel anything."

"I don't believe you, Adam Blackburn. Aidan Barton."

"That I'm dead? Or that I'm some old man who wrote endless letters to the woman he loved and lost?"

"You're both, and you're one and the same. I don't believe that you can't feel anything, otherwise you wouldn't be here by my side. You came back for me. Just as I felt last night . . . that Venture came back to Aidan. I saw her . . . in my reflection. All of us, we found each other in that farmhouse because we're all the same."

"You can't be sure."

"I am."

"Vanessa, no, I came to say good-bye."

"I'm cold."

"Vanessa, hang on."

"I don't want to," she said. "I want what we had. I want to know if it's all true."

"You don't know that forever is what we'll get. It's too great a leap. If you give up now, we can't guarantee where the world takes us next. We . . . you, you can't take that chance. I think the letters filled our minds with crazy fantasy, that the love that existed between Aidan and Venture could inspire us to head to tomorrow. But there's no tomorrow for me, only for you. You have way too much to live for, the world is out there for you to discover."

"I've seen it, more than I ever dreamed. What I have left to discover is you, rediscover," she said, gazing into his blue eyes that sparkled like the azure sea. What she saw beneath them was sunshine, white clouds that blazed across a blazing sky, no more rain and no more thunder, just a new morning filled with promise, a fresh start. In her mind they were beside the lake, and the water was lapping against the sandy shores and they were together, safe and secure and free of the rocky terrain that loomed nearby. She desired what those knowing eyes revealed, a window to some other

place she'd never thought possible, where they could be together . . .

"We need to be together. All of us," she suddenly said.

"Vanessa, no, we had our time . . ."

A smile widened across Vanessa's face. "I'm cold."

"No . . . Vanessa, fight it."

But his voice was fuzzy again, a hazy glaze settling over
her eyes. She allowed them to close and then she felt a jerk
of her body, a violent seizure that knocked her eyes back
open. She looked up to find the medic hovering over,
scrambling, screaming for help.

"She's going into cardiac arrest," he yelled, "somebody
get over here . . ."

She felt the cold sensations rip through her body. She
saw things, so many things. In her mind, flipping, flickering
images of the dance, of Danny's funeral, of Adam in New
York, of Reva and Mrs. Stillwell-Abramson and the beautiful capitals of the world in which she'd lived and thrived and
died a little death, and then quaint old Danton Hill and the
rocky pier called Mercer's Point where she and Adam had
once decided they no longer wished to stake a claim to in-
nocence, where they came together in a tender, desperate
moment that maybe never should have happened, except it
had and the result was . . .

Her eyes closed. She felt hands upon her, pumping at
her, hitting her chest.

They were reviving her.

But they wouldn't, that's what she decided.

She would take a chance.

She would take that leap of faith into the netherworld.
She would follow her heart. She would do as Venture would
have done.

She had to believe, to trust that whatever had happened
to her had all been for a reason. The screaming voices of

those misunderstood folks trying to revive her echoed in her soggy brain, their sounds fading like the sirens she'd heard earlier today when she'd awakened in the farmhouse after sleeping in the strong arms of the man whom she . . .

. . . say it, she thought, say it. He has to know, even though you couldn't say it before, it wasn't the right time but now it had to be done. Here was the defining, ultimate moment of her life and perhaps its last one too, its final breath. That's when she again opened her eyes and what she saw, well, it was the most beautiful thing ever.

Sunshine, bright, glowing,

For the first time, warmth.

There she saw a face shining down on her.

"Adam," she said. "It's you . . . Aidan."

He smiled and it was the smile she'd waited so many months to see, as she sat upon the beach and stared at the quiet waters of the lake. A smile she never thought she would see again. Not in this lifetime or those she'd patiently waited through.

"Yes, Aidan, that's me. But I'm Adam too."

"Am I Venture? How can that be, how can I be anyone other than Vanessa?"

"You are Venture, and you are Vanessa, and perhaps you've been others too."

"You found me."

"More like you found me, saved me, after all this. Sitting in the homeroom class so many years ago. I couldn't be sure, because how could I? I was just a kid, and what did I know of love in this life, much less a love that defied the ages? But I knew I had to know more about you, and that one day our paths would cross again. Who could ever have imagined how . . ."

"Or why."

"No, we know why, we know because destiny mapped

out our lives even when we couldn't see it, or listen. The world meant for us to find each other, to be together . . . someday, one day, when both of us were ready to believe. Are you, Vanessa, are you ready for what was denied us all this time?"

Hesitation played no part in her decision. She nodded. She said, "Yes."

She reached out, touched his cheek. Her hand felt like it went through him. "Are you real?"

"Real enough. For you, for me," he responded.

"I love you," she said. "Adam."

"I love you too, my sweet, effervescent Vanessa," he said, and she felt his kiss.

She allowed his strong arms to encircle her. She realized she was no longer held captive on the gurney, or by the sea for that matter, she was free of their hold, perhaps free of all worldly constraints. And yet here he was, and here she was, they were together, and the horror of the accident was gone. She could barely remember the hard impact or being rescued, nearly being brought back to the living. This moment was perfect—this was how it should be. She kissed him back, and he kissed her again, fiercely, their embrace like one more dance, and this time she actually thought she could hear music, real music that allowed her heart to swell and her body to sway and for the man she adored to sweep her off her feet and into a world of reds and purples where nothing existed but the two of them. The four of them.

Yet they weren't alone.

A sound came toward them, feet upon the soft ground.

They turned.

From out of the wild, ripened cornstalks came a small figure. She was adorable, with a smile that brightened everything around them, her hair shimmering with the color of golden wheat and her cheeks apple-like, red and rosy. She extended her hands, both of them, waiting for them each to take hold of her.

"But who are you?" Vanessa asked, bending down to gaze upon the beautiful girl.

"Of course you know," the girl said.

Vanessa gasped, holding her hand to her beating chest. Her heart, ceaseless in the other world, threatened to leap from her body, so filled with an overwhelming love was it. She wasn't alive but somehow she was, vibrantly so, she could feel and she could touch and she could reach out and hold this lovely little creature. She could feel her heart swell with pride and amazement. She could feel tears fall from her cheeks like rain and she did nothing to stop them.

"Elizabeth Grace," Vanessa whispered. Tremulous, heaving sobs escaped her mouth, yet, combined with joyous laughter, managed to echo across the sky. "My lovely little girl, it's you, and . . . my . . . how perfect you are."

"So beautiful," Adam breathed, his face filled with the wonder of just what was possible in this world, "just beautiful . . . both of you . . . my God, this is . . . can it be real?"

"I don't know how. But yes, it's as real as we want it to be."

"Come with me," said the little girl, turning to gaze up at Adam. "Both of you."

"Me too?" Adam said with some surprise to his voice.

"Of course, how silly. That's how it's supposed to happen, that's how it was supposed to be long, long ago," she said with an innocent but knowing giggle that sounded so much like her mother's. "Now, take hold of my hand. I've been waiting too long for your loving touch. Let's go, it's not very far. I have a place to show you. Do you like swing sets?"

Adam nodded. "Very much so."

"But, sweetie," Vanessa said, crouching down so her expression met the little girl's eyes. They were emerald green too, a mirror of her mother's. "Where are you taking us?"

What she said was so simple, but so telling, and so very right.

"Someplace where it's warm and the sun shines all the time and there's happiness, where stars beam when you want them to and comets soar past you."

"And where is that?"

"Easy," the magical child said. "Beyond the storm."

And that's when she placed herself between Adam and Vanessa, scrunching her tiny nose up at the both of them, a miniaturized, glowing version of the woman named Vanessa Massey. Vanessa took hold of the little girl's hand, and the man named Adam Blackburn followed her lead, and together, the three of them began to walk, venturing toward the cornfields, which right now—in this very moment in time—glowed in the encroaching sun, opening up and welcoming them into a world where nothing was known and everything was new.

ACKNOWLEDGMENTS

Beyond the Storm exists because of the generosity of many people.

Much of the first draft of the novel was written in Brussels, Belgium, and so I send huge thanks to Steven Tallman and Yuri Michielsen for the use of their gorgeous apartment in the Saint-Gilles neighborhood and for providing Vanessa a haven.

Thanks to Susan Kunz and Wolfgang Joensson, who, over drinks in Paris, France, during that same trip, helped breathe life into Vanessa's sense of wanderlust.

Thanks also to Audrey LaFehr (my editor!) and Steve Marquart, without whom I'd never have met the above people. You invited me to places in Europe I could only dream about, and what do I do? Write another novel set in Upstate New York.

Thanks to Liz Fleming, who allowed me to take a break from the writing when I landed in London, England, toward the end of my trip. And a break translates to pints at the local pub.

Lastly, thanks to the Fayetteville-Manlius High School Class of 1982 for helping to inspire a story about a reunion. All those glamorous cities, and ultimately where do I end up? Home. Not bad.

BEYOND THE STORM

Joseph Pittman

About This Guide

The suggested questions are included to enhance
your group's reading of Joseph Pittman's
Beyond the Storm.

DISCUSSION QUESTIONS

1. Vanessa and Adam seem to have very little in common when they attend the prom. But years later, what life issues have bonded them?

2. How is Vanessa's personality like Venture's? How is it not?

3. How is Adam's personality like Aidan's? How is it not?

4. What are your thoughts on why, after the accident, Vanessa is always feeling a chill, while Adam seems fine despite the piece of glass in his forehead?

5. How did the author's "then" and "now" structure inform the novel? Did it drive the narrative and create a sense of mystery, or did it frustrate you in wanting to know all Vanessa was holding back?

6. Do you think the discovery of the old trunk upstairs in the cupola helped convince Vanessa and Adam that they were Venture and Aidan in a previous life?

7. Food and drink (especially wine) play a role in the book. How do the bare cupboards play into their isolation, and how do the cornfields release them?

8. Do you think the sexual nature of their relationship was impulsive, an attempt at burying the hurt, or an unconscious acknowledgment of their connection?

Do you think both had sex on their mind when they decided to attend the reunion?

9. The storm never seems to let up. Did it strike you as odd that a fierce thunderstorm like that would linger for so long? How was the storm another character in the book?

10. Adam has a fear of death from nearly the first page. Discuss his memories of old Mrs. Woodson and how they informed his thoughts on death and his rather cool approach to learning of his own at the end.

11. Who is Elizabeth Grace, and where is she leading Vanessa and Adam? What are your thoughts on reincarnation?

12. Given the choice Vanessa had to make, at the end of the book, what would you do?